KNOCK DOWN
and
BONECRACK

Dick Francis has written forty-one international best-sellers and is widely acclaimed as one of the world's finest thriller writers. His awards include the Crime Writers' Association's Cartier Diamond Dagger for his outstanding contribution to the crime genre, and an honorary Doctorate of Humane Letters from Tufts University of Boston. In 1996 Dick Francis was made a Mystery Writers of America Grand Master for a lifetime's achievement and in 2000 he received a CBE in the Queen's Birthday Honours list.

KNOCK DOWN

INTRODUCTION

At Newmarket horse sales one October a friend told me that all bloodstock agents were crooks. I listened rather vaguely to the catalogue of accusations, learning about the price-fixing rings and the blackmailing extortions which drove the sale prices of thoroughbreds up and down artificially.

In January, casting about belatedly for the core of a novel I ought already to have started, I remembered my friend's cynical comments and sought her out, this time paying concentrated attention to the various scams she revealed.

Fortuitously I then heard of a small package tour being organized to fly British and Irish racehorse owners and bloodstock agents to the week-long bloodstock sales at Hialeah, Florida. Without hesitation I added my wife's and my name to the list, and we set out in a party of about twenty to spend glorious days by the sea in the sun, and fascinating warm evenings watching the glossy horses sold under bright lights.

We listened and asked questions, our eyebrows risin

to the hairline as even the bloodstock agents themselves told us how to cheat the bloodstock breeders out of a fortune.

We returned to February snow and, very late but at last, I invented my ex-jockey honest bloodstock agent, Jonah Dereham, thrusting him into a series of violent confrontations with a racketeering pack determined to force him to be as corrupt as themselves. Good versus evil in pretty basic terms!

In the recognition that no individual life is without sadness and tribulations, I often give my chief characters experiences of shadows and regrets. I burdened Jonah Dereham with an alcoholic brother to whom he felt tied by an exasperated but immutable love, and I made this brother a working cog in the plot so that he was not there simply to embarrass.

I like self-reliant women who don't need to bang a feminist drum. I gave Jonah Dereham a silver-cool woman and waited to see, as I went along, how the relationship would work out. It's always more interesting, to me, not to know every single outcome of my stories too far in advance.

Of course my Newmarket sales friend had got it wrong, and of course she wildly exaggerated: not all bloodstock agents are crooks. The central message of *Knock Down*, however, is still valid and clear . . . *Caveat emptor*.

CHAPTER ONE

Mrs Kerry Sanders looked like no Angel of Death.

Mrs Kerry Sanders looked like a rich, cross, American lady opening a transparent umbrella against a spatter of cold rain.

'This,' she said in disbelief, 'is *Ascot* goddam *Sales*?'

She was small and exquisitely packaged in suede with mink trimmings. Her skin put peaches to rout and her scent easily prevailed over British October weather and a hundred nearby horses. With forty years behind her she wore assurance as naturally as diamonds; and she wore diamonds like crusty knuckledusters across the base of all her fingers.

'*Ascot?*' she said, her voice brimming with overtones of silk hats, champagne and Royal Lawns. 'This depressing dump?'

'I did try to warn you,' I said with mild apology.

She gave me a sharp, unfriendly glance. 'You did say it was like something out of Dickens.'

I looked across at the primitive sale ring: metres in diameter, open to the skies. A patch o field grass in the centre encircled by an asphalt path for the horses to walk on, and surrounding that, for the comfort of the customers, an elementary wooden shelter, backed and roofed with planks.

Plans for a bright new tomorrow were already past the drawing board stage, but on that day the future warm brick building with civilized armchairs was still a twinkle in the architect's eye. The only available seating was a six-inch-wide wooden shelf running round the inside wall of the shelter at hip height, upon which few people ever rested for long owing to the local numbness it induced.

Throughout the sale ring's wooden O the wind whistled with enthusiasm, but it was just possible when it was raining to find dry patches if you beat everyone else to them first.

'It used to be worse,' I said.

'Impossible.'

'There used to be no shelter at all.'

She diagnosed the amusement in my voice and if anything it made her more annoyed.

'It's all very well for you. You're used to a rough life.'

'Yes . . . Well,' I said. 'Do you want to see this horse?'

'Now that I'm here,' she said grudgingly.

To one side of the sale ring, and built to a specifica-
as Upstairs as the wooden circle was Downstairs,
magnificent turn-of-the-century stable yard,
nd tidy, with rows of neat-doored boxes round

a spacious quadrangle. There was intricate stone carving on the arches into the yard, and charming little ventilation turrets along the roofs, and Mrs Kerry Sanders began to look more secure about the whole excursion.

The horses stabled in these prime quarters were in general those offered for sale last on the programme. Unfortunately the horse she had insisted on inspecting before I bought it for her came earlier and with a small sigh I wheeled her round in the opposite direction.

Thunder clouds immediately gathered again in the blue-green eyes, and two vertical lines appeared sharply between her eyebrows. Before her lay an expanse of scrubby wet grass with rows of functional black wooden stabling on the far side. The rain fell suddenly more heavily on the shiny umbrella, and the fine-grained leather of her boots was staining dark and muddy round the edges.

'It's too much,' she said.

I simply waited. She was there by her own choice, and I had used absolutely no pressure for or against.

'I guess I can see it in the ring,' she said, which was no way to buy a horse. 'How long before they sell it?'

'About an hour.'

'Then let's get out of this goddam rain.'

The alternative to the open air was the moder? new wooden building housing coffee urns at or and a bar at the other. The Sanders nose ` automatically at the press of damp human?

3

and I noticed, as one does when seeing through the eyes of visitors, that the board floor was scattered more liberally than usual with discarded plastic drinking cups and the wrappers from the sandwiches.

'Gin,' Kerry Sanders said belligerently without waiting to be asked.

I gave her a brief meant-to-be-encouraging smile and joined the scrum to the bar. Someone slopped beer down my sleeve and the man in front of me bought five assorted drinks and argued about his change: there had to be better ways, I thought resignedly, of passing Wednesday afternoons.

'Jonah,' said a voice in my ear. 'Not like you, chum, to chase the booze.'

I glanced back to where Kerry Sanders sat at a small table looking disgusted. The other eyes at my shoulder followed in her direction and the voice chuckled lewdly. 'Some lay,' he said.

'That chicken,' I said, 'is a customer.'

'Oh sure. Sure.' The hasty retreat from offence, the placatory grin, the old-pals slap on the shoulder, I disliked them all yet was aware they were only the desperate papering over no self-confidence. I had known him for years and we had jumped many a fence alongside: Jiminy Bell, one-time steeplechase jockey, ently drifting around horse places hoping for hand-Where, but for the grace ...

k?' I suggested, and pitied the brightening eyes.
' he said. 'Large, if you could.'

4

I gave him a treble and a fiver. He took both with the usual mix of shame and bravado, consoling himself inwardly with the conviction that I could afford it.

'What do you know of the Ten Trees Stud?' he asked, which was much like asking what one knew of the Bank of England. 'I've been offered a job there.'

If it had been a good job, he wouldn't be asking my opinion. I said, 'What as?'

'Assistant.' He made a face over the brandy, not from the taste but from the realities of life. 'Assistant stud groom,' he said.

I paused. It wasn't much.

'Better than nothing, perhaps.'

'Do you think so?' he asked earnestly.

'It's what you are,' I said. 'Not what you do.'

He nodded gloomily, and I wondered if he were thinking as I was that it was really what you had *been* that mattered when you came face to face with the future. Without his ten years as a name in the sports pages he would have settled happily for what he now saw as disgrace.

Through a gap in the crowd I saw Kerry Sanders staring at me crossly and tapping her fingers on the table.

'See you,' I said to Jiminy Bell. 'Let me know how you get on.'

'Yeah . . .'

I elbowed back to the lady. Gin and jollying soften the sales' impact and eventually she recovered s of the fizz with which she had set out from London in my car. We had come to buy a steeplechaser as a gift for a young man, and she had made it delicately clear that it was not the young man himself that she was attached to, but his father. Pre-marital negotiations, I gathered, were in an advanced stage, but she had been reticent about names. She had been recommended to me, and me to her, by a mutual American acquaintance, a bloodstock agent called Pauli Teksa, and until two days earlier I had not known of her existence. Since then, she had filled my telephone.

'He will like it, don't you think?' she asked now for the seventh or eighth time, seeking admiration more than reassurance.

'It's a fantastic present,' I said obligingly, and wondered if the young man would accept it cynically or with joy. I hoped for her sake he would understand she wanted to please him more than bribe him, even if a bit of both.

'I think,' I said, 'that I ought to go over and take a quick look at the horse before it comes into the ring, just to make sure it hasn't bowed any tendons or grown any warts since I saw it last.'

She glanced out at the rain. 'I'll stay here.'

'Right.'

I squelched down to the drab old stables and found Box 126 with Lot 126 duly inside, shifting around on s straw and looking bored. Lot 126 was a five-year-hurdler which someone with a macabre sense of humour had named Hearse Puller, and in a way one could see why. Glossy dark brown all over, he was slightly flashy-looking, holding his head high as if preening. All he needed was a black plume on his head and he'd have been fine for Victorian trips to the cemetery.

Kerry Sanders had stipulated that her gift should be a young, good-looking past winner, with cast-iron future prospects. Also that in all its races it should never have fallen. Also that it should be of a calibre pleasing to the father even though it was to be given to the son. Also that it should be interesting, well bred, sensible, brave, bursting with health and keen to race: in short, the perfect chaser. Also that it should be bought by Friday which was the young man's birthday. Also it should cost no more than six or seven thousand dollars.

That had been the gist of her first call to me on Monday afternoon. She had conceived the idea of the gift at two o'clock, found my name by two-ten, and talked to me by two-twenty. She saw no reason why I should not put the same sort of hustle on and seemed delighted when I suggested Ascot Sales. Which was, of course, before she went there.

No one buys the perfect novice steeplechaser for seven thousand dollars. Most of my time since Monday had been taken both by persuading her to settle for a 50 per cent reduction on perfection and by searching through the Ascot catalogue for a cut-price paragon.

had come up finally with Hearse Puller, knowing that she would object to the name. It had no breeding to speak of but I had seen it race and knew it had guts, which was half the battle, and it was trained by a nervy trainer which meant it might do better somewhere more relaxed.

I felt the Hearse Puller legs and peered at the tonsils and went back and told Kerry Sanders that her money was on the way.

'You think we'll get him, then?' she asked.

'As long as no one else wants him very badly.'

'Do you think they will?'

'Can't tell,' I said, and wondered how many times every year I had this same conversation. Nothing warned me there was anything different this time.

The rain had slackened to drizzle by the time we went over to the ring but even so it was difficult to find room for Kerry Sanders in a dry spot. No one in the rain-coated assembly looked much except miserable. They stood with hunched shoulders, coat collars turned up, hands in pockets, the usual collection of bloodstock agents, racehorse trainers, breeders and hopeful would-be purchasers all out on the same trail of winners and loot.

Lot 122, a sad-looking chestnut, plodded round the asphalt path and failed to reach his reserve despite the auctioneer's cajoling. I told Kerry Sanders I would be back in a minute, and went to watch 126 being led round in the collecting ring as he waited his turn. He carried himself well enough but he looked a little too excited and I thought that the rain was probably hiding the fact that he was sweating.

'You interested in that black peacock?' said a voice at my shoulder, and there again was Jiminy Bell, following the direction of my eyes and giving me the benefit of the treble brandy at close quarters.

'Not specially,' I said, and knew he couldn't have read anything from my face. Nothing like bloodstock dealing for encouraging an expression to make poker players look indiscreet.

Hearse Puller pranced past and I switched my attention to 127 coming along next.

'Now that one,' Jiminy said approvingly. 'Bit of class there.'

I grunted non-committally and turned towards him. He made way for me with a half-aggressive half-ingratiating smile, a short man with greying hair, deeply wrinkled skin, and teeth too good to be true. Four or five years out of the saddle had put weight on him like a padded coat and all his past pride in being able to do a job well had evaporated from his general carriage and the way he held his head. But feel sorry for him as I might, I had no intention of telling him in advance in which direction my interest lay: he was well into the stage of trotting off with the news to the vendor and asking a commission for bidding the price up high.

'I'm waiting for number 142,' I said, and as soon as I walked off he started busily looking it up in the catalogue. When I glanced briefly back he was staring after me in amazement so I looked up 142 out of curiosity and found it was a crib-biting point-to-pointer, still a maiden at ten.

Laughing inwardly I rejoined Kerry Sanders and watched the determined auctioneer wring twelve hundred pounds out of the UK Bloodstock Agency for the sinewy chestnut mare who was Lot 125. As she was led out I felt Kerry Sanders stir beside me with her intentions showing to all and sundry like a flourish of trumpets. Inexperienced customers always did this if they came to the sales and it cost them a good deal of money.

Hearse Puller was led into the ring and the auctioneer checked his number against his notes.

'Bit on the leg,' a man behind us said disparagingly.

'Is that bad?' Kerry Sanders asked anxiously, overhearing.

'It means his legs are long in proportion to his body. It's not ideal, but some good chasers are like that.'

'Oh.'

Hearse Puller tossed his head and regarded the scene with eyes filled with alarm, a sign of waywardness which made me wonder if that were the basic reason for selling him.

Kerry Sanders' anxiety grew a little.

'Do you think he'll be able to manage him?'

'Who?'

'His new owner, of course. He looks damn wild.'

The auctioneer began his spiel, reeling off the gelding's origins and history. 'Who'll start me at a thousand? A thousand anywhere? Come along now, he'd look cheap at that wouldn't he? A thousand? Well, five hundred then. Someone start me at five hundred . . .'

I said to Kerry Sanders, 'Do you mean the young man is going to ride him himself? In races?'

'Yes.'

'You didn't tell me that.'

'Didn't I?' She knew she hadn't.

'Why didn't you, for heaven's sake?'

'Five hundred,' said the auctioneer. 'Thank you, sir. Five hundred I have. That's nowhere near his value. Come along now. Five hundred. Six. Thank you, sir. Six . . . Seven . . . Eight . . . against you, sir . . .'

'I just . . .' She hesitated, then said, 'What difference does it make?'

'Is he an amateur?'

She nodded. 'But he's got what it takes.'

Hearse Puller was no armchair ride and I would be doing my job badly if I bought him for the sort of amateur who bumped around half fit. The customer's insistence on the horse never having fallen suddenly made a lot of sense.

'Twelve hundred. Fourteen. Against you at the back, sir. Fourteen. Come along now, you're losing him . . .'

'You'll have to tell me who it's for,' I said.

She shook her head.

11

'If you don't, I won't buy it for you,' I said, trying with a smile to take the discourtesy out of the words.

She stared at me. 'I can buy it myself.'

'Of course.'

The auctioneer was warming up. 'Eighteen . . . can I make it two thousand? Two thousand, thank you, sir. Selling all the time now. Two thousand . . . against you in front . . . Shall I say two thousand two? Two thousand one . . . thank you, sir. Two thousand one . . . Two . . . Three . . .'

'It will be too late in a minute,' I said.

She came to a decision. 'Nicol Brevett, then.'

'Jeez,' I said.

'Buy it then. Don't just stand there.'

'All done?' said the auctioneer. 'Selling at two thousand eight hundred. Selling once . . . all done then?'

I took a breath and waved my catalogue.

'Three thousand . . . New bidder. Thank you, sir . . . Against you in front. Can I make it three thousand two?'

As often happens when a fresh bidder comes in at the last moment the two contestants soon gave up, and the gavel came down at three thousand four.

'Sold to Jonah Dereham.'

Jiminy Bell was staring at me slit-eyed from the other side of the ring.

'What's that in dollars?' said my client.

'About seven thousand five hundred.'

We left the wooden shelter and she raised the umbrella again although the drizzle had all but ceased.

'More than I authorized you to spend,' she said, without great complaint. 'And your commission on top, I guess?'

'Five per cent,' I nodded.

'Ah well . . . In the States you wouldn't buy a three-legged polo pony for that money.' She gave me a small smile as nicely judged as a tip and decided to walk on to wait in my car while I completed the paper work and arranged for the onward transport of Hearse Puller. He was to be stabled for the night in my own back yard and delivered to his new owner on the birthday morning.

Nicol Brevett . . . A surprise like a wasp at the honey, harmless unless you touched it on the stinging side.

He was a hard, forceful young man who put his riding cards on the table and dared the professionals to trump them. His obsessive will to win led him into ruthlessness, rudeness and rows. His temper flared like a flame thrower. No one could deny his talent, but where most of his colleagues won friends and races, Nicol Brevett just won races.

Hearse Puller was within his scope as a rider and if I were lucky they would have a good season together in novice chases: and I thought I would need to be lucky because of Brevett senior, whose weight could be felt all over the Turf.

My respect for Kerry Sanders rose several notches. Any woman who could interest Constantine Brevett to the point of matrimony had to be of a sophistication to put Faberge eggs to shame, and I could well understand her coyness about naming him. If any announcements concerning him were to be made, he would want to make them himself.

Constantine covered with velvet the granite core which showed in rocky outcrops in his son, and from brief racecourse meetings over the past few years I knew his social manners to be concentrated essence of old-boy network. The actions which spoke truer had repeatedly left a wake of smaller operatives who sadly wished they had never been flattered by his attention. I didn't know exactly what his business was, only that he dealt in property and thought in millions, and was now trying to build up the best collection of horses in the country. I had guessed it was being best that interested him more than the actual horses.

When I was ready to leave the sales the best thing of the day was due to come up in the ring, so it seemed that everyone was flocking in one direction to watch it while I went in the other towards the cars. I could see Kerry Sanders sitting waiting, her head turned towards me behind the rain-speckled glass. Two men were leaning on the car beside mine, cupping their hands over matches while they lit cigarettes.

When I passed them, one of them picked up some sort of bar from the bonnet of the car and hit me a crunching blow on the head.

Dazed and astonished I staggered and sagged and

saw all those stars they print in comic strips. Vaguely I heard Kerry Sanders shouting and opening the door of my car, but when the world stopped whirling a little I saw that she was still sitting inside. Door shut, window open. Her expression as much outrage as fright.

One of the men clutched my right arm which probably stopped me falling flat on my face. The other calmly stood and watched. I leaned against the car next to mine and weakly tried to make sense of it.

'Muggers,' Kerry Sanders said scathingly. I thought she said 'buggers' with which I agreed, but finally understood what she meant.

'Four pounds,' I said. 'Only got four pounds.' It came out as a mumble. Indistinct.

'We don't want your money. We want your horse.'

Dead silence. They shouldn't have hit my head so hard if they wanted sense.

Kerry Sanders made things no clearer. 'I've already told you once,' she said icily, 'that I intend to keep him.'

'You told us, but we don't believe you.'

The one doing the talking was a large cheerful man with a bouncer's biceps and frizzy mouse-brown hair standing round his head like a halo.

'A fair profit, I offered you,' he said to Kerry. 'Can't say fairer than that, now can I, darlin'.'

'What the hell,' I said thickly, 'is going on?'

'See now,' he said, ignoring me. 'Three thousand six. Can't say fairer than that.'

Kerry Sanders said no.

Frizzy Hair turned his reasonable smile on me.

'Look now, lover boy, you and the lady is going to sell us the horse. Now we might as well do it civilized like. So give her some of your expensive advice and we'll be on our way.'

'Buy some other horse,' I said. Still a mumble.

'We haven't got all afternoon, lover boy. Three thousand six. Take it.'

'Or leave it,' I said automatically.

Kerry Sanders almost laughed.

Frizzy Hair dug into an inner pocket and produced wads of cash. Peeling a few notes away from one packet he threw the bulk of it through the car window onto Kerry Sanders' lap, followed by three closely taped packets which he didn't count. The lady promptly threw the whole lot out again and it lay there in the mud of the car park, lucre getting suitably filthy.

The haze in my head began to clear and my buckling knees to straighten. Immediately, sensing the change, Frizzy Hair shed the friendly persuader image in favour of extortionist, grade one.

'Let's forget the games,' he said. 'I want that horse and I'm going to get it. See?'

He unzipped the front of my rain-proof jacket.

I made a mild attempt at freeing myself from the other man's grasp, but my coordination was still shot to pieces. The net result was nothing except a fresh whirling sensation inside my skull, and I'd been knocked out often enough in the past to know that the time of profitable action was still a quarter of an hour ahead.

Under my jacket I wore a sweater, and under that a shirt. Frizzy Hair slid his hand up between these two layers until his fingers encountered the webbing strap I wore across my chest. He smiled with nasty satisfaction, yanked up the sweater, found the buckle on the strap, and undid it.

'Now you see, don't you, lover boy,' he said, 'how I'm going to get that horse?'

CHAPTER TWO

I sat in the driving seat of my car leaning my head against the window. Kerry Sanders sat beside me with the muddy packets of money on her expensive suede lap and unadulterated exasperation in her manner.

'Well, I couldn't just sit there and watch them putting you through a wringer,' she said crossly. 'Someone had to get you out of that fix, didn't they?'

I said nothing. She had stepped out of the car and picked up the money and told the thugs to leave me alone. She said they could have the goddam horse and much good might it do them. She had not tried screaming for help or running away or anything equally constructive, but had acted on the great modern dictum that you became less of a hospital case if you gave in to threats of violence right away.

'You looked as grey as death,' she said. 'What did you expect me to do? Sit and applaud?'

I didn't answer.

'What's the matter with your goddam arm, anyway?'

'It dislocates,' I said. 'The shoulder dislocates.'

18

'All the time?'

'Oh no. Not often. Only if it gets into one certain position. Then it falls apart, which is very boring. I wear the strap to prevent that happening.'

'It isn't dislocated now, is it?'

'No.' I smiled involuntarily. I tended not to be able to sit comfortably in cars whenever it went out.

'Thanks to you,' I added.

'As long as you realize.'

'Mm.'

They had taken the certificate of sale out of my pocket and had made Kerry Sanders write a receipt for the cash. Then they had simply walked away towards the centre of operations to claim their prize. Kerry Sanders had not felt like trying to stop them and I had still hardly been able to put one foot in front of the other with any certainty, and the one sure thing on that unsure afternoon was that Frizzy Hair and his pal would waste no time in driving off with Hearse Puller to destinations unknown. No one would question their right to the horse. Rapid post-sale sales were common.

'Why?' she said for the twentieth time. '*Why* did they want that goddam horse? Why *that* one?'

'I absolutely don't know.'

She sat fidgeting.

'You said you'd be able to drive by four.'

I glanced at the clock on the dashboard. Five past.

'Right.' I removed my head from the window and gave it a small tentative shake. Reasonable order seemed to have returned in that department so I started the engine and turned out towards London. She made a rapid assessment of my ability to drive and relaxed a shade after we had gone half a mile without hitting anything. At that point grievance took over from shock.

'I'm going to complain,' she said with vigour.

'Good idea. Who to?'

'Who to?' She sounded surprised. 'To the auctioneers, of course.'

'They'll commiserate and do nothing.'

'Of course they will. They'll have to.'

I knew they wouldn't. I said so.

She turned to look at me. 'The Jockey Club, then. The racing authorities.'

'They have no control . . . no jurisdiction . . . over the sales.'

'Who does, then?'

'No one.'

Her voice sharpened with frustration. 'We'll tell the police.'

'If you like.'

'The Ascot police?'

'All right.'

So I stopped at the police station and we told our story. Statements were taken and signed and no doubt filed as soon as we left, because as an overworked sergeant tiredly pointed out, we had not been robbed. A bang on the head, very nasty, very reprehensible, a lot of it about. But my wallet hadn't been stolen, had it? Not even my watch? And these rough customers had actually given Mrs Sanders a *profit* of two hundred pounds. Where was the crime in that, might one ask?

We drove away, me in resignation, Kerry Sanders in a boiling fury.

'I will not be pushed around,' she exploded. 'Someone . . . *someone* has got to do something.'

'Mr Brevett?' I suggested.

She gave me one of her sharp glances and noticeably cooled her voice.

'I don't want him bothered with this.'

'No,' I said.

We drove ten miles in thoughtful silence. She said eventually, 'Can you find me another horse by Friday?'

'I could try.'

'Try, then.'

'If I succeed can you guarantee that no one else will knock me on the head and pinch it?'

'For a man who's supposed to be tough,' she said, 'you're soft.'

This dampening opinion led to a further five miles of silence. Then she said, 'You didn't know those two men, did you?'

'No.'

'But they knew you. They knew about your shoulder.'

'They did indeed.'

'You'd thought of that, had you?' She sounded disappointed.

'Mm,' I said.

I steered with care through the London traffic and stopped outside the Berkeley Hotel, where she was staying.

'Come in for a drink,' she said. 'You look as if you could use one.'

'Er ...'

'Aw, c'mon,' she said. 'I won't eat you.'

I smiled. 'All right.'

Her suite looked out over Hyde Park with groups of riding-school ponies trotting in the Row and knots of household cavalry practising for state occasions. Late afternoon sunshine slanted into the lilac and blue sitting-room and made prisms of the ice-cubes in our glasses.

She protested over my choice.

'Are you sure you want Perrier?' she said.

'I like it.'

'When I said come up for a drink, I meant ... a *drink*.'

'I'm thirsty,' I said reasonably. 'And a touch concussed. And I'm driving.'

'Oh.' Her manner changed subtly. 'I understand,' she said.

I sat down without being asked. It was all very well having had extensive experience of bangs on the head, but this had been the first for three years and the interval had not improved my speed of recovery.

She gave me a disillusioned glance and took off her

beautiful, muddied coat. Underneath she wore the sort of simplicity only the rich could afford on the sort of shape that was beyond price. She enjoyed quietly my silent appreciation and took it naturally as the most commonplace courtesy.

'Now look,' she said. 'You haven't said a goddam thing about what happened this afternoon. Now what I'd like is for you to tell me just what you think those men were up to, back there.'

I drank the fizzy water and fractionally shook my head.

'I don't know.'

'But you must have ideas,' she protested.

'No . . .' I paused. 'Did you tell anyone you were going to Ascot Sales? Did you mention me? Did you mention Hearse Puller?'

'Hey, now,' she said, 'it was you they were after, not me.'

'How do we know?'

'Well . . . your shoulder.'

'Your horse.'

She moved restlessly across the room, threw the coat over a chair and came back. The slim boots had dirty water marks round the edges of the uppers which looked incongruous against the pale mauve carpet.

'I told maybe three people,' she said. 'Pauli Teksa was the first.'

I nodded. Pauli Teksa was the American who had given Kerry Sanders my name.

'Pauli said you were an honest bloodstock agent and therefore as rare as fine Sundays.'

'Thanks.'

'Then,' she said pensively, 'I told the guy who fixes my hair.'

'Who what?'

'Hairdresser,' she said. 'Right downstairs here in the hotel.'

'Oh.'

'And I had lunch with Madge yesterday . . . Lady Roscommon. Just a friend.'

She sat down suddenly opposite in an armchair with a blue and white chintz cover. A large gin and French had brought sharp colour to her cheeks and a lessening in her slightly dictatorial manner. I had the impression that for the first time she was considering me as a man instead of as an employee who had fallen down (more or less literally) on the job.

'Do you want to take your coat off?' she asked.

'I can't stay,' I said.

'Well then . . . Do you want more of that goddam water?'

'Please.'

She refilled my glass, brought it back, sat down.

'Don't you ever drink?' she said.

'Not often.'

'Alcoholic?' she said sympathetically.

I thought it odd of her to ask such a personal question, but I smiled, and said, 'No.'

She raised her eyebrows. 'Nearly all the non-drinkers I know are reformed alcoholics.'

'I admire them,' I said. 'But no. I was hooked on Coke at six. Never graduated.'

'Oh.' She seemed to lose interest in me. She said, 'I am on the committee of a private hospital back home.'

'Which dries out drunks?'

She didn't care for the bluntness. 'We treat people with a problem. Yes.'

'Successfully?'

She sighed. 'Some.'

I stood up. 'You can't win them all.' I put the empty glass on a side-table and went ahead of her to the door.

'You'll let me know if you find another horse?' she said.

I nodded.

'And if you have any thoughts about those two men?'

'Yes.'

I drove slowly home and put the car in the garage in the stable yard. The three racehorses there moved around restlessly in their boxes, mutely complaining because I was two hours late with their evening feed. They were horses in transit, waiting to be shipped by air to foreign buyers; not my horses but very much my responsibility.

I talked to them and fondled their muzzles, and straightened their boxes and gave them food and water and rugs against the October night, and finally, tiredly, took my own throbbing head into the house.

There was no wife there waiting with a smiling face and a hot tempting dinner. There was, however, my brother.

His car was in the garage next to mine, and there were no lights anywhere in the house. I walked into the kitchen, flicked the switch, washed my hands under the hot tap in the sink, and wished with all my heart that I could off-load my drinking problem on to Kerry Sanders and her do-good hospital.

He was in the dark sitting-room, snoring. Light revealed him lying face down on the sofa with the empty Scotch bottle on the carpet near his dangling hand.

He didn't drink often. He tried very hard, and he was mostly the reason I stayed off it, because if I came home with alcohol on my breath he would smell it across the room, and it made him restless. It was no hardship for me, just a social nuisance, as Kerry Sanders was by no means alone in concluding that non-drinkers were ex-alcoholics. One had to drink to prove one wasn't, like natural bachelors making an effort with girls.

We were not twins, though much alike. He was a year older, an inch shorter, better looking and not so dark. People had mistaken us for each other continually when we had been young, but less so now at thirty-four and thirty-five.

I picked up the empty bottle and took it out to the dustbin. Then I cooked some scrambled eggs and sat down at the kitchen table to eat, and over coffee and aspirin and a sore head put up a reasonable fight against depression.

There was much to be thankful for. I owned outright the house and stable yard and ten acres of paddocks, and after two years' slog I was beginning to make it as an agent. On the debit side I had a busted marriage, a brother who lived off my earnings because he couldn't keep a job, and a feeling that Frizzy Hair was only the tip of an iceberg.

I fetched a pen and a sheet of paper and wrote three names.

Pauli Teksa.

Hairdresser.

Lady Roscommon (Madge).

None looked a winner in the villainy stakes.

For good measure I added Kerry Sanders, Nicol Brevett, Constantine Brevett and two smiley thugs. Shake that lot together and what did we get? A right little ambush by someone who knew my weakest spot.

I spent the evening trying by telephone to find a replacement for Hearse Puller. Not easy. Trainers with horses the owners might sell were not keen to lose them from their yards, and I could give no guarantee that Nicol Brevett would leave his horse with its present trainer. Bound by Kerry Sanders, I could not even mention his name.

I reread the Ascot Sale catalogue for the following day but there was still nothing suitable, and finally with a sigh offered my custom to a bloodstock dealer called Ronnie North, who said he knew of a possible horse which he could get if I would play ball.

'How much?' I said.

'Five hundred.'

He meant that he would sell me the horse for a price. I would then charge Kerry Sanders five hundred pounds more . . . and hand the five hundred over to North.

'Too much,' I said. 'If you get me a good one for two thousand I'll give you a hundred.'

'Nuts.'

'A hundred and fifty.' I knew he would probably acquire the horse for maybe fifteen hundred pounds, and sell it to me for double: he always considered he had wasted his time if he made less than 100 per cent profit. Squeezing a large chunk more from my client was just icing on the cake.

'And,' I said, 'before we go any further, I want to know about it.'

'Do me a favour.'

He was afraid that if I knew who owned the horse I would go direct to the source, and cut him out altogether. I wouldn't have done that, but he would, and he judged me by himself.

I said, 'If you buy it and I don't like it, I won't take it.'

'It's what you want,' he said. 'You can trust me.'

I could perhaps trust his judgement of a horse, though that was absolutely all. If the horse hadn't been for Nicol Brevett I might have taken a chance and bought blind, but in this case I could not afford to.

'I have to OK it first.'

'Then no deal,' he said succinctly and disconnected.

I chewed the end of my pencil and thought about the bloodstock jungle which I had entered with such innocence two years earlier. It had been naïve to imagine that all it took to be a bloodstock agent was a thorough knowledge of horses, an intimate relationship with the stud book, hundreds of acquaintances in the racing industry and a reasonable head for business. Initial surprise at the fiddles I saw all around me had long since passed from revulsion to cynicism, and I had grown a thick skin of self-preservation. I thought that sometimes it was difficult to perceive the honest course, and more difficult still to stick to it, when what I saw as dishonesty was so much the general climate.

I understood, after two years, that dishonesty was much a matter of opinion. There were no absolutes. A deal I thought scandalous might seem eminently reasonable to others. Ronnie North saw nothing wrong at all in milking the market for every possible penny: and moreover he was likeable to meet.

The telephone rang. I picked up the receiver.

'Jonah?'

He was back, as I'd thought he might be.

'The horse is River God. You have it for three thousand five hundred with five hundred on top.'

'I'll call you back.'

I looked up the River God form and consulted a jockey who'd ridden it a few times, and finally dialled Ronnie North.

'All right,' I said. 'Subject to a vet's report, River God will do well.'

He said with elaborate resignation, 'I told you, you can trust me.'

'Yeah. I'll give you two thousand five hundred.'

'Three thousand,' he said. 'And that's rock bottom. With five hundred to come.'

'One fifty,' I said positively, and compromised at a hundred more.

River God, my jockey friend had said, belonged to a farmer in Devon who had bought it unbroken at three years old as a point-to-point prospect for his son. Between them they'd done a poor job of the breaking and now the son couldn't control the result. 'He's a ride for a pro,' said my informant, 'but he's quite fast and a natural jumper, and they haven't managed to cock that up.'

I stood up, stretched, and as it was by then half past ten, decided to tell Kerry Sanders in the morning. The room I used as an office, lined with bookshelves and fitted cupboards, was half functional, half sitting-room, and mostly what I thought of as home. It had a lightish brown carpet, red woollen curtains and leather armchairs, and one big window which looked out to the stable yard. When I had tidied away the books and papers I'd been using I switched off the powerful desk lamp and stood by the window, looking out from darkness to moonlight.

Everything was quiet out there, the three lodgers patiently waiting for their aeroplane from Gatwick Airport five miles down the road. They should have been gone a week since and the overseas customers were sending irritable cables, but the shipping agents muttered on about unavoidable delays and kept saying the day after tomorrow.

'The day after tomorrow never comes,' I said, but they didn't think it funny.

I used the yard as a staging post and seldom kept horses there more than a night or two. They were a tie, because I looked after them myself, and I did that because until recently I had not been earning enough to think of employing anyone else.

In my first year in the business I had negotiated fifty sales, and in my second ninety-three, and during the past three months I had been almost constantly busy. Given a bit of luck, I thought, like, say, buying a Derby winner for five thousand as a yearling . . . just some such impossible bit of luck . . . I might yet achieve tax problems.

I left the office and went to the sitting-room. My brother Crispin was still where I'd left him, face down, snoring, spark out. I fetched a rug and draped it over him, knowing he wouldn't wake for hours, and that when he did he would be in his usual violent hangover temper, spewing out his bitter resentments like untreated effluent.

We had been orphaned when I was sixteen and he seventeen, first by a riding accident which killed our mother, and then three months later by a blood clot in Father. Abruptly, almost from one week to the next, our lives changed to the roots. We had been brought up in comfort in a house in the country, with horses to ride and a cook and gardener and stablemen to do the work. We went to expensive boarding schools and thought it natural, and holidayed on grouse moors in Scotland.

The glitter had by no means been founded on gold. Solicitors gravely told us that our parent had mortgaged all he possessed, had borrowed on his life assurance, had sold the family treasures and was only a Degas sketch away from bankruptcy. He had, it appeared, been living on the brink of disaster for several years, always finding a last-minute goody to send to Sotheby's. When his debts had been paid and house, horses, cook, gardener, stablemen and all had vanished into limbo, Crispin and I, without close relatives, were left with no home to go to and precisely one hundred and forty-three pounds each.

The school had been understanding but not to the point of keeping us without fees. We had finished the Easter term, but that was that.

It had affected Crispin more than me. He had been aiming for university and the law and could not bring himself to settle for the generously offered Articles in the grave solicitor's office. My more practical nature saved me from such torments. I faced prosaically the fact that from now on I would need to work to eat, totted up my assets which proved to be a thin body, good health and a certain facility on horseback, and got myself a job as a stable lad.

Crispin had been furious with me but I'd been happy. I was not academic. Stable life, after the confines of school, had been a marvellous freedom. I never regretted what I'd lost.

I left him snoring and went upstairs to bed, thinking about our different fates. Crispin had tried stock-broking and insurance and felt he had not been appreciated, and I, in becoming a jockey, had found total fulfilment. I always reckoned I'd had by far the best of it and didn't begrudge anything I could do to compensate.

My bedroom, like the office, looked out to the yard, and except when it was freezing I slept with the window open. At twelve-thirty I woke from the depths with the sudden instant awareness of the subconscious hitting the alarm switch.

I lay tinglingly awake, listening at full stretch, not knowing what I'd heard but sure that it was wrong.

Then unmistakably it came again. The scrape of a

hoof on a hard surface. The clop of horse shoes where
they had no business to be at that time of night.

I flung back the duvet and jumped to the window.

No movement down there in the moonlit yard. Just
a yawning black oblong which should have been filled
by a firmly closed stable door.

I cursed with a sinking heart. The most valuable of
my lodgers, all seventy thousand pounds' worth, was
out loose on the dangerous roads of Surrey.

CHAPTER THREE

He wasn't comprehensively insured, because his new owner had jibbed at the high premium. He wasn't finally paid for, because of a complicated currency transfer. I had had to guarantee the money to the vendor when I didn't actually have it, and if I didn't get that two-year-old back fast and unscratched the financial hot waters would close over my head. The foreign buyer was a ruthless man who would stop his cheque if the horse were damaged and my own insurers wouldn't pay up for anything less than death, and reluctantly at that.

Sweater, jeans, boots went on at high speed and I ran downstairs fumbling to do up the buckles of the strap which anchored my shoulder. In the sitting-room Crispin still snored. I shook him, calling his name. No response. The stupor persisted.

I stopped in the office to telephone the local police.

'If anyone reports a horse in their back garden, it's mine.'

'Very good,' said a voice. 'Saves time to know.'

Out in the yard there was no sound. The two-year-old had been already on the road when I woke, because it was metal on tarmac I'd heard, not the soft familiar scrunch on weedy gravel.

No sound on the road. It lay empty in the moonlight for as far as I could see.

He could be peacefully grazing the verge a few yards beyond my sight.

He could be halfway to the express line of the electric railway or on the dual carriageway to Brighton or on the main runway at the airport.

He could be crashing down rabbit holes in the local scrubby woodland.

I sweated in the cold night air. Seventy thousand bloody pounds I didn't have and couldn't raise.

Looking for a loose horse at night by car had high built-in-failure factors. One couldn't hear his movements and with his dark coat one could hit him as soon as see him. One could startle him into panic, into crashing through a fence, tearing himself on barbed wire, skidding to his knees, damaging beyond repair the slender bones and tendons of his legs.

I hurried back through the yard, picked up a bridle and a halter from the tackroom, and ran on out to the nearest paddock. There somewhere in the dim dappled light was the pensioned-off steeplechaser I used as a hack. Dozing on his feet and dreaming of long-past Gold Cups.

Climbing the rails I whistled to him in a trill through

36

my teeth, the sound he responded to when he felt like it.

'Come on, boy,' I called. 'Come here you bugger, for God's sweet sake.' Come. Just come. But the field looked empty.

I whistled again, despairing.

He ambled over with all the urgency of a museum. Sniffed at my fingers. Resignedly allowed me to put on his bridle. Even stood moderately still when I led him to the gate and used it as usual as a mounting block. Jogging on his bare back, I trotted him through the yard, and at the gate let him choose his own direction.

Left lay the main roads and right the woods. He chose the right, but as I urged him on I wondered if he had gone that way because I subconsciously wanted it. Horses, highly telepathic, needed little steering.

If the two-year-old were in the woods he wasn't under the wheels of a twenty-ton lorry. If he were in the woods he could be calmly eating leaves from the branches and not sticking his feet down rabbit holes ...

After half a mile, where the narrow road began to wind upward and the tangle of beech and bramble and evergreen grew thicker, I reined in my 'chaser, stood him still, and listened.

Nothing. Only the faint sound of moving air, hardly as much as a rustle. My mount waited, uninterested and unexcited. He would have known if the two-year-old had been near. He was telling me indirectly that he wasn't.

I went back, trotting him fast on the softer verge. Past the stable gate, where he wanted to turn in. Down the road to the village and across the moonlit green.

I tried to comfort myself with the thought that horses didn't usually go far when they got loose from their stable. Only as far as the nearest succulent grass. They wandered and stopped, wandered and stopped, and only if something frightened them would they decamp at a gallop. The trouble was they were so easily frightened.

There was grass enough on the village green, but no two-year-old. I stopped again on the far side, listening.

Nothing.

Worried and dry-mouthed I went on towards the junction with the main road, where the village swept abruptly out into the three-lane double highway of the A23.

How could I, I thought, how could I have been so stupid as not to bolt the stable door. I couldn't remember not doing it, but then I couldn't remember doing it either. It was one of those routine actions one did automatically. I couldn't imagine not flicking the bolt when I left the box. I'd been doing it all my working life. I was not insured against my own negligence. How could I possibly . . . how could I ever . . . have been stupid enough not to bolt that door?

Even after midnight there was too much traffic on the Brighton road. Definitely not a place for horses.

I reined in again, and almost immediately my 'chaser

lifted his head, pricked his ears, and whinnied. He twisted to the right, towards the oncoming headlights, and whinnied again. Somewhere out of sight he could hear or sense another horse, and not for the first time I envied that extra-human perception.

Hurrying, I set off southwards along the green edge, hoping against hope that it was the right horse ahead and not a lay-by full of gypsy ponies.

In the distance there was suddenly a horrific screech of tyres, some wildly scything headlights, a sickening bang and a crash of breaking glass.

My mount let out a whinny that was more a shriek. His rider felt sick.

Oh God, I thought. Oh dear God.

I slowed to a walk and found I was trembling. There were shouts ahead and cars pulling up, and I rubbed my hand over my face and wished I didn't have to face the next bit. Not the next hour, the next day or the next year.

Then, unbelievably, a shape detached itself from the jumble of light and dark ahead. A shape moving very fast, straight towards me, and *clattering*.

Hooves drummed on the hard surface with the abandon of hysteria. The two-year-old raced past at a forty-mile-an-hour full-stretched gallop, going as if the Triple Crown depended on it.

Swamped with relief that at least he was still undamaged, and blotting out fears for the car which had crashed, I swung my 'chaser round and set off in pursuit.

It was an unequal contest: an ageing jumper against a hot-blooded sprinter. But my anxiety was spur enough for my mount. He was infected by it and aroused, and achieved a pace that was madness on that sort of surface.

The two-year-old, sensing us behind him, could have taken up the challenge and raced harder, but in fact he seemed to be reassured, not galvanized by the approach of another horse, and although he showed no sign of stopping he allowed me gradually to move alongside.

I came up on his outside, with him on my left. He had worn no headcollar in the stable and although I had brought a halter it would have taken a circus stunt man to put it on at such a gallop, let alone an unfit ex-jockey with three fused vertebrae and a shoulder which came apart with one good tug.

We were nearly back to the fork in the village. Straight ahead lay a major roundabout with crossing traffic, and the thought of causing a second accident was too appalling. Whatever the risk to the two-year-old, he had simply got to be directed into the village.

I squeezed my 'chaser to the left until my leg was brushing the younger horse's straining side, and I kicked my toe gently into his ribs. I did it three or four times to give him the message, and then when we came to the fork kicked him most insistently and pulled my own mount quite sharply onto him, leaning to the left.

The two-year-old veered into the fork without losing his balance and as positively as if he had been ridden. He fled ahead again into the village, no doubt because once off the main road I had instinctively slowed down. One couldn't take the narrow bends flat out.

The two-year-old discovered it the hard way. He skidded round the corner to the green, fought to keep his feet under him, struck sparks from his scrabbling shoes, tripped over the six-inch-high edge of the turf, and fell sprawling in a flurry of legs. Dismounting and grabbing the 'chaser's reins I ran towards the prostrate heap. My knees felt wobbly. He couldn't, I prayed, have torn a tendon here on the soft green grass, with so much agonizing danger all behind him.

He couldn't.

He hadn't. He was winded. He lay for a while with his sides heaving, and then he stood up.

I had put the halter on him while he was down, and now led him and the 'chaser, one in each hand, along the lane to the yard. Both of them steamed with sweat and blew down their nostrils; and the hack, having been bridled, dropped foamy saliva from his mouth; but neither of them walked lame.

The moonlight was calming, quiet and cool. In the yard I hitched the 'chaser to a railing and led the two-year-old back to his box, and realized there for the first time that he was no longer wearing his rug. Somewhere on his escapade he had rid himself of it. I fetched another and buckled it on. By rights I should have walked him round for another half-hour to cool him down, but I hadn't time. I went out, shut his door, and slammed home the bolt, and simply could not understand how I could have left it undone.

I backed the car out of the garage and drove through the village and down the main road. There was a fair crowd now at the scene of the crash, and people waving torches to direct the traffic. When I pulled on to the grass and stopped one of the self-elected traffic directors told me to drive on, there were enough onlookers already. I told him I lived near by and perhaps could help, and left him to move along the next fellow.

Across in the north-bound lane also the traffic was on the move, as the wreckage was all on the near side. With something like dread I crossed over and joined the group at the heart of things. Car headlights threw them into sharp relief, bright on one side, dark on the other. All men, all on their feet. And one girl.

It was her car that was most smashed. One side of it seemed to have hit the metal post of the advance signpost to the village and the backside of it had been rammed by a dark green Rover which stood askew across the roadway spilling water from its dented radiator and frosty fragments from its windscreen.

The owner of the Rover was stamping about in

loquacious fury, shouting about women drivers and that it was not his fault.

The girl stood looking at the orange remains of an MGB GT which had buried itself nose first into the ditch. She wore a long dress of a soft floaty material, white with a delicate black pattern and silver threads glittering in the lights. She had silver shoes and silver-blond hair which hung straight to her shoulders, and she was bleeding.

At first I was surprised that she was standing there alone, that the masculine onlookers were not wrapping her in rugs, binding up her wounds and generally behaving protectively, but when I spoke to her I saw why. She was in icy command of herself, as cool and silver as the moonlight. Despite the oozing cut on her forehead and the smears she had made trying to wipe it, despite the much heavier stain on her right arm and the scarlet splashes down the front of the pretty dress, she somehow repelled help. And she was not as young as she looked at first sight.

'She cut right across me,' the Rover driver was shouting. 'Swerved right across me. I didn't have a chance. She went to sleep. That's what she did. And now she gives us all this crap about a horse. I ask you. A horse! Swerved to avoid a horse. She went to sleep. She dreamed the horse. The silly *bitch*.'

Shock took people like that sometimes, and to be fair he had had a bad fright.

I said to the girl, 'There was a horse.'

She looked at me without eagerness.

'Of course there was,' she said.

'Yes . . . He got loose from my stable and strayed up here on to the road.'

I was immediately the focus of a hedge of accusing eyes and also the new target for the Rover driver's ire. He had really been quite restrained with the girl. He knew a lot of words one seldom heard even on a racecourse.

In a gap in the tirade the girl spoke. She had one hand pressed against her abdomen and a strained look on her face.

'I need,' she said distinctly, 'to go to the bathroom.'

'I'll take you to my house,' I said. 'It's not far.'

The Rover driver was against it. She should stay until the police arrived, which would be at any second, he said. But some of the men showed that they understood what such an occasion could do to the viscera and silently parted to let her go with me across to my car.

'If the police want her,' I said, 'tell them she's at Jonah Dereham's house. First turn left, through the village, a house and stable yard out on the far side, on the right.'

They nodded. When I looked back I could see most of them returning to their own cars and driving away, and only one or two staying to support the Rover man.

She said nothing on the short journey. There was

sweat on her face as well as blood. I drew up outside the kitchen and led her inside without delay.

'The cloakroom is there,' I said, showing her the door.

She nodded and went inside. White walls, bright unshaded light bulb, gumboots, waterproofs, two framed racing photographs and an ancient shotgun. I left her to this uncosy decor and went outside again to where my 'chaser still patiently stood hitched to the railing.

I patted him and told him he was a great fellow. Fetched him a couple of apples from the tackroom and led him back to his paddock. He hadn't galloped so fast or felt such excitement since the day they cheered him home up the hill at Cheltenham. He snorted with what was easy to read as pride when I released him and trotted away on springy ankles like a yearling.

She was coming out of the cloakroom when I returned. She had washed the streaked blood off her face and was dabbing the still unclotted cut on her forehead with a towel. I invited her with a gesture back to the kitchen and she came with the same marked and unusual composure.

'What you can give me now,' she said, 'is a large drink.'

'Er . . . How about some hot strong tea?'

She stared. 'No. Brandy.'

'I haven't any.'

She gestured impatiently. 'Whisky, then. Gin. Anything will do.'

'I'm afraid,' I said apologetically, 'that I haven't anything at all.'

'Do you mean,' she said in disbelief, 'that you have no alcohol of any sort in this house?'

'I'm afraid not.'

'Oh my God,' she said blankly. She sat down suddenly on the kitchen chair as if her knees had given way.

I said, 'Tea is honestly better when you're injured. I'll make you some.'

I went over to the kettle and picked it up to fill it.

'You bloody fool,' she said. Her voice was a mixture of scorn, anger and, surprisingly, despair.

'But . . .'

'But nothing,' she said. 'You let your stupid horse out and it nearly kills me and now you can't even save me with a bloody drink.'

'Save you?' I echoed.

She gave me a cutting glance. Same mix: scorn, anger, despair. She explained the despair.

'Look . . . I've been to a party. I was driving myself home. Now thanks to you and your stupid horse there's been an accident and even though it wasn't my fault the police will be along with their little breath tests.'

I looked at her.

'I'm not drunk,' she said unnecessarily. 'Nowhere near it. But I'd be over the eighty milligrammes. Even eight-one is enough. And I can't afford to lose my driving licence.'

My horse had got her into the mess. I suppose I should do my best to get her out.

'All right,' I said. 'I'll fix it.'

'Wake a neighbour,' she said. 'But do it quick, or the police will be here.'

I shook my head. I went out to the dustbin and retrieved the empty Scotch bottle.

'No time for neighbours,' I said. 'And it would look too deliberate.' I fetched a glass and gave it to her. Then I held the empty bottle under the tap, splashed in a thimbleful of water, swilled the water around and finally dripped it into the glass.

'Do you think,' she said ominously, 'that this is going to fool anybody?'

'Don't see why not.'

I put the empty bottle on the kitchen table and returned to the kettle. 'And we'd better get your cuts seen to.'

She blotted her forehead again and looked indifferently at the crimson state of her right forearm. 'I suppose so,' she said.

While the kettle boiled I telephoned my own doctor and explained the situation.

'Take her to the Casualty Department at the Hospital,' he said. 'That's what they're there for.'

'She's pretty,' I said. 'And you'd make a better job of it.'

47

'Dammit, Jonah, it's half past one,' he said, but he agreed to come.

The tea was made and brewing by the time the police arrived with their little breath tests. They accepted mugs with sugar and milk and sniffed sourly into the whisky bottle and the glass in the girl's hand. Didn't she know she shouldn't have a drink before she had blown into the breathalyser? She shook her head tiredly and indicated that she hadn't given it a thought.

Tests within fifteen minutes of alcohol intake were not acceptable as evidence. They filled in the time by taking down her view of the facts.

'Name, miss?'

'Sophie Randolph.'

'Married?'

'No.'

'Age?'

'Thirty-two.' No feminine hesitation. Just a fact.

'Address?'

'Primrose Court, Scilly Isles Drive, Esher, Surrey.'

'Occupation?'

'Air traffic controller.'

The policeman's pen remained stationary in the air for five seconds before he wrote it down. I looked at the girl; at Sophie Randolph, unmarried, thirty-two, air traffic controller, a woman accustomed to working on equal terms among males, and I remembered her instinctive reaction to the men at the scene of the crash: even in a crisis she repelled protective cosseting because in everyday life she could not afford it.

She gave them a straightforward statement. She had been to dinner with friends near Brighton. She left at twelve-fifteen. At about twelve-fifty she was driving in good visibility at forty-five miles an hour, listening to all-night radio. A horse suddenly emerged into the road from the central area of bushes. She braked hard but had no chance to stop. She steered sharply to the left to avoid the horse. She had passed the Rover a mile or so back and did not realize he was still so close behind her. The Rover struck the back of her car, slewing it round. Her car then bounced off a signpost at the side of the road, and slid to a stop in the ditch. She had been shaken. She had been wearing a seat belt. She had been slightly cut by broken glass.

One of the policemen asked what she had had to drink during the evening. In the same calm factual voice she itemized sherry before dinner, wine with.

Eventually they got her to blow into the bag. She did so without anxiety.

The policeman who took the bag from her gave the crystals a sharp scrutiny and raised his eyebrows.

'Well, miss,' he said. 'Unofficially I can tell you that if you hadn't drunk that whisky you'd have been on the right side. It isn't much over, even now.'

'I'm not really surprised,' she said, and that at least was true.

'You'd be amazed the number of people who try to drink before we test them.'

'Do they really?' She sounded tired, and as if evasive tactics had never come into her orbit. The police packed up their notes and their bottle kit, gave me a lecture about letting animals get loose, and in their own good time went away.

Sophie Randolph gave me the beginnings of a smile. 'Thanks,' she said.

CHAPTER FOUR

She slept in my bed and I slept in Crispin's, and Crispin slept on, unknowing, on the sofa.

She had been stitched up neatly by the doctor but had been more concerned that he should take care of her dress. She had insisted that he unpick the seam of her sleeve rather than rip the material to get to her wound, and I had smiled at the meticulous way he had snipped through the tiny threads to please her.

'My arm will mend itself,' she explained. 'But the dress won't, and it was expensive.'

The cut, once revealed, had been jagged and deep, with fragments of glass embedded. She watched with interest while he anaesthetized it locally and worked on the repairs, and by the end I was wondering just what it would take to smash up such practised self-command.

The morning found her pale and shaky but still basically unruffled. I had been going to tell her to stay in bed but when I came in at eight-thirty after feeding and mucking out the lodgers she was already down in

51

the kitchen. Sitting at the table, wearing my dressing-gown and slippers, smoking a cigarette and reading the newspaper. There were dark smudges round her eyes and most of the thirty-two years were showing in her skin. I thought that very probably her bandaged arm was hurting.

She looked up calmly when I came in.

'Hullo,' I said. 'Like some coffee?'

'Very much.'

I made it in the filter pot. 'I was going to bring it to you upstairs,' I said.

'I didn't sleep too well.'

'Not madly surprising.'

'I heard you out in the yard. Saw you from the window, and thought I might as well come down.'

'How about some toast?' I asked.

She said yes to the toast and yes also to three strips of crispy bacon to go with it. While I cooked she looked round the workmanlike kitchen and finally asked the hovering question. 'Are you married?'

'Divorced.'

'Some years ago, I would guess.'

I grinned. 'Quite right.' Married, repented, divorced, and in no hurry to make another mistake.

'Can you lend me any clothes I won't look ridiculous in?'

'Oh . . . a jersey. Jeans. Would that do?'

'Lovely with silver shoes,' she said.

I sat down beside her to drink my coffee. She had a

face more pleasant than positively beautiful, a matter of colouring and expression more than bone structure. Her eyebrows and eyelashes were brownish blond, eyes hazel, mouth softly pink without lipstick.

Her composure, I began to understand, was not aggressive. It was just that she gave no one any chance to patronize or diminish her because she was female. Understandable if some men didn't like it. But her colleagues, I thought, must find it restful.

'I'm very sorry,' I said, 'about my horse.'

'So you damn well ought to be.' But there was none of the rancour she would have been entitled to.

'What can I do to make amends?'

'Are you offering a chauffeur service?'

'By all means,' I said.

She munched the toast and bacon. 'Well . . . I'll need to see about getting my car towed away. What's left of it. Then I'd be grateful if you could drive me to Gatwick Airport.'

'Do you work there, then?' I asked, surprised.

'No. At Heathrow. But I can hire a car at Gatwick. Special discount . . . goes with the job.'

She was using her right hand to cut the toast, and I saw her wince.

'Do you have to work today?' I asked.

'Nothing wrong with my voice,' she said. 'But probably not. I'm on stand-by from four this afternoon for twelve hours. That means I just have to be home in my flat, ready to take over at an hour's notice in case anyone is ill or doesn't turn up.'

'And what are the chances?'

'Of working? Not high. Most stand-bys are just a bore.'

She drank her coffee left-handed.

'And you?' she asked. 'What do you do?'

'I'm a bloodstock agent.'

She wrinkled her forehead. 'I have an aunt who says all bloodstock agents are crooks.'

I smiled. 'The big firms wouldn't thank her for that.'

'Do you work for a firm?'

I shook my head. 'On my own.'

She finished the toast and fished a packet of cigarettes out of my dressing-gown pocket.

'At least you smoke,' she said, flicking my lighter. 'I found these in your bedroom... I hope you don't mind.'

'Take what you like,' I said.

She looked at me levelly and with a glint of amusement.

'I'll give you something instead. That man in the Rover, do you remember him?'

'Who could fail to!'

'He was doing about forty until I tried to pass him. When I was level with him he speeded up.'

'One of those.'

She nodded. 'One of those. So I put my foot down and passed him and he didn't like it. He kept weaving around close behind me and flashing his headlights and generally behaving like an idiot. If he hadn't been distracting me I might have seen your horse a fraction sooner. The crash was just as much his fault as your horse's.'

'Well,' I said. 'Thank you too.'

We smiled at each other, and all the possibilities suddenly rose up like question marks, there in the kitchen over the crumbs of toast.

Into this subtle moment Crispin barged with the sensitivity of a tank. The kitchen door crashed open and in he came, crumpled, unshaven, ill and swearing.

'Where the bloody hell have you hidden the whisky?'

Sophie looked at him with predictable calm. Crispin didn't seem to notice she was there.

'Jonah, you vicious sod, I'll cut your bloody throat if you don't give it back at bloody once.' It was his tragedy that he was more than half-serious.

'You finished it last night,' I said. 'The empty bottle's in the dustbin.'

'I did no such bloody thing. If you've poured it down the drain I'll bloody strangle you.'

'You poured it down your throat,' I said. 'And you'd better have some coffee.'

'Stuff your effing coffee.' He strode furiously round the kitchen, wrenching open cupboards and peering inside. 'Where is it?' he said. 'Where have you put it, you stinking little stable boy?'

He picked up a bag of sugar and threw it on the floor. The paper burst and the crystals scattered in a frosty swathe. He pulled several tins out to look behind them, dropping them instead of putting them back.

'Jonah, I'll kill you,' he said.

I heated him some coffee and put the mug on the table. A packet of rice and another of cornflakes joined the mess on the floor.

He gave up the search with a furious slam of a cupboard door, sat down at the table and stretched for his coffee. His hand was shaking as if he were ninety.

He seemed to see Sophie for the first time. His gaze started at her waist and slowly travelled up to her face.

'Who the bloody hell are you?'

'Sophie Randolph,' she said politely.

He squinted at her. 'Jonah's bloody popsy.'

He swung round to me, a movement which upset his semicircular canals and brought on an obvious wave of nausea. I hoped urgently he was not going to vomit, as on other vile occasions in the past.

'You lecherous bastard,' he said. 'All you had to do was ask me to go out. I'd have gone out. You didn't have to get me drunk.'

The easy tears began to roll down his cheeks. And after the self-pity, the promises, I thought. Always the same pattern.

'You got yourself drunk,' I said.

'You shouldn't have given me the Scotch,' he said. 'It was your bloody fault.'

'You know damn well I never gave you any Scotch.'

'You just put it here on the table and left it here for me to find. If that's not giving it to me, then what is?'

'You'd convince yourself it grew on a tree in the garden. You went out and bought it.'

'I tell you I didn't,' he said indignantly. 'I just found it on the table.'

He managed to get the mug to his mouth without spilling the contents.

I considered him. If by some extraordinary chance he was telling the truth, someone wished him very ill. But as far as I knew he had no active enemies, just bored acquaintances who tended to cross the road at his approach and disappear into convenient doorways. On balance I thought it more likely he had bought the bottle somewhere and was trying to shift the blame. The days when I could effortlessly believe what he said were ten years back.

'As God's my judge, Jonah, it was here on the table.' A couple more tears oozed out. 'You never believe a bloody word I say.'

He drank half the coffee.

'I'd never buy whisky,' he said. 'Sour bloody stuff.'

Once the craving took him he would drink whatever he could get hold of. I'd known him pass out on creme de menthe.

He worked on the grudge that I didn't believe him until he was back to full-scale anger. With a sudden half-coordinated swing he hurled his mug of coffee across the room where it shattered against the wall. Brown rivulets trickled downwards on the floor.

He stood up, upsetting his chair, his head lowered aggressively.

'Give me some bloody money.'

'Look . . . Go to bed and sleep it off.'

'You stupid sod. I need it. You and your goody-goody airs. You've no bloody idea. You don't begin to understand. You've pinched my whisky. Just give me some bloody money and go stuff yourself.'

Sophie Randolph cleared her throat.

Crispin swung violently around to her to forestall any adverse suggestion she might make, and that time the sudden movement took his nausea out of control. At least he had enough self-respect left not to sick up in her face: he bolted for the back door and we could hear his troubles out in the yard, which was quite bad enough.

'He's my brother,' I said.

'Yes.'

She seemed to need no further explanation. She looked around at the debris. 'Will he clear that up?'

'No chance,' I said, smiling. 'I'll do it later, when he's asleep. If I do it too soon it enrages him . . . he would just make a worse mess.'

She shook her head in disapproval.

'He isn't like this all the time,' I said. 'He goes weeks sometimes without a drink.'

Crispin came back looking greener than ever.

'Money,' he said aggressively.

I stood up, went along to the office, and returned with five pounds. Crispin snatched it out of my hands.

'The pub isn't open yet,' I observed.

'Bugger you.' Crispin's gaze swung round to include Sophie. 'Bugger you both.'

He lurched out of the door and through the window we watched him walk a slightly pompous path to the gate, trying to behave like a country gent and forgetting that he still wore yesterday's clothes and yesterday's beard.

'Why did you give him the money?'

'To save him stealing it.'

'But . . .' She stopped doubtfully.

I explained. 'When the craving's on him, he'll do literally anything to get alcohol. It's kinder to let him have it with some shred of dignity. He'll be drunk all today and tonight but maybe by tomorrow it will be over.'

'But the pub . . .'

'They'll let him in,' I said. 'They understand. They'll sell him a bottle and send him home again when he shows signs of passing out.'

Although to my mind she would have been better off in bed, Sophie insisted that she should be out seeing to her car. She compromised finally to the extent of letting me ring the local garage, where I was known, and arranging the salvage. Then, dressed in jeans and sweater two sizes too big, she spent most of the morning sitting in the squashy leather armchair in the office, listening to me doing business on the telephone.

Kerry Sanders was pleased about River God and didn't quibble about the price.

'That's more like it,' she said. 'I never did go for that goddam name Hearse Puller.'

'Well . . . I can have him fetched from Devon any time, so where and when would you like him delivered?'

'I'm visiting with the family this weekend.' Even now, I noticed, she avoided using their names. 'I'll be going down there for lunch and I'd like the horse van to arrive at around four-thirty.'

'Certainly,' I said. 'What address?'

'Don't you have it?'

I said I could find it, no doubt.

She came across with the information reluctantly, as if imparting a secret. A village in Gloucestershire, as open as the day.

'OK. Four-thirty on the dot,' I said.

'Will you be there yourself?'

'No. I don't usually.'

'Oh.' She sounded disappointed. 'Well . . . could you make it?'

'You wouldn't need me.'

'I'd sure like it,' she said, her voice hovering uncertainly between cajolery and demand, and I realized that for all her assurance she was still unsure about this gift.

'You mean,' I said, 'to perform introductions?'

'Well. I guess so.'

Nicol Brevett, this is River God. River God, meet Nicol Brevett. Howdy partner, shake a hoof.

'All right,' I said. 'I'll arrive with the horse.'

'Thanks.' Again the mixture in her voice. Partly she definitely thought I ought to jump to it when asked, and partly she was genuinely relieved I had agreed. I thought she was crazy to marry into a family which made her nervous, and I wondered why they had that effect on her.

'Have you heard any more about those two men?' she asked.

'No.' Apart from a sore spot when I brushed my hair, I had forgotten them. Too much seemed to have happened since.

'I'd like you to find out why they took that horse.'

'I'd like to know, sure,' I said. 'But as to finding out ... If you care enough, how about hiring the Radnor Halley Agency? They'd do it.'

'Private detectives?'

'Specialists in racing,' I said.

'Yes, well. But ... I don't know ...'

It came back every time to the way she reacted to the Brevetts.

'I'll do my best,' I said, and she was pleased, but I had no confidence at all.

I spoke next to a transport firm in Devon, arranging that they should pick up River God early the following morning, and meet me at three o'clock beyond Stroud. What was the ultimate destination, they asked, and with sudden caution I didn't give it. Ten miles beyond our rendezvous, I said, and I would show them the way. I put the receiver down feeling slightly foolish, but the loss of Hearse Puller had been no joke.

I telephoned the Devon farmer and asked him to send a man with River God to look after him, and also to produce him well groomed with his feet and shoes in good condition. The farmer said he hadn't the time to be bothered, and I said that if the horse looked too rough he'd get him straight back. He grunted, groused, agreed, and hung up.

'You sounded very tough on him,' Sophie said with a smile.

'Horses straight from small farms sometimes look as if they've been pulling a plough . . .'

She lit a cigarette, the bandaged arm moving stiffly.

'I've got some codeine,' I said.

She twisted her mouth. 'Then I'd like some.'

I fetched the pain-killers and a glass of water.

'Are you everyone's nurse?' she said.

'Mostly my own.'

While I had been telephoning, she had taken note of the racing photographs on the walls.

'Those are of you, aren't they?' she asked.

'Most of them.'

'I've heard of you,' she said. 'I don't go racing myself, but my aunt has a stud farm, and I suppose I see your name in newspapers and on television.'

'Not any more. It's nearly three years since I stopped.'

'Do you regret it?'

'Stopping?' I shrugged. 'Everyone has to, sometime.' Especially when on the receiving end of six months in a spinal brace and severe warnings from gents in white coats.

She asked if I would drive her along to where she had crashed so that she could see the place in daylight.

'Sure,' I agreed. 'And I want to look for the rug my horse got rid of on his travels, though it's bound to be torn. Pity he lost it, really, as it's a light fawn . . . much easier to see in the dark than his own bay coat.'

She stubbed out her cigarette but before we could move the telephone rang.

'Hi, Jonah,' said a cheerful American voice. 'How did the sale go?'

'Which one?' I asked.

'Well . . . I guess the one for Kerry. You know. Kerry Sanders.'

'Oh sure,' I agreed. 'Only I've bought two for her. Didn't she tell you?'

'Uh uh. Only that you were off to Ascot for some nag with a God-awful name.'

Pauli Teksa. I pictured him at the other end of the line, a short, solidly built man in his early forties, bursting with physical and mental energy and unashamedly out to make money. I had met him only a few times and thought his most outstanding quality was the speed with which he reached decisions. After a session with him one felt as if one had been carried along irresistibly by a strong tide, and it was only afterwards that one wondered if any of his instant assessments ever turned out to be wrong.

He was over in England for the Newmarket Yearling Sales, a bloodstock agent on a large scale in the States keeping tabs on the worldwide scene.

We had had a drink together in a group of others at Newmarket the previous week, and it was because of that and other equally casual meetings that he had, I supposed, given my name to Kerry Sanders.

I told him what had become of Hearse Puller. Out of the corner of my eye I could see Sophie listening with her mouth open in incredulity. Pauli Teksa's astonishment was tempered by greater cynicism about the world we both moved in, but even he was outraged at the use of force.

'Pressure,' he said vigorously. 'Even unfair pressure. Sure. But *violence . . .*'

'I'm surprised she didn't tell you.'

'I've been out of town since Tuesday. Just got back from Ireland. Guess she couldn't reach me.'

'Anyway,' I said. 'No great harm done. She made a profit on Hearse Puller and I bought her another horse instead.'

'Yeah, but you sure ought to raise a hell of a ruckus over what went on back there at Ascot.'

'I'll leave it to Mrs Sanders.'

'It sure makes me feel bad that it was I who got you into this mess.'

'Never mind,' I said.

'But I'm glad you managed to do a deal for her in the end.' He paused, his voice heavy with meaning.

I smiled wryly at the telephone. 'You're saying you want a cut of the commission?'

'Jonah, fella,' his voice sounded hurt, 'did I ask?'

'I learn,' I said. 'I learn.'

'Two per cent,' he said. 'A gesture. Nothing more. Two per cent, Jonah. OK?'

'OK,' I said, sighing. The 2 per cent, which sounded so little, was in fact two-fifths of my fee. I should have charged Kerry Sanders more than 5 per cent, I thought. Silly me. Except that 5 per cent was fair.

It was no good refusing Pauli. The remaining 3 per cent was better than nothing, even with a bang on the head thrown in, and there was goodwill involved. Pauli on my side was a good future prospect. Pauli against, a lousy one.

By the time I put the receiver down Sophie had shut her mouth and regained her calm. She raised her eyebrows.

'Hey ho for a quiet life in the country.'

'Quiet is internal,' I said.

*

Up on the main road the orange MG dangled like a crumpled toy at the rear of the breakdown truck. Sophie watched with regret as it was towed away, and picked up a bent silver hub cap which fell off in the first few feet.

'I liked that car,' she said.

The Rover had already gone. All that remained after distance swallowed the breakdown truck were some black brake marks on the road and a pathetic heap of swept-up glass.

Sophie threw the hub cap into the ditch, shrugged off her regrets, and said we would now look for my rug.

We found it not very far away and across on the far side of the road, a damp, haphazard heap half-hidden by bushes. I picked it up expecting a complete ruin, as horses mostly rid themselves of their rugs by standing on one edge and becoming so frightened by the unexpected restraint that they tear the cloth apart in a frenzy to get free. Horses standing quietly in stables almost never shed their rugs, but horses loose among bushes could do it easily.

'What's the matter?' she said.

I looked up. 'There's nothing wrong with it.'

'Well, good.'

'Yes,' I said doubtfully. Because I didn't see how any horse could get out of his rug by undoing the three fastening buckles, one across the chest, the others

under the stomach; and on this rug, which was totally
undamaged, the buckles were quite definitely undone.

CHAPTER FIVE

Sophie was adamant about returning home, the steel in her character showing little spikes when I tried to persuade her to give my number to the people who might call her out on stand-by. She unbent to the extent of grilled chicken for lunch in the still untidy kitchen, and at Gatwick Airport she even allowed me to pay the deposit for her hired car, though this was entirely because she had set out to the dinner party without cheque book or identification and felt less than impressive in my clothes. I said I liked pale blue socks with silver sandals. She said I was a bloody fool. I wished very much that she wasn't going.

Crispin's return from the pub coincided with mine from Gatwick. He was maudlin, bleary-eyed, expansive, waving his arms around in large gestures and clutching a full bottle of gin. According to him he didn't know how I put up with him, I was the salt of the earth, the salt of the effing earth, he didn't care who knew it.

'Sure,' I said.

He belched. I wondered if one struck a match whether gin fumes would ignite like gas.

He focused on the remains of chicken and said he wanted some.

'You won't eat it,' I said.

'I will.' He squinted at me. 'You'll cook for a bloody popsy but not for your own brother.'

I put another piece in the griller. It smelled good, looked good, and he didn't eat it. He sat at the table, picked it up in his fingers and took a couple of small bites before pushing the plate away.

'It's tough,' he said.

He lit a cigar. It took six matches, a lot of squinting and a variety of oaths.

We'd been through so many cures. Six weeks in a private nursing home drying out with a psychiatrist listening daily to his woes had resulted in precisely one month's sobriety. Then, having been scooped by the police from a Park Lane gutter, he woke in a public ward and didn't like it. I told him I wasn't riding races just to keep him in trick cyclists. He said I didn't care about him. The whole hopeless circus had been going on for years.

Sophie telephoned at nine o'clock that evening. Her voice sounded so immediately familiar that it was incredible to think I had known her for less than twenty-four hours.

' . . . Just to thank you for everything . . .'

'For crashing your car?'

'You know what I mean,' she said.

'How's the arm?'

'Oh, much better. Look . . . I don't have a lot of time. I have to go to work after all . . . rather a nuisance but it can't be helped.'

'Say you don't feel up to it.'

She paused. 'No. It wouldn't really be true. I slept for hours when I got home and honestly I feel fine now.'

I didn't argue. I already knew it was impossible to persuade her against her will.

She said, 'How are your knight-in-shining-armour instincts?'

'Rusty.'

'I could provide Brasso.'

I smiled. 'What do you want done?'

'Yes. Mm. Well, when it comes to the point, I don't know that I've got any right to ask.'

'Will you marry me?' I said.

'*What* did you say?'

'Er . . .' I said. 'Never mind. What was it you wanted done?'

'Yes,' she said.

'Yes what?'

'Yes, I will. Marry you.'

I stared across the office, seeing nothing. I hadn't meant to ask her. Or had I? Anyway, not so soon. I swallowed. Cleared my throat.

'Then . . . you've a right to ask anything.'

'Good,' she said crisply. 'Button your ears back.'

'They're buttoned.'

'My aunt . . . the one who has the stud farm . . .'

'Yes,' I said.

'I've been talking to her on the telephone. She's in a grade-one tizzy.'

'What about?'

'To be honest, I don't exactly understand. But she lives near Cirencester and I know you are going over that way tomorrow with Mrs Sanders' horse . . . and . . . well . . . I suppose I sort of vaguely offered your help. Anyway, if you've got time to call on her, she'd be grateful.'

'All right,' I said. 'What's her name?'

'Mrs Antonia Huntercombe. Paley Stud. Her village is Paley, too. Near Cirencester.'

'Right.' I wrote it down. 'Are you working tomorrow evening?'

'No. Saturday morning.'

'Then . . . I could come to your place . . . on my way home . . . to tell you how I got on with her.'

'Yes.' Her voice was tentative, almost embarrassed. 'I live . . .'

'I know where you live,' I said. 'Somewhere at the end of the five-furlong straight of Sandown Racecourse.'

She laughed. 'If I lean out, I can see the stands from the bathroom window.'

'I'll be there.'

71

'I've got to go now, or I'll be late.' She paused, then she said doubtfully, 'Did you mean it?'

'Yes,' I said. 'I think so. Did you?'

'No,' she said. 'It's silly.'

Friday morning saw the long-delayed departure of the seventy thousand-pound two-year-old, who seemed to have suffered no harm from his nocturnal junket. I knew, as I thankfully dispatched him with his two slightly less valuable fellows, that I had been luckier than I deserved, and I still sweated at the thought of that headlong gallop down the main road.

Crispin, that Friday morning, lay in the customary coma on his bed. I rang the doctor, who said he would look in on his rounds.

'How's the girl I stitched?' he asked.

'Gone home. Gone to work.'

'A lot of starch in that one.'

'Yes.'

I thought about her every ten minutes or so. A cool girl I had kissed once, on the cheek in the afternoon, standing beside a hired car in Gatwick Airport. She had done nothing in return but smile. One couldn't call it love. Recognition, perhaps.

Mid-morning I set off for Gloucestershire and without much trouble found the aunt's stud farm at Paley. As a business breeding venture it had all the first-sight marks of imminent skids: weeds in the gravel, an unmended fence, tiles off the stable roof and paint too old to keep out the rain.

The house itself was a pleasant Cotswold stone affair with too much creeper on the walls. I knocked on the front door, which was open, and was told by a rich voice to come in. Dogs greeted me in the hall, a whippet, a labrador, two bassets and a dachshund, all displaying curiosity tempered by good manners. I let them sniff and lick, and they'd know me next time, I thought.

'Come in, come in,' called the voice.

I went further, to the door of a long sitting-room where much-used antique furniture stood on elderly Persian rugs. Padded and pelmeted curtains and silk lampshades and Staffordshire china dogs all spoke of enough money somewhere in the past, but the holes in the flowery chintz sofa covers were truer of the present.

Antonia Huntercombe sat in an armchair fondling yet another dog. A Yorkshire terrier, a walking hearth-rug. She was a woman of about sixty with strong facial bones and an air of first-class stoicism in the face of titanic submersion.

'Are you Jonah Dereham?'

'Mrs Huntercombe?'

She nodded. 'Come in and sit down.'

At closer quarters the voice was fruity in the lower notes and punctiliously articulated. She did not seem

73

over-friendly considering that I was supposed to be there to offer help.

'Excuse me not getting up,' she said. 'Little Dougal here is not very well, and I don't want to disturb him.'

She stroked the hearthrug soothingly. One couldn't see which end of it was which.

'Sophie asked me to call,' I said.

'Can't see what good you can do,' she said forbiddingly. 'And besides, you're one of *them*.'

'One of who?'

'Bloodstock agents.'

'Oh,' I said. Several shades of light began to dawn.

She nodded grimly. 'I told Sophie it was no good asking you for help, but she insisted that I should at least tell you my complaints. She's a very forceful girl, Sophie.'

'She is indeed.'

Antonia Huntercombe looked at me sharply. 'She seems to think well of you. She telephoned to find out how I was, but she talked mostly of you.'

'Did she?'

She nodded. 'Sophie needs a man. But not a crook.'

I thought privately that few young women needed a man less than Sophie but quarrelled only with the second half of the pronouncement.

'I'm not a crook.'

'Hmph.'

I said, 'I looked you up in the books, before I came. You've got one good stallion, Barroboy, but he's getting old now, and one young one, Bunjie, who might be better if he were keener on his job. You have eight brood mares, the best being Winedark who came third in the Oaks. She was bred last year to a top sire, Winterfriend, and you sent the resulting filly as a year-ling to Newmarket Sales last week. She fetched only eighteen hundred guineas because of a heart murmur, which means that you lost a lot of money on her, as the stud fee was five thousand in the first place and then there is all her keep and care and overheads . . .'

'It was a lie,' she said fiercely.

'What was?'

'That the filly had a heart murmur. She didn't. Her heart is as sound as a bell.'

'But I was there at the sales,' I said. 'I remember hearing that the Winterfriend filly would never race and might be doubtful even as a brood mare. That's why no one bid for her.'

'That's why, right enough.' Her voice was bitter. 'But it wasn't true.'

'You'd better tell me who spread such a rumour,' I said. 'Who and why.'

'Who is easy. All you crooked sharks calling yourself bloodstock agents. Bloodsucking agents more like. As for *why* . . . need you ask? Because I won't give you kick-backs.'

She was referring to the practice which had grown up among some agents of going to a breeder before a sale and saying, in effect: 'I'll bid your horse up to a good price if you give me a share of what you get.' Far more intimidating was the follow-up: 'And if you don't agree to what I suggest I'll make sure no one bids for your horse and if you sell it at all it will be at a loss.' Dozens of small breeders were coughing up the kick-backs just to keep themselves in business and Mrs Antonia Huntercombe's difficulties were what happened if they didn't.

I knew all about it. I knew that the big, reputable firms never asked for kick-backs at all, and that individual agents' kickbacks varied from nil to nearly extortionate.

'I was offered eight thousand for the filly,' Mrs Huntercombe said bitterly. 'I was to give back half of anything she made over that price.' She glared at me. 'I refused to agree. Why should I? She cost eight thousand to produce. They wanted half of any profit I made. And for doing what? Nothing at all except bidding in a sale ring. No work, no worry, no thought and care. It's downright wicked to come and demand half of my profit.'

'Who was it?'

'I'm not going to tell you. You're one of them, and I don't trust you.'

'So you sent her to the sales to take her chance.'

'She should have made at least ten thousand. At least.' She glared at me. 'Don't you agree?'

'Twelve or fourteen, I would have thought.'

'Of course she should.'

'Didn't you put a reserve on her?' I asked.

'Reserves are a racket in themselves,' she said furiously. 'But no, I didn't. There was no reason why she shouldn't make her price. Her breeding, her looks . . . you couldn't fault her.'

'And you didn't go with her to Newmarket?'

'It's so far. And there's too much to do here. I sent a groom with her. I couldn't believe . . . I simply couldn't believe it when she went for eighteen hundred. I didn't hear that story about a heart murmur until two days afterwards when the man who bought her rang up to ask for the vet's report.'

I thought about the general lack of prosperity about the place.

'You needed her to make a good profit?' I suggested.

'Of course I did. She was the best foal I've had for years.'

'But not the first request for a kick-back?'

'The worst,' she said. 'I've told them all . . . I always tell them . . . they've no right to what they do nothing to earn . . . but this time . . . it was *wicked*.'

I agreed with her. I said, 'And for some time your yearlings have not been fetching good prices?'

'For two years,' she said fiercely. 'You're all in it. You know I won't give kick-backs so you won't bid for my horses.'

She was wrong about us all being in it. I had bought several bargains at various sales when half my rivals had turned their backs. Bargains for me and my clients, disasters for the people who'd bred them. And it was always the small breeder, the honest or naïve breeder who lost, because the big firms could look after themselves and others were crooks too and had some scandalous tricks of their own.

The kick-back system probably stemmed from the Irish 'luck penny': if you bought a horse from an Irishman he gave you back a penny of your money for luck. A penny! What a laugh.

There was no harm in a breeder giving an agent a thank-you present for getting him a good price for his horse. The harm came when the agent demanded it first. The crime came when he demanded it with threats and carried them out when he was refused.

Rumours rocketed round sale rings with the speed of light. I had heard the Winterfriend filly had a heart murmur ten minutes before she was sold, and I had believed it like everyone else.

I had often been told that the kick-back lark was on the increase. Some breeders made the best of it and some positively welcomed it, because it more or less guaranteed a good price for their horses. Only the Mrs Huntercombes who wouldn't play ball were coming to grief.

'Well?' she said belligerently. 'Sophie said to ask your advice. So what is it?'

I was too much of a realist for Aunt Antonia. I knew she wouldn't like what I would say, but I said it all the same.

'You've three choices. The first is to pay the kick-backs. You'd be better off in the end.'

'I won't.' She narrowed her eyes in anger. 'That's exactly what I would have expected from one of you.'

'The second,' I said, 'is to sell your stud, raise a mortgage on the house and live on an annuity.'

The anger grew. 'And just how do I get a fair price for my stallions and mares? And as for a mortgage . . . I already have one.' From the way she said it I guessed it was the largest she could get.

'Third,' I said, 'you could go every time to the sales when you sell a horse. Put a sensible reserve on it and get a friend to help with starting the bidding. Take a vet with you bristling with certificates. Tell the agents from the big firms, and as many other people as you can reach, whatever they may hear to the contrary, your horse is in good health, and offer to repay instantly if it is found to be not.'

She stared at me. 'I haven't the strength. It would be exhausting.'

'You sell only six or seven a year.'

'I am too old. I have high blood pressure and my ankles swell up.'

It was the first really human thing she'd said. I smiled at her. She did not smile back.

'It's the best I can do,' I said, standing up.

'Don't shut the front door when you go out,' she said. 'Or I'll have to get up to open it for the dogs.'

*

It was barely five miles from Paley to where I had arranged to meet the horsebox bringing River God from Devon. I had expected to reach the rendezvous first, but from some distance away I could see a blue box already parked in the designated place.

I had chosen one of those useful half-moons carved by road-straightening programmes where the loop of old country road remained as a leafy lay-by. There was one other car there, an old green Zodiac station wagon, which hadn't been cleaned for weeks. I passed it and the horsebox, and stopped in front, getting out to go back to talk to the driver.

Talking to the driver had to be postponed, as he was otherwise engaged. I found him standing with his back to that side of the box which faced away from the gaze of passing motorists on the main road. He was standing with his back to the box because he could retreat no further. Before him, adopting classic threatening poses, were two men.

I knew them well enough. I had met them at Ascot. Frizzy Hair and his mate.

They hadn't expected to see me either and it gave me at least an equal chance. I picked up the nearest weapon to hand, which was a nice solid piece of branch fallen from one of the road-lining trees, and positively raced to the attack. If I'd stopped to think I might not have done it, but fury is a great disregarder of caution.

My face must have been an accurate mirror of my feelings. Frizzy Hair for one indecisive moment looked mesmerized, horrified, paralysed by the spectacle of a normally moderate man rushing at him murderously, and because of it he moved far too slowly. I cracked the branch down on him with a ferocity that frightened me as much as him.

He screeched and clutched at the upper reaches of his left arm, and his mate made an equally comprehensive assessment of my general intentions and bolted towards the green wagon.

Frizzy Hair followed him, flinging nothing into the battle but one parting verbal shot.

'It won't help you.'

I ran after him, still holding the stick. He was going like a quarter horse and the mate was already in the driving seat with the motor turning over.

Frizzy Hair gave me a sick look over his shoulder, scrambled into the passenger seat and slammed the door. Short of being dragged along the highway I could see no way of stopping them: but I could and did take a quick look at the mud-coated number plate as they shot away, and before I could forget it I fished out pen and paper and wrote it down.

I went much more slowly back to the driver, who was staring at me much as if I were a little green man from outer space.

''Struth,' he said. 'I thought you was going to kill 'em.'

Hell hath no fury like the vanquished getting his own back.

I said, 'What did they want?'

'Blimey . . .' He pulled out a crumpled handkerchief and wiped his face. 'Didn't you even know?'

'Only in general,' I said. 'What in particular?'

'Eh?' He seemed dazed.

'What did they want?'

'Got a fag?'

I gave him one and lit for us both. He sucked in the smoke as if it were oxygen to the drowning.

'I s'pose you are . . . Jonah Dereham?' he said.

'Who else?'

'Yeah . . . I thought you were smaller, like.'

Five feet nine inches. Eleven stone. Couldn't be more average. 'A lot of jump jockeys are taller,' I said.

He began to look less stirred up. He ran his tongue round his teeth and seemed to feel a fresh flow of saliva to a dry mouth.

'What did they want?' I asked for the third time.

'That one you hit . . . with all that fluffy sort of hair . . . it was him did the talking.'

'What did he say?'

'Rum sort of bloke. All smiley. Came up to me cab as nice as you please asking for the loan of a spanner for 'is broken-down car.' He stopped to look at the empty road along which the broken-down car had vanished at high speed.

'Yeah . . . Well, see, I reached back to the tool kit

and asked what size. Come and look see, he said. So I jumped down from me cab. And then, see, he sort of grabbed me and shoved me back against the side of the box. And he never let off smiling. Creepy bastard. So then he says, look mate, there's someone as wants this horse more than you do.'

'I suppose he didn't say who?'

'Eh? No. He just says there's someone as wants him more than you do, so I says it isn't mine in the first place and he says not to make jokes . . . and him laughing his bleeding head off all the time.'

'What else did he say?'

'Nothing else. 'Struth, he didn't have time. Well, he did say as how I'd better let him take the horse peaceful like if I didn't want me ribs kicked in . . . well, I ask you . . . who would?'

Who indeed? 'So then what?'

'That's when you came belting into them like they'd raped your sister.'

'They didn't say just how they proposed to take the horse?'

He stared. 'No. I didn't ask. I s'pose they meant to drive off with the whole bleeding lot.' The idea offended him. 'Bleeding bastards,' he said.

'Did they offer to pay for it?'

''Struth, you don't half have some funny ideas.'

I wondered if they would have done, if I'd given them time. I wondered if I would have found the box driver clutching the cash plus another two hundred profit, and no River God in sight.

I sighed and stubbed out my cigarette.

'Let's look at the cargo,' I said, and climbed aboard the box.

The farmer had done a smartening up job along the lines of paint over rust. The feet had been seen to: the shoes were patently new, and the newly trimmed hooves had been darkened with oil. The mane and tail had been brushed out, and the coat was clean. On the other hand, there was a lot too much hair everywhere which spoke of little or no regular grooming; too much mane growing between the ears, too many whiskers around the muzzle, hairs too long on the chest, hairs sticking out everywhere instead of lying down neat and flat. The whole mess was shrouded by a tatty rug with two holes in it; and there was no attendant in sight.

'I asked the farmer to send a groom,' I said.

'Yeah. He said he didn't have nobody to spare. If you ask me he isn't fit to keep a pit pony, much less a racehorse. When I got there, you'd hardly credit it, there was this poor bleeding animal standing in the yard tied up to the outside of the stable door, and there was this big bleeding pool of water all round him on the ground. Shivering, he was. I reckon they just hosed him down to get all the muck off. The farmer said he was sweating, that was why his coat looked damp. I ask you, who did he think he was kidding. I made him give me the rug to put on the poor bleeder. He didn't want mc to take it in case I didn't bring it back.'

'OK,' I said. 'Let's get him out.'

He was surprised. 'What, out here on the road?'

'That's right,' I agreed.

'But he's warm enough now. He's dried off, like, on the journey up.'

'All the same . . .' I said, and helped the box driver, who said his name was Clem, unload River God. *Deus ex machina*, I thought irrelevantly, and nothing much about this one either was divine.

I removed the rug, folded it, and returned it to the box. Then with Clem holding the horse's farm-stained headcollar I went along to my car and took off my jacket, and in shirt sleeves collected from the boot my bag of gear.

'What are you going to do?' Clem asked.

'Tidy him up.'

'But I had to meet you at three . . . you were early but it's a quarter past already.'

'I left time enough,' I said. 'We're not due until four-thirty.'

'Did you reckon he'd look this rough, then?'

'Thought he might.'

Once I was committed to turning up with the horse I was also committed to defend what he looked like. I took out hand clippers, two pairs of scissors, a heavy steel comb and some wax tapers, and set to work.

Clem held the horse's head and watched while with

comb in one hand and lighted taper in the other I worked on the rough coat, singeing off all the too-long, sticking out hair which in a good stable would have been removed by daily brushing. The tiny candle flame was too small to disturb the horse, who felt no fear or pain, and he looked a lot less like a throwback to a carthorse when I'd finished. Next I clipped out the mane between his ears and over his withers, then snipped off the worst of the whiskers round his muzzle, and with a large pair of scissors finally straightened the bottom of his tail.

''Struth,' Clem said. 'He looks a different horse.'

I shook my head. Nothing but care, good food and brushing could bring a shine to that coat. He looked like a poor boy after a haircut, tidy but still poor.

Before we loaded him up again I wound neat dark blue bandages round his forelegs and buckled on the clean rug I'd brought from my own yard. Eliza Doolittle off to the ball, I thought, but it was the best I could do.

CHAPTER SIX

Kerry Sanders looked from Nicol to Constantine in carefully camouflaged anxiety while they inspected her gift. One of Brevett's own men was showing him off, trotting him now and then or making him stand with his legs arranged as for a photograph.

River God could move, I'd give him that. A good strong walk and a straight collected trot. Nothing to be ashamed of in that department.

Constantine was saying comfortingly, 'My dear girl, I realize you got him at very short notice. I'm sure he'll make up into a very good performer one of these days. Look at those legs . . . the bone is there.'

'I hope he'll win for Nicol,' she said.

'Of course he will. He's a very lucky boy to be given such a generous present.'

The lucky boy himself drew me aside and said abrasively, 'Couldn't you have found me something better?'

I had ridden against him often enough in races, at the end of my career and the beginning of his, and he knew me as well and as little as any jockey in the changing room.

'She gave me two days . . . and its form isn't bad.'

'Would you have ridden it?'

'Definitely. And if it turns out no good, I'll sell it for you later.'

He sucked his teeth.

'It did quite well in a bad stable,' I said. 'It should improve a mile in yours.'

'D'you think so?'

'Give it a try.'

He smiled sourly. 'And don't look a gift horse in the teeth?'

'She wanted to please you,' I said.

'Huh. Buy me, more like.'

'Happy birthday,' I said.

He turned to watch Kerry Sanders talking to his father, the neat, small, feminine figure overshadowed by the large, protecting, paternal male. As before, the Sanders wrappings were as uncluttered as gold bricks and the slanting autumn sunlight drew fire from the diamond knuckledusters.

'At least she's not after his money,' Nicol said. 'I had her checked out. She's way ahead.'

For an also-ran, Constantine was not doing so badly. Clem's horsebox stood on a clear quarter-acre of front drive with Clem himself fidgeting around for a signal that he could set off home. There were buildings along two sides of the mini parade ground, a modern garage and stable block at one end set at right angles to a much older, slightly austere stone house. Not quite a mansion, but more than enough for two.

The outside surface was being cleaned, with nearly one third showing warm cream instead of forbidding grey. One could see that it would look a good deal more welcoming when it was finished, but the effect meanwhile was undignified piebald. One should not, I reflected, ever make the mistake of thinking one would catch its master at such public disadvantage.

Nicol strode over to the man leading River God and the man nodded and took the horse away to the stables.

Kerry Sanders looked a fraction disappointed until Nicol rejoined her and said, 'Thought I'd just try it. Can't wait, you see.'

River God came back with saddle and bridle, and Nicol swung easily onto his back. He trotted him a little round the gravel and then took him through a gate into a railed field alongside and quickened the pace to a working canter. Constantine Brevett watched with heavy good humour, Kerry Sanders with hope, Clem with impatience and I with relief. Whatever I thought of his financial methods, Ronnie North had delivered the goods.

Nicol came back, handed the reins to the stableman, and strode over and kissed Kerry Sanders with enthusiasm on the cheek.

'He's great,' he said. His eyes shone. 'Absolutely great.'

Her face filled with joy enough to melt the hardest case. Nicol took note of it, and as she and his father turned away to return to the house he gave me a twisted smile and said, 'See? I'm not always a bastard.'

'And besides,' I said, 'the horse is better than he looks.'

'Cynical sod. It's got a mouth like the back end of a rhino.'

'A ride for a pro, I was told.'

'The first nice thing you've ever said to me.' He laughed. 'Come on in and have a drink.'

'Just a sec . . .' I turned away to go over to Clem to give him a fiver and send him off home and found Nicol following me to double the ante. Clem took both notes with cheerfulness, hopped up into the cab and rolled away to the gate.

Champagne stood ready in tulip-shaped glasses in the sitting-room to which Nicol led the way, the last rays of sun making the bubbles glisten like silver in liquid gold. Constantine handed us a glass each and we drank rather pompously to Nicol's health. He gave me a private, irreverent grin and greatly to my surprise I began to like him.

We sat in cloud nine armchairs and Constantine fussed over Kerry Sanders. She glowed with happiness, the peach bloom cheeks as fresh as a child's. It was extraordinary, I thought, how clearly and quickly the mental state of a woman showed in her skin.

'You almost didn't get a horse at all,' she told Nicol.

'The most infuriating thing happened to the first one Jonah bought.'

They listened to the saga in bewilderment, and I added to it by saying that the same two thugs had tried a repeat with River God.

Constantine took up a heavily authoritarian stance which went well with his smooth silver hair and thick black spectacle frames, and assured Kerry that he would see they got their just deserts. As it was fairly likely I had broken Frizzy Hair's arm I thought he had probably got his already, but I had no quarrel with any plans Constantine might have for finding out what was going on. He had the weight to lean heavily in places where I had none.

'What do you think, Jonah?' Nicol asked.

'Well . . . I can't believe either Hearse Puller or River God would themselves be the cause of so much action. They came from widely different places, so it can't be anyone close to them resenting them being sold. It seems even crazier when you think that we'll find out who bought Hearse Puller as soon as he's entered in a race. Even if he's changed hands more than once we should be able to trace him back.'

Constantine shook his head heavily and spoke from personal knowledge. 'Easy enough to cover up a sale if you know how.'

'Maybe someone simply wanted to stop Kerry giving me a horse,' Nicol said.

'But why?' Kerry asked. 'Why should they?'

No one knew. 'Who did you tell about River God?' I asked her.

'After last time? You must be crazy. At least when you got another horse I had the sense not to shout it around.'

'You didn't tell Lady Roscommon or your hairdresser or Pauli Teksa? None of the same people as last time?'

'I sure did not. I didn't see Madge or the hairdresser guy, and Pauli was out of town.'

'Someone knows,' Nicol said. 'So who did you tell, Jonah?'

'No one. I didn't tell the man I bought it from who it was for, and I didn't tell the transport firm where they were taking it.'

'Someone knew,' Nicol said again, flatly.

'Do you have any particularly bad friends?' I asked him.

'The professional jockeys all hate my guts.'

'And the amateurs?'

He grinned. 'Them too, I dare say.'

Constantine said, 'However jealous the other riders might be of Nicol's success, I cannot see any single one of them going around buying up or stealing horses simply to prevent Nicol riding winners.'

'They'd have a job,' Nicol said.

Constantine's voice was resonant and deep and filled the room to overflowing. Nicol had the same basic equipment but not the obvious appreciation of his own

92

power, so that in him the voice was quieter, more natural, not an announcement of status.

'What about Wilton Young?' he said.

Constantine was ready to believe anything of Wilton Young. Constantine saw only one threat to his bid to dominate British racing, and that was a bullet-headed Yorkshireman with no social graces, a huge mail-order business and the luck of the devil with horses. Wilton Young trampled all over people's finer feelings without noticing them and judged a man solely on his ability to make brass. He and Constantine were notably alike in ruthlessness and it was no doubt immaterial to their flattened victims that one streamroller was smoothly oiled while the other was roughly clanking.

'Of course,' Constantine said, his face filling with anger. 'Wilton Young.'

'The two men didn't have Yorkshire accents,' I said.

'What's that got to do with it?' Constantine demanded.

'Wilton Young makes a point of having York-shiremen working for him. He looks down on everyone else.'

'Arrogant little pipsqueak,' Constantine said.

'I can't honestly see him taking such trouble to stop Mrs Sanders giving Nicol a horse for his birthday.'

'Can't you?' Constantine looked down his nose as if he could believe half a dozen more improbable things before breakfast. 'He'd do anything he could think of to irritate me, however petty.'

'But how could he have known I was buying the horse for Nicol?'

He took barely three seconds to come up with an answer. 'He saw you at the sales with Kerry, and he has seen her at the races with me.'

'He wasn't at the sales,' I said.

He struggled impatiently. 'All you mean is that you didn't see him.'

I doubted if it were possible to be in so small a place as Ascot Sales' paddock and not know whether Wilton Young was there or not. He had a voice as loud as Constantine's and a good deal more piercing, and he was not a man who liked to be overlooked.

'Anyway,' Nicol said, 'I'll bet his bloodstock agent was there. That carrot-headed little Yorkshireman who buys his horses.'

I nodded. 'So was your own chap, Vic Vincent.'

Constantine had nothing but praise for Vic Vincent.

'He's bought me some great yearlings this time. Two he bought at Newmarket last week ... classic colts, both of them. Wilton Young will have nothing to touch them.'

He went on at some length about the dozen or so youngsters which according to him were about to sweep the two-year-old board, patting himself on the back for having bought them. Vic Vincent was a great judge of a yearling. Vic Vincent was a great fellow altogether.

Vic Vincent was a great fellow to his clients, and

that was about where it ended. I listened to Constantine singing his praises and drank my champagne and wondered if Vic Vincent thought me enough of a threat to his Brevett monopoly to whip away any horse I bought for the family. On balance I doubted it. Vic Vincent looked on me as Wilton Young looked on non-Yorkshiremen: not worth bothering about.

I finished the champagne and found Kerry Sanders watching me. For signs of alcoholism, I supposed. I smiled at her and she smiled a little primly back.

'Kerry my dear, you couldn't do better, another time, than to consult Vic Vincent . . .'

'Yes, Constantine,' she said.

From Gloucester to Esher I thought about Frizzy Hair a little and Sophie Randolph a lot. She opened her door with the composure all in place and greeted me with a duplicate of the Gatwick kiss, cheek to cheek, a deal too chaste.

'You found me, then,' she said.

'How long have you lived here?'

'Just over a year.'

'So you weren't here when I used to race next door.'

'No,' she said. 'Come in.'

She looked different. She was wearing another long dress, not white and black and silver this time, but a glowing mixture of greens and blues. The cut on her forehead had crusted over and her system had recovered from the state of shock. Her hair looked a warmer gold, her eyes a deeper brown, and only the inner self-reliance hadn't changed a lot.

'How's your arm?' I asked.

'Much better. It itches.'

'Already? You heal fast.'

She shut the door behind me. The small lobby was an offshoot of the sitting-room which opened straight ahead, warm, colourful and full of charming things.

'It's pretty,' I said, and meant it.

'Don't sound so surprised.'

'It's just . . . I thought perhaps your room might be more bare. A lot of smooth empty surfaces, and space.'

'I may be smooth but I'm not empty.'

'I grovel,' I said.

'Quite right.'

There were no aeroplanes on her walls, but she wore a little gold one on a chain round her neck. Her fingers strayed to it over and over again during the evening, an unconscious gesture from which she seemed to gain confidence and strength.

A bottle of white wine and two glasses stood ready on a small silver tray.

She gestured towards them non-committally and said, 'Would you like some? Or don't you ever?'

'When Crispin is drunk,' I said, 'I drink.'

'Well, hallelujah.' She seemed relieved. 'In that case, take your jacket off, sit on the sofa, and tell me how you got on with my aunt.'

She made no mention at all of my invitation to marry. Maybe she had decided to treat it as a joke, and yesterday's joke at that. Maybe she was right.

'Your aunt,' I said, 'wouldn't take my advice if I showed her the way to Heaven.'

'Why not?' She handed me a glass and sat down comfortably opposite in an armchair.

I explained why not, and she was instantly angry on her aunt's behalf.

'She was swindled.'

'I'm afraid so.'

'Something must be done.'

I sipped the wine. Light, dry, unexpectedly flowery, and definitely not supermarket plonk.

'The trouble is,' I said, 'that the kick-back system is not illegal. Far from it. To many it is a perfectly sensible business method and anyone who doesn't take advantage of it is a fool.'

'But to demand half her profit . . .'

'The argument goes that an agent promised a large kick-back will raise the auction price much higher than it might have gone, so the breeder positively benefits. Some breeders don't just put up with having to pay the kick-backs, they offer to do so. In those cases everyone is happy.'

'Except the person who buys the horse,' she said severely. 'He comes off badly. Why do the buyers stand for it?'

'Ah,' I said. 'What clients don't know would sink a battleship.'

She looked disapproving. 'I don't like the sound of your profession.' She added, in the understatement of the year, 'It isn't straightforward.'

'What sort of agent you are depends on how you see things,' I said. 'Honesty is your own view from the hill.'

'That's immoral.'

I shook my head. 'Universal.'

'You're saying that honesty in the bloodstock business is only a matter of opinion.'

'And in every business, every country, every era, since the world began.'

'Jonah, you talk nonsense.'

'How about marriage?'

'What are the kick-backs?'

'Oh God,' I said. 'You learn fast.'

She laughed and stood up. 'I'm a lousy cook but if you stay I'll give you a delicious dinner.'

I stayed. The dinner came out of frozen packs and would have pleased Lucullus; lobster in sauce on shells and duck with almonds and honey. The freezer was the largest item in the small white kitchen. She stocked it up every six months, she said, and did practically no shopping in between.

Afterwards, over coffee, I told her about Frizzy Hair turning up to take River God. It did nothing much to improve her view of my job. I told her about the flourishing feud between Constantine Brevett and Wilton Young, and also about Vic Vincent, the blue-eyed boy who could do no wrong.

'Constantine thinks the yearlings he's bought must be good because they were expensive.'

'It sounds reasonable.'

'It isn't.'

'Why not?'

'Year after year top prices get paid for the prize flops.'

'But why?'

'Because,' I said, 'yearlings haven't been raced yet, and no one knows whether they will actually be any good. They make their price on their breeding.' And that too could be rigged, though I didn't think I had better tell her.

'This Vic Vincent . . . he's been paying high prices for good breeding?'

'High prices for moderate breeding. Vic Vincent is costing Constantine a packet. He's the biggest kick-back merchant of the lot, and getting greedier every minute.'

She looked more disgusted than horrified. 'My aunt was right about you all being crooks.'

'Your aunt wouldn't tell me who demanded half her profits . . . if you ring her again, ask her if she's ever heard of Vic Vincent, and see what she says.'

'Why not right now?'

She dialled her aunt's number, and asked, and

listened. Antonia Huntercombe spoke with such vehemence that I could hear her from the other side of the room, and her words were earthy Anglo-Saxon. Sophie made a face at me and nearly burst out laughing.

'All right,' she said, putting down the receiver. 'It was Vic Vincent. That's one of life's little mysteries cleared up. Now what about the rest?'

'Let's forget them.'

'Let's absolutely not. You can't just forget two fights in three days.'

'Not to mention a loose horse.'

She stared. 'Not the one . . .'

'Well,' I said. 'I might have believed that I hadn't shut a stable door properly for the first time in eighteen years, but not that a horse could get out of his rug by undoing the buckles.'

'You said . . . he was darker without his rug.'

'Yes.'

'You mean . . . someone took off his rug and shooed him out in front of my car . . . just to cause a crash?'

'To injure the horse,' I said. 'Or even to kill it. I'd have been in very great trouble if you hadn't reacted so quickly and missed him.'

'Because you would have been sued for your horse causing an accident?'

'No. The law is the other way round, if anything. Loose animals are no one's fault, like fallen trees. No . . . The way the insurance on that horse was fixed, I could have lost seventy thousand pounds if he'd been damaged but not dead. And that,' I added fervently, 'is a position I am never going to be in again.'

'Have you *got* seventy thousand pounds?'

'Along with six castles in Spain.'

'But . . .' She wrinkled her forehead. 'Letting that horse loose means that whoever it is is attacking you personally. Not Kerry Sanders or the Brevetts . . . but you.'

'Mm.'

'But why?'

'I don't know.'

'You must have some idea.'

I shook my head. 'As far as I know I've done no one any harm. I've thought about little else for two days but I can't think of anyone with a big enough grudge to go to all this trouble.'

'What about small grudges?'

'Dozens of them, I dare say. They flourish like weeds.'

She looked disapproving.

'You get them everywhere,' I said mildly. 'In every working community. Schools, offices, convents, horse shows . . . all seething with little grudges.'

'Not in control towers.'

'Oh yeah?'

'You're a cynic.'

'A realist. How about marriage?'

She shook her head with a smile that took the suggestion still as a joke, and her hand strayed for the twentieth time to the little gold aeroplane on its slender chain.

'Tell me about him,' I said.

Her eyes opened wide with shock. 'How did you . . .?'

'The aeroplane. You wear it for someone else.'

She looked down at her hand and realized how often she held it in just that position, touching the talisman.

'I . . . He's dead.'

She stood up abruptly and carried the coffee pot out to the kitchen. I stood also. She came back immediately with the calm friendly face, no grief showing and no encouragement either. She gestured to me to sit down again and we took our former places, me on the sofa, her in an adjacent armchair. There was a lot of space beside me on the sofa, but no way of getting her to sit there before she was ready.

'We lived together,' she said. 'For nearly four years. We never bothered to marry. It didn't seem to matter. At the beginning we never expected it to last . . . and it just grew more and more solid. I suppose we might have taken out a licence in the end . . .'

Her eyes looked back into the past.

'He was a pilot. A first officer on Jumbos, always on long trips to Australia . . . We were used to being apart.'

Still no emotion in her voice. 'He didn't die in an aeroplane.' She paused. 'Eighteen months ago yesterday he died in a hospital in Karachi. He had a

102

two-day rest stop there and developed an acute virus infection . . . It didn't respond to antibiotics.'

I looked at her in silence.

'I was mad to say I would marry you,' she said. A smile twitched the corners of her eyes. 'It was just . . . a rather nice bit of nonsense.'

'A nonsense a day is good for the digestion.'

'Then you certainly will never get ulcers.'

We looked at each other. A moment like that in the kitchen, but this time with no Crispin to interrupt.

'Would you consider,' I said, 'coming to sit on the sofa?'

'Sit on it. Not lie on it.'

Her meaning was plain.

'All right.'

She moved to the sofa without fuss.

'I'll say one thing for you,' she said. 'When you make a contract, you keep it.'

'How do you know?'

'Too proud not to.'

'Beast.'

She laughed. She put her head on my shoulder and her mouth eventually on mine, but it was more a matter of warmth than of kindling passions. I could feel the withdrawal lying in wait only a fraction below the surface, a tenseness in the muscles warning me how easily I could go too far.

'Stop worrying,' I said. 'A contract's a contract, like you said.'

'Is this enough for you?'

'Yes.'

She relaxed a good deal. 'Most men nowadays think dinner leads straight to bed.'

Most men, I reflected, had exactly the right idea. I put my arm round her and shoved the most basic of urges back into its cave. I had won a lot of waiting races in my time. Patience was an old friend.

She lifted her head off my chest and rubbed her cheek.

'Something's scratching me.'

I explained about the dislocating shoulder, and the strap I wore to keep it anchored in place. She traced the line of webbing across my chest and rubbed her fingers on the scratching buckle.

'How does it work?'

'A small strap round my arm is linked to the one round my chest. It stops me lifting my arm up.'

'Do you wear it always?'

I nodded. 'Mm.'

'Even in bed?'

'Not this one. A softer one.'

'Isn't it a nuisance?'

'I'm so used to it I never notice.'

She looked up at my face. 'Couldn't you get it fixed? Isn't there an operation?'

'I'm allergic to scalpels.'

'Reasonable.'

She stretched for a cigarette and I lit it, and we

sat side by side talking about her job, and mine, her childhood and mine, her tastes in books and places and people, and mine.

Exploration, not conflagration.

When the time was right I kissed her again. And went home.

CHAPTER SEVEN

I spent most of the next week in Newmarket, staying with a trainer friend for the sales and the races.

Crispin, sober and depressed, had sworn to stay off drink in my absence and find a job, and as usual I had assured him he had the will power to do both. Experience always proved me wrong, but to him the fiction was a prop.

Sophie had worked awkward hours all weekend and Monday but said she would come down to my house for lunch the next Sunday, if I would like. I could bear it, I said.

The whole mob was at Newmarket. All the blood-stock agents, big and small. All the trainers with runners, all the jockeys with mounts, all the owners with hopes. All the clients with their cheque books ready. All the breeders with their year's work at stake. All the bookies looking for mugs. All the Press looking for exclusives.

I had commissions for eleven yearlings if I could find good ones at the right price, and in most cases my clients' money was already in my bank. I should have been feeling quietly pleased with the way business was expanding but found instead a compulsive tendency to look over my shoulder for Frizzy Hair.

The fact that nothing else had happened over the weekend had not persuaded me that nothing would. The attacks still seemed senseless to me, but someone somewhere must have seen a point to them, and the point was in all likelihood still there.

Crispin had sworn on everything sacred from the Bible to his 2nd XV rugger cap that he had found the bottle of whisky standing ready and uncapped on the kitchen table, and had smelled it as soon as he went through the door. At the tenth vehement repetition, I believed him.

Someone knew about my shoulder. Knew about my brother. Knew I kept horses in transit in my yard. Knew I was buying a horse for Kerry Sanders to give to Nicol Brevett. Someone knew a damn sight too much.

The Newmarket sale ring would have suited Kerry Sanders: a large, enclosed amphitheatre, warm, well lit and endowed with tip-up armchairs. At ground level round the outside, under the higher rows of seating, were small offices rented by various bloodstock agents. Each of the large firms had its own office, and also a few individuals like Vic Vincent. One had to do a good deal of business to make the expense worth it, though the convenience was enormous. I would have arrived, I thought, when I had my own little office at every major sale ring. As it was I did my paperwork as usual in the margins of the catalogue and conducted meetings in the bar.

I turned up on the first day, Tuesday, before the first horse was sold, because often there were bargains to be had before the crowds came, and was buttonholed just inside the gate by Ronnie North.

'I got your cheque for River God,' he said. 'Now tell me, wasn't that just what you wanted?'

'You should have seen it.'

He looked pained. 'I saw it race last spring.'

'I shouldn't think it had been groomed since.'

'You can't have everything for that money.'

He was a small whippet of a man, as quick on his feet as in his deals. He never looked anyone in the face for long. His eyes were busy as usual, looking over my shoulder to see who was arriving, who going and what chance of the quick buck he might be missing.

'Did he like it?' he asked.

'Who?'

'Nicol Brevett.'

Something in my stillness drew his attention. The wandering eyes snapped back to my face and he took rapid stock of his indiscretion.

I said, 'Did you know it was for Nicol before you sold it to me?'

'No,' he said, but his fractional hesitation meant 'yes'.

'Who told you?'

'Common knowledge,' he said.

'No, it wasn't. How did you know?'

'Can't remember.' He showed signs of having urgent business elsewhere and edged three steps sideways.

'You just lost a client,' I said.

He stopped. 'Honest, Jonah, I can't tell you. Leave it at that, there's a pal. More than my life's worth to say more, and if you want to do me a favour you'll forget I mentioned . . .'

'A favour for a favour,' I said.

'What?'

'Start the bidding for number four.'

'You want to buy it?'

'Yes,' I said.

He looked at me doubtfully. No one who wanted to buy liked to show eagerness by making the first bid, but on the other hand no astute bloodstock dealer ever told another which horse he was after. I produced all the earnest naivety I could muster and he smirked a little and agreed to bid. When he had darted off I slowly followed, and saw him from across the paddock talking excitedly to Vic Vincent.

Together they turned the first few pages of the catalogue and read the small print. Vic Vincent shook his head. Ronnie North talked quickly, but Vic Vincent shook his head even harder.

I shrugged. All I'd proved was that Ronnie North wouldn't do me a favour without clearing it with Vic

Vincent. It didn't follow that it was Vic Vincent who had told him that River God was for Nicol Brevett.

The first few horses were being led up from the stables to the collecting rings, and I leaned on the rails and took a close look at number four. A chestnut colt grown out of proportion with a rear end too tall for its front. Time would probably right that but would do little to improve the narrow head. Its breeding was fairly good, its full sister had won a decent race, and it was being offered for sale by Mrs Antonia Huntercombe of Paley Stud.

'Morning, Jonah,' said a voice half behind me.

I turned. Jiminy Bell, half ingratiating, half aggressive, as at Ascot. A great one for arriving unheard at one's elbow. He looked pinched with cold in the brisk wind because his overcoat was too thin for the job.

'Hullo,' I said. 'Care to earn a tenner?'

'You're on.' No hesitation at all.

'Start the bidding on number four.'

'What?' His mouth stayed open with surprise.

'Go up to two thousand.'

'But you never . . . you never . . .'

'Just this once,' I said.

He gulped, nodded, and presently disappeared. He was less obvious than Ronnie North, but in a remarkably short time he too fetched up beside Vic Vincent, and he too got the emphatic shake of the head.

I sighed. Sophie's Aunt Antonia was about to make another loss. For Sophie's sake I had tried to ensure her a good price, but if Vic Vincent had put the evil eye on the colt I was going to get it for almost nothing. I thought on the whole that I had better not buy it. I wouldn't be able to explain it to either Sophie or her aunt.

Very much to my surprise I found Vic himself drifting round to my side. He rested his elbows on the rails beside me, and nodded a greeting.

'Jonah.'

'Vic.'

We exchanged minimal smiles that were more a social convention than an expression of friendship. Yet I could have liked him, and once had, and still would have done had he not twice pinched my clients by telling them lies.

It was so easy to believe Vic Vincent. He had a large, weather-beaten face with a comfortable double chin and a full mouth which smiled easily and turned up at the corners even in repose. A lock of reddish-brown hair growing forward over his forehead gave him a boyish quality although he must have been forty, and even his twinkling blue eyes looked sincere.

The bonhomie was barely skin deep. When I protested about my lost clients he had laughed and told me that all was fair in love, war and bloodstock, and if I didn't like the heat to get out of the kitchen but he would stoke up the fire as much as he liked.

He turned up his sheepskin coat collar round his

ears and banged one thickly gloved hand against the other.

'Parky this morning.'

'Yes.'

'I heard you had a spot of bother at Ascot,' he said.

'That's right.'

'Constantine Brevett told me.'

'I see.'

'Yeah.' He paused. 'If Mrs Sanders wants any more horses, you'd better let me get them.'

'Did Constantine say so?'

'He did.'

He watched the first horses walk round the ring. Number four looked reasonable from behind but scratchy in front.

'I bought a colt just like that, once,' Vic observed. 'I thought his shoulders would develop. They never did. Always a risk when they grow unevenly.'

'I suppose so,' I said. Poor Antonia.

He stayed a few more seconds, but he had delivered his two messages as succinctly as if he'd said straight out, 'Don't step on my toes, and don't buy that colt.' He gave me the sort of reinforcing nod that the boss gives the cowed and ambled bulkily away.

The loudspeakers coughed and cleared their throats and said, 'Good morning everyone, the sale is about to begin.'

I went inside. Apart from four or five earnestly suited auctioneers in their spacious rostrum the place was deserted. Electric lights augmenting the daylight shone brightly on tiers of empty seats, and the sand on the circular track where the merchandise would walk was raked fine and flat. The auctioneers looked hopefully towards the door from the collecting ring and Lot 1 made its apologetic appearance attended by a few worried-looking people who were apparently its vendors.

There was no bid. No one there bidding. Lot 1 made its way through the far door and the worried people went after it.

There was no bid for Lot 2 and ditto for Lot 3. British auctioneers tended to arrange their catalogues so that the potential money-makers came up in mid-session, and small studs like Antonia's got the cold outer edges.

Lot 4 looked better under bright lights. All horses always did, like jewellery, which was why auctioneers and jewellers spent happily on electricity.

The auctioneer dutifully started his sale while clearly expecting nothing to come of it. He stretched the price up to one thousand without one genuine bid, at which point I rather undecidedly waved my catalogue. Antonia would be livid if I got it for a thousand.

'Thank you, sir,' he said, sounding surprised, and picked 'Eleven hundred' expertly out of the totally empty ranks of seats facing him.

Glory be, I thought. The aunt had had the sense to slap on a reserve. I made it twelve, the auctioneer said thirteen, and between us we limped up to his own bid of nineteen.

'You're losing him,' said the auctioneer warningly.

Three or four people came in from the outside and stood near me on the edge of the track where Lot 4 plodded patiently round and round. Everyone outside could hear on the loudspeakers how the sale was going, and some had come in to see.

I wondered how high Antonia had made the reserve. Two thousand was all I would give for that colt. If she wanted more she could have him back.

I nodded to the auctioneer. He fractionally relaxed, said smoothly, 'Two thousand ... Selling all the time now ...' His gaze went past me to the people who had just come in. 'Shall I say two thousand one ...?'

No one said two thousand one. He made a few more efforts to no avail and Jonah Dereham got the colt.

I turned round. Behind me stood Vic Vincent, looking like thunder.

'Jonah,' he said. 'I want to talk to you.'

'Sure, Vic, how about coffee?'

He brushed the suggestion aside. He took me strongly by the arm in a mock-friendly gesture and practically propelled me out of the door.

'Now look,' he said.

'What's the matter?'

'I told you that colt was no good.'

'I'm grateful for your interest.'

He glared at me. 'How much is Mrs Huntercombe giving you?'

'It's cold out here,' I said.

He looked near to fury.

'She's giving you nothing,' he said.

'I haven't asked her to.'

'That's the point, you stupid sod. We must all stick together. We must all let the breeders know that we all stick together. Do you understand what I'm saying? We can't have you working for less than the rest of us. It's not fair on us. You'll make more money yourself too if we all stick together. It makes sense. Do you follow me?'

'Yes,' I said. All too well.

'Mrs Huntercombe and people like her must be made to understand that unless they reward us properly we are not interested in buying their horses.'

'I follow you,' I said.

'Good. So you'll go along with us in future.' A positive statement, not a question.

'No,' I said.

There may be quicker ways of stirring up hornets, but I doubt it. The rage flowed out of him like a tangible force. He was so near to explosive physical assault that his arms jerked and his weight shifted to his toes. Only the gathering sales crowd stopped him lashing out. He flicked glances left and right, saw people watching, took an almighty and visible grip on his feelings and put the frustrated violence into words.

'If you don't join us we'll ruin you.'

There was no mistaking the viciousness in that voice, and the threat was no idle boast. People found it easy to believe Vic Vincent. The two clients I had already lost to him had believed I cheated them because Vic Vincent had told them so. He could stop the sale of a good filly just by saying she had a heart murmur. He could no doubt smash my growing business with a rumour just as simple and just as false. A bloodstock agent was only as secure as his clients' faith.

I could think of no adequate answer. I said, 'You used not to be like this,' which was true enough but got me nowhere.

'I'm telling you,' he said. 'You play ball or we'll get you out.'

He turned on his heel and walked jerkily away, the anger spilling out of the hunched shoulders and rigid legs. Ronnie North and Jiminy Bell circled round him like anxious satellites and I could hear his voice telling them, low, vigorous and sharp.

Within an hour most of the bloodstock agents knew of the row and during the day I found out who my friends were. The bunch I had said I wouldn't join drew their skirts away and spoke about me among themselves while looking at me out of the corners of their eyes. The chaps in the big firms treated me exactly as usual, and even one or two with approval, as officially they frowned on exorbitant kick-backs.

The uncommitted in the no man's land between were the most informative.

I had coffee and a sandwich with one of them, a man who had been in the game longer but was in much my position, more or less established and just beginning to prosper. He was distinctly worried and cheered up not at all when I confirmed what Vic had threatened.

'They've approached me as well,' he said. 'They didn't say what would happen if I didn't join them. Not like with you. They just said I would be better off if I did.'

'So you would.'

'Yes ... but ... I don't know what to do.' He put down his sandwich half finished. 'They're getting so much worse.'

I said I'd noticed it.

'There used to be just a few of them,' he said. 'When I started, only a few. But lately they're getting so powerful.'

'And so greedy,' I said.

'That's it,' he said in eager agreement. 'I don't mind a little extra on the side. Who does? It's just that ... they've started pushing so hard. I don't know what to do ... I don't like their methods and I can't afford ...' He stopped, looked depressed, and went on slowly, 'I suppose I could just not bid when the word goes round. There wouldn't be much harm in that.'

The make-the-best-of-it syndrome. The buttress of

every tyrant in history. He took his worries away and later I saw him smiling uneasily with Vic.

During the day I bought one more yearling, bidding against one of the big firms and securing it for a fair price. However extensively Vic's tentacles might stretch, they had not reached every breeder in the country, or at any rate not yet. Neither he nor his friends showed any interest in my second purchase.

Towards the end of the day one of my regular clients arrived with a flashy girl in one hand and a cigar in the other: Eddy Ingram, member of the well-heeled unemployed.

'Staying for the week,' he said cheerfully, waving the cigar in a large gesture. 'How about you joining me and Marji for dinner tomorrow night?'

'I'd like to.'

'Great, great.' He beamed at me, beamed at Marji. An overgrown schoolboy with a nature as generous as his inheritance. I thought him a fool and liked him a lot. 'Have you found me a couple of good 'uns, then?' he asked.

'There's one tomorrow . . .'

'You buy it. Tell me after.' He beamed again. 'This lad,' he said to Marji, 'he's bought me four horses and they've all shown a profit. Can't complain about that, can you?'

Marji smiled sweetly and said, 'Yes, Eddy,' which was a fair measure of her brain-power.

'Don't forget now. Dinner tomorrow.' He told me

where and when, and I said I would see him at the races or the sales before that, if not both.

He beamed and led Marji away to the bar and I wished there were more like him.

In the morning I bought him a well-bred filly for eleven thousand pounds, outbidding one of Vic Vincent's cronies. As none of his bunch looked upset, I guessed that one or all of them jointly would be collecting a kick-back from the breeder. Even though they hadn't bought the horse they would collect just for raising the price.

By mid-morning the crowd had swelled tremendously and almost every seat in the amphitheatre was taken. Two highly bred colts, due to come up towards noon, were bringing in the punters on their way to the races and the town's wives with their shopping baskets and the semi-drunks from the bars. None had the slightest intention of buying, but there was an irresistible fascination in seeing huge sums being spent. I watched the two star attractions stalk grandly round the collecting ring and then with the tide moved inside for the actual sale. No seats vacant near the door. I leaned against one of the dividing partitions and found myself next to Pauli Teksa. Short, tough, American. Wearing a wide-shouldered light blue overcoat.

'Hi,' he said. 'How're you doing?'

'Fine. And you?'

'Grand... I hear Nicol Brevett liked his horse. Kerry called me.'

'Did she tell you we nearly lost that one too?'

'She sure did. That's some mystery you've got there.'

His attention, however, was not on Kerry or me or the problem of our disappearing purchases, but on the sale in hand. Heavy scribblings and calculations surrounded the high-bred colts in his catalogue, and it looked as though one American agent at least was about to try for a slice of British bloodstock.

The double doors from the collecting ring opened and the first of the colts was led in. The crowd stirred expectantly. The auctioneers put their best man forward. Pauli Teksa cleared his throat.

I glanced at his face. Nothing relaxed about it. Strong features, hard muscles beneath the skin, a face of resolution and decision, not of kindness and compassion. He had crinkly black hair receding at the temples and smoky grey eyes which could move faster than thought.

'The first of two colts by Transporter.' The auctioneer trotted through his spiel. ' . . . Offered for sale by the Baylight Stud . . . Someone start me at ten thousand.'

Someone started him at five. When the price rose to ten, Pauli Teksa started bidding. I owed him something, I thought, for giving me Kerry Sanders' commission, however oddly it had turned out.

'I wouldn't buy that colt if I were you,' I said.

'Why not?' He raised the price another two thousand with his eyebrows.

'Because of its colour.'

'Nothing wrong with its colour. Perfectly good chestnut.' Another two thousand.

I said, 'Transporter has sired about three hundred horses and that's the only chestnut. All the rest are dark bay or light brown.'

'So?' Another two thousand.

'So I wouldn't bet on the paternity.'

Pauli stopped bidding abruptly and turned towards me with an intent, concentrated expression.

'You sure do your homework.'

I watched the chestnut colt going round the sand track while the price rose to forty thousand.

'I've seen a lot of Transporter's progeny,' I said. 'And they don't look like that.'

The auctioneer looked over to Pauli inquiringly. 'Against you, sir.'

Pauli shook his head, and the bidding went on without him.

'This guy from New Zealand,' he said. 'When he was over stateside, he asked me to buy him a Transporter colt at Newmarket if one came up, and ship it out to him so he could mix the blood line with his stock.'

I smiled and shook my head.

'How much do you want?' Pauli said.

'What do you mean?'

'For the information.'

'Well . . . nothing.'

Pauli looked at me straightly. 'You're a goddam fool,' he said.

'There's things besides money,' I said mildly.

'No wonder these other guys are against you!'

'What have you heard?' I asked curiously.

'Why don't you go along with them?'

'I don't like what they're doing.'

He gave me an old-man-of-the-world look and told me I'd get hurt if I didn't go along with the crowd. I said I would chance it. I was a triple goddam fool, he said.

The chestnut colt made fifty-six thousand pounds. The second potential star seller came into the ring looking as a Transporter should, dark bay with a slightly narrow neck and sharp pelvic bones high on the rump.

'What about this one?' Pauli demanded.

'The real McCoy.'

'You slay me.'

He bid for it but dropped out at his authorized limit of fifty thousand. I reflected upon how terribly easy it was to influence a sale. Pauli had believed me on two counts, first against the chestnut and then for the bay, and had acted unhesitatingly on what I'd said. Just so had others with Vic Vincent. Who could blame anyone at all for heeding off-putting advice when so much money was at risk.

At fifty-two thousand all the big firms had dropped out and the bidding had resolved itself into a straight contest between Vic Vincent and the carrot-headed Yorkshireman, Fynedale, who bought for Wilton Young. Constantine Brevett, I suddenly saw, had brought his smooth hair and dark-framed spectacles into the arena and was standing at Vic's shoulder talking urgently into his ear.

Wilton Young's man was nodding away as if he had the whole mint to call on. Constantine was looking both piqued and determined. Yearlings that cost more than sixty thousand were not a great financial proposition, even with the stud potential from Transporter, and I guessed that against anyone but Wilton Young he would have dropped out long ago.

At seventy thousand he began to scowl. At seventy-five he shook his head angrily and stalked out of the sale ring. The carrot-headed Fynedale winked at Vic Vincent.

Pauli Teksa said, 'Say, that was some figure.'

'Too much,' I agreed.

'I guess pride comes expensive.'

It did, I thought. All sorts of pride came expensive, in one way or another.

He suggested a drink and with the sale's main excitement over we joined the general exodus barwards.

'Seriously, Jonah,' Pauli said, glass in hand and strong features full of friendly conviction. 'There's no place any more for the individualist in the game. You either have to join a big firm or else come to an agreement with the small men like yourself and act together as a body. You can't buck the system . . . not if you're out for profits.'

'Pauli, stop trying,' I said.

'I don't want to see you in big trouble, fellah.'

'Nothing will happen,' I said, but he shook his head, and said he was afraid for me, he surely was. I was too honest for my own good.

CHAPTER EIGHT

Constantine, Kerry and Nicol were all at the track that
afternoon, to see Constantine's colt start favourite for
the big race. Constantine was in such a bad mood that
they would have had more fun in a dentist's waiting-
room, and soon after they arrived Nicol detached
himself from the general gloom and joined me with a
grimace.

'That bloody Wilton Young...'

We strolled over to see the runners for the apprentice race walk round the parade ring.

'Tell your father to console himself with the thought
that Wilton Young has probably poured his money
down the drain.'

'Do you think so?'

'How many horses earn anything like seventy-five
thousand?'

'He's convinced it'll win the Arc de Triomphe.'

'More likely a consolation race at Redcar.'

Nicol laughed. 'That'll cheer him up.'

I asked him how River God was doing and he said

he was eating well and already looking better. He asked if I had found out why Frizzy Hair had wanted his horses and I said I hadn't. We spent two or three chunks of the afternoon together, cementing an unexpected friendship.

Vic Vincent took a note of it and disliked what he seemed to see as a threat to his Brevett monopoly. Even Nicol noticed the blast of ill will coming my way.

'What have you done to upset Vic?' he asked.

'Nothing.'

'You must have done *something*.'

I shook my head. 'It's what I won't do,' I said, 'and don't ask what it is, because I can't tell you.'

He sniffed. 'Professional secret?'

'Sort of.'

He gave me the flashing sideways grin. 'Like when you knew I was lying my head off to keep a race on an objection, and you didn't split?'

'Well . . .'

'Yeah,' he said. 'I remember, even if you don't. You finished fourth. You listened to me giving my owner a right lot of codswallop and you never said a word.'

'You'd won the race.'

'Yeah . . . and they'd have taken it off me if you'd given me away.'

'It was a long time ago.'

'All of three years.' He grinned. 'The leopard still has the same claws.'

'Spots.'

126

'Claws.' The grin came and went. 'You were a ferocious bastard to ride against.'

'No.'

'Oh sure. Milk and honey on the ground and a bloody nuisance as an opponent.' He paused. 'I'll tell you . . . I learned something from you. I learned not to go around squealing when things weren't fair. . . . I learned to shrug off small injustices and get on with the next thing and put my energies in the future instead of rabbiting about the past. I learned not to mind too much when things went against me. And I reckon I owe you a lot for that.'

'You just paid it,' I said.

I leaned later alone against the rails of the balcony on the Members' roof and looked down to where Vic Vincent was moving desultorily from group to group. Talking, smiling, taking notes, nodding, patting people on the back. He looked pleasant, knowledgeable and useful. He looked boyish, harmless and trustworthy. He wore a heavy tweed suit and a slightly dandified dark red shirt with a white collar and tie, and no hat on the reddish-brown hair.

I wondered why he had recently grown so aggressively rapacious. He had been successful for a long time and as one of the top one-man bands he must have been handling about two million pounds' worth of business every year. At a flat 5 per cent that meant a hundred thousand stayed with him, and even after heavy expenses and taxes he must have been well off.

He worked hard. He was always there, standing in the bitter winds round the winter sale rings, totting up, evaluating, advising, buying, laying out his judgement for hire. He was working even harder now that he was going around intimidating breeders in far-flung little studs. Something had recently stoked up his appetite for money to within a millimetre of open crime.

I wondered what.

Pauli Teksa rapturized about Newmarket and compared it favourably with every American track from Saratoga to Gulf Stream Park. When pinned down by my scepticism he said he guessed he liked Newmarket because it was so *small*. And *quaint*. And so goddam *British*. The stands at Newmarket were fairly new and comfortable; but I reflected wryly that small, quaint and British usually meant hopelessly inadequate seating, five deep in the bars and not enough shelter from the rain.

He liked the Heath, he said. He liked to see horses running on grass. He liked the long straight course. He liked right-handed races. He'd always liked Newmarket, it was so quaint.

'You've been here before?' I asked.

'Sure. Four years ago. Just for a look-see.'

We watched an untidy little jockey squeeze home

after five furlongs by a shorter margin than he ought, and on the way down from the stands found ourselves alongside Constantine and Kerry.

She introduced the two men to each other, the big silver-haired man of property and the short wide-shouldered American. Neither took to the other on sight. They exchanged social politeness, Constantine with more velvet than Pauli, but in less than two minutes they were nodding and moving apart.

'That guy sure thinks a lot of himself,' Pauli said.

Wilton Young arrived in a helicopter a quarter of an hour before the big race. Wilton Young had his own pilot and his own Bell Ranger, which was one up on the Brevett Rolls, and he made a point of arriving everywhere as noticeably as possible. If Constantine thought a lot of himself, Wilton Young outstripped him easily.

He came bouncing through the gate from the air strip straight across the paddock and into the parade ring, where his fourth-best three-year-old was on display for the contest.

The loud Yorkshire voice cut through the moist October air like a timber saw, the words from a distance indistinct but the overall sound level too fierce to be missed.

Constantine stood at the other end of the parade ring towering protectively over the little knot of Kerry, his trainer and his jockey, and trying to look unaware that his whole scene had just been stolen by the poison ivy from the skies.

Nicol said in my ear, 'All we want now is for Wilton Young's horse to beat Father's,' and inevitably it did. By two lengths. Easing up.

'He'll have apoplexy,' Nicol said.

Constantine, however, had beautiful manners even in defeat and consoled his trainer in the unsaddling enclosure without appearing to notice the ill-bred glee going on six feet away, in the number one slot.

'It always happens,' Nicol said. 'The one you least want to win is the one which does.'

I smiled. 'The one you choose not to ride . . .'

'They make you look a bloody fool.'

'Over and over.'

At the end of the afternoon I drove from the race-course, which lay a mile out on the London road, down into the town again, taking the right-hand turn to the sale paddocks. Nicol came with me, as Constantine was returning with Kerry to his hotel to lick his wounds in private, and we went round the stables looking at the dozen or so yearlings I had noted as possibles. He said he was interested in learning how to buy his own horses so that he wouldn't have to rely on an agent all his life.

'More like you, I'd be out of business,' I said.

There was a filly by On Safari that I liked the look of, a big, deep-chested brown mare with a kind eye. She had speed in her pedigree and her dam had produced three two-year-old winners already, and I thought that if she didn't fetch an astronomical amount she would do very nicely for Eddy Ingram.

She was due to come up about an hour after the evening session started, and I filled in the time by buying two moderate colts for a thousand each for a trainer in Cheshire.

With Nicol still in tow I went outside to watch the On Safari filly walk round the collecting ring. She walked as well as she looked and I feared that Eddy Ingram's limit of fifteen thousand might not be enough.

Jiminy Bell did his appearing act, sliding with a wiggle into the space between Nicol and myself as we stood by the rail.

'Got a note for you,' he said.

He thrust a folded piece of paper into my hand and vanished again even before I could offer him a drink, which was as unlikely as a gatecrasher leaving before the food.

I unfolded the paper.

'What's the matter?' Nicol said.

'Nothing.'

I put the paper into my jacket pocket and tried to take the grimness out of my face. The message was written in capital letters and allowed for no mistakes.

DON'T BID FOR 182.

'Jonah . . . you're as tense as a high wire.'

I looked at Nicol vaguely. He said again, 'For God's sake, what's the matter?'

I loosened a few muscles and said flippantly, 'If you've got to go, you've got to go.'

'Go where?'

'I expect I'll find out.'

'I don't understand you.'

'Never mind,' I said. 'Let's go and see this filly sold.'

We went into the big circular building and sat in the section of seats nearest the door, the section crowded as usual with breeders, agents and an all-sorts mixture of racing people. Ronnie North was in the row behind us. He leaned forward and spoke into the space between our heads.

'The word is that the On Safari filly is likely to be sterile. Some infection or other... No good as a breeding prospect, they say. Such a pity.'

Nicol looked startled and disappointed on my behalf. He asked Ronnie one or two questions but Ronnie shook his head sadly and said he didn't know details, only that he'd heard it on the best authority.

'She wouldn't be worth so much in that case,' Nicol said, turning back to me.

'Not if it's true.'

'But ... don't you think it is?'

'I don't know.'

Lot 180 was being sold. There was so little time. 'Got some business,' I said to Nicol. 'See you later.'

I scudded to the telephone. The On Safari filly came from an Irish stud I'd scarcely heard of, and it took two precious minutes for the Irish service to find me the number. Could they ring it at once, I asked.

'Half an hour's delay.'

'If it isn't at once it will be too late.'

'Hold on . . .'

There were clicks and distant voices and then suddenly, clearly, a very Irish voice saying 'Hello?'

I asked if the On Safari filly had ever had an infection or an assessment of fertility.

'Well now,' said the voice, deliberating slowly. 'I wouldn't know about that now. I wouldn't know anything about the horses, do you see, because I'm just here minding the children until Mr and Mrs O'Kearey get home on the train from Dublin . . . they'll be home in an hour, so they will. They'll be able to answer your question in an hour.'

When I got back the filly was already being led round and the bidding, such as it was, had started. The seat beside Nicol had been taken. I stood in the chute through which the horses were led into the ring and listened to the auctioneer assuring everyone that she had a clean bill of health.

A man beside me shook his head dubiously. I glanced at him. A senior partner from one of the big firms. He stared morosely at the filly and made no move to buy her.

A couple of people in the crowd had taken the price up to six thousand five hundred, and there she stuck. The last bidder began to look intensely worried and

obviously didn't want her. I guessed he was acting for
the breeder and would have to buy the filly back if she
didn't fetch a better price.

'Six thousand five ... any advance on six thousand
five? She's on the market ...' He looked round the
ranks of bloodstock agents and took note of the shut-
tered impassive faces. 'Six thousand five once then. Six
thousand five twice ... All done?' He raised his gavel
and I lifted my hand.

'Six thousand six.'

The last bidder's face relaxed in pure relief. Several
heads turned in my general direction, looking to see
who had bid, and the senior partner beside me stirred
and said out of the corner of his mouth, 'They say she's
sterile.'

'Thank you,' I said.

No one else made a move. The auctioneer tried
harder for another hit but without result, and knocked
her down with a shake of the head.

'Jonah Dereham,' he announced, writing it down.

A ripple like a shudder went through the small group
round Vic Vincent. I didn't wait to hear what they had
to say but beat it hastily down to the stables to see
about transport. On the way back an hour and a strong
cup of coffee later I came face to face with Eddy
Ingram who said loudly and without a smile that he
had been looking for me.

'If you've bought that On Safari filly for me,' he said
positively, 'you can forget it.'

The bright lights around the collecting ring shone on a face from which most of the good nature had evaporated. The delectable Marji registered scorn.

'She's bound to be fast, with that breeding,' I said.

'I've been told she's infected and sterile.' He was angry about it. Not the usual beaming Eddy at all. 'You're not spending my money on rubbish like that.'

'I haven't bought you a dud yet, Eddy,' I said. 'If you don't want this filly, well, fair enough, I'll find someone who does. But she's a bargain at that price and I'd have liked you to benefit.'

'But she's sterile. And you knew it before you bid for her. You weren't acting in my best interests.'

'Ah,' I said. 'Now there's a nice phrase. Not acting in your best interests. Who said that?'

His eyes flickered. 'I don't see . . .'

'I do,' I said drily.

'Anyway . . .' He shrugged off his doubts. 'Anyway, I'll take the one you bought for me this morning, but I don't want you to get me any more.'

Someone had been very quickly persuasive, but then Eddy was gullible and a fool. I wondered whether all my clients would desert with such speed.

Eddy came out with the clincher which had alienated him fastest. 'You didn't think I would find out she was sterile. You thought you'd collect your 5 per cent from me for buying her even though you knew she was probably useless.'

'How do you know she's sterile?' I asked.

'Vic says so.'

'And is Vic going to buy your horses in future?'

He nodded.

'Good luck to you, Eddy,' I said.

He still hovered indecisively. 'You haven't denied it.'

'I did not buy that filly just to get 5 per cent.'

He began to look unhappy. 'Vic said you'd deny it and I'd be a fool to believe you ...'

'Vic's a persuasive fellow,' I said.

'But you've bought me four good ones ...'

'You sort it out, Eddy. Think it over and let me know.'

I walked away and left him.

An hour later I again telephoned Ireland.

'Is she *what*?'

I took my eardrum away from the receiver and winced.

'Of course she's not sterile.' The Irish voice yelled out as if crossing the Irish Sea without benefit of wires. 'She's never had a day's illness since she was foaled. Where the devil did you hear that?'

'At the sales.'

'What?' Alarm joined the indignation. 'How much did she make?'

I told him. I removed the receiver a good ten inches and still had no difficulty in hearing. Vic Vincent's victims all seemed to be endowed with good lungs.

'I told a neighbour of mine to bid up to ten thousand and I'd be sure to pay him back if he had to buy her.'

'His nerve broke at six thousand five,' I said.

'I'll murder him.' He sounded as if he meant to. 'I told that Vic Vincent fellow I didn't need his help, I'd get my own bidding done thank you very much, and now look. Now look.' He gurgled.

'What did Vic offer?' I asked.

'He said he'd raise the filly to ten thousand, and if it made more than that he wanted half. *Half!* I ask you. I offered him one fifth and that's a bloody liberty, even that much. He said half or nothing so I said nothing and go to hell.'

'Will you do what he wants next time?'

'Next time!' The idea of a next and a next and a next time slowly sank in. 'Well . . .' Some of the fire went out. There was a long pause and when he finally spoke it was clear he had thought of the advantages of Vic's help and realized what refusing him might cost. 'Well now,' he said. 'Perhaps I will.'

When next I saw Eddy Ingram he was beaming away at Vic, and Marji likewise. All three of them in a little huddle, as thick as thieves.

I reflected uncharitably that I was in no way bound to tell Eddy there was nothing wrong with the filly. If she turned out to be the best brood mare of the century it would serve him damn well right.

*

Towards the end of the evening, after Nicol had left to have dinner, my arm was grabbed by a man who said fiercely, 'I want to talk to you,' and such was the readiness of my flight reflexes that I nearly hit and ran before I realized that his grievance was not with me. He was, he said, the breeder of the Transporter colt which Wilton Young's agent Fynedale had bought for seventy-five thousand pounds. He nearly spat the words out and did not look as one should if one's produce were among the top prices in the sales.

He insisted that he should buy me a drink and that I should listen to him.

'All right,' I said.

We stood in a corner of the bar drinking brandy and ginger ale while the bitterness poured out of him like acid.

'I heard Vic Vincent's out to get you. That's why I'm telling you this. He came down to my place last week and bought my colt for thirty thousand.'

'Oh did he,' I said.

Private sales before the auctions were not supposed to take place. Every horse in the catalogue had to appear in the sale ring unless excused by a vet's certificate, because otherwise, as the auctioneers complained with some reason, the buyers and sellers would just use their catalogue as a free information and advertising medium, and not send their horses to the auction at all. The auctioneers produced the catalogue and set up the sales, and wanted their 10 per cents for their trouble. At one or two sales the catalogue had not been produced until the very last minute because of the number of private bargains which had been struck at other times before the auction.

Late catalogues made my job a lot more difficult. On the other hand I knew that some breeders were avoiding paying the auctioneers' commission by selling privately for a good sum and then doing everything they could to keep the auction price at rock bottom. One couldn't blame the auctioneers for fighting back.

'Vic gave me a double promise,' said the breeder, his lips tight with fury. 'He said they wouldn't bid the price up to thirty thousand if nobody else was trying to buy.'

'So that you wouldn't have to pay the full commission to the auctioneers?'

He stared. 'Nothing wrong in that, is there? Business is business.'

'Go on,' I said.

'He said that if the price went up to fifty thousand he would give me half of everything over thirty.'

He drank, nearly choking himself. I watched.

'And then . . . then . . .' He spluttered, hardly able to get the words out. 'Do you know what he has the gall to say? He says our agreement only went as far as fifty thousand. Everything over that, he takes it *all*.'

I admired the beauty of it in an odd sort of way.

'Was the agreement in writing?' I asked.

'Yes,' he said furiously.

'Unfortunate.'

'*Unfortunate!* Is that all you have to say?'

I sighed. 'Why didn't you let the colt take its chance at the sale instead of selling to Vic first?'

'Because he didn't think it would make as much as thirty at auction, but he had a client who would give that much, and he said I might as well benefit.'

'Have you ever dealt with Vic before?' I asked curiously.

'Not directly. No. And to be honest, I was flattered when he came to my place specially . . . *Flattered!*'

He crashed his empty glass with a bang onto one of the small tables scattered in the bar. A man sitting at the table looked up and waved a beckoning arm.

'Join the club,' he said.

I knew him slightly; a small-scale trainer from one of the northern counties who came down south occasionally to buy new horses for his owners. He knew as much about horses as any agent, and I reckoned his owners had been lucky he could buy for them himself as it saved them having to pay an agent's commission.

He was lightly smashed, if not drunk.

'That bastard,' he said. 'Vic Vincent. Join the anti-Vic Vincent club.'

The breeder, hardly attending, said, 'What are you talking about?'

'Can you beat it?' the trainer asked of the world in general. 'I've bought horses for an owner of mine for years. Damn good horses. Then what happens? He

140

meets Vic Vincent and Vic persuades him to let him buy him a horse. So he buys it. And then what happens? Then I buy him a horse, like I've always done. And then what happens? Vic Vincent complains to my owner, saying I shouldn't buy the horses because it does him, Vic Vincent, out of the fair commission he would be getting if he bought them. Can you believe it? So I complain to my owner about him buying horses through Vic Vincent because I like to train horses I choose, not horses Vic Vincent chooses, and then what do you think happens?'

He threw his arms wide theatrically and waited for his cue.

'What happens?' I supplied obligingly.

'Then my owner says I'm not being fair to Vic Vincent and he takes his horses away from me and sends them to another trainer that Vic Vincent picked out for him and now between them they're rooking my owner right and left, but he doesn't even realize, because he thinks horses must be twice as good if they cost twice as much.'

The breeder listened in silence because he was deep anyway in his own grudges; and I listened in silence because I believed every incredible word of it. People who bought racehorses could be more easily conned than any old lady parting with her savings to a kind young man on the doorstep. People who bought race-horses were buying dreams and would follow anyone who said he knew the way to the end of the rainbow.

A few had found the crock of gold there, and the rest never gave up looking. Someone ought to start a Society for the Protection of Gullible Owners, I thought, smiling, with Constantine and Wilton Young as its first cases.

The breeder and the trainer bought large refills and sat down to compare wounds. I left them to their sorrows, went back to the ring, and bid unsuccessfully for a well-grown colt who went to Vic Vincent for nearly double my authorized limit.

The underbidder was Jiminy Bell. I saw Vic giving him a tenner afterwards and patting him on the back. Some other Gullible Owner would be paying Vic. It was enough to make you laugh.

Vic was not laughing, however, in the car park.

I was fishing out my keys to unlock the car door when someone shone a torch straight at my face.

'Turn that bloody thing off,' I said.

The light went out. When the dazzle cleared from my eyes there were six or seven men standing round me in a ring at a distance of six feet.

I looked at them one by one. Vic Vincent and the carrot-headed Yorkshireman Fynedale, Ronnie North and Jiminy Bell. Three others I met every day at the sales.

All deadly serious.

'What have we here?' I said. 'A lynch mob?'

No one thought it funny. Not even me.

CHAPTER NINE

Vic said, 'You're going to have to be told, Jonah.'

'Told what?'

There were people within shouting distance, going to their cars. I thought maybe I would shout, but not perhaps just yet.

The seven men took a small step forwards almost as if moved by a signal. I stood with my back against my car and thought I was getting tired of being attacked in car parks. Have to travel more by train.

'You're going to do what we tell you, whether you like it or not.'

'No,' I said. 'I am not.'

They took another step and stood in a solid wall, shoulder to shoulder. If I reached out I could touch them.

'You'll fall over yourselves in a minute,' I said.

They didn't like me trying to make a joke of them. The anger Vic had throttled earlier rose up again in his face and none of his clients would have recognized their friendly neighbourhood bloodsucker. A vein in his forehead swelled and throbbed.

The Yorkshireman Fynedale put his shoulder in front of Vic's as if to hold him back.

'You're more trouble than you're worth,' he told me, 'and you might as well get this straight. You're not to bid when we say not. Right?'

Vic elbowed him back. Vic didn't like his lieutenant usurping the role of number one thug.

'If we get rough, you've asked for it,' he said.

'Get,' I said, 'what do you call that bang on the head at Ascot? A friendly pat?'

He snapped out, 'That wasn't us,' and instantly regretted it. His face closed like a slammed door.

I glanced round the ring of faces. Some of them didn't know what had happened at Ascot. But Vic did. Fynedale did. Ronnie North and Jiminy Bell did . . .

'Who was it?'

'Never you mind. You just reckon you've had a taster. And you bloody will do what you're told.'

They all looked so furiously intent that I wanted to laugh: but when they suddenly wheeled away and went off to their own cars I found I didn't want to laugh after all. I stood where they'd left me and breathed in deep lungfuls of winter night. However ludicrous I might think it that some perfectly ordinary citizens should threaten to beat me up if I didn't join their strong-arm union, their collective menace had been real enough.

All I suddenly wanted was a cigarette.

*

144

There were few cars left in the park, but the one next to mine turned out to be Pauli Teksa's.

'Jonah?' he said, peering at me through the dim lighting.

'Hullo.'

'You're just standing there smoking?'

'Yeah.'

'Want to come to my place for a bite to eat?'

By tacit consent my dinner date with Eddy and Marji had lapsed, but my hosts for the week were not expecting me back. If I wanted to eat at all it might as well be in company.

'Couldn't think of anything better,' I said.

He was staying in a pub outside Newmarket which put on late dinners especially for people after the sales. The cosy bar and dining-room were full of familiar faces and the general conversation was predictable.

He moved his strong, stocky body through the crowd with ease, and there was some quality about him which parted the crush like Moses and the Red Sea. I watched him being served at the bar at once where others had waited longer and saw that the others acknowledged rather than resented his priority. I wondered what it must be like to be Pauli, generating such natural and unconscious power.

We ate smoked salmon and then roast pheasant, and drank Chateau Haut Badon 1970, which was my choice, not his, as he said Americans knew goddam all about

French wines and he was no exception. He preferred bourbon, he said.

'All these guys here,' he said over coffee, waving a hand at the other crowded tables. 'They kinda like you.'

'You imagine it.'

'Nope.' He gave me a cigar from a crocodile case with gold mountings. A Havana. He inhaled the smoke deeply, and sighed, and said the only good thing ever to come out of Cuba was its cigars and life in the States was hardly worth living now they were banned. He had stocked up in England, he said. He was going to smuggle a hundred or so through in his baggage.

'You looked a bit shook up back there in the car park,' he said.

'Did I?'

'Those guys I saw standing round you when I came out of the gate. They friends of yours?'

'Business acquaintances.'

He smiled sympathetically. 'Ganging up on you, eh? Well I sure did warn you.'

'You sure did,' I said, smiling back.

He looked at me assessingly. 'They don't seem to have made it stick.'

'No.'

'You want to take care, fellah,' he said earnestly. 'Remember you got bashed at Ascot.'

'Tonight's lot said they didn't do that.'

He was surprised. 'They said . . .?'

I nodded. 'They clammed up as soon as they'd said

it. It might be true in a way, because the two men who took Hearse Puller and tried to get River God aren't regulars on the racing scene. I'd never seen them before. But at a guess . . . tonight's crowd supplied the basic information.'

'How do you mean?'

'Between them they knew everything the two strangers knew.'

'What sort of things?'

His strong face was intent, receptive, helpful. I told him about the two-year-old getting loose on the main road, and about Crispin's whisky.

He was astounded. I said, 'Of the people there tonight, Jiminy Bell knew about my dicey arm as he'd seen the strap often enough in the changing room, when we were both jockeys. Ronnie North knew I'd bought River God, because he'd sold it to me. Vic Vincent knew I kept horses in transit in my yard. Any of them could have known I have an alcoholic brother, it's no secret. All of them were at Ascot the day I bought Hearse Puller. It's quite clear they could have supplied the info if they'd wanted to. The trouble is that I simply don't see the point.'

He carefully edged half an inch of ash off the end of his cigar and took his time over replying.

'I'll tell you what they might have been after,' he said.

'What?'

'To soften you up.'

'What?' I laughed. 'You can't be serious.'

He shrugged. 'It's possible. They rough you up a little. Nothing you'd make too much of a fuss of. Kick you around a bit. Then they give out with the threats . . . Join us or else.'

I shook my head. 'It can't be that simple.'

'Why not?'

'Because I'm not that much of a threat to them. Why should they go to all that trouble?'

He leaned back in his chair, smiling gently through the Cuban smoke. 'Don't you know the classic law of the invader, fellah? Single out the strongest guy around and smash him. Then all the weaker crowd come to heel like lambs.'

'Vic has invaded like the Mongol hordes,' I agreed, 'but I'm by no means the strongest guy around.'

'You sell yourself short, fellah.'

'Don't be a nut.'

He shook his head. 'I back my own judgement. Make my decisions. Buy my horses. Quick. Snap.' He snapped his fingers. 'And I don't get things wrong.'

The circus left Newmarket after the races on Saturday.

By that time relations between Vic and myself were if possible worse. He had instructed me not to bid on five occasions: three of those yearlings I hadn't wanted anyway, and the other two I bought. The mood of the mob had hardened to the point where I was careful to keep out of lonely car parks.

By Saturday Vic had warned Constantine that I was not a good companion for Nicol. Constantine had warned Nicol, and Nicol, grinning over a sandwich, had warned me.

Wilton Young had become the owner of three more yearlings at near-record prices and Fynedale was smirking from ear to ear.

Constantine had pretended not to be mortified, and had cheered up considerably when his horse beat Wilton Young's in the Cesarewitch.

Eddy Ingram asked to have the On Safari filly after all as he had discovered on his own account that she was undamaged, but I had already passed her on to another client and felt regrettably unsympathetic when I told him so.

On the business side I had had quite a good week in spite of all Vic's threats, but I drove away down the A11 to London with a deep sigh of relief.

The relief lasted until I turned down towards the village at home.

The village was in a turmoil with all the people out of the houses, and the street blocked with cars, bicycles, prams and kids. The time was ten past eight. The cause of the upheaval was a bright glow in the night sky with leaping flames and flying sparks, and I knew at once and without hope that the place on fire was mine.

It was impossible to drive there. I left my car and went forward on foot, competing it seemed to me with every man, woman and wheelchair in the parish. The nearer I got the more I had to push, and it was a six-deep seething mass which was being held back by a portable barrier placed across the gateway. I squeezed round one end of it to get into the yard and was roughly told to get out by a busy fireman.

'It's my bloody house,' I snapped. 'I've just got home.'

'Oh.' He paused fractionally. 'The wind's against us, I'm afraid. We're doing our best.'

I looked around me and took stock.

The stables were alight and gone. Bright orange from end to end. Flames shot up high from what had been the roof, roaring and crackling like thunder and lightning shaken together in some demoniacal cocktail. The heat was incredible. Smoke swirled everywhere, stinging the eyes. It was like being on the wrong side of a giant bonfire, and I could see what he had meant by the wind. It was blowing showers of bright splintery sparks like rain onto the still black bulk of the house.

Half the firemen were trying to damp down the stables. The rest, back to back and cramped for room, were focusing on what might still be saved. Silver jets of water swept the tiles and the back face of the house and poured through my bedroom window, which was broken.

There were two fire engines, both of them through the other side of the yard, out in the paddock. I wondered stupidly what they were doing there, and then realized they were pumping water directly from the brook, which ran along one side. Not a very big brook, I thought uneasily. The long, narrow yard itself was a sea of puddles and hoses and men in black helmets doing a difficult job efficiently, part-time firemen who'd left their Saturday-night beer in the local and come out enthusiastically to try to save my house. It was crazy to think of their beer at a time like that, but I did.

The fireman I'd spoken to before said sympathetically that I'd had a hell of a homecoming. He said that there was never much hope for places like stables and farms, once they caught fire, not if there was any hay or straw stored there. Burned like tinder, he said.

'We sent for another appliance,' he said. 'It ought to have been here by now.' He had almost to shout for me to hear.

'The road's blocked right back into the village,' I said.

He looked resigned, which was not what I felt.

'Sorry about your car,' he shouted.

'What car?'

He swept an arm round to the garage at the end of

the stable block and pointed. The remains of Crispin's car were burning in there like a skeleton.

I caught the fireman by the arm.

'Where's my brother?' I shouted. 'He's here ... Where is he?'

He shook his head. 'The place was empty. We checked. The fire hadn't got such a hold when we came and there was no danger inside the house then.'

'He might be asleep.'

'No one could have slept through this lot, mate,' he shouted, and looking and listening to the disaster, one could see his point.

'I'll have to make sure.'

'Come back,' he yelled. 'You can't go in there now. You'll suffocate.'

He fielded me forcibly on my way to the kitchen door. I said we must find my brother.

He began to tell me again that he wasn't there.

'He might be dead drunk.' It was no time to save Crispin's face. 'Unconscious.' And he might have walked down to the pub and be sitting there obliviously over his sixth double gin; but I couldn't waste time finding out.

'Oh.' The fireman pulled me through the scrum of men and hoses to the nearest fire engine and thrust a breathing pack into my arms.

'Put it on,' he said. 'The lights will be shot to hell by now and you can find him quicker than I can, if he's there.' He gave me a helmet and gloves and we ran over to the house, with me struggling to fasten everything on.

The house was unbelievably full of smoke, dark, pungent, hot and oily. The only light was from the flames outside, which meant that all the far rooms were filled with black fog. It stung in my eyes worse than ever and made them water. I straightened the breathing mask over them and tried to see where I was going.

'Where would he be?' yelled the fireman.

'Maybe the sitting-room. This way.'

We blundered down the passage and into the pitch-black room. Impossible to see. I felt all over the sofa, the armchairs, and the floor around, which was where he usually passed out.

No Crispin.

'No good.'

We went upstairs. Everything was very hot indeed up there and the smoke was, if anything, denser. Patches of woodwork round the doors were charred, as if they had already burnt, but there were no actual flames.

I couldn't find him anywhere in his bedroom, which was dark, or in mine, which glowed vividly orange through the smoke and was as drenching as a tropical rainstorm from the water pouring through the window.

'He isn't here,' shouted the fireman.

'Bathroom . . .' I said.

'Hurry. The roof's smouldering.'

The bathroom door was shut but not locked. I

opened it, took one step, and tripped over Crispin's feet.

The air in there was clearer. The fireman pushed past me, threw Crispin over his shoulder as if he were a child, and went out of the house faster than I could with no burden.

He laid Crispin on a patch of wet grass because there was nowhere else to put him. I pulled off the breathing mask and looked down at him anxiously.

'Is he alive?'

'Don't know. Put your mask on him.'

He started at once giving Crispin artificial respiration by the method of pulling his arms backwards over his head, while I clipped on the mask and checked the air flow.

Without pausing the fireman glanced up at the staring crowd at the gate and at the rows of faces looking over the hedge for as far down the road as the flames lit them, and I could read his mind as if he'd spoken. The third appliance, an ambulance, doctor, police . . . no other vehicle was going to reach us until the village went home.

The roof down the half of the stables nearest us fell in with a roar and a sudden out-gushing of sizzling heat. The fireman raised his eyes from his exertions on Crispin and said encouragingly, 'Now if the rest of that roof falls in quickly, the house has more of a chance.'

I looked up. The incendiary shower of sparks had diminished, but the house looked more than ever as if it would burst all over into flames in explosive spontaneous combustion. Despite all their efforts the eaves at the far end were blackly burning.

Crispin showed not the slightest sign of life, but when I felt for his pulse, it was there. Faint and slow, but there.

I nodded to the fireman in relief, and he stopped the respiration. He watched Crispin's chest. There was no perceptible movement. The fireman slid his hand inside Crispin's clothes, to feel his ribs. Nothing. He shook his head, and went back to pumping.

'I can do that,' I said.

'Right.'

I took his place and he went back to help with the fire, and the hot, roaring, smoky nightmare seemed to go on and on and on.

Crispin lived and they more or less saved the house.

At some point that I wasn't quite clear about the police arrived, and soon afterwards an ambulance took my still unconscious brother away to a more thorough decoking.

The first thing the firemen told the police was that it looked like arson, and the first thing the police asked me was had I started it.

'I wasn't even here.'

'Have you got any money troubles?'

I looked at them incredulously. Standing there in all that shambles with thick, hot smoke still pouring off the damp and blackening embers they were stolidly conducting inquiries.

'Is that all the help you can give?' I said, but their manner said plainly enough that they weren't there to give help.

It seemed the final unreality on that disjointed night that they should believe I had brought such destruction on myself.

By dawn one of the fire engines had gone but the other was still there, because, the firemen told me, with old houses you never knew. Sometimes a beam would smoulder for hours, then burst into flames and start the whole thing over again.

They yawned and rolled up hoses, and smoked cigarettes which they stubbed out carefully in little flat tins. Relays of tea in thermos flasks came up from the village and a few cautious jokes grew like flowers on the ruins.

At nine I went down to the pub to borrow the telephone and caught sight of myself in a mirror. Face streaked with black, eyes red with smoke and as weary as sin.

I told Sophie not to come, there wouldn't be any lunch. She would come anyway, she said, and I hadn't the stamina to argue.

The pub gave me a bath and breakfast. My clothes smelled horrible when I put them on again, but nothing to the house and yard when I got back. Wet burnt wood, wet burnt straw, stale smoke. The smell was acrid and depressing, but the departing firemen said nothing could be done, things always smelled like that after blazes.

Sophie came, and she was not wearing the gold aeroplane.

She wrinkled her nose at the terrible mess and silently put her arm through mine and kissed me. I felt more comforted than I had since childhood.

'What's left?' she said.

'Some wet furniture and a tin of peanuts.'

'Let's start with those.'

We went through the house room by room. Watery ash and stale smoke everywhere. My bedroom had a jagged black corner open to the sky where the roof had burnt right through, and everything in there was past tense. I supposed it was lucky I had had some of my clothes with me in Newmarket.

There was an empty gin bottle in Crispin's room, and another in the bathroom.

In the office the ash covered everything in a thick, gritty film. The walls were darkened by smoke and streaked with water and my rows of precious, expensive and practically irreplaceable form books and stud records would never be the same again.

'What are you going to do?' Sophie said, standing on the filthy kitchen floor and running one finger through the dust on the table.

'Emigrate,' I said.

'Seriously?'

'No . . . Seriously, the pub opens in five minutes and we might as well get drunk.'

CHAPTER TEN

We rolled home happily at two o'clock and found the police there. Two of them, one a constable, one with the shoulder badges of Chief Inspector.

'Enjoying yourself, Mr Dereham?' the Chief Inspector said sarcastically. 'Celebrating on the insurance money, are you?'

It seemed, however, that this opening was more a matter of habit than threat, because they had not after all come to accuse, but to ask and inform.

'Chilly out here, sir,' the Chief Inspector said, looking up pointedly at the dull wintery sky.

'Chilly indoors now too,' I said. 'The central heating oil tank was in the stables.'

'Ah,' he said. 'Yes, exactly.'

He chose all the same to go indoors, so I took them into the office and fetched a duster for the chairs. The duster merely smeared the dirt. I had to fetch others for them to spread out and sit on.

'Tell us about your enemies, Mr Dereham,' said the Chief Inspector.

'What enemies?'

'Exactly, sir. What enemies do you have?'

'I didn't know I had any who would set fire to my stable.'

'You may not have known it before, sir, but you know it now.'

I silently nodded.

'Give us a name, sir.'

'I don't think I can. But it isn't the first thing that's happened.' I told them about Hearse Puller, and about my loose two-year-old, and he asked immediately why I hadn't reported these things to the police.

'I did report the Ascot incident,' I said, thanking Kerry's indignation. 'And as for the horse . . . some of your men came here after the accident, but I didn't think then that the horse had deliberately been let loose, I thought I'd just been careless.'

As they had thought the same thing they could hardly quarrel with that. The Chief Inspector also knew perfectly well that they wouldn't have called out the reserves if I'd turned up with the unbuckled rug.

'Well, sir,' he said. 'It seems you were lucky this time. We have a witness. A fourteen-year-old boy who'd been up in the woods at the end of your lane. He was going home. He says he saw what he saw from the lane, but I reckon he'd come here to help himself to what was lying around loose. He says he knew you were away in Newmarket. Anyway, he said he saw a man go into the store-room in the stable block and he heard him making metallic noises in there, and thought it odd that whoever it was had not switched on the lights. He seems to know his way round your stables pretty well. He saw the man strike a match and bend down. Then the man came out of the stable and hurried away along the lane to the village. The boy didn't try to intercept him, but went to the store-room and switched on the light.'

The Chief Inspector paused, with a fine sense of theatre. His riveted audience waited impatiently for him to get on with it.

'He took one look and retreated without delay. He says the pipe from the oil storage tank at the back of the stove was broken and the oil was coming out onto the floor. Standing in the pool of oil was a cardboard box, and on that there was a large firework. A golden shower, he says. He observed that the touch paper was red and smoking. He did not advance into the store-room, he says, because in his opinion anyone who had done so would have needed his brains examined, that is if his brains hadn't been burning with the rest of him.'

Sophie laughed at this verbatim bit of reporting. The Chief Inspector permitted himself the smallest of smiles.

'Anyway, sir, it seems he then made best speed down the village to tell his mum to call the Fire Brigade, which, once he had convinced her, she did. When the firemen arrived here the oil tank had exploded and the stables, being built internally largely of wood, were hopelessly alight. The firemen say that if they had arrived much later they could not have saved the house.'

He smiled lopsidedly. 'They usually ruin what they only just save.'

'The house is fine,' I said.

'Good. Now what young Kenneth saw is not evidence that you didn't set the whole thing up yourself. People often arrange to have fires start while they themselves have an unbreakable alibi.'

Sophie started to protest. The Chief Inspector gave her an amused glance, and she stopped abruptly.

'All right, miss. This time it's different. This time we know a bit more. Young Kenneth gave us a description of the man he saw.'

'But it was dark,' I said.

'Something about the man was very distinctive. Apart from that, we found the car he came in. After everyone had gone home last night there were two cars left in the village street. One was yours. One was a Zodiac station wagon, and the man Kenneth had seen here was reported as having been observed trying to start it, failing to do so, kicking its wheels in disgust, and walking towards the main road, presumably to thumb a lift. Upon examining the station wagon we found two things. One was that the starter motor had jammed and that was why it would not start. The other was that the number plates did not coincide with the number written on the licence. We checked the licence. The car belongs to a Mr Leonard Williamson who says a young fellow took it away from him. He was asked if he knew the young fellow's name and eventually he said he did. The young fellow was a Mr Frederick Smith. We went to the home of Mr Frederick Smith and invited him to come down here and help with our inquiries.'

'Or in other words,' I said smiling, 'Leonard Williamson shopped Fred Smith who is now swearing blue murder in one of your cells.'

The Chief Inspector said primly, 'We would like you to come and see if you know him.'

It was Frizzy Hair.

He looked hard, arrogant and unrepentant. The taunting smile he gave his victims had become a taunting sneer for his captors, and the way he sprawled on a chair with his legs spread wide was a statement of defiance.

You could see at once why young Kenneth had been able to describe him. On his left arm from biceps to knuckles he wore a large white plaster cast.

He stared boldly at me without recognition.

'Hello, lover boy,' I said.

The Chief Inspector looked at me sharply.

'So you do know him.'

'Yes. He attacked me at Ascot.'

163

'I never.'

'Mrs Kerry Sanders saw you.'

He blinked. Remembered. Narrowed his eyes with a snap and gave me a look that would have done credit to a crocodile.

'You broke my bleeding elbow.'

'I never,' I said.

'I hear your stable burnt,' he said viciously. 'Pity you weren't in it.'

The Chief Inspector drew me back to his office.

'He's got form as long as your arm,' he said cheerfully. 'Well known on his own patch, is Fred Smith.'

'Someone's paying him,' I said.

'Oh yes. But we've no chance of him telling us who it is. He's hard as nails. The Fred Smiths of this world never grass.' He sounded as if he admired him for it. 'He'll do his time, but he'll tell us nothing.'

Sophie came with me to see Crispin, who was sick and sorry for himself in the local hospital. His skin was pallid and sweaty, he coughed with a hand pressed to his chest, and his eyes showed that the gin level had ebbed as far as maximum agony. Like an axe chopping his brain, he'd once described it.

The first thing he said when he saw us was, 'Give me a bloody drink. They won't give me a bloody drink.'

I produced a small bottle of orange juice. He stared ~t it balefully.

'You know what I bloody mean.'

'Yes,' I said. 'Vitamin C. Marvellous for hangovers.' I poured the orange juice into a glass and gave it to him. A nurse watched approvingly from across the room. Crispin sniffed it crossly, tasted it, and drank the lot. He lay back against his pillows and closed the swimmy eyes.

'Bloody orange juice,' he said.

He lay for a minute or two as if asleep, but then with his eyes still shut said, 'I hear you saved my bloody life.'

'Not exactly.'

'Near enough . . . Don't expect me to be grateful.'

'No.'

Another long pause. 'Come and fetch me tomorrow morning,' he said. 'About noon, they said.'

'All right.'

'As for now, you can bugger off.'

Sophie walked away with me down the ward with her disgust escaping like steam.

'Why on earth do you put up with him?'

'He's my brother.'

'You could kick him out.'

'Would you?'

She didn't answer. When it came to the point, one couldn't.

I thought of him lying there in his acute self-made misery, a lonely, defeated man in a private hell. He'd had girlfriends once but not any more. There was no

165

one except me between him and the gutter, and I knew he relied on me as if I'd been a solid wall.

'Isn't there any cure?' Sophie said.

'Oh yes. One certain cure. The only one.'

'What is it?'

'Wanting to be cured.'

She looked at me dubiously. 'Does that make sense?'

'He would automatically be cured if his urge to be cured was stronger than his urge to drink.'

'But sometimes it is,' she said. 'You said he some-times doesn't drink for weeks.'

I shook my head. 'He always means to drink again. He just postpones it, like a child saving its sweets.'

We collected my car and drove off towards the ill-smelling cinders.

'I thought it was a disease,' she said.

'An addiction. Like football.'

'You've been at the nonsense again.'

'Under the influence of football,' I said, 'you can tear railway carriages apart and stampede people to death.'

'More people die of alcohol,' she protested.

'I expect you're right.'

'You're having me on.'

I grinned.

'I thought there was a drug that could cure it,' she said.

'You mean antabuse?'

'What's that?'

'Some stuff which makes alcohol taste disgusting. Sure, it works. But you've got to want to stop drinking in the first place, otherwise you don't take it.'

'Crispin won't?'

I nodded. 'You're so right. Crispin won't.'

'How about Alcoholics Anonymous?' she asked.

'Same thing,' I said. 'If you want to stop drinking, they're marvellous. If you don't, you keep away from them.'

'I never thought about it like that.'

'Lucky old you.'

'Pig.'

We went a mile or so in companionable silence.

'All the same,' she said, 'I've always been told it was an illness. That you couldn't help it. That one drink sets off a sort of chain reaction.'

'It isn't the one drink. It's the wanting to drink. Alcoholism is in the mind.'

'And in the legs.'

I laughed. 'OK, it invades the body. In fact the bodies of ultra-persistent alcoholics become so adjusted chemically to the irrigation that a sudden cut-off in the supply can cause epileptic fits.'

'Not . . . in Crispin?'

'No. Not so bad. But when he says he needs a bloody drink . . . he needs it.'

Which was why the drink I'd given him had been only half orange juice and the other half gin.

*

We stood in the yard for a while with the last of daylight fading over the cooling embers of the stables.

'What are you thinking?' Sophie said.

'Oh . . . That I'd like to break Fred's Smith's other elbow. Also his knees, toes, ankles and neck.'

'In that order,' she said, nodding.

I laughed, but the inner anger remained. This time the assault had been too much. This had gone beyond a skirmish to a major act of war. If Pauli Teksa were by any chance right and Vic or someone besides him were trying to frighten me off the scene they were having the opposite effect. Far from persuading me to go along with Vic's schemes they had killed the tolerance with which I had always regarded them. In my own way I could be as bloody-minded as frizzy Fred Smith. Vic was going to wish he had left me alone.

I turned away from the ruins. I would rebuild what had been lost. Soon, and better, I thought.

'Where are you planning to sleep?' Sophie asked.

I looked at her in the dusk. Smooth silver hair. Calm sky-reflecting eyes. Nothing but friendly interest.

Where I was planning to sleep was going to need more welcome than that.

'Could I borrow your sofa?' I said.

A pause.

'It's not long enough,' she said.

Another pause. I looked at her and waited.

A smile crept in around her eyes.

'Oh, all right. You gave me your bed . . . I'll give you mine.'

'With you in it?'

'I don't suppose you burnt your bedroom just to get there?' she asked.

'I wish I could say yes.'

'You look smug enough as it is,' she said.

We drove sedately to Esher, she in her car, me in mine. We ate a sedate dinner out of her freezer, and watched a sedate old movie on her box.

She was also in a way sedate in bed. The inner composure persisted. She seemed to raise a mental eyebrow in amusement at the antics humans got up to. She was quiet, and passive.

On the other hand she left me in no doubt that I gave her pleasure; and what I gave, I got.

It was an intense, gentle love-making. A matter of small movements, not gymnastics. Of exquisite lingering sensations. And done, on her part also, without reservation.

She lay afterwards with her head on my shoulder.

She said, 'I can't stay here till morning.'

'Why not?'

'Have to be at Heathrow on duty by six o'clock.'

'Fine time to say so.'

I could feel her smile. 'Better than ten minutes ago.'

I laughed in my nose. 'The off-put of the century.'

She rubbed her hand lazily over my chest. 'I'll think of this when I'm up in the tower.'

'You'll knit the approaches.'

'No.' She kissed my skin. 'I'm on departures. I tell them when to take off.'

'When?'

'And where. But not what.'

I smiled. Shut my eyes in the warm dark.

'You don't take your strap off even for love-making,' she said, running her fingers along inside the soft crepe bandage I slept in.

'Especially,' I said. 'Very high-risk activity for dislocating shoulders.'

'You speak from experience?'

'You might say so.'

'Serve you right.'

We slid slowly, contentedly, to sleep.

CHAPTER ELEVEN

At Ascot Sales on Wednesday Vic and his pals closed their ranks when they saw me coming, and moved in my direction in a body.

I met them halfway. Like something out of *High Noon*, I thought frivolously. All we lacked were the Sheriff's badge and the guns.

'I warned you,' Vic said.

They all stared at me. I looked at them one by one. Vic all open aggression, the rest in various shades from satisfied spite to a trace of uneasiness.

'People who play with fire get burnt,' I said.

Vic said, 'We didn't do it.'

'Quite right. Fred Smith did. And he's not telling who paid him. But you and I know, don't we Vic?'

He looked extraordinarily startled. '*You* know?' he exclaimed. 'You couldn't.' He considered it and shook his head. 'You don't.'

'But *you* know,' I said slowly. 'And if it isn't you . . . who is it?'

Vic gave a fair imitation of a clam.

171

'You just do as we tell you and nothing else will happen,' he said.

'You've got your psychology all wrong,' I said. 'You bash me, I'll bash back.'

Jiminy Bell said to Vic, 'I told you so.'

Vic gave him a reptilian glance. Jiminy was a great one for losing friends and not influencing people.

Ronnie North stood on one side of their battalion commander and the carrot-headed Fynedale on the other. Neither of them looked either impressed or worried about my vaguely stated intentions.

'How about a truce?' I suggested. 'You leave me entirely alone, and I'll leave you.'

Six upper lips curled in unison.

'You can't do a damn thing,' Vic said.

I bought four horses for various clients uninfected by Vic, and went home. Crispin, morosely sober, had spent the day watching a demolition gang shift the burnt rubble of the stables into lorries. The stale smell persisted, and the air was full of dust and fine ash, but the hard concrete foundations had been cleared and cleaned in some places and looked like the first outlines of the future.

He was sitting in the office drinking fizzy lemonade in front of a television programme for children. Two days had seen rapid action by the electricity people, who had insulated all burnt-through wires and restored the current, and by the Post Office, who had reconnected me with the outer world. With help from the village I had cleaned up the office and the kitchen and borrowed dry beds, and even if the house was partly roofed by tarpaulin and as sodden as an Irish bog, it was still where I lived.

'About twenty people telephoned,' Crispin said. 'I've had a bloody awful day answering the damn thing.'

'Did you take messages?'

'Couldn't be bothered. Told them to ring again this evening.'

'Have you eaten anything?'

'Someone brought you an apple pie from the village,' he said. 'I ate that.'

I sat down at the desk to make a start on the ever-present paperwork.

'Get me some lemonade?' I asked.

'Get it yourself.'

I didn't, and presently with an ostentatious sigh he went out to the kitchen and fetched some. The thin, synthetic fizz at least took away the taste of brick dust and cinders, though as usual I wished someone would invent a soft drink with a flavour of dry white wine. A great pity all soft drinks were sweet.

During the evening apart from answering the post-poned inquiries and finalizing various sales I made three more personal calls.

One was to the breeder of the Transporter colt which Vic had bought for thirty thousand and let go to Wilton Young for seventy-five.

One was to Nicol Brevett. And one to Wilton Young himself.

As a result of these the breeder met Nicol the next day in Gloucester, and on the Friday morning I drove them both to see the mail order tycoon in Yorkshire.

The row between Wilton Young and his carrot-headed agent at Doncaster races that Saturday could be heard from Glasgow to The Wash. Along with everyone else I listened avidly and with more general satisfaction.

Wilton Young had not wanted to believe he had been made a fool of. What man would? I was wrong, he said. His agent Fynedale would never conspire with Vic Vincent to drive the price of a colt up by thousands so that he, Wilton Young, would shell out, while they, the manipulators, split the lolly between them.

I hadn't said much at the interview. I'd left it all to the breeder. The furious indignation he'd been exploding with at Newmarket had deepened into a bitter consuming resentment, and he had pounced like a starving cat on the opportunity of doing Vic a lot of no good.

Nicol himself had been astounded and angry on his father's behalf and had sat next to me all the way to Yorkshire saying he couldn't believe it at regular intervals. I was sure Nicol's surprise was genuine but I privately doubted whether Constantine's would be. Nicol's father was quite subtle enough to make Wilton

Young pay and pay and pay for the privilege of outbidding a Brevett. That was, of course, if his pride would allow so private a victory, and on that point I was in a fog.

Wilton Young and Fynedale stood on the grass in front of the weighing-room shouting at each other as if oblivious of the fascinated audience of five thousand. Wilton Young attacked like a tough little terrier and Fynedale's temper burnt as flaming bright as his hair. One or two stewards hovered on the perimeter looking nervous about the outcome and the jockeys on their way out to the first race went past with smiles like water-melon slices.

' . . . bare-faced bloody fraud,' Wilton Young was shouting, the Yorkshire accent thick and blunt. 'I tell thee straight, no one makes a bloody monkey out of me and gets away with it. You don't buy no more horses for me, I tell thee straight. And I want back from you every penny you've swindled out of me these past two years.'

'You've no bloody chance,' scoffed Fynedale, driving nails into his own coffin with the recklessness of all hotheads. 'You paid a fair price for those horses and if you don't like it you can bloody lump it.'

'A fair price to you and that damned Vic Vincent is every penny you can screw out of people who trust you. All right, I've been a right bloody fool, but that's all finished, I tell you straight.' He stabbed the air with

175

his forefinger, emphasizing every angry word. 'I'll sue you for that money, see if I don't.'

'Don't bother. Tha'll not win.'

'Enough mud'll stick on you to save any other mugs wasting their brass. I tell thee straight, mister, by the time I've finished every single person in this country is going to know they pay through the bloody nose for every horse you buy them.'

'I'll bloody sue you for libel,' Fynedale yelled.

'And it'll be bloody worth it.'

'I'll take you for millions,' Fynedale screamed, almost jumping up and down with fury.

'You do already.'

The row hotted up in noise level and degenerated to straight abuse, and when the race began the unprintable insults rose in volume above the commentary. Along with many others I was chuckling so much I couldn't hold my race-glasses still enough to watch the distant runners. Nicol, standing beside me, had tears running down his cheeks.

'Oh my God,' he said, gasping for breath. 'What is a fat-arsed hyena-faced blood-sucking son of a sodding bitch?'

'A mongrel,' I said.

'Oh don't. It hurts.' He pressed a hand to his heaving ribs. 'It's too much.'

Even after the main row was over little eddies of it persisted all afternoon, both Wilton Young and Fynedale separately being anxious to air their grievances loudly to all who would listen. Wilton Young's fore-finger stabbed the air as if he were poking holes in it and Fynedale's voice took on a defensive whine. I kept away from them for most of the time but before the end they both came looking for me.

Wilton Young said, 'Like a bloody piece of quick-silver, you are. I keep seeing you in the distance and then when I go that way you've disappeared.'

'Sorry,' I said.

'You were right and I was wrong. There you are then.' He made a large gesture of magnanimity, letting me know how generous he thought himself to be making such an admission. 'The little tyke was swind-ling me. Like you said. All legal like, mind. I've been told this afternoon I won't have a chance of getting anything back.'

'No,' I said.

'Cut your losses, that's what I always say. Any line in my mail order business that's not pulling its weight, I scrap it. Same with employees, see?'

'I see.'

'You don't approve. I can see it in your face. You're soft, lad, you'll never get anywhere.'

'Depends where you want to go,' I said.

He stared, then laughed. 'Right, then. You go to the sales next week and buy me a horse. Any horse you think is good. Then we'll see.'

'Good for what?'

'A fair return for outlay.'

'In cash terms?'

'Naturally in cash terms. What else is there?'

If he didn't know, I couldn't tell him.

'I wasn't born in Yorkshire,' I said.

'What the hell has that got to do with it?'

'You only employ Yorkshiremen.'

'And look where it bloody got me. No, lad, you buy me a good horse and I'll overlook you being born in the wrong place.'

Nicol drifted near and Wilton Young gave him a stare suitable for the son of his dearest enemy, even if the two of them had the common bond of victims.

'Another thing you can do for me,' Wilton Young said to me, stabbing the inoffensive air. 'Find me a way of taking that effing Fynedale for every penny he screwed out of me. I tell thee straight, I'll not rest till I'm satisfied.'

I hesitated, but I'd already gone a long way down the road. I said slowly, 'I do know . . .'

He seized on it. 'What? What do you know?'

'Well . . .' I said. 'You remember those three horses you sent out to race in South Africa?'

'Damned waste of good money. They had useful form here, but they never did any good in Durban. The climate was all wrong. And of course they couldn't come back because of the quarantine laws.'

'One died soon after it arrived in South Africa,' I said. 'And the other two never saw a racecourse.'

He was surprised. 'How the hell do you know?'

'They went by sea,' I said.

'They didn't then,' he interrupted positively. 'They went by air. Had a bad flight, by all accounts.'

'They went by sea,' I said. 'I sent two horses out there, and they went on the same boat. I sent a groom with mine, and quantities of food. Your three travelled alone for three weeks with no one to look after them. They were shipped with a total of half a ton of hay, and not even good hay at that. No oats, bran, or horse cubes. Just a starvation ration of poor hay, and no one to see that they even got that. The man I sent looked after them as best he could and gave them enough of my food to keep them alive, but when they reached Durban they were in such a poor state that they were almost not allowed into the country.'

He listened in disbelief. 'I sent them by air,' he repeated.

'You thought you did. I read in the *Sporting Life* that they'd flown out to Durban. But when my man came back, he told me what had really happened.'

'But I paid for air . . . I paid more than four thousand quid.'

'And who did you pay?'

'By God.' He looked murderous. 'I'll screw him to the wall, I tell thee straight.'

'Get a lawyer to do it,' I said. 'I'll tell him which ship it was, and give him the name and address of the groom I sent.'

.

'By God, I will,' he said. He turned on his heel and hurried off as if going to do it there and then.

Nicol said, 'When you start a fire you do it properly.'

'They shouldn't have burnt my stable.'

'No,' he said. 'That was a bad mistake.'

Fynedale's anger was in a different category altogether. He caught me fiercely by the arm outside the weighing-room and his face made me determine to stay in well-lit, populated places.

'I'll kill you,' he said.

'You could have had a truce,' I said.

'Vic will kill you.'

It sounded ridiculous. Fynedale might do at a pinch, but Vic wasn't the killing sort.

'Don't be silly,' I said. 'You two can't even light your own fires. And Fred Smith won't kill me for you, he's in clink.'

'Someone else will.'

'Jiminy Bell?' I suggested. 'Ronnie North? You're all good at using threats but you need a Fred Smith to carry them out. And Fred Smiths don't grow on trees.'

'We keep telling you,' he said fiercely. 'We didn't pay Fred Smith. We didn't tell him to burn your yard. We didn't.'

'Who did?'

'Vic did. No . . . Vic didn't.'

'Sort it out.'

'Vic reported that you wouldn't play ball. He said you needed a bloody good lesson.'

'Reported to who?'

'How do I know?'

'You ought to find out. Look where he's got you. Out of a cushy job with Wilton Young and into a nasty prosecution for fraud. You're a bloody fool to let someone you don't know get you into such a mess.'

'*You* got me into the mess,' he yelled.

'You bash me, I bash back.'

The message at last got through, and the result on him was the same as it had been on me. Aggression created counter-aggression. The way full-scale wars started. He expressed no sorrow. Made no apologies. No offer of amends. Instead he said again and with increased intention, 'I'll kill you.'

Nicol said, 'What are you going to do next?'

'Pork pie and a bottle of Coke.'

'No, you ass. I mean . . . about Vic.'

'Stoke up his kitchen fire.' Nicol looked mystified. I said, 'He told me once if I didn't like the heat . . .'

'To stay out of the kitchen.'

'Right.'

The cold, dank winter afternoon seeped under my anorak and my feet were freezing. Nicol's face looked pale blue. A little kitchen heat would have come as no harm.

'How?'

'Not sure yet.'

181

It had been comparatively easy to break up the entente between Wilton Young and Fynedale, for the two hot-headed Yorkshire tempers had needed only a small detonation to set them off. Detaching Constantine from Vic might take longer. Constantine was not as bluntly honest as Wilton Young, and in his case face-saving might have priority.

'There's also someone else,' I said.

'Who?'

'Don't know. Someone helping Vic. Someone who engaged Fred Smith to do the dirty work. I don't know who . . . but I won't stop until I find out.'

Nicol looked at me speculatively. 'If he could see the look on your face he'd be busy covering his tracks.'

The trouble was, his tracks were far too well covered already. To find him, I'd have to persuade him to make fresh ones. We went into the snack bar for the warmth as much as the food and watched the fifth race on closed-circuit television.

Nicol said, 'Do you know of any other fiddles Vic and Fynedale have got up to?'

I smiled. 'One or two.'

'What?'

'Well . . . there's the insurance premium fiddle.'

'What's that?'

'I shouldn't be telling you.'

'Things have changed. You don't owe them a scrap of loyalty any more.'

I wryly agreed. 'Well . . . Say you sell a horse to

an overseas customer. You tell him you can arrange insurance for the journey if he sends the premiums. So he sends the premiums, and you pocket them.'

'Just like that?'

'Just like that.'

'But what happens if the horse dies on the way? Surely you have to pay up out of your own money?'

I shook my head. 'You say you were very sorry you couldn't arrange the insurance in time, and you send the premiums back.'

'By God.'

'By the time you've finished you should be more clued up than your father,' I said with amusement.

'I should damn well hope so. Vic's been taking him for one almighty ride.'

'*Caveat emptor*,' I said.

'What does that mean?'

'Buyer beware.'

'I know one buyer who'll beware for the rest of his life, and that's me.'

The next week at the Newmarket Mixed Sales I bought a two-year-old colt for Wilton Young.

He was there himself.

'Why that one?' he demanded. 'I've looked him up. He's run in three races and never been nearer than sixth.'

'He'll win next year as a three-year-old.'

'How do you know?'

'Scorchmark's progeny need time to grow. It's no good being impatient if they don't win at two. He's being sold by an impatient owner and he's been trained by a two-year-old specialist. They both wanted quick results, and Singeling wasn't bred for that. Next summer he'll win.'

'He didn't cost very much,' he said disparagingly.

'All the better. One good prize and he'll be making you that profit.'

He grunted. 'All right. I said buy me a horse, and you've bought it. I won't go back on my word. But I don't think that Singeling is any bloody good.'

Owing to the natural loudness of his voice this opinion was easily overheard, and a little while later he sold Singeling himself to someone who disagreed with him.

With typical bluntness he told me about it. 'He offered me a good bit more than you paid. So I took it. I didn't reckon he'd be much good, that Singeling. Now, what do you have to say to that?'

'Nothing,' I said mildly. 'You asked me to buy you a horse which would give you a good return in cash terms. Well . . . it has.'

He stared. He slapped his thigh. He laughed. Then a new thought struck him and he looked suddenly suspicious. 'Did you find another buyer and send him to offer me a profit?'

'No,' I said, and reflected that at least he seemed to be learning.

'I'll tell you something,' he said grudgingly. 'This chap I sold it to . . . when we'd shaken hands on it and it was too late for me to back out, he said . . . I tell thee straight . . . he said any horse Jonah Dereham picked as a good prospect was good enough for him.'

'Flattering,' I said.

'Ay.' He pursed his mouth and screwed up his eyes. 'Maybe I was too hasty, getting rid of that Singeling. I reckon you'd better buy me another one, and I'll keep it, even if it's got three legs and a squint.'

'You positively ask to be cheated,' I said.

'You won't cheat me.'

'How do you know?'

He looked nonplussed. Waved his arm about. 'Everybody knows,' he said.

Vic was not his confident, cheerful self. He spent a great deal of his time drawing people into corners and talking to them vehemently, and in due course I learned that he was saying I was so desperate for clients I was telling outright lies about sincere men like Fynedale, and that I had a fixed obsession that he, Vic Vincent, had set fire to my stables, which was mad as well as wicked because the police had arrested the man who had really done it. I supposed the extent to which people believed his version was a matter of habit: his devotees never doubted him, or if they did they kept it to themselves.

Vic and Pauli Teksa stood alone together on the far side of the collecting ring, with Vic's tongue working overtime. Pauli shook his head. Vic spoke faster than ever. Pauli shook his head again.

Vic looked around him as if to make sure he was not being overheard, then advanced his head to within three inches of Pauli's, his red-brown forward-growing hair almost mingling with Pauli's crinkly black.

Pauli listened for quite a while. Then he drew back and stood with his head on one side, considering, while Vic talked some more. Then slowly again he shook his head.

Vic was not pleased. The two men began to walk towards the sale building: or rather, Pauli began to walk and Vic, unsuccessfully trying to stop him, had either to let him go or go with him. He went, still talking, persuading, protesting.

I was standing between them and the sale building. They saw me from four paces away, and stopped. Vic looked as lividly angry as I'd ever seen him, Pauli as expressionless as a concrete block.

Vic gave Pauli a final furious look and strode away.

Pauli said, 'I plan to go home tomorrow.'

There were some big American sales the next week. I said, 'You've been here a month, I suppose . . .'

'Nearer five weeks.'

'Has it been a successful trip?'

He smiled ruefully. 'Not very.'

We went together for a cup of coffee, but he seemed preoccupied.

'I'd sure like to have bought a colt by Transporter,' he said.

'There'll be another crop next year.'

'Yeah . . .'

He said nothing more about me going along with the crowd, with conforming unless I got hurt. What he did say, though, with his mind clearly on his recent encounter, was, 'You don't want to stir up that Vic Vincent more than you can help.'

I smiled.

He looked at the smile and read it right. He shook his head.

'He's an angry man, and angry men are dangerous.'

'That makes two of us,' I said.

He soberly consulted his stock of inner wisdom and came up with a cliche. 'It's easier to start something than to stop it.'

CHAPTER TWELVE

Wilton Young came to the following Doncaster Sales not to buy but to see some of his horses-in-training sold. Cutting his losses, he said. Weeding out all those who'd eaten more during the just-ended flat season than they'd earned. He slapped me jovially on the back and told me straight that slow horses ate as much as fast, and he, Wilton Young, was no meal ticket for flops.

'Profit, lad,' he boomed. 'That's what it's all about. Brass, lad. Brass.'

I bought one of his cast-offs, a three-year-old colt with little form and a reputation for kicking visitors out of his box. I got him cheap for a Sussex farmer who couldn't afford more.

His ex-owner said disparagingly, 'What did you buy that for? It's no bloody good. If that's what you buy, what the hell will you buy for me?'

I explained about the poorish farmer. 'He'll geld it and hack it about the farm. Teach it to jump. Make it a four-year-old novice hurdler by April.'

'Huh.'

Second-rate jumpers were of less account than marbles to self-made tycoons with cheque books open for Derby prospects. I realized that whatever his fury against Fynedale he was still expecting to pay large sums for his horses. Perhaps he needed to. Perhaps he felt a reflected glory in their expense. Perhaps he wanted to prove to the world how much brass he'd made. Conspicuous consumption, no less.

Which meant that to please him best I would have to buy an obviously good horse at a shade above what I thought it worth. Given a bargain like Singeling he had rid himself of it within an hour, and for all his twinge of regret afterwards he would be likely to do the same again. Accordingly I picked out the pride of the sale, a two-year-old with near-classic expectations, and asked if he would like it.

'Ay,' he said. 'If it's the best, I would.'

'It'll fetch at least twenty thousand,' I said. 'How far do you want me to go?'

'It's your job. You do it.'

I got it for twenty-six, and he was delighted.

Fynedale was not.

From across the ring his eyes looked like stark black holes in his chalk-white face. The carrot hair on top flamed like a burning bush. The hate vibrated in him so visibly that if I could have seen his aura it would have been bright red.

*

189

Constantine had brought Kerry to the Friday sales, although the chief purpose of their journey to Yorkshire was to see Nicol try out River God in Saturday's novice chase.

Constantine was saying authoritatively to whomever would listen that keeping a large string of horses in training was becoming impossibly expensive these days, and that he thought it a prudent time to retrench. Only fools, he intimated, were still ready to buy at the inflated prices of recent months.

I saw Vic Vincent go across to greet them when they came. Amicable handshakes. Smiles with teeth. A good deal of window dressing to establish that whatever some people might think of their agents, Constantine was satisfied with his.

Nicol came and leaned beside me on the rail of the collecting ring.

'I told him,' he said. 'I said Vic had been rooking him of thousands. Vic and Fynedale, pushing up the prices and splitting the proceeds.'

'What happened?'

He looked puzzled. 'Nothing. He didn't say much at all. I got the impression . . . I know it's silly . . . but I got the impression he already knew.'

'He's nobody's fool,' I said.

'No . . . but if he knew, why did he let Vic get away with it?'

'Ask him.'

'I did. He simply didn't answer. I said I supposed he

would ditch him now and he said I supposed wrong. Vic could pick horses better than any other single agent, he said, and he had no intention of cutting himself off from his advice.'

We watched the merchandise walk round the collecting ring. Nothing in the current bunch looked worth the outlay.

Nicol said gloomily, 'They think I'm a traitor for listening to you at all. You're absolutely *persona non grata* with my parent.'

Predictable. If Constantine wasn't going to admit he'd been swindled, he wouldn't exactly fall on the neck of the person who'd publicly pointed it out.

'Is he really cutting down on his string?' I asked.

'Heaven knows. He's not noticeably short of the next quid, though some big deal or other fell through the other day, which irritated him more than somewhat.' He gave me a quick sideways sardonic glance. 'My new step-mama will be able to maintain us in the style to which we are accustomed.'

'Why don't you turn professional?' I asked with mild reproof. 'You're good enough.'

I had, it seemed, touched him on a jumpy nerve. He said angrily, 'Are you trying to tell me I should earn my own living?'

'Not really my business.'

'Then keep your trap shut.'

He shifted abruptly off the rail and walked away. I didn't watch him go. A minute later he came back.

'You sod,' he said.

'I try.'

'You bloody well succeed.'

He hunched his shoulders inside his sheepskin coat. 'Professional jockeys aren't allowed to own horses in training,' he said.

'Nothing to stop them running in your father's name.'

'Shut up,' he said. 'Just shut up.'

I shut.

I came face to face with Vic by accident, he coming out of the sale building, I going in. He was moderately triumphant.

'You've got nowhere,' he said.

'Because you'll soon find another stooge to replace Fynedale?'

His mouth compressed. 'I'm admitting nothing.'

'How wise.'

He gave me a furious look and stalked away. He'd said nothing this time about me toeing the line or else. Perhaps because with Fynedale out of action there was no effective line to toe. Perhaps the or else campaign was temporarily in abeyance. Nothing in his manner persuaded me it was over for ever.

Having Wilton Young for a client positively galvanized my business. During that one Friday I received as many inquiries and definite commissions as in any past

whole month, mostly from Northern trainers with bustling would-be owners who like Wilton Young had made
their own brass.

As one trainer for whom I'd ridden in the past put
it, 'They know eff-all about horses but the money's
burning their fingers. All they want is to be sure they're
getting the best possible. That they're not being done.
Get me ten good two-year-olds and I'll see you right.'

Both Vic and Fynedale noticed the constant stream
of new clients and the swelling of my order book: they
would have to have been blind not to. The effect on
them was the reverse of joyful. Vic's face grew redder
and Fynedale's whiter and as time wore on neither of
them was capable of ordinary social conversation.

Finally it worried me. All very well prospering in
front of their eyes, but when success could breed envy
even in friends, in enemies it could raise spite of Hima-
layan proportions. Several of my new customers had
transferred from Fynedale and one or two from Vic,
and if I'd wanted a perfect revenge, I'd got it: but
revenge was a tree with sour fruit.

Between Vic and Fynedale themselves things were
no better. Under Constantine's faithful umbrella Vic
had disowned his former lieutenant and had been heard
to say that if he had realized what Fynedale was up to
he would of course have had nothing to do with it.
Antonia Huntercombe and the breeder of the Transporter colt would have been interested.

Probably the fact that Fynedale had two directions

for hatred exhausted him to immobility. He stood about looking dazed, in a trance, as if Vic's perfidy had stunned him. He shouldn't have been so surprised, I thought. Vic always lied easily. Always had. And had always had the gift of the good liar, that people believed him.

On the Saturday afternoon River God won the novice chase by a short head thanks entirely to Nicol's riding. I watched the triumphant unsaddling party afterwards and noted that Vic was there too, oozing bonhomie in Nicol's direction and being very man-of-the-world with Constantine. His big, boyish face was back to its good-natured-looking normal, the manner easy again, and confident. Kerry Sanders patted his arm and Constantine's heavy black spectacles turned repeatedly in his direction.

All sweetness and light, I thought uncharitably. Vic would always bounce back like a rubber ball.

From habit I went to watch the next race from the jockeys' box, and Nicol climbed the steps to my side.

'Well done,' I said.

'Thanks.'

The runners came out into the course and jauntily ambled down in front of the stands. Eight or nine, some of them horses I'd once ridden. I felt the usual tug of regret, of nostalgia. I wouldn't entirely get over it, I thought, until there was a completely new generation of horses. While my old partners were still running, I wanted to be on them.

Nicol said with surprised discovery, 'You wish you were still riding!'

I mentally shook myself. It was no good looking back. 'It's finished,' I said.

'No more crashing falls. No more booing crowds. No more bloodyminded trainers telling you you rode a stinking race and engaging a different jockey next time.'

'That's right.'

He smiled his quick smile. 'Who'd wish it on a dog?'

The runners assembled, the tapes flew up, the race went away. They were experienced hurdlers, crafty and fast, flicking over the low obstacles without altering their stride. Even though I dealt mostly with young stock for the Flat, I still liked watching jumpers best.

'If I suggested to Father I would be a pro, he'd have a fit.'

'Particularly,' I said 'if you mentioned me in connection.'

'God, yes.'

The runners went down the far side and we lifted race-glasses to watch.

'Vic looks happy today,' I said.

Nicol snorted. 'Father told him to go to the States after Christmas and buy Kerry some colt called Phoenix Fledgling.'

'With her money?'

'Why?'

'He was saying yesterday he was cutting down. So

today he has a hundred thousand quid lying about loose?'

'So much?' He was surprised.

'It could be even more.'

'Would Father know?' Nicol asked doubtfully.

'Vic would,' I said.

Nicol shook his head. 'I don't know what they're up to. Thick as thieves again today.'

The runners turned into the straight. Positions changed. The favourite came through and won smoothly, the jockey collected, expert, and totally professional.

Nicol turned to me abruptly.

'If I could ride like *that*, I'd take out a licence.'

'You can.'

He stared. Shook his head.

'You do,' I said.

Crispin had been sober since the fire. Sober and depressed.

'My life's a mess,' he said.

As usual during these periods he sat every night in my office while I got through the paperwork and did the inevitable telephoning.

'I'm going to get a job.'

We both knew that he wouldn't. Those he wanted, he couldn't keep. Those he could keep, he despised.

'You can have one here,' I said. 'At this rate, I'll

have to get help with the paperwork. I can't cope with it all.'

'I'm not a bloody typist,' he said scornfully.

'You can't type.'

'We all know I'm absolutely useless. No need to rub it in.'

'You can keep the accounts, though. You know all about figures.'

He thought it over. Unreliable he might be, but not untrained. If he wanted to he could take over the financial half of the office load and do it well.

'I'll see,' he said.

Outside in the yard the demolition work was nearly finished. Plans for the new stables lay on my desk, drawn up at high speed by a local architect from the scribbled dimensions I'd given him. Depending on the time it took the Council to pass them, I'd be open for business again by the summer.

The rebuilding of the roof of the house was due to be started the following week. Rewiring from stern to stern had to be done after that, and there were several fallen ceilings to be replastered. Despite day and night oil heaters astronomicalizing my fuel bills in every room, the damp and the damp smell persisted. Repainting lay a long way ahead. It would take almost a year, I reckoned, to restore in full what had been done to intimidate me.

Vic had not seen the damage he'd caused and maybe he could put it comfortably out of his mind, but I came home to it night after night. He might forget, but he had made sure that I didn't.

Sophie had had two weeks of night shift, telling departing freight flights where to get off.

'What are you doing tomorrow?' she asked on the telephone.

'Day or night?'

'Day.'

'Damn.'

She laughed. 'What's wrong with the day?'

'Apart from anything else . . . I have to go to Ascot Sales.'

'Oh.' A pause. 'Couldn't I come with you?'

'If you don't mind me working.'

'I'd love it. See all the little crooks doing the dirty. And Vic Vincent . . . will I see him?'

'I'm not taking you,' I said.

'I won't bite him.'

'Can't risk it.'

'I promise.'

When I picked her up at nine she was still yawning from five hours' sleep and a system geared to waking at noon. She opened her door in jeans, sweater, toast and honey.

'Come in.' She gave me a slightly sticky, sweet-tasting kiss. 'Coffee?'

She poured two cups in her tiny kitchen. Bright

sunshine sliced through the window, giving a misleading report of the freezing day outside, where the north-west wind was doing its Arctic damnedest.

'You'll need warm boots,' I said. 'And sixteen layers of insulation. Also a nose muff or two and some frost-bite cream.'

'Think I'll stay at home and curl up with a good television programme.'

When wrapped up she looked ready for Outer or even Inner Mongolia and complained that the padding made her fat.

'Ever seen a thin Eskimo?'

She tucked the silver hair away inside a fur-lined hood. 'So everyone has problems.'

I drove to the Ascot sale ring. Sophie's reaction, although forewarned, was very much like Kerry's.

'*Ascot*,' she said.

'At least today it isn't raining.'

She huddled inside the fat-making layers. 'Thank God you insisted on the igloo bit.'

I took her down to the stables where there were several horses I wanted to look at, the underfoot conditions that day rock hard, not oozing with mud. She dutifully stuck her head inside each box to look at the inmates, though her claim to know less about horses than quantum mechanics was quickly substantiated.

'Do they see two views at once, with their eyes on opposite sides of their head like that?'

'Their brains sort it out,' I said.

'Very confusing.'

'Most animals look sideways. And birds. And fish.'

'And snakes in the grass,' she said.

Some of the horses had attendants with them. Some didn't. Some had attendants who had vanished temporarily to the refreshment room. Everywhere lay the general clutter of stables in the morning: buckets, muck sacks, brushes, bandages, haynets and halters, mostly in little clumps either outside or inside each box door. Most of the early lot numbers had stayed overnight.

I asked for three or four horses to be led out of their boxes by their attendants to get an idea of how they moved. They trotted obligingly along and back a wider piece of ground, the attendant running alongside holding them by the head on a short rope. I watched them from behind and from dead ahead.

'What do you look for?' Sophie said.

'Partly whether they dish their feet out sideways.'

'Is that good?'

I shook my head, smiling. 'The fastest ones generally don't do it.'

We went up to the O-shaped sale ring, where the wind whistled through with enthusiasm and the meagre crowd of participants stamped their feet and tucked their hands under their armpits. Ronnie North was there, breathing our clouds of steam and wiping a running nose; and Vic was there, dandified in a belted white shiny jacket with a blue shirt underneath.

While he was deep in conversation with a client I pointed him out to Sophie.

'But he looks *nice*,' she objected.

'Of course he does. Hundreds of people love him.'

She grinned. 'Such sarcasm.'

I bought two three-year-old fillies for a client in Italy and Vic watched broodingly from directly opposite.

Sophie said, 'When he looks at you like that . . . he doesn't look nice at all.'

I took her to warm up over some coffee. It occurred to me uneasily and belatedly that maybe I had not been clever to bring her to Ascot. It had seemed to me that Vic was as much interested in Sophie herself as in what I was buying, and I wondered if he were already thinking of ways to get at me through her.

'What's the matter?' Sophie said. 'You've gone very quiet.'

'Have a doughnut?'

'Yes please.'

We munched and drank, and I checked ahead through the catalogue, making memory-jogging notes about the horses we had seen in their boxes.

'Does it go on like this all day?' Sophie asked.

'A bit boring for you, I'm afraid.'

'No . . . Is this what you do, day after day?'

'On sales days, yes. Other days I fix up deals privately, or go to the races, or see to things like transport and insurance. Since last week I've barely had time to cough.' I told her about Wilton Young and the consequently mushrooming business.

'Are there a lot of horses for sale?' she said doubtfully. 'I wouldn't have thought there were enough for so many people all to be involved in buying and selling.'

'Well . . . In Britain alone there are at present about seventeen thousand thoroughbred brood mares. A mare can theoretically have a foal every year, but some years they're barren and some foals die. I suppose there must be about nine thousand new foals or yearlings on the market every season. Then there are about twenty thousand horses in training for flat races, and heaven knows how many jumpers, but more than on the Flat. Horses which belong to the same people from birth to death are exceptions. Most of them change hands at least twice.'

'With a commission for the agent every time?' Her expression held no approval.

I smiled. 'Stockbrokers work for commission. Are they more respectable?'

'Yes.'

'Why?'

'I don't know. Don't confuse me.'

I said, 'France, Italy and especially America are all at it in the bloodstock business hammer and tongs. There are about thirteen hundred stud farms in the British Isles and thousands more round the world.'

'All churning out horses . . . and only so that people can gamble.'

I smiled at her still disapproving expression. 'Everyone needs some sort of fantasy on their bread.'

She opened her mouth and shut it, and shook her head. 'I can never decide whether you are very wise or an absolute fool.'

'Both.'

'Impossible.'

'Dead easy, I'm afraid. Most people are.'

We went back to the ring and watched Vic and Ronnie North beat up the price of a weedy four-year-old hurdler to twice the figure his form suggested. Vic would no doubt be collecting a sizeable kick-back from the seller along with the commission from his client, and Ronnie North looked expansively pleased both with his status as underbidder for this one horse and with life in general.

Fynedale's successor, it seemed to me, had been elected.

Fynedale himself, I noticed, had arrived in the ring in time to see what was happening. He seemed to be in much the same state as before, white-faced, semi-dazed and radiating unfocused hatred.

Sophie said, 'He looks like gelignite on the boil.'

'With luck he'll explode all over Vic.'

'You're pretty heartless . . . he looks ill.'

'Buzz off and mother him then,' I said.

'No thanks.'

We looked at some more horses and I bought

another; we had some more coffee and the wind blew even colder. Sophie, however, seemed content.

'Nose needs powdering,' she said at one point. 'Where will I meet you?'

I consulted the catalogue. 'I'd better look at eighty-seven and ninety-two, in their boxes.'

'OK. I'll find you.'

I looked at eighty-seven and decided against it. Not much bone and too much white around the eye. There was no one with him. I left his box, bolted both halves of the door and went along to ninety-two. There I opened the top half of the door and looked inside. No attendant there either, just patient Lot 92 turning an incurious gaze. I opened the bottom half of the door and went in, letting them swing shut behind me. Lot 92 was securely tied by a headcollar to a ring in the wall, but it was too cold for open doors.

The horse was a five-year-old hurdler being sold for a quick profit while he still showed promise of being useful at six. I patted his brown flank, ran my hand down his legs, and took a good close look at his teeth.

When the door opened and closed I paid no especial attention to whatever had come in. It should have been an attendant for the horse or another like me inspecting the goods at close quarters.

It wasn't.

No instinct made me look up as I let go of the

hurdler's mouth, stroked his nose and stood back for a final appraisal.

I saw only a flash in the air. Felt the thud in my chest. And knew, falling, that the white face of Fynedale was coming forward to finish the job.

CHAPTER THIRTEEN

He had thrown at me like a lance the most lethal of all stable equipment. A pitchfork.

The force behind his arm knocked me off my feet. I lay on my side on the straw with the two sharp prongs embedded and the long wooden handle stretched out in front.

He could see that in spite of a deadly accurate throw and all the hate that went into it he still hadn't killed me. The glimpse I got of his distorted face convinced me that he intended to put that right.

I knew the pitchfork had gone in, but not how far. I couldn't feel much. I jerked it out and rolled over and lay on it face down, burying it under me in the straw. He fell on me, pulling, clutching, dragging, trying to get at it, and I simply lay on it like a log, not knowing what else to do.

The door opened again and light poured in from outside. Then a voice shouting. A girl's voice.

'Help . . . Someone help . . .'

I knew dimly from under the flurry of Fynedale's

exertions that it was Sophie. The troops she mobilized came cautiously to the rescue. 'I say . . .' said a well-bred voice plaintively, and Fynedale took no notice.

'Here. What's going on?'

The voice this time was tough and the owner tougher. Hands began to pull Fynedale off me and then others to help me, and when I took my nose out of the straw I could see three men trying to hold on to Fynedale while Fynedale threw them off like pieces of hay.

He crashed out through the door with my rescuers in pursuit, and when I got from my knees to my feet the only audience was Sophie.

'Thank you,' I said with feeling.

'Are you all right?'

'Yes . . . I think so.'

I bent down and picked up the pitchfork.

'What's that?'

'He threw it at me,' I said.

She looked at the stiletto prongs and shuddered. 'Good job he missed.'

'Mm.' I inspected the two small tears in the front of my anorak. Then I slowly unzipped it and put a hand inside, exploring.

'He did miss, didn't he?' said Sophie, suddenly anxious.

'Direct hit. Don't know why I'm not dead.'

I said it lightly and she didn't believe me, but it was the truth. I could feel the soreness of a tear in my skin and the warm stickiness of blood, but the prongs had not gone through to heart or lungs, and the force with which they'd landed had been enough to get them there.

I smiled idiotically.

'What is it?' Sophie asked.

'Thank the Lord for a dislocating shoulder . . . The pitchfork hit the strap.'

Unfortunately for Fynedale two policemen in a patrol car had come to the sales on some unrelated errand, but when they saw three men chasing another they caught the fugitive out of habit. Sophie and I arrived to find Fynedale sitting in the police car with one policeman while the other listened to the three chasers saying that if Jonah Dereham wasn't a hospital case it was because they had saved him.

I didn't argue with that.

Sophie with unshaken composure told them about the pitchfork, and the policeman, having taken a quick look inside my anorak, told me to go and find a doctor and then come along to the local station to make a statement. I reckoned it would be the same nick I'd been to with Kerry: there would be a certain amount of doubtful eyebrow-raising over a man who got himself attacked twice in the same small sales paddock within six weeks.

At the nearest doctor's surgery the damage resolved itself into one long slit over a rib. The doctor, a girl of less than thirty, swabbed away prosaically and said that ten days earlier she'd been called to attend a farm worker who'd driven a pitchfork right through his own foot. Boot and all, she added.

I laughed. She said she hadn't meant to be funny. She had nice legs but no sense of humour. My own amusement rather died when she pointed out the state of the buckle on my strap, which she'd taken off to get at the cut. The buckle was bent. The mark of the prong showed clearly.

'One prong hit the buckle. The other went into you but slid along against a rib. I'd say you were exceptionally lucky.'

I said soberly, 'I'd say so too.'

She stuck on some plaster, gave me a couple of anti-infection injections, and refused my offer of a fee.

'On the National Health,' she said sternly, as if offering to pay were immoral. She handed me the strap. 'Why don't you get that shoulder repaired?'

'Can't spare the time... and I'm allergic to hospitals.'

She gave my bare chest and arms a quick glance. 'You've been in a few. Several of your bones have been fractured.'

'Quite so,' I agreed.

She allowed herself a sudden small smile. 'I recognize you now. I've seen you on television. I backed your horse once in the Grand National when I was a student. I won six pounds and spent it on a book on blood diseases.'

'Glad to have been of service,' I said.

'I shouldn't wear that strap for a week or so,' she said. 'Otherwise it will rub that wound and prevent it healing.'

'All right.'

I thanked her for her skill, dressed, collected Sophie from the waiting-room, and drifted along to the police station. Once again Sophie was offered a chair to sit on. She showed signs of exasperated patience and asked if I would be long.

'Take my car,' I said contritely. 'Do some shopping. Go for a walk to Windsor Park.'

She considered it and brightened. 'I'll come back in an hour.'

The police wanted a statement from me but I asked if I could first speak to Fynedale.

'Speak to him? Well ... there's no law against it. He hasn't been charged yet.' They shook their heads dubiously. 'He's in a violent state, though. Are you sure you want to?'

'Certain.'

They shrugged. 'This way, then.'

Fynedale was in a small, bare interview-room, not sitting beside the table on one of the two plain wooden chairs, but standing in the centre of the largest available clear space. He vibrated still as if strung as tight as piano wire and a muscle jumped spasmodically under his left eye.

The room, brown paint to waist height, cream above, had no windows and was lit by electric light. An impassive young policeman sat on a chair just inside the door. I asked him and the others to leave me and Fynedale to talk alone. Fynedale said loudly, 'I've nothing to bloody say to you.'

The policemen thought I was being foolish, but eventually they shrugged and went away.

'Sit down,' I said, taking one of the chairs by the table and gesturing to the other.

'No.'

'All right, don't.' I pulled out cigarettes and lit one. Whatever was said about cancer of the lungs, I thought, there were times worth the risk. I drew the smoke down and was grateful for its comfort.

Fynedale began pacing around in jerky little strides.

'I *told* you I'd kill you,' he said.

'Your good luck that you didn't.'

He stopped dead. 'What did you say?'

'If you had, you'd have spent ten years inside.'

'Bloody worth it.' He went back to pacing.

'I see Vic's got another partner,' I said.

He picked up a chair and threw it viciously against the wall. The door opened immediately and the young policeman stepped hurriedly in.

'Please wait,' I said. 'We've hardly started.'

He looked indecisively at Fynedale, the fallen chair,

and me sitting calmly smoking, and decided that perhaps after all it would be safe to leave. The door closed quietly behind him.

'Vic's done the dirty on you, I reckon,' I said.

He circled behind me. The hairs on my neck bristled. I took another lungful of smoke and didn't look round.

'Getting you into trouble and then ditching you.'

'It was you got me into trouble.' The voice was a growl in the throat.

I knew that any tenseness in my body would react on him and screw him up even tighter, but it took a fair amount of concentration to relax every muscle with him out of sight behind my head. I tried to make my voice slow, thoughtful, persuasive, but my mouth was as dry as a Sunday in Salt Lake City.

'Vic started it,' I said. 'Vic and you. Now it's Vic and Ronnie North. You and I . . . we've both come off worst with Vic . . .'

He reappeared jerkily into my field of vision. The carrot hair looked bright orange under the electric bulb. His eyes alternately shone with manic fire when the light caught them and receded into secretive shadows when he bent his head. Sophie's remarks about gelignite on the boil came back to me; and his instability had if anything increased.

'Cigarette?' I suggested.

'Get stuffed.'

It was better when I could see him.

I said, 'What have you told the police?'

'Nothing. Bloody nothing.'

'Did they get you to make a statement?'

'That they bloody did not.'

'Good,' I said. 'That simplifies things.'

'What the hell are you on about?'

I watched the violence and agitation in every physical movement. It was as if his muscles and nerves were acting in spasms, as if some central disorganization were plucking wires.

I said, 'What is upsetting you most?'

'Most?' he yelled. 'Most? The fact that you're bloody walking in here as cool as bloody cucumbers, that's what. I tried to kill you. *Kill you*.'

He stopped as if he couldn't explain what he meant, but he'd got his message across to me loud and clear. He had taken himself beyond the edge of sense in his compulsion to do me harm, and there I was, proving that it had all been for nothing. I guessed that he badly needed not to have failed entirely. I took off my jacket and explained about the strap and buckle saving my life. I undid my shirt, showed him the plaster, and told him what lay underneath.

'It hurts,' I said truthfully.

He stopped pacing and peered closely at my face. 'Does it?'

'Yes.'

He put out his hand and touched me. I winced.

He stood back, bent and picked up the chair he'd thrown, set it on its feet on the far side of the table, and sat down opposite me. He stretched for the packet of cigarettes and lighter which I'd left lying, and lit one with hands still shaking with tension.

I left my shirt undone and falling open. He sat smoking jerkily, his eyes flicking every few seconds to the strip of plaster. It seemed to satisfy him. To reassure. Finally to soothe. He smoked the whole cigarette through without speaking, but the jerky movements gradually quietened, and by the time he threw the stub on the floor and twisted his foot on it the worst of the jangle had disappeared.

'I'll make a bargain with you,' I said.

'What bargain?'

'I'll say the pitchfork was an accident.'

'You know bloody well it wasn't.'

'I know. You know. The police know. But there were no witnesses ... If I swear it was an accident there would be no question of you being even charged with attempted murder, let alone tried and convicted.'

He thought it over. There were a lot of little twitches in the muscles of his face, and the skin stretched gauntly over the cheekbones.

'You don't actually want to do time, do you?' I asked.

'No.'

'Suppose we could get you off all the hooks ... Assault, fraud, the lot.'

'You couldn't.'

'I could keep you out of jail, that's for sure.'

214

A long pause. Then he said, 'A bargain. That means you want something in return.'

'Mm.'

'What, then?'

I ran my tongue round my teeth and took my time over replying.

'I want . . .' I said slowly, 'I want you to talk about the way you and Vic tried to make me join your ring.'

He was surprised. 'Is that all?'

'It'll do for a start.'

'But you know. You know what Vic said to you.'

'I don't know what he said to *you*.'

He shrugged in bewilderment. 'He just said if you wouldn't go along with us, we'd break you.'

'Look,' I said, 'the price of your freedom is every word, every scrap of conversation that you can remember. Especially everything about that ally of Vic's who got my stable burnt.'

'I told you . . . I don't know.'

'If you want to get out of here, you're going to have to do better than that.'

He stared across the table. I saw his understanding of my offer deepen. He looked briefly round the bleak, crowding walls of the little interview-room and shivered. The last vestiges of the exalted murderous state evaporated. He looked smaller and colder and no danger to anybody.

'All right,' he said. 'I reckon I don't owe Vic any

more. I'll not go to jail just to save his bloody skin. I'll tell you what I can.'

It took three more cigarettes and a lot of pauses, but he did his best.

'I reckon it started about six weeks ago. I mean, for some time before that Vic had said a few things about you being the biggest danger on the horizon, you were pretty good as an agent and dead honest, and he thought you might drain off some of the business which he'd otherwise corner.'

'Room for us all,' I murmured.

'Not what Vic thought. Anyway, about six weeks ago he said it was time to bust you once and for all.' He thought for a while, sucking deep on his cigarette. 'See, Vic and I and some of the others had this thing going . . .'

'The kick-backs system,' I said.

'Ay. All right, so goody-goody sods like you can look down their noses and sniff, but it's not illegal and it does a lot of people a lot of bloody good.'

'Some people.'

'All right, so the client pays over the odds, so what? Anyway, as Vic always says, the higher the prices the more commission the auctioneers get and the better they like it, so they're just as bad, running things up as far as they bloody can.'

They also had a duty to the seller, I thought, but it wasn't the time to argue.

'Well, there we were, running this little ring and

doing better and better out of it and then one day ...
I suppose it was just before the first yearling sales at
Newmarket ...' He paused, looking back in his mind.
His voice died away.

'What happened?' I prompted.

'Vic was sort of ... I don't know ... excited and
scared ... both at once.'

'Vic was scared?' I said sceptically.

'Ay, he was. Sort of. Sort of excited, though. Like
someone had put him up to something he wanted to
do but knew he shouldn't.'

'Like stealing apples?'

He brushed off the childish parallel. 'These were no
apples. Vic said we'd make so much money that what
had gone before was only peanuts. He said there was
a deal we could do with a breeder that had a colt by
Transporter that was a perfect peach ...'

'Was it Vic's own idea?' I asked.

'I thought so ... I don't know ... Anyway, it worked
a dream. He gave me five thousand quid just for
bidding, and he made twenty out of it himself.'

'By my reckoning he made thirty.'

'Oh no ...' He stopped, surprised, then went on
more slowly. 'No ... I remember him saying ... ten
thousand pounds went to the bloke who wrote the
agreement that Vic got the breeder to sign. I said I
thought it was a lot, but Vic says you have to pay for
expert advice.'

'Does he often pay for expert advice?'

He nodded. 'All the time.'

'Cheerfully?'

'What? Of course.'

'He isn't being blackmailed?'

He looked scornful. 'I'll say not. You can't see any piddling little blackmailer putting one over on Vic.'

'No . . . but what it amounts to is that Vic is collecting huge kick-backs from breeders and other vendors, and out of that he is paying his own kick-backs to someone else for expert advice.'

He frowned. 'I suppose you could say so.'

'But you don't know who?'

'No.'

'How long would you say he had been receiving this advice?'

'How the hell do I know? A year. Two. About that.'

'So what was different about the last six weeks?'

'You were. All of a sudden Vic says it's time to get rid of you. Either that or make you back down and take your cut with the rest of us. We all thought you'd come in with us with a bit of pressure. Well, see, it didn't make sense you holding out. Only do yourself a lot of harm. Jiminy Bell, he says now he told us you'd never agree, but he bloody didn't. That little sod, he said then that you were pretty soft really. A soft touch, he always said. Always good for a sob-story. So now he says he told us you were a tough nut, the squirmy little liar.'

'Does Vic see this friend of his every day?'

218

'Couldn't say.'

'Well . . . think.'

He thought. 'I'd say that most days he either sees him or talks on the phone. See, Vic always gets things done quickly, like pinching that horse you bought at Ascot . . .'

'How was that done?'

He blinked. Shifted uneasily on his chair. I shoved the cigarettes across and tried to look as if the whole question was quite impersonal.

'Er . . .' he said. 'Vic said you were buying a horse for Mrs Sanders and he couldn't have that, she was marrying Constantine Brevett and he was Vic's exclusive territory.'

'When did he say that?'

'At the sales the day you bought Hearse Puller.'

'Had he already fixed it up with Fred Smith?'

He hesitated. 'He knew Fred Smith was going to take away whatever horse you bought. Yes.'

'Did Vic himself fix it with Fred Smith?'

'See, I don't really know. Vic said he didn't, but I don't know, he'd say his grandmother was a pigmy if it suited him.'

'Ronnie North,' I said slowly. 'Did he know Fred Smith?'

Fynedale's face twisted into the sardonic sneer. 'Old mates, weren't they?'

'Were they?'

'Well . . . Ronnie, he came from Stepney way, same

as Fred Smith. Ronnie started in the horse coping business in the old days when they sold horses on market days in all the big towns. He started as a boy, helping his dad. Bloody lot of gypsies if you ask me. Up to every damn trick in the book, is Ronnie. But bright, see? Got brains, Ronnie has.'

'Ronnie sold me the next horse I bought for Kerry Sanders.'

'Ay. Him and Vic, laughing themselves sick about it, they were. Then Ronnie afterwards said you needed a bloody lesson, busting Fred Smith's arm.'

'Did you yourself ever meet Fred Smith?'

'I saw him, like. Saw him at Ascot, with Ronnie. Ronnie pointed you out to him. We all did, see?'

'I see.'

'Then, well, with River God it was dead easy, wasn't it? Ronnie found which transport firm you'd engaged and got them to tell him their instructions, and he just sent Fred Smith to pick you off on the lay-by.'

'Ronnie sent him?'

'Ronnie . . . or Vic.' He shrugged. 'One of them.'

'Not Vic's unknown friend?'

'Might have been, I suppose.' He didn't think it made much difference. 'We weren't going to steal River God, see? Fred Smith had the money for it. He was going to make you take it, like at Ascot.'

'And River God was going back to Ronnie North?'

'Ay.'

'Then why did he agree to sell it to me in the first place?'

He said with exaggerated patience as if talking to a dim child, 'See, he wasn't going to, first off. Then he rings Vic and says you're looking for another horse instead of Hearse Puller. Then Vic rings back and says sell you River God and it'll be a good opportunity of bashing you up a bit more.'

'Did you actually hear either of these calls?'

'Eh?' He shook his head. 'I don't live in Vic's pocket, do I? No, Vic told me.'

I thought for a while. 'All right,' I said, 'which of you thought of burning my yard?'

He shifted his chair abruptly so that he was no longer facing me, but spoke to the bare walls.

'See . . . Vic said . . . a real smash, and you'd cave in. See . . . he saw you talking to that Transporter breeder . . . and that trainer whose owner he'd swiped . . . in the bar, see?'

'Yes.'

'Ay. Well then, Vic says this time no messing, you've got to be put right out of action, because this expert friend of his has thought up a fiddle to make the Transporter colt look like hay-seeds, only he wouldn't tell Vic what it was while you were still around at the sales. Vic said this expert was afraid you would make a public fuss which would mean everyone would be a lot more careful about buying horses in future and that was the last thing they wanted. So Vic said you either had to join in or be got rid of and you'd made it crystal clear you wouldn't join in, so it was your own bloody fault you got your yard burnt.'

I grunted: 'And what happened afterwards?'

'Well, there you bloody were at the sales as if nothing had happened. The whole thing had been a flop and Fred Smith was in jail and Vic was furious because he couldn't start the new fiddle. He said he'd just have to go on with the kick-backs and anyway we'd been doing pretty well out of those for two years so it didn't seem too bad.'

He swung round again, his face full of renewed anger.

'And then you had to bugger the whole thing up by ratting to Wilton Young.'

'Calm down,' I said flatly. 'Did you expect me to go on meekly taking whatever you cared to dish out?'

He looked indecisive. 'Don't know.'

You know now, I thought.

'Are Vic and his expert friend still planning this new big fiddle for some time in the future?'

'Ay. They are. Today... Today?' He seemed suddenly astounded that it was only that morning that he had gone to Ascot Sales.

'Today... I could have killed Vic... I told him I could kill him... and kill you too... and he said... why didn't I just kill you, then he could get on with the fiddle... and he was bloody laughing... but I reckon now he meant to egg me on.'

'I expect he did,' I said.

'Ay. He'd be rid of you and me too. He'd have the whole bloody field to himself.'

He leaned his elbows on the table and picked up my lighter and fidgeted with it.

'Here,' he said. 'I'll tell you something. You can put Vic in the same boat as you did me.'

'Do you mean . . . had up for fraud?'

'Ay . . . Makes shipping horses by sea instead of air look like kids' stuff.'

'Tell me, then.'

He looked up. 'You meant it straight, didn't you, about getting me out of here?'

'I did.'

He sighed. 'Reckon I can trust you. And that's a bloody laugh, for a start.'

He threw down the lighter and leaned back.

'Right, then,' he said. 'Vic swindled the High Power Insurance Company out of a hundred and fifteen thousand quid.'

CHAPTER FOURTEEN

'Are you sure?' I said.

'Positive.'

'Can you prove it?'

'I reckon *you* could, if you wanted to.'

'How did he do it?'

'See . . . it was about three years ago . . . he shipped a four-year-old stallion out to Japan. Polyprint, it was called.'

I said, 'I remember that. It died on the way.'

'Ay. It did. And Vic had insured it for a hundred and fifteen thousand for the journey, with himself to collect if anything happened to the horse.'

'Nothing especially unusual in that.'

'No. And he insured it a week before it was due to go. That is what made the insurance firm pay up. Because a week before the horse set off, Vic couldn't have known it was going to die, because a vet had been over it from nose to arse and given it the OK, and it was the High Power Company's own vet, which strung them up proper.'

'I can't remember what it died of . . .'

'Tetanus,' he said. 'Three days by air to Japan. They took it out of Gatwick looking as right as rain . . . it walked up the ramp into the aircraft as quiet as you please. By the time they got to the Middle East it was sweating something chronic. Next stop, they got it out and walked it around, but it was staggering a bit. Next stop they had a local vet waiting. Tetanus, he said. So they cabled the insurance company and they wanted to send their own man out to take a look. See, there was a lot of brass involved. Anyway he never went because the horse died while he was still in England getting cholera jabs or something. So Vic claims the money, and the High Power has to pay up.'

'Did Vic travel with the horse himself?'

'No. He was right here in England.'

'So . . . where was the fraud?'

'Ah . . . See, the horse that set off for Japan and died of tetanus, that horse wasn't Polyprint.'

He lit a cigarette, absorbed in his story.

'It was a horse called Nestegg.'

I stared at him. 'Nestegg is standing at stud in Ireland.'

'Ay,' he said. 'And that's Polyprint.'

The gaunt face twisted into the ghost of a smile. 'See, Vic bought Nestegg because he had a client who wanted it. Nestegg was six and had won a few long-distance races, and this client had a small stud and wanted a stallion that wouldn't cost too much. Well, Vic bought Nestegg for ten thousand and was going to pass him on for fifteen, and then this client just dropped down dead one afternoon and the widow said nothing doing, she didn't want to know. Vic wasn't much worried because Nestegg wasn't bad, really.'

He took a few deep puffs, sorting things out.

'One evening I was at Vic's place near Epsom and we looked round the yard, like one does. He shows me Polyprint, who's due to set off to Japan the next day. Big bay horse. Full of himself. Then, three boxes along, there was Nestegg. Another bay, much the same. We went in and looked at him and he was standing there all hunched up and sweating. Vic looked him over and said he would go out and see him again later, and if he was no better he would get the vet in the morning. Then we went into Vic's house for a drink, and then I went home.'

He looked at me broodingly.

'So the next day off goes this horse to Japan and dies of tetanus two days later. Next time I saw Vic he sort of winks at me and gives me a thousand quid in readies, and I laughed and took it. Then later he sold this bay which he still had, which was supposed to be Nestegg but was really Polyprint, he sold him to a stud in Ireland for seventeen thousand. He wouldn't have made a penny if he'd sent Polyprint off to Japan and got a vet to try to save Nestegg. Just by swapping those two horses when he had the chance, he made himself a proper packet.'

'And it gave him a taste for more easy money in large amounts?'

'Ay . . . It was after that that he latched on to the kick-backs in a big way. He asked me to help . . . Tell you the truth, I was glad to.'

'And he found this expert,' I said.

'Ay . . .' He hesitated. 'It was maybe the other way round. Vic more or less said this chap had come to him and suggested more ways Vic could make money.'

'He hadn't done so badly on his own,' I observed.

'Well . . . Polyprint was a one-off, see. You couldn't work that again. He only did it because he realized Nestegg had tetanus and would die pretty quickly if he wasn't treated and even maybe if he was. See, tetanus isn't that common. You couldn't have two die of it on journeys when they were heavily insured, even if you could infect them on purpose, which you can't. Vic walked that horse around all night to keep it moving and fed it a bucketful of tranquillizers so that it looked all right when it was loaded on to the plane at Gatwick. But to get another one to die on a journey you'd have to fix some sort of accident. The insurance people would be dead suspicious, and even if they paid up they might afterwards refuse to insure you altogether and you couldn't risk that. But the thing about this expert chap was that nearly everything he suggested was legal. Vic said it was like property development and land speculation. You could make a great deal of money without breaking the law if you knew how to set about it.'

The police were understandably sour about my assertion that I had fallen on the pitchfork by accident and that Fynedale was as innocent of assault as a bunch of violets. They argued and I insisted, and half an hour later Fynedale stood outside on the pavement shivering in the wind.

'Thanks,' he said briefly. He looked shrunken and depressed.

He huddled inside his jacket, turned on his heel, and walked away up the street to the railway station. The carrot hair was a receding orange blob against the dead copper leaves of a beech hedge.

Sophie was waiting by the kerb, sitting in the driving seat of my car. I opened the passenger-side door and slid in beside her.

'Will you drive?' I said.

'If you like.'

I nodded.

'You look bushed,' she said. She started the engine, shifted the gears, and edged out into the road.

'Couldn't beat Muhammad Ali right now.'

She smiled. 'How did it go?'

'Like a torrent, once he'd started.'

'What did you learn?'

I thought, trying to put everything into its right order. Sophie drove carefully, flicking glances across, waiting for an answer.

I said, 'Vic swindled an insurance company very neatly, about three years ago. Some time after that someone who Fynedale calls an expert sought Vic out and suggested a sort of alliance, in which Vic would extort money in various more or less legal ways and pay a proportion of it to the expert. I imagine this expert guessed Vic had swindled the insurance and was therefore a good prospect for a whole career of legal robbery.'

'There's no such thing as legal robbery.'

I smiled. 'How about wealth taxes?'

'That's different.'

'Taking by law is legal robbery.'

'Ah well . . . go on about Vic.'

'Vic and the expert started redistributing wealth in no uncertain terms, chiefly into their own pockets but with enough pickings to entice six or seven other agents into the ring.'

'Fynedale?' Sophie said.

'Yes. Especially Fynedale, as he knew about the original insurance swindle. It just seems to have been my bad luck that I started being an agent at about the time Vic and the expert were warming things up. Pauli Teksa had a theory that Vic and his friends wanted me out of the way because I was a threat to their monopoly, and from what Fynedale says I should think he might have been right, though I thought it was nonsense when he suggested it.'

I yawned. Sophie drove smoothly, as controlled at the wheel as everywhere else. She had taken off the fur-lined hood, and the silver-blond hair fell gently to her shoulders. Her profile was calm, efficient, content. I thought that probably I did love her, and would for a long time. I also guessed that however often I might ask her to marry me, in the end she would not. The longer and better I knew her, the more I realized that she was by nature truly solitary. Lovers she might take, but a bustling family life would be alien and disruptive. I understood why her four years with the pilot had been a success: it was because of his continual long absences, not in spite of them. I understood her lack of even the memory of inconsolable grief. His death had merely left her where she basically liked to be, which was alone.

'Go on about Vic,' she said.

'Oh . . . well . . . They started this campaign of harassment. Compulsory purchase of Hearse Puller at Ascot. Sending Fred Smith down to my place to do what harm he could, which turned out to be giving Crispin whisky and letting loose that road-hogging two-year-old. Arranging for me to buy and lose River God. When all that, and a few bits of intimidation from Vic himself, failed to work, they reckoned that burning my stable would do the trick.'

'Their mistake.'

'Yeah . . . well . . . they did it.' I yawned again. 'Fred Smith, now. Vic and the expert needed some muscle. Ronnie North knew Fred Smith. Vic must have asked Ronnie if he knew anyone suitable and Ronnie suggested Fred Smith.'

'Bingo.'

'Mm . . . You know something odd?'

'What?'

'The insurance company that Vic swindled was the one Crispin used to work for.'

Sophie made us tea in her flat. We sat side by side on the sofa, bodies casually touching in intimate friendship, sipping the hot reviving liquid.

'I ought to sleep a bit,' she said. 'I'm on duty at eight.'

I looked at my watch. Four-thirty, and darkening already towards the winter night. It had seemed a long day.

'Shall I go?'

She smiled. 'Depends how sore you are.'

'Sex is a great anaesthetic.'

'Nuts.'

We went to bed and put it fairly gently to the test, and certainly what I felt most was not the stab along my rib.

The pattern as before: sweet, intense, lingering, a vibration of subtle pleasure from head to foot. She breathed softly and slowly and smiled with her eyes, as close as my soul and as private as her own.

Eventually she said sleepily, 'Do you always give girls what suits them best?'

I yawned contentedly. 'What suits them best is best for me.'

'The voice of experience . . .' She smiled drowsily, drifting away.

We woke to the clatter of her alarm less than two hours later.

She stretched out a hand to shut it off, then rolled her head over on the pillow for a kiss.

'Better than sleeping pills,' she said. 'I feel as if I'd slept all night.'

She made coffee and rapid bacon and eggs, because to her it seemed time for breakfast, and in an organized hurry she offered her cheek in goodbye on the pavement and drove away to work.

I watched her rear lights out of sight. I remembered I had read somewhere that air traffic controllers had the highest divorce rates on earth.

Wilton Young came to Cheltenham races the following day in spite of the basic contempt he held for steeple-chasing because of its endemic shortage of brass. He came because the rival tycoon who was sponsoring the day's big race had asked him, and the first person he saw at the pre-lunch reception was me.

'What are you doing here?' he said bluntly.

'I was invited.'

'Oh.'

He didn't quite ask why, so I told him. 'I rode a few winners for our host.'

He cast his mind back and gave a sudden remembering nod. 'Ay. So you did.'

A waiter offered a silver tray with glasses of champagne. Wilton Young took one, tasted it with a grimace, and said he would tell me straight he would sooner have had a pint of bitter.

'I'm afraid I may have some disappointing news for you,' I said.

He looked immediately belligerent. 'Exactly what?'

'About Fynedale.'

'Him!' His eyes narrowed. 'Any bad news about him is good news.'

I said, 'The man I sent to South Africa says he can't swear the extra horses he looked after on the way were yours.'

'You seemed sure enough that he would.'

'He says he had the impression they were yours, but he couldn't be sure.'

'That'll not stand up in court.'

'No.'

He grunted. 'I'll not sue, then. I'll not throw good brass after bad. Suing's a mug's game where there's any doubt.'

His plain honesty rebuked me for the lie I'd told

him. My man had been absolutely positive about the horses' ownership: he'd seen the papers, I reckoned my promise to get Fynedale off was fully discharged and from there on he would have to take his chances.

'What's past is past,' Wilton Young said. 'Cut your losses. Eh, lad?'

'I guess so,' I said.

'Take my word for it. Now, look here. I've a mind to buy an American horse. Tough, that's what they are. Tough as if they came from Yorkshire.' He wasn't joking. 'There's one particular one I want you to go and buy for me. He comes up for sale soon after Christmas.'

I stared at him, already guessing.

'Phoenix Fledgling. A two-year-old. Ever heard of it?'

'Did you know,' I said, 'that Constantine Brevett is after it too?'

He chuckled loudly. 'Why the hell do you think I want it? Put his bloody superior nose out of joint. Eh, lad?'

The bloody superior nose chose that precise moment to arrive at the reception, closely accompanied by the firm mouth, smooth grey hair, thick black spectacle frames and general air of having come straight from some high-up chairmanship in the City.

As his height and booming voice instantly dominated the assembly, I reflected that the advantage always seemed to go to the one who arrived later: maybe if Constantine and Wilton Young both realized it they would try so hard to arrive after each other that neither would appear at all, which might be a good idea all round. Constantine's gaze swept authoritatively over the guests and stopped abruptly on Wilton Young and me. He frowned very slightly. His mouth marginally compressed. He gave us five seconds' uninterrupted attention, and then looked away.

'Has it ever occurred to you,' I said slowly, 'that it might just be *your* nose that *he's* putting out of joint?'

'Don't be daft.'

'How many times have you had to outbid him to get a horse?'

He chuckled. 'Can't remember. I've beaten him more times than he's sold office blocks.'

'He's cost you a great deal of money.'

The chuckle died. 'That was bloody Fynedale and Vic Vincent.'

'But ... what if Constantine approved ... or even planned it?'

'You're chasing the wrong rabbit, I tell thee straight.'

I chewed my lower lip. 'As long as you're happy.'

'Ay.'

Nicol won the amateurs' race by some startlingly aggressive tactics that wrung obscenities from his opponents and some sharp-eyed looks from the stewards. He joined me afterwards with defiance flying like banners.

'How about that, then?' he said, attacking first.

'If you were a pro on the Flat you'd have been suspended.'

'That's right.'

'A proper sportsman,' I said drily.

'I'm not in it for the sport.'

'What then?'

'Winning.'

'Just like Wilton Young,' I said.

'What do you mean?'

'Neither of you cares what winning costs.'

He glared. 'It cost you enough in your time in smashed-up bones.'

'Well ... maybe everyone pays in the way that matters to them least.'

'I don't give a damn what the others think of me.'

'That's what I mean.'

We stood in silence, watching horses go by. All my life I'd stood and watched horses go by. There were a lot worse ways of living.

'When you grow up,' I said, 'you'll be a bloody good jockey.'

'You absolute sod.' The fury of all his twenty-two pampered years bunched into fists. Then with the speed of all his mercurial changes he gave me instead the brief, flashing, sardonic smile. 'OK. OK. *OK*. I just aged five years.'

He turned on his heel and strode away, and although I didn't know it until afterwards, he walked straight into the Clerk of the Course's office and filled out an application form for a licence.

Vic didn't come to Cheltenham races. I had business with him, however, so after a certain amount of private homework I drove to his place near Epsom early on the following morning.

He lived as he dressed, a mixture of distinguished traditional and flashy modern. The house, down a short well-kept drive off a country by-road on the outskirts of Oxshott Woods, had at heart the classically simple lines of early Victorian stone. Stuck on the back was an Edwardian outcrop of kitchens and bathrooms and to one side sprawled an extensive new single-storey wing which proved to embrace a swimming pool, a garden-room, and a suite for guests.

Vic was in his stable, a brick-built quadrangle standing apart from the house. He came out of its archway, saw me standing by my car and walked across with no welcome written plain on his large unsmiling face.

'What the hell do you want?' he said.

'To talk to you.'

The cold sky was thick with clouds and the first heavy drops spoke of downpours to come. Vic looked irritated and said he had nothing to say.

'I have,' I said.

It began to rain in earnest. Vic turned on his heel

and hurried away towards the house, and I followed him closely. He was even more irritated to find me going in with him through his own door.

'I've nothing to say,' he repeated.

'You'll listen, then.'

We stood in a wide passage running between the old part of the house and the new, with central heating rushing out past us into the chilly air of Surrey. Vic tightened his mouth, shut the outer door, and jerked his head for me to follow.

Money had nowhere been spared. Large expanses of pale blue carpeting stretched to the horizon. Huge, plushy sofas stood around. Green plants the size of saplings sprouted from Greek-looking pots. He probably had a moon bath, I thought, with gold taps: and a water bed for sleep.

I remembered the holes in Antonia Huntercombe's ancient chintz. Vic's legal robbery had gone a long way too far.

He took me to the room at the far end of the hallway, his equivalent of my office. From there the one window looked out to the pool, with the guest-rooms to the left, and the garden-room to the right. His rows of record books were much like mine, but there ended the resemblance between the two rooms. His had bright new paint, pale blue carpet, three or four Florentine mirrors, Bang and Olufsen stereo and a well-stocked bar.

'Right,' Vic said. 'Get it over. I've no time to waste.'

'Ever heard of a horse called Polyprint?' I said.

He froze. For countable seconds not a muscle twitched. Then he blinked.

'Of course.'

'Died of tetanus.'

'Yes.'

'Ever heard of Nestegg?'

If I'd run him through with a knitting needle he would have been no more surprised. The stab went through him visibly. He didn't answer.

'When Nestegg was foaled,' I said conversationally, 'there was some doubt as to his paternity. One of two stallions could have covered the dam. So the breeder had Nestegg's blood typed.'

Vic gave a great imitation of Lot's wife.

'Nestegg's blood was found to be compatible with one of the stallions, but not with the other. Records were kept. Those records still exist.'

No sign.

'A full brother of Polyprint is now in training in Newmarket.'

Nothing.

I said, 'I have arranged a blood test for the horse now known as Nestegg. You and I both know that his blood type will be entirely different from that recorded for Nestegg as a foal. I have also arranged a blood test for Polyprint's full brother. And his blood type will be entirely compatible with the one found in the supposed Nestegg.'

'You *bugger*.' The words exploded from him, all the more forceful for his unnatural immobility.

'On the other hand,' I said, 'the tests have not yet been made, and in certain circumstances I would cancel them.'

His breath came back. He moved. 'What circumstances?' he said.

'I want an introduction.'

'A what?'

'To a friend of yours. The friend who drew up the agreement that the breeder of the Transporter colt signed. The friend who decided to burn my stable.'

Vic moved restlessly.

'Impossible.'

I said without heat, 'It's either that or I write to the High Power Insurance people.'

He fidgeted tensely with some pens lying on his desk.

'What would you do if you met . . . this friend?'

'Negotiate for permanent peace.'

He picked up a calendar, looked at it unseeingly, and put it down.

'Today's Saturday,' I said. 'The blood tests are scheduled for Monday morning. If I meet your friend today or tomorrow, I'll call them off.'

He was more furious than frightened, but he knew as well as I did that those blood tests would be his first step to the dock. What I didn't know was whether Vic, like Fred Smith, would swallow the medicine with, so to speak, his mouth shut.

Vic said forcefully, 'You'd always have that threat over me. It's bloody blackmail.'

'Sort of,' I agreed.

Ripples of resentment screwed up his face. I watched him searching for a way out.

'Face to face with your friend,' I said. 'Five minutes will do. That's not much when you think what you stand to lose if I don't get it.' I gestured round his bright room and out to the luxurious pool. 'Built on Polyprint's insurance, no doubt.'

He banged his fist down on the desk, making the pens rattle.

'Bloody Fynedale told you,' he shouted. 'It must have been. I'll murder the little rat.'

I didn't exactly deny it, but instead I said matter-of-factly, 'One calculation you left out . . . my brother Crispin worked for High Power.'

CHAPTER FIFTEEN

Crispin stood in the yard at home looking miserable and broody. I stopped the car on my return from Vic's and climbed out to meet him.

'What's the matter?' I said.

'Oh . . .' He swung an arm wide in inner frustration, indicating the flattened stable area and the new scaffolding climbing up to the burnt part of the roof.

'All this . . . If I hadn't been drunk it wouldn't have happened.'

I looked at him. 'Don't worry about it.'

'But I do. If I'd been around . . . if there had been lights on in the house . . . that man wouldn't have set fire . . .'

'You don't know that he wouldn't,' I said.

'Stands to reason.'

'No. Come on in, it's cold out here.'

We went into the kitchen and I made coffee. Crispin's mood of self-abasement flickered on fitfully while he watched me put the water and coffee grounds into the percolator.

'It would have been better if you had let me die.'

'It was a good job you passed out in the bathroom,' I said. 'It was the only room which had natural ventilation through an airbrick.'

He wasn't cheered. 'Better if I'd snuffed it.'

'Want some toast?'

'Stop bloody talking about food. I'm saying you should have let me die.'

'I know you are. It's damn silly. I don't want you dead. I want you alive and well and living in Surrey.'

'You don't take me seriously.' His voice was full of injured complaint.

I thought of all the other conversations we'd had along those lines. I ought to have let him drown in the bath, the time he went to sleep there. I ought to have let him drive into a tree, the time I'd taken his car keys away. I ought to have let him fall off the Brighton cliffs, the time he tottered dizzily to the edge.

Blaming me for not letting him die was his way of laying all his troubles at my door. It was my fault he was alive, his mind went, so it was my fault if he took refuge in drink. He would work up his resentment against me as a justification for self-pity.

I sighed inwardly and made the toast. Either that day or the next he would be afloat again on gin.

There was no word from Vic. I spent all day working in the office and watching racing on television, with Crispin doing his best to put his mind to my accounts.

'When you worked for High Power,' I said, 'did you

243

have anything to do with a claim for a horse called Polyprint?'

He sniffed. 'You know damn well I was in Pensions, not Claims.'

'Just thought you might have heard . . .'

'No.'

We drank Coke and fizzy lemonade and coffee, and I grilled some lamb chops for supper, and still Vic didn't telephone.

Same thing the next morning. Too much silence. I bit my nails and wondered what to do if my lever didn't work: if Vic wouldn't tell and the friend wouldn't save him. The blood-typing tests could go ahead and chop Vic into little pieces, but the friend would be free and undiscovered and could recruit another lieutenant and start all over again, like cancer.

I wandered round the place where the stable had been, desultorily kicking at loose stones.

A car turned into the yard, one I didn't know, and from it stepped a total stranger. Tall, young, blond. Surely this couldn't be Vic's friend, I thought: and it wasn't. There were two other people in the car with him, and from the back of it stepped Sophie.

'Hi . . .' She grinned at my face. 'Who were you expecting? The bailiffs?'

She introduced the friends, Peter and Sue. They were all on their way to lunch with Sue's parents, but if I liked she could stop off with me and they would pick her up on their way back.

244

I liked. The friends waved and went, and Sophie tucked her arm through mine.

'How about marriage?' I said.

'No.'

'Why not?'

'Because you like oysters and I don't.'

I smiled and steered her into the house. It was as good an answer as any.

Crispin was highly restless and not in the least pleased to see her.

'I'll go for a walk,' he said. 'I can see I'm not wanted.'

'You'll stay right where you are and pour us some Cokes,' I said firmly. We looked at each other, both knowing that if he went for a walk it would lead to the pub.

'All right,' he said abruptly. 'You bloody bully.'

I cooked the lunch: steaks and grilled tomatoes. Crispin said that Sophie ought to do it and Sophie said you should never interfere in someone else's kitchen. They looked at each other with unfriendly eyes as if each wishing that the other wasn't there. Not the most relaxed of Sunday lunch parties, I thought: and Vic telephoned with the coffee.

'My friend will meet you,' he said. 'For five minutes only. Like you said.'

'Where?' I asked.

'Here. At my house. Six o'clock.'

'I'll be there,' I said.

His voice held a mixture of instructions and anxiety. 'You'll cancel those blood tests?'

'Yeah,' I said. 'After the meeting, I will.'

I went back to the kitchen. Sophie was smoking and Crispin glowered at his coffee as if it were an enemy. When we were alone he often stacked the plates in the dishwasher but I knew he wouldn't do it while she was there. He took it for granted that if there was a woman in the room she would do the household chores, even if she were a guest. Sophie saw no reason to do jobs she disliked, and her host's jobs at that, simply because she was female. I watched the two of them with a sad sort of amusement, my liability of a brother and the girl who wouldn't be my wife.

During the afternoon Peter and Sue rang to say they were staying overnight with Sue's parents and consequently couldn't take Sophie home. Would I mind frightfully driving her home myself.

I explained to Sophie that I had an appointment near Epsom.

'That's all right,' she said. 'I'll wait in the car while you do your business, and we can go on to my place after.'

A flicker of caution made me uneasy. 'I'm going to see Vic Vincent,' I said.

'Is he likely to be as lethal as Fynedale?'

I smiled. 'No.'

'And don't forget it was a good job I was with you at Ascot.'

'I haven't.'

'Well, then.'

So I took her.

Crispin followed us out to the car. 'I suppose you won't be back till bloody morning,' he said.

'Whether I am or not, you'll be all right.'

He looked at me in desperation. 'You know I bloody won't.'

'You can be if you want to,' I said persuasively.

'Sod you, Jonah.'

He stood and watched us as I started the car and drove away. As usual he had made me feel a grinding guilt at leaving him to struggle alone. As usual I told myself that if he were ever to beat the drink he would have to stay off it when I wasn't there. I simply couldn't be beside him every minute of his life.

We drove towards Epsom. We were early, by design. Vic had said six o'clock, but I thought that a preliminary scout around might be prudent. The friend, whoever he was, had already sent a load of trouble my way, and I had a minimum of faith that all would henceforth be caviar and handshakes.

I drove fifty yards past the entrance to Vic's drive, and pulled up on the grass verge with Sophie's door pressed close against the hedge. I switched off the lights and turned to her.

'When I go, lock my door behind me,' I said. 'And don't get out of the car.'

'Jonah ... You really do think Vic might be lethal.'

'Not Vic. But he might have someone else with him ... I don't know. Anyway, I'll be much happier if I'm sure you're sitting here snug and safe.'

'But ...'

'No buts.' I kissed her lightly. 'I'll be back in half an hour or so. If I'm not here by six-thirty, drive on into Epsom and raise a posse.'

'I don't like it.'

'Put the rug round you, or you'll get cold.'

I slid out of the car and watched her lock the door. Waved. Smiled as if I were going to the circus. Went away.

The night was not pitch dark. Few nights are. My eyes adjusted to the dimness and I went quietly through the gateway and up alongside the drive, walking on the grass. I had worn for the occasion a black sweater and dark trousers, black rubber-soled shoes. I pulled a pair of gloves from my pocket and put them on. I had dark brown hair, which helped, and apart from the pale blob of my face I must have looked much at one with the shadows.

There were two cars outside the front of Vic's house, both of them unfamiliar. A Ford Cortina and a Jaguar XJ 12.

I drifted round the house towards the pool, hoping and guessing that Vic used his office, as I did, as the natural place to take his friends. Most of the house was in darkness. Vic's window shone with light. Round one, I thought.

Carefully I skirted the pool and approached under the protection of the dark overhang of the roof over the guest suite keeping tight against the wall. Faint light from the sky raised a sheen on the unruffled pool water. There was no wind, no sound except from an occasional car on the road. I edged with caution closer.

Vic's window was hung with thick fawn-coloured crusty net in clustered folds. I found that one could see a certain amount when trying to look through it straight ahead, but that slanting vision was impossible. It also seemed possible that as the curtaining was not opaque, anyone inside could see through it to someone moving about outside. Inconvenient for peeping Toms.

I crawled the last bit, feeling a fool. The window stretched down to within eighteen inches of the paving stone. By the time I reached the wall I was flat on my stomach.

Vic was walking around the room, talking. I risked raising my eyes over the level of the sill, but to little purpose. All I could clearly see was a bit of the table which stood near the window and a distant piece of Florentine mirror. I shifted sideways a little and looked again. A sliver of bookcase and a chair leg. Another shift. More bookcase, and a quick impression of Vic moving.

His voice came through the glass whenever he walked near the window. I put my head down and listened to unconnected snatches.

' . . . Polyprint and Nestegg . . . bloody dynamite . . .'

' . . . what does it matter how he found out? How did you find out in the first place . . .'

' . . . beating him up wouldn't have worked either. I told you . . . burning his place hurt him more . . .'

' . . . you can't put pressure on a wife and children if he hasn't got any . . .'

' . . . brother . . . no good . . . just a lush . . .'

I shifted along on my stomach and looked again. Another uninformative slice of furnishings.

I couldn't see who Vic was talking to nor hear the replies. The answering voice came to me only as a low rumble, like a bass drum played quietly. I realized in the end that its owner was sitting against the window wall but so far to the left that unless he moved I was not going to be able to see him from where I was. Never mind, I thought. I would see him face to face soon enough. Meanwhile I might as well learn as much as I could. There might be a gem for the bargaining session ahead.

' . . . can't see any other way out . . .' Vic said.

The reply rumbled briefly.

Vic came suddenly close to the window. I buried my face and stretched my ears.

'Look,' he said. 'I more or less promised him you would meet him.'

Rumble rumble, seemingly displeased.

'Well I'm damn well not going inside just to save him from knowing who you are.'

Rumble rumble.

'Damn right I'll tell him.'

Rumble rumble rumble.

Vic hadn't been exactly frank, I thought. He hadn't told his rumble-voiced friend that I was due there at six o'clock. Vic was going to hand the friend to me on a plate whether the friend liked it or not. I smiled in the dark. Round two.

'I don't give a damn about your reputation,' Vic said. 'What's so bloody marvellous about your reputation?'

A long rumble. Infuriating not to be able to hear.

Vic's voice in reply sounded for the first time as if he were stifling doubts.

'Of course I agree that business is founded on trust . . .'

Rumble rumble.

'Well, it's too bad because I'm not bloody going to jail to save your reputation, and that's flat.'

Rumble.

Vic moved across the window from right to left, but I could still hear him clearly.

'Where are you going?' His voice suddenly rose sharply into anxiety. 'What are you doing? No . . . No . . . My God . . . Wait . . .' His voice went higher and louder. 'Wait . . .'

The last time, he screamed it. 'Wait . . .'

There was a sort of cough somewhere inside the room and something heavy fell against the window. I raised my head and froze in absolute horror.

Vic was leaning back against the glass. The net curtain all around him was bright scarlet.

While I watched he twisted on his feet and gripped hold of the curtain for support. On the front of his lilac shirt there was an irregular scarlet star.

He didn't speak. His grip slackened on the curtains. I saw his eyes for a second as he fell.

They were dead.

Without conscious thought I got to my feet and sprinted round to the front of the house. It's easy enough looking back to say that it was a mad thing to do. At the time all I thought was that Vic's murdering friend would get clean away without me seeing who he was. All I thought was that I'd set Vic up to flush out the friend, and if I didn't see who it was he would have died for nothing. The one thing I didn't think was that if the friend saw *me*, he would simply shoot me too.

Everything happened too fast for working out probabilities.

By the time I had skirted the pool and the garden-room the engine of one of the cars in the drive was urgently revving. Not the big Jaguar. The Cortina. It reversed fiercely in an arc to point its nose to the drive.

I ran. I came up to it from behind on its left side. Inside the car the dark bulk of the driver was shifting the gears from reverse to forward. I put my hand on the handle of the rear door, wanting to open it, to make him turn his head, see who he was, to stop him, fight

him, take his gun away, hand him over to justice ...
heaven knows.

The Cortina spurted forward as if flagged off the
grid and pulled my arm right out of its socket.

CHAPTER SIXTEEN

I knelt on the ground in the familiar bloody agony and thought that a dislocated shoulder was among the ultimates.

What was more, there were footsteps coming up the drive towards me.

Scrunch scrunch scrunch.

Inexorable.

All things have to be faced. I supported my left elbow in my right hand and waited, because in any case I could barely move, let alone run away.

A figure materialized from the darkness. Advanced to within six feet. Stopped.

A voice said, 'Have you been run over?'

I nearly smiled. 'I thought I told you to stay in the car.'

'You sound funny,' Sophie said.

'Hilarious.'

She took two paces forward, stretching out her hands.

'Don't touch me,' I said hastily.

'What's the matter?'

I told her.

'Oh God,' she said.

'And you can put it back.'

'What?'

'Put my shoulder back.'

'But . . .' She sounded bewildered. 'I can't.'

'Not here. In the house.'

She had no idea how to help me up. Not like jump jockeys' wives, I thought briefly, for whom smashed up husbands were all in the day's work. I made it to my feet with the loss of no more than a pint of sweat. Various adjectives occurred to me. Like excruciating.

One foot gingerly in front of the other took us to the door that Vic's friend had left open, the door to the hallway and the office. Light spilled out of it. I wondered if there was a telephone anywhere except in the office.

We went very slowly indoors with me hunched like Quasimodo.

'Jonah!' Sophie said.

'What?'

'I didn't realize . . . you look . . . you look . . .'

'Yeah,' I said. 'I need you to put it back.'

'We must get a doctor.'

'No . . . the police. Vic Vincent's been shot.'

'*Shot*.' She followed my gaze to Vic's office and went along there to take a look. She returned several shades paler, which made two of us.

'It's . . . awful.'

'See if you can find another telephone.'

She switched on several lights. There was another telephone on a table flanked by a sofa and a potted palm.

'Call the police,' I said.

She dialled three nines. Told them a man had been killed. They would come at once, they said. She put the receiver down and turned towards me purposefully.

'I'm going to dial again for an ambulance.'

'No. You do it. It has to be done now. At once.'

'Jonah . . . don't be stupid. How can I? You need professional help. A doctor.'

'I need a doctor like yesterday's news. Look . . . doctors don't put shoulders back. By the time they arrive all the muscles have gone into spasms, so they can't. They send you to hospital in bloody jerking ambulances. The hospitals sit you around for hours in casualty departments. Then they send you for X-rays. Then they trundle you to an operating theatre and by then they have to give you a general anaesthetic. It takes about four hours at the best of times. Sunday evenings are not the best of times. If you won't do it . . . I . . . I . . .' I stopped. The prospect of those long hours ahead was enough to scare the saints.

'I can't,' she said.

'I'll tell you how . . .'

She was appalled. 'You must have a doctor.'

I muttered under my breath.

'What did you say?' she demanded.

'I said . . . God give me a woman of strength.'

She said in a low voice, 'That's unfair.'

I went slowly past her through the hall into the open-plan dining-room and sat gingerly on one of the hard straight-backed chairs. What I felt was beyond a joke.

I shut my eyes and thought about Vic's friend. Thought about the glimpse of him I'd had in the split second before he blasted off and took my comfort with him. There had been a seepage of light from the house's open door. Enough to show me the shape of a head.

There had been little time for certainty. Only for impression. The impression remained in my mind indelibly.

Sophie said, 'Jonah . . .'

I opened my eyes. She was standing in front of me, huge-eyed and trembling.

I'd wanted to know what could break up her colossal composure. Now I knew. One man shot to death and another demanding an unimaginable service.

'What do I do?' she said.

I swallowed. 'It will take ten minutes.'

She was shocked. Apprehension made her eyes even bigger.

'If you mean it . . .' I said.

'I do.'

'First instruction . . . smile.'

'But . . .'

257

'Six deep breaths and a big smile.'

'Oh Jonah.' She sounded despairing.

'Look,' I said. 'I don't want you messing about with my precious body unless you go back to being your normal confident, relaxed, efficient, hard-hearted self.'

She stared. 'I thought you were past talking. You're a fraud.'

'That's better.'

She took me literally. Six deep breaths and a smile. Not a big smile, but something.

'OK,' I said. 'Put your left hand under my elbow and hold my wrist with your right.'

I shifted an inch or two back on the seat until the base of my spine was firmly against the chair back. She very tentatively stepped close in front of me and put her hands where I'd said. For all her efforts I could see she still did not believe she could help.

'Look . . . Do it slowly. You can't wrench it back. When you get my arm in the right position, the top of the bone will slide back into the socket . . . Do you understand?'

'I think so.'

'Right . . . there are three stages. First, straighten my arm out, slightly to the side. Then keep my wrist out and pull my elbow across my chest . . . it will look awkward . . . but it works. If you pull hard enough the top of the bone will come in line with the socket and start to slide into it. When it does that, fold my wrist up and over towards my right shoulder . . . and my arm will go back where it ought to be.'

She was in no way reassured.

'Sophie . . .'

'Yes?'

I hesitated. 'If you do it, you'll save me hours of pain.'

'Yes.'

'But . . .' I stopped.

'You're trying to say,' she said, 'that I'm going to hurt you even worse, and I mustn't let it stop me.'

'Attagirl.'

'All right.'

She began. Straightened my arm out, slowly and carefully. I could feel her surprise at the physical effort it demanded of her: an arm was a good deal heavier than most people realized and she had the whole weight of it in her hands.

It took five minutes.

'Is that right?' she said.

'Mm.'

'Now do I pull your elbow across?'

'Mm.'

Always the worst part. When she'd gone only a short way I could feel her trembling. Her fingers under my elbow shook with irresolution.

I said, 'If you . . . drop my elbow . . . now . . . I'll scream.'

'Oh . . .' She sounded shattered but her grip tightened blessedly. We proceeded, with no sound but heavy breathing on both sides. There was always a point at which progress seemed to end and yet the arm was still out. Always a point of despair.

We reached it.

'It's no good,' she said. 'It isn't working.'

'Go on.'

'I can't do it.'

'Another . . . half inch.'

'Oh, no . . .' But she screwed herself up and went on trying.

The jolt and the audible scrunch when the bone started to go over the edge of the socket astounded her.

'Now . . .' I said. 'Wrist up and over . . . not too fast.'

Two more horrible crunches, the sweetest sounds on earth. Hell went back into its box. I stood up. Smiled like the sun coming out.

'That's it,' I said. 'Thank you very much.'

She was bewildered. 'Do you mean . . . the pain goes away . . . just like that.'

'Just like that.'

She looked at the transformation she'd wrought in me. Her eyes filled with tears. I put my right arm round her and held her close.

'Why don't you get the bloody thing fixed?' she said.

'You won't catch me having any more orthopaedic operations if I don't absolutely have to.'

She sniffed the tears away. 'You're a coward.'

'All the way.'

I walked with her to Vic's office. We stood in the doorway, looking in. He lay by the window, face down, the back of his purple shirt a glistening crimson obscenity.

Whatever he had done to me, I had done worse to him. Because of the pressure I'd put on him, he was dead. I supposed I would never outlive a grinding sense of responsibility and regret.

'I half saw who killed him,' I said.

'Half?'

'Enough.'

The indelible impression made sense. The pattern had become plain.

We turned away.

There was a sound of a car drawing up outside, doors slamming, two or three pairs of heavy feet.

'The police,' Sophie said in relief.

I nodded. 'Keep it simple, though. If they start on Vic's and my disagreements we'll be here all night.'

'You're immoral.'

'No . . . lazy.'

'I've noticed.'

The police were their usual abrasive selves, saving their store of sympathy for worthier causes like old ladies and lost kids. They looked into the office, tele-phoned for reinforcements and invited us in a fairly hectoring manner to explain what we were doing there. I stifled an irritated impulse to point out that if we'd chosen we could have gone quietly away and left someone else to find Vic dead. Virtue's own reward was seldom worth it.

Both then and later, when the higher ranks arrived, we gave minimum information and kept quiet in between. In essence I said, 'There were no lights on in the front of the house when I arrived. I know the house slightly. I walked round to the side to see if Vic was in his office. I had a tentative arrangement to see him for five or six minutes at six o'clock. I was driving Miss Randolph home to Esher and called in at Vic's on the way, parking outside on the road and walking up the drive. I saw him in his office. I saw him fall against the window, and then collapse. I hurried round to the front to try to get into the house to help him. A light-coloured Ford Cortina was starting up. It shot away in a hurry but I caught a glimpse of the driver. I recognized the driver.'

They listened to my identification impassively, neither pleased nor sceptical. Did I see a gun, they asked. There was no gun in Vic's office.

'No,' I said. 'Nothing but the driver's head.'

They grunted and turned to Sophie.

'Jonah left me in his car,' she said. 'Then this other car came crashing out of the drive at a reckless speed. I decided to see if everything was all right. I walked up here and found Jonah in front of the house. The house door was open, so we went inside. We found Mr

Vincent lying in his office. We telephoned immediately to you.'

We sat for nearly three hours in Vic's beautiful dining-room while the end of his life was dissected by the prosaic professionals for whom murder was all in the day's work. They switched on every light and brought more of their own, and the glare further dehumanized their host.

Maybe it was necessary for them to think of him as a thing, not a person. I still couldn't.

I was finally allowed to take Sophie home. I parked outside and we went up to her flat, subdued and depressed. She made coffee, which we drank in the kitchen.

'Hungry?' she said. 'There's some cheese, I think.'

We ate chunks of cheese with our fingers, absent-mindedly.

'What are you going to do?' she said.

'Wait for them to catch him, I suppose.'

'He won't run . . . he doesn't know you saw him.'

'No.'

She said anxiously, 'He doesn't . . . does he?'

'If he'd seen me he'd have come back and shot us both.'

'You think the nicest thoughts.'

The evening had left smudgy circles round her eyes. She looked more than tired: over-stretched, over-strained. I yawned and said I ought to be going home, and she couldn't disguise her flooding relief.

I smiled. 'You'll be all right alone?'

'Oh yes.' Absolute certainty in her voice. Solitude offered her refuge, healing and rest. I didn't. I had brought her a car crash, a man with a pitchfork, a bone-setting and a murder. I'd offered an alcoholic brother, a half-burnt home and a snap engagement. None of it designed for the well-being of someone who needed the order and peace of an ivory control tower.

She came with me down to the car.

'You'll come again?' she said.

'When you're ready.'

'A dose of Dereham every week . . .'

'Would be enough to frighten any woman?'

'Well, no.' She smiled. 'It might be bad for the nerves, but at least I'd know I was alive.'

I laughed and gave her an undemanding brotherly kiss. 'It would suit me fine.'

'Really?'

'And truly.'

'I don't ask for that,' she said.

'Then you damn well should.'

She grinned. I slid into the driving seat. Her eyes looked calmer in her exhausted face.

'Sleep well,' I said. 'I'll call you tomorrow.'

It seemed a long way home. My shoulder ached: a faint echo, but persistent. I thought with longing of a stiff brandy and stifled a sigh at the less reviving prospect of Coke.

When I got back the house was dark.

No lights, no Crispin.

Hell, I thought. He had no car any more; no transport but his feet. The one place his feet could be trusted to take him was straight to the source of gin.

I parked outside the kitchen as usual, opened the unlocked back door, went in, switched on the lights, and shouted through the house.

'Crispin?' No answer. 'Crispin.'

Total silence.

Swearing under my breath I went along to the office, intending to telephone the pub to ask what state he was in. If he were too far gone, I'd drive up and fetch him. I had picked up the receiver and begun to dial when I heard the door behind me squeak on its hinges.

So he hadn't gone after all. I turned with the beginnings of a congratulatory smile.

It wasn't Crispin who had come in. I looked at the heavy pistol with its elongated silencer, and like Vic the urgent words which shaped in my mind were no and my God and wait.

CHAPTER SEVENTEEN

'Put the telephone down,' he said.

I looked at the receiver in my hand. I'd dialled only half the number. Pity. I did as he said.

'I saw you at Vic's,' I said. 'I told the police.'

The gun merely wavered a fraction. The round black hole still faced my heart. I'd seen what it had made of Vic, and I had no illusions.

'I guessed you were there,' he said.

'How?'

'A car parked by the hedge ... Saw it when I left. About twelve miles on I realized it was yours. I went back ... the place was crawling with police.'

My tongue felt huge and sluggish. I looked at the gun and could think of nothing useful to say.

'You and Vic,' he said. 'You thought you had me in a corner. Too bad. Your mistake.'

I swallowed with difficulty. 'I saw you,' I repeated, 'and the police know.'

'Maybe. But they'll have trouble making it stick when you're not alive to give evidence.'

I looked desperately around for a way of diverting him. For a weapon to attack him with.

He smiled faintly. 'It's no good, Jonah. It's the end of the road.'

He straightened his arm to the firing position adopted by people who knew what they were about.

'You won't feel much,' he said.

The door behind him swung on its hinges while he was already beginning to squeeze the trigger. The sudden shift of my attention from sick fascination at the round hole from which death was coming to a point behind his back was just enough to jerk his hand.

Enough was enough.

The flame spat out and the bullet missed me.

Crispin stood in the doorway looking with horror at the scene. In one hand he waved a heavy green bottle of gin.

'The old heave-ho,' he said distinctly.

He wasn't drunk, I thought incredulously. He was telling me to go right back to a rugger tackle we'd perfected in boyhood. Instinctively, faster than thought, I feinted at our visitor's knees.

The gun came round and down towards me and Crispin hit him hard on the head with the gin bottle.

The pistol swung away from me and fired, and I snapped up and lifted the only heavy object within reach, which was my typewriter. I crashed it down with all my strength in the wake of the gin bottle, and the visitor sprawled on the floor with blood gushing from his scalp and the typewriter ribbon rolling across his unconscious face and away to the wall.

'You old crazy loon,' I said breathlessly, turning to Crispin. 'You old blessed . . .'

My voice died away. Crispin half sat, half lay on the floor with his hand pressed to his side.

'Crispin!'

'I'm . . . not . . . drunk,' he said.

'Of course not.'

'I think . . . he shot me.'

Speechlessly I knelt beside him.

He said, 'Was he the one . . . who burnt the yard?'

'Yes.'

'Hope . . . you killed him.'

His body sagged. I caught him. Eased him down to the floor and with one hand grabbed a cushion for his head. His pressing fingers relaxed and fell away, and there on the waistband of his trousers was the spreading patch of blood.

'I'm . . . floating,' he said. He smiled. 'It's better . . . than . . . being drunk.'

'I'll get a doctor,' I said.

'No . . . Jonah . . . Don't leave me . . . you sod.'

I didn't leave him. Three minutes later, without speaking again, he left me.

I closed his eyes gently and got stiffly to my feet, trying to fold numbness around me like a coat.

The pistol lay where it had fallen. I pushed it carefully with my toe until it was completely out of sight under the low-slung armchair. I didn't want the visitor waking to grab it again.

The visitor hadn't moved. I sat on the edge of my desk and looked down at the two of them, the unconscious and the dead.

Time enough, I thought, to call in those more or less constant companions, the busy and probing police. A quarter of an hour sooner or later, what did it matter. There was nothing any more to be gained. Too much had been irrevocably lost.

I didn't care how much damage I'd done with the typewriter. The head I'd busted with it looked more bloody than dented, but I felt a strong aversion to exploring. In all my life I had never wanted to kill anyone; had never thought I could come within a mile of it. I had not even intended to kill with the typewriter, but only to stun. I sat quietly on the desk and shook with fury inside, and wished I could have that blow back again, so that I could make it heavier, avenging and fatal.

Whatever my brother had been, he had been my brother. No one had the right to kill him. I think at that moment I felt as primitive as the Sicilians.

From greed the visitor had set out to destroy me. Not because I'd done him any harm. Simply because I stood in his plundering way. He'd sent me a message: join or be flattened, an ultimatum as old as tyranny.

My own fault, as they had tirelessly pointed out, if the answer I'd chosen was flatten and be damned.

Kerry Sanders had been only a convenient door. Had she not thought of her equine birthday present, another way would have been found. The intention was the activating force. The means were accidental.

I remembered what Pauli Teksa had said at dinner that evening at Newmarket. I remembered his exact words. The classic law of the invader was to single out the strongest guy around and smash him, so that the weaker crowd would come to heel like lambs.

At various times I had thought of the man who lay on my carpet as 'someone', as the expert, as Vic's friend, as the driver, and as the visitor; Pauli's word – the invader – suited him best.

He had invaded the bloodstock game with gangster ethics. Invaded Vic's life and business as a dangerous ally. Invaded mine as a destroyer.

The fact that I did not feel that I filled the role he'd cast me in had not mattered. It was the invader's view which had mattered. My bad luck that he'd seen me as the strongest guy around.

There was no way of winning against a determined invader. If you gave in at once, you lost. If you fought to the death you still lost, even if you won. The price of victory was sore.

Pauli Teksa had said, just before he went back to America, that it was easier to start things than to stop them. He had been warning me that if I lashed back at Vic I could find myself in even more trouble than before.

He had been right.

But he had been speaking also of himself.

Pauli Teksa, the invader, lay face down on my carpet, my broken typewriter beside his bloody head.

The stocky, tough, wide-shouldered body looked a solid hunk of bull muscle. The crinkly black hair was matted and running with red. I could see half of his face; the strong distinctive profile with the firm mouth now slackly open, the swift eye shut.

His hands lay loosely on the floor, one each side of his head. He wore two thick gold rings. A gold and platinum wrist-watch. Heavy gold cufflinks. The tip of the gold mountain he had siphoned off through Vic.

I thought it likely that his British venture had been an extension of activities at home. The super-aggressive kick-back operation had been too polished to be a trial run. Maybe he had set up Vic-equivalents in other countries. Maybe Vics in South America and Italy and Japan were rooking the local Constantines and Wilton Youngs for him and driving the Antonia Huntercombes to despair.

Vic and Fynedale had been amateurs, compared with him. Fynedale working himself into a white murdering

271

manic state. Vic nearing apoplexy with easy rage. Pauli stayed cool and used his eyes and made his snap decisions, and when he saw the need to kill he did it without histrionics. An unfortunate necessity, best done quickly.

He had even with macabre kindness told me I wouldn't feel much, and I believed him. I'd heard shot people say all they had felt was a sort of thud, and hadn't realized they were wounded until afterwards. If you were shot through the heart there was no afterwards, and that was that.

He had himself urged me several times to throw in my lot with Vic, and to go along with the crowd. He'd warned me of the dangers of holding out. He'd given me the advice as a friend, and behind the smile there had been an enemy as cold as bureaucracy.

I realized slowly that perhaps at one point he had in fact done his best to stop what he'd started. He had said no to some demand of Vic's, and he had gone home to America. But by then it was too late because in burning my stable he had switched me from tolerance to retaliation. Bash me, I bash back. The way wars started, big and small.

On the floor, Pauli stirred.

Not dead.

Across the room the gin bottle lay where Crispin had dropped it. I shoved myself off the desk and went over to pick it up. If Pauli were to return to consciousness, groggy or not, I'd trust him as far as I could throw the Empire State Building. A reinforcing clunk with green glass would be merely prudent.

I looked closer at the bottle. It was full. In addition the seal was unbroken.

I returned to the desk and set the bottle on it, and looked down with impossible grief at my brother. I knew that I had needed him as much as he needed me. He was at the roots of my life.

Pauli stirred again. The urge to finish off what I'd started was almost overwhelming. No one would know. No one could tell whether he'd been hit twice or three times. Killing someone who was trying to kill you was justifiable in law, and who was to guess that I'd killed him ten minutes later.

The moment passed. I felt cold suddenly, and old and lonely and as tired as dust. I stretched out a hand to the telephone, to call the cops.

It rang before I touched it. I picked up the receiver and said dully, 'Hello?'

'Mr Crispin Dereham?' A man's voice, educated.

'I'm his brother,' I said.

'Could I speak to him?'

'I'm afraid . . .' I said, 'he's . . . unavailable.'

'Oh dear.' The voice sounded warmly sympathetic. 'Well . . . this is Alcoholics Anonymous. Your brother telephoned us earlier this evening asking for help, and we promised to ring him back again for another chat . . .'

He went on talking for some time, but I didn't hear a word he said.

BONECRACK

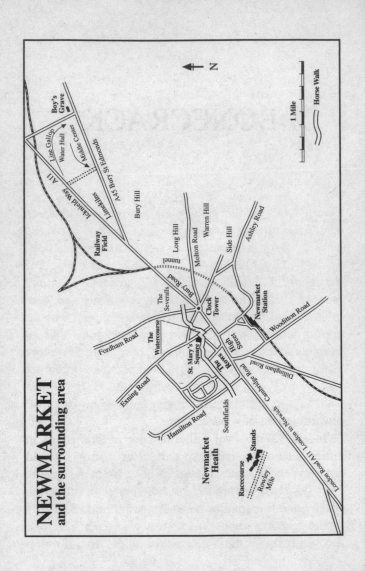

NEWMARKET
and the surrounding area

INTRODUCTION

Unsatisfactory father–son relationships interest me to such an extent that book reviewers have speculated in their columns about my own personal experiences, opining that I must have suffered badly at home. For the record, I actually had a loving, amusing, faithfully married father who enjoyed female company and, with my mother, brought up my brother and myself with an appropriate amount of no-nonsense strictness and an absolute absence of punishment. There were never any unresolvable hang-ups at any stage between my father and myself. I had a good childhood, and in due course tried to give the same upbringing to both my own two rewarding and now adult sons.

Indeed, if my own father-and-son relationships in either generation had been painful or stormy I would not have been able to write about them in fiction. Only because they are for me imaginary can I describe cruelty and domination between parent and child.

Bonecrack is about two fathers who each have one son, and about the inter-relationships that develop between the four of them when one of the fathers strives for total power over both of the sons.

This theme could have been clothed in many garments and set in any age, any country. I decided to put it here and now in Newmarket against a background of horse-racing; dressing the scene with bone-breaking bullies and letting them loose to try to invade, conquer and devastate a solidly respectable racing stable.

The narrator, Neil Griffon, is one of the sons. I gave him a background in business, not in racing, and endowed him with a subtle, intuitive mind, directly opposite to the straightforward evil of the invading enemy father. Griffon subverts direct aggression by not responding as expected and by finding a back-door way to resolve his dilemmas.

The interplays and undercurrents of the father-and-son struggles fascinated me throughout the writing of *Bonecrack*, even while I filled the pages with action, danger and splendid horses.

CHAPTER ONE

They both wore thin rubber masks.

Identical.

I looked at the two identical faceless faces in tingling disbelief. I was not the sort of person to whom rubber-masked individuals up to no good paid calls at twenty to midnight. I was a thirty-four-year-old sober-minded businessman quietly bringing up to date the account books at my father's training stables in Newmarket.

The pool of light from the desk lamp shone squarely upon me and the work I had been doing, and the two rubber-faces moved palely against the near-black panelling of the dark room like alien moons closing in on the sun. I had looked up when the latch clicked, and there they were, two dim figures calmly walking in from the hall of the big house, silhouetted briefly against the soft lighting behind them and then lost against the panelling as they closed the door. They moved without a squeak, without a scrape, on the bare polished floor. Apart from the unhuman faces, they were black from head to foot.

1

I picked up the telephone receiver and dialled the first of three nines.

One of them closed in faster, swung his arm, and smashed downwards on the telephone. I moved my finger fractionally in time with the second nine all but complete, but no one was ever going to achieve the third. The black gloved hand slowly disentangled a heavy police truncheon from the mangled remains of the Post Office's property.

'There's nothing to steal,' I remarked.

The second man had reached the desk. He stood on the far side of it, facing me, looking down to where I still sat. He produced an automatic pistol, without silencer, which he pointed unwaveringly at the bridge of my nose. I could see quite a long way into the barrel.

'You,' he said. 'You will come with us.'

His voice was flat, without tone, deliberate. There was no identifiable accent, but he wasn't English.

'Why?'

'You will come.'

'Where to?'

'You will come.'

'I won't, you know,' I said pleasantly, and reached out and pressed the button which switched off the desk lamp.

The sudden total darkness got me two seconds' advantage. I used them to stand up, pick up the heavy angled lamp, and swing the base of it round in an arc in the general direction of the mask which had spoken.

There was a dull thump as it connected, and a grunt. Damage, I thought, but no knock-out.

Mindful of the truncheon on my left I was out from behind the desk and sprinting towards the door. But no one was wasting time batting away in the darkness in the hope of hitting me. A beam of torchlight snapped out from his hand, swung round, dazzled on my face, and bounced as he came after me.

I swerved. Dodged. Lost my straight line to the door and saw sideways the rubber-face I'd hit with the lamp was purposefully on the move.

The torch beam flickered away, circled briefly, and steadied like a rock on the light switch beside the door. Before I could reach it the black gloved hand swept downwards and clicked on the five double wall brackets, ten naked candle bulbs coldly lighting the square wood-lined room.

There were two windows with green floor-length curtains. One rug from Istanbul. Three unmatched William and Mary chairs. One sixteenth-century oak chest. One flat walnut desk. Nothing else. An austere place, reflection of my father's austere and spartan soul.

I had always agreed that the best time to foil an abduction was at the moment it started: that merely obeying marching orders could save present pain but not long-term anxiety: that abductors might kill later, but not at the beginning, and that if no one's safety was at risk, it would be stupid to go without a fight.

Well, I fought.

I fought for all of ninety seconds more, during which time I failed to switch off the lights, to escape through the door, or to crash out through the windows. I had only my hands and not much skill against the truncheon of one of them and the threat of a crippling bullet from the other. The identical rubber-faces came towards me with an unnerving lack of human expression, and although I tried, probably unwisely, to rip one of the masks off, I got no further than feeling my fingers slip across the tough slippery surface.

They favoured in-fighting, with their quarry pinned against the wall. As there were two of them, and they appeared to be experts in their craft, I got such a hammering in that eternal ninety seconds that I soundly wished that I had not put my abduction-avoiding theories into practice.

It ended with a fist in my stomach, the pistol slamming into my face, my head crashing back against the panelling, and the truncheon polishing the whole thing off somewhere behind my right ear. When I was next conscious of anything, time had all too clearly passed. Otherwise I should not have been lying face down along the back seat of a moving car with my hands tied crampingly behind my back.

For a good long time I believed I was dreaming. Then my brain came further awake and made it clear that I wasn't. I was revoltingly uncomfortable and also extremely cold, as the thin sweater I had been wearing indoors was proving a poor barrier to a freezing night.

4

My head ached like a steam hammer. Bang, bang, bang.

If I could have raised the mental energy I would have been furious with myself for having proved such a push-over. As it was, only uncomplicated responses were getting anywhere, like dumb unintelligent endurance and a fog-like bewilderment. Of all the candidates for abduction, I would have put myself among the most unlikely.

There was a lot to be said for a semi-conscious brain in a semi-conscious body. *Mens blotto in corpore ditto* ... the words dribbled inconsequentially through my mind and a smile started along the right nerve but didn't get as far as my mouth. My mouth anyway was half in contact with some imitation leather upholstery which smelled of dogs. They say many grown men call out for their mothers in moments of fatal agony, and then upon their God: but anyway I hadn't had a mother since I was two, and from then until seven I had believed God was someone who had run off with her and was living with her somewhere else ... (God took your mother, dear, because he needed her more than you do) which had never endeared him to me, and in any case this was no fatal agony, this was just a thumping concussion and some very sore places and maybe a grisly future at the end of the ride. The ride meanwhile went on and on. Nothing about it improved. After several years the car stopped with a jerk. I nearly fell forwards off the seat. My brain came alert with a jolt and my body wished it hadn't.

The two rubber-faces loomed over me, lugged me out, and literally carried me up some steps and into a house. One of them had his hands under my armpits and the other held my ankles. My hundred and sixty pounds seemed to be no especial burden.

The sudden light inside the door was dazzling, which seemed as good a reason as any for shutting one's eyes. I shut them. The steam hammer had not by any means given up.

They dumped me presently down on my side, on a wooden floor. Polished. I could smell the polish. Scented. Very nasty. I opened my eyes a slit, and verified. Small intricately squared parquet, modern. Birch veneer, wafer thin. Nothing great. A voice awakening towards fury and controlled with audible effort spoke from a short distance above me.

'*And who exactly is this?*'

There was a long pin-dropping silence during which I would have laughed, if I could. The rubber-faces hadn't even pinched the right man. All that battering for bloody nothing. And no guarantee they would take me home again, either.

I squinted upwards against the light. The man who had spoken was sitting in an upright leather armchair with his fingers laced rigidly together over a swelling paunch. His voice was much the same as Rubber-Face's: without much accent, but not English. His shoes, which were more on my level, were supple, handmade, and of Genoese leather.

Italian shape. Not conclusive: they sell Italian shoes from Hong Kong to San Francisco.

One of the rubber-faces cleared his throat. 'It is Griffon.'

The remains of laughter died coldly away. Griffon is indeed my name. If I was not the right man, they must have come for my father. Yet that made no more sense: he was, like me, in none of the abduction-prone professions.

The man in the armchair, with the same reined-in anger, said through his teeth, 'It is not Griffon.'

'It is,' persisted Rubber-Face faintly.

The man stood up out of his armchair and with his elegant toe rolled me over on to my back.

'Griffon is an old man,' he said. The sting in his voice sent both rubber-faces back a pace as if he had physically hit them.

'You didn't *tell* us he was old.'

The other rubber-face backed up his colleague in a defensive whine and a different accent. This time, down-the-scale American. 'We watched him all evening. He went round the stables, looking at the horses. At every horse. The men, they treated him as boss. He is the trainer. He is Griffon.'

'Griffon's assistant,' he said furiously. He sat down again and held on to the arms with the same effort as he was holding on to his temper.

'Get up,' he said to me abruptly.

I struggled up nearly as far as my knees, but the rest was daunting, and I thought, why on earth should I bother, so I lay gently down again. It did nothing to improve the general climate.

'Get up,' he said furiously.

I shut my eyes.

There was a sharp blow on my thigh. I opened my eyes again in time to see the American-voiced rubber-face draw back his foot for another kick. All one could say was that he was wearing shoes and not boots.

'Stop it.' The sharp voice arrested him mid-kick. 'Just put him in that chair.'

American Rubber-Face picked up the chair in question and placed it six feet from the armchair, facing it. Mid-Victorian, I assessed automatically. Mahogany. Probably once had a caned seat, but was upholstered now in pink flowered glazed chintz. The two rubber-faces lifted me up bodily and draped me around so that my tied wrists were behind the back of the chair. When they had done that they stepped away, just as far as one pace behind each of my shoulders.

From that elevation I had a better view of their master, if not of the total situation.

'Griffon's assistant,' he repeated. But this time the anger was secondary: he'd accepted the mistake and was working out what to do about it.

It didn't take him long.

'Gun,' he said, and Rubber-Face gave it to him.

He was plump and bald, and I guessed he would take no pleasure from looking at old photographs of himself. Under the rounded cheeks, the heavy chin, the folds of eyelids, there lay an elegant bone structure. It still showed in the strong clear beak of the nose and in the arch above the eye sockets. He had the basic equipment of a handsome man, but he looked, I thought fancifully, like a Caesar gone self-indulgently to seed: and one might have taken the fat as a sign of mellowness had it not been for the ill will that looked unmistakably out of his narrowed eyes.

'Silencer,' he said acidly. He was contemptuous, irritated, and not suffering his rubber-faced fools gladly.

One rubber-face produced a silencer from his trouser pocket and Caesar began screwing it on. Silencers meant business where naked barrels might not. He was about to bury his employees' mistake.

My future looked decidedly dim. Time for a few well-chosen words, especially if they might prove to be my last.

'I am not Griffon's assistant,' I said. 'I am his son.'

He had finished screwing on the silencer and was beginning to raise it in the direction of my chest.

'I am Griffon's son,' I repeated. 'And just what is the point of all this?'

The silencer reached the latitude of my heart.

'If you're going to kill me,' I said, 'you might at least tell me why.'

My voice sounded more or less all right. He couldn't see, I hoped, that all my skin was prickling into sweat.

An eternal time passed. I stared at him: he stared back. I waited. Waited while the tumblers clicked over in his brain: waited for three thumbs-down to slot into a row on the fruit machine.

Finally, without lowering the gun a millimetre, he said, 'Where is your father?'

'In hospital.'

Another pause.

'How long will he be there?'

'I don't know. Two or three months, perhaps.'

'Is he dying?'

'No.'

'What is the matter with him?'

'He was in a car crash. A week ago. He has a broken leg.'

Another pause. The gun was still steady. No one, I thought wildly, should die so unfairly. Yet people did die unfairly. Probably only one in a million deserved it. All death was intrinsically unfair: but in some forms more unfair than in others. Murder, it forcibly seemed to me, was the most unfair of all.

In the end, all he said, and in a much milder tone, was, 'Who will train the horses this summer, if your father is not well enough?'

Only long experience of wily negotiators who thundered big threats so that they could achieve their real aims by presenting them as a toothless anticlimax kept me from stepping straight off the precipice. I nearly, in relief at so harmless an enquiry, told him the truth: that no one had yet decided. If I had done, I discovered later, he would have shot me, because his business was exclusively with the resident trainer at Rowley Lodge. Temporary substitutes, abducted in error, were too dangerous to leave chattering around.

So from instinct I answered, 'I will be training them myself,' although I had not the slightest intention of doing so for longer than it took to find someone else.

It had indeed been the crucial question. The frightening black circle of the silencer's barrel dipped a fraction: became an ellipse: disappeared altogether. He lowered the gun and balanced it on one well-padded thigh.

A deep breath trickled in and out of my chest in jerks, and the relief from immediate tension made me feel sick. Not that total safety loomed very loftily on the horizon. I was still tied up in an unknown house, and I still had no idea for what possible purpose I could be a hostage.

The fat man went on watching me, went on thinking. I tried to ease the stiffness which was creeping into my muscles, to shift away the small pains and the throbbing headache, which I hadn't felt in the slightest when faced with a bigger threat.

The room was cold. The rubber-faces seemed to be snug enough in their masks and gloves, and the fat man was insulated and impervious, but the chill was

11

definitely adding to my woes. I wondered whether he had planned the cold as a psychological intimidation for my elderly father, or whether it was simply accidental. Nothing in the room looked cosily lived in.

In essence it was a middle-class sitting-room in a smallish middle-class house, built, I guess, in the nineteen thirties. The furniture had been pushed back against striped cream wallpaper to give the fat man clear space for manoeuvre: furniture which consisted of an uninspiring three-piece suite swathed in pink chintz, a gate-legged table, a standard lamp with parchment-coloured shade, and a display cabinet displaying absolutely nothing. There were no rugs on the highly polished birch parquet, no ornaments, no books or magazines, nothing personal at all. As bare as my father's soul, but not to his taste.

The room did not in the least fit what I had so far seen of the fat man's personality.

'I will release you,' he said, 'on certain conditions.'

I waited. He considered me, still taking his time.

'If you do not follow my instructions exactly, I will put your father's training stables out of business.'

I could feel my mouth opening in astonishment. I shut it with a snap.

'I suppose you doubt that I can do it. Do not doubt. I have destroyed better things than your father's little racing stables.'

He got no reaction from me to the slight in the word 'little'. It was years since I had learned that to rise to slights was to be forced into a defensive attitude which only benefited my opponent. In Rowley Lodge, as no doubt he knew, stood eighty-five aristocrats whose aggregate worth topped six million pounds.

'How?' I asked flatly.

He shrugged. 'What is important to you is not how I would do it, but how to prevent me from doing it. And that, of course, is comparatively simple.'

'Just run the horses to your instructions?' I suggested neutrally. 'Just lose to order?'

A spasm of renewed anger twisted the chubby features and the gun came six inches off his knee. The hand holding it relaxed slowly, and he put it down again.

'I am not', he said heavily, 'a petty crook.'

But you do, I thought, rise to an insult, even to one that was not intended, and one day, if the game went on long enough, that could give me an advantage.

'I apologize,' I said without sarcasm. 'But those rubber masks are not top level.'

He glanced up in irritation at the two figures standing behind me. 'The masks are their own choice. They feel safer if they cannot be recognized.'

Like highwaymen, I thought: who swung in the end.

'You may run your horses as you like. You are free to choose entirely . . . save in one special thing.'

I made no comment. He shrugged, and went on.

'You will employ someone who I will send you.'

'No,' I said.

'Yes.' He stared at me unwinkingly. 'You will employ this person. If you do not, I will destroy the stable.'

'That's lunacy,' I insisted. 'It's pointless.'

'No, it is not,' he said. 'Furthermore, you will tell no one that you are being forced to employ this person. You will assert that it is your own wish. You will particularly not complain to the police, either about tonight, or about anything else which may happen. Should you act in any way to discredit this person, or to get him evicted from your stables, your whole business will be destroyed.' He paused. 'Do you understand? If you act in any way against this person, your father will have nothing to return to, when he leaves the hospital.'

After a short, intense silence, I asked, 'In what capacity do you want this person to work for me?'

He answered with care. 'He will ride the horses,' he said. 'He is a jockey.'

I could feel the twitch round my eyes. He saw it, too. The first time he had really reached me.

It was out of the question. He would not need to tell me every time he wanted a race lost. He had simply to tell this man.

'We don't need a jockey,' I said. 'We already have Tommy Hoylake.'

'Your new jockey will gradually take his place.'

Tommy Hoylake was the second best jockey in Britain and among the top dozen in the world. No one could take his place.

'The owners wouldn't agree,' I said.

'You will persuade them.'

'Impossible.'

'The future existence of your stable depends on it.'

There was another longish pause. One of the rubber-faces shifted on his feet and sighed as if from boredom, but the fat man seemed to be in no hurry. Perhaps he understood very well that I was getting colder and more uncomfortable minute by minute. I would have asked him to untie my hands if I hadn't been sure he would count himself one up when he refused.

Finally I said, 'Equipped with your jockey, the stable would have no future existence anyway.'

He shrugged. 'It may suffer a little, perhaps, but it will survive.'

'It is unacceptable,' I said.

He blinked. His hand moved the gun gently to and fro across his well-filled trouser leg.

He said, 'I see that you do not entirely understand the position. I told you that you could leave here upon certain conditions.' His flat tone made the insane sound reasonable. 'They are, that you employ a certain jockey, and that you do not seek aid from anyone, including the police. Should you break either of these agreements the stable will be destroyed. But . . .' He spoke more slowly, and with emphasis, '. . . If you do not agree to these conditions in the first place, you will not be freed.'

I said nothing.

15

'Do you understand?'

I sighed. 'Yes.'

'Good.'

'Not a petty crook, I think you said.'

His nostrils flared. 'I am a manipulator.'

'And a murderer.'

'I never murder unless the victim insists.'

I stared at him. He was laughing inside at his own jolly joke, the fun creeping out in little twitches to his lips and tiny snorts of breath.

This victim, I supposed, was not going to insist. He was welcome to his amusement.

I moved my shoulders slightly, trying to ease them. He watched attentively and offered nothing.

'Who then', I said, 'is this jockey?'

He hesitated.

'He is eighteen,' he said.

'*Eighteen* . . .'

He nodded. 'You will give him the good horses to ride. He will ride Archangel in the Derby.'

Impossible. Totally impossible. I looked at the gun lying so quiet on the expensive tailoring. I said nothing. There was nothing to say.

When he next spoke there was the satisfaction of victory in his voice alongside the careful non-accent.

'He will arrive at the stable tomorrow. You will hire him. He has not yet much experience in races. You will see he gets it.'

An inexperienced rider on Archangel . . . ludicrous.

So ludicrous, in fact, that he had used abduction and the threat of murder to make it clear he meant it seriously.

'His name is Alessandro Rivera,' he said.

After an interval for consideration, he added the rest of it.

'He is my son.'

CHAPTER TWO

When I next woke up I was lying face down on the bare floor of the oak-panelled room in Rowley Lodge. Too many bare boards everywhere. Not my night.

Facts oozed back gradually. I felt woolly, cold, semiconscious, anaesthetized . . .

Anaesthetized.

For the return journey they had had the courtesy not to hit my head. The fat man had nodded to the American rubber-face, but instead of flourishing the truncheon he had given me a sort of quick pricking thump in the upper arm. After that we had waited around for about a quarter of an hour during which no one said anything at all, and then quite suddenly I had lost consciousness. I remembered not a flicker of the journey home.

Creaking and groaning I tested all articulated parts. Everything present, correct, and in working order. More or less, that is, because having clanked to my feet it became advisable to sit down again in the chair by the desk. I put my elbows on the desk and my head in my hands, and let time pass.

Outside, the beginnings of a damp dawn were turning the sky to grey flannel. There was ice round the edges of the windows, where condensed warm air had frozen solid. The cold went through to my bones.

In the brain department things were just as chilly. I remembered all too clearly that Alessandro Rivera was that day to make his presence felt. Perhaps he would take after his father, I thought tiredly, and would be so overweight that the whole dilemma would fold its horns and quietly steal away. On the other hand, if not, why should his father use a sledgehammer to crack a peanut? Why not simply apprentice his son in the normal way? Because he wasn't normal, because his son wouldn't be a normal apprentice, and because no normal apprentice would expect to start his career on a Derby favourite.

I wondered how my father would now be reacting, had he not been slung up in traction with a complicated fracture of tibia and fibula. He would not, for certain, be feeling as battered as I was, because he would, with supreme dignity, have gone quietly. But he would none the less have also been facing the same vital questions: which were, firstly, did the fat man seriously intend to destroy the stable if his son did not get the job, and secondly, how could he do it.

And the answer to both was a king-sized blank.

It wasn't my stable to risk. They were not my six

million pounds' worth of horses. They were not my livelihood, nor my life's work.

I could not ask my father to decide for himself: he was not well enough to be told, let alone to reason out the pros and cons.

I could not now transfer the stable to anyone else, because passing this situation to a stranger would be like handing him a grenade with the pin out.

I was already due back at my own job and was late for my next assignment, and I had only stop-gapped at the stable at all because my father's capable assistant, who had been driving the Rolls when the lorry jack-knifed into it, was now lying in the same hospital in a coma.

All of which added up to a fair-sized problem. But then problems, I reflected ironically, were my business. The problems of sick business were my business.

Nothing at that moment looked sicker than my prospects at Rowley Lodge.

Shivering violently, I removed myself bit by bit from the desk and chair, went out to the kitchen, and made myself some coffee. Drank it. Moderate improvement only.

Inched upstairs to the bathroom. Scraped off the night's whiskers and dispassionately observed the dried blood down one cheek. Washed it off. Gun-barrel graze, dry and already healing.

Outside, through the leafless trees, I could see the lights of the traffic thundering as usual up and down

Bury Road. These drivers in their warm moving boxes, they were in another world altogether, a world where abduction and extortion were something that only happened to others. Incredible to think that I had in fact joined the others.

Wincing from an all-over feeling of soreness, I looked at my smudge-eyed reflection and wondered how long I would go on doing what the fat man had told me to. Saplings who bent before the storm lived to grow into oaks.

Long live oaks.

I swallowed some aspirins, stopped shivering, tried to marshal a bit more sense into my shaky wits, and struggled into jodhpurs, boots, two more pullovers, and a windproof jacket. Whatever had happened that night, or whatever might happen in the future, there were still those eighty-five six million quids' worth downstairs waiting to be seen to.

They were housed in a yard that had been an inspiration of spacious design when it was built in 1870 and which still, a hundred-plus years later, worked as an effective unit. Originally there had been two blocks facing each other, each block consisting of three bays, and each bay being made up to ten boxes. Across the far end, forming a wall joining the two blocks, were a large feed-store room, a pair of double gates, and an equally large tack room. The gates had originally led into a field, but early on in his career, when success struck him, my father had built on two more bays, which formed another small enclosed yard of twenty-five boxes. More double gates opened from these, now, into a small railed paddock.

Four final boxes had been built facing towards Bury Road, on to the outside of the short west wall at the end of the north block. It was in the furthest of these four boxes that a full-blown disaster had just been discovered.

My appearance through the door which led directly from the house to the yard galvanized the group which had been clustered round the outside boxes into returning into the main yard and advancing in ragged but purposeful formation. I could see I was not going to like their news. Waited in irritation to hear it. Crises, on that particular morning, were far from welcome.

'It's Moonrock, sir,' said one of the lads anxiously. 'Got cast in his box, and broke his leg.'

'All right,' I said abruptly. 'Get back to your own horses, then. It's nearly time to pull out.'

'Yessir,' they said, and scattered reluctantly round the yard to their charges, looking back over their shoulders.

'Damn and bloody hell,' I said aloud, but I can't say it did much good. Moonrock was my father's hack, a pensioned-off star-class steeplechaser of which he was uncharacteristically fond. The least valuable inmate of the yard in many terms, but the one he would be most upset to lose. The others were also insured. No one, though, could insure against painful emotion.

I plodded round to the box. The elderly lad who looked after him was standing at the door with the light from inside falling across the deep worried wrinkles in his tortoise skin and turning them to crevasses. He looked round towards me at my step. The crevasses shifted and changed like a kaleidoscope.

'Ain't no good, sir. He's broke his hock.'

Nodding, and wishing I hadn't, I reached the door and went in. The old horse was standing up, tied in his usual place by his head-collar. At first sight there was nothing wrong with him: he turned his head towards me and pricked his ears, his liquid black eyes showing nothing but his customary curiosity. Five years in head-line limelight had given him the sort of presence which only intelligent highly successful horses seem to develop: a sort of consciousness of their own greatness. He knew more about life and about racing than any of the golden youngsters round in the main yard. He was fifteen years old and had been a friend of my father's for five.

The hind leg on his near side, towards me, was perfect. He bore his weight on it. The off-hind looked slightly tucked up.

He had been sweating: there were great dark patches on his neck and flanks; but he looked calm enough at that moment. Pieces of straw were caught in his coat, which was unusually dusty.

Soothing him with her hand, and talking to him in a common-sense voice, was my father's head stable hand, Etty Craig. She looked up at me with regret on her pleasant weather-beaten face.

'I've sent for the vet, Mr Neil.'

'Of all damn things,' I said.

She nodded. 'Poor old fellow. You'd think he'd know better, after all these years.'

I made a sympathetic noise, went in and fondled the moist black muzzle, and took as good a look at his hind leg as I could without moving him. There was absolutely no doubt: the hock joint was out of shape.

Horses occasionally rolled around on their backs in the straw in their boxes. Sometimes they rolled over with too little room and wedged their legs against the wall, then thrashed around to get free. Most injuries from getting cast were grazes and strains, but it was possible for a horse to twist or lash out with a leg strongly enough to break it. Incredibly bad luck when it happened, which luckily wasn't often.

'He was still lying down when George came in to muck him out,' Etty said. 'He got some of the lads to come and pull the old fellow into the centre of the box. He was a bit slow, George says, standing up. And then of course they could see he couldn't walk.'

'Bloody shame,' George said, nodding in agreement.

I sighed. 'Nothing we can do, Etty.'

'No, Mr Neil.'

She called me Mr Neil religiously during working hours, though I'd been plain Neil to her in my childhood. Better for discipline in the yard, she said to me once, and on matters of discipline I would never contradict her. There had been quite a stir in Newmarket when my father had promoted her to head lad, but as he had explained to her at the time, she was loyal, she was knowledgeable, she would stand no nonsense from anyone, she deserved it from seniority alone, and had she been a man the job would have been hers automatically. He had decided, as he was a just and logical person, that her sex was immaterial. She became the only female head lad in Newmarket, where girl lads were rare anyway, and the stable had flourished through all the six years of her reign.

I remembered the days when her parents used to turn up at the stables and accuse my father of ruining her life. I had been about ten when she first came to the yard, and she was nineteen and had been privately educated at an expensive boarding school. Her parents with increasing bitterness had arrived and complained that the stable was spoiling her chances of a nice suitable marriage; but Etty had never wanted marriage. If she had ever experimented with sex she had not made a public mess of it, and I thought it likely that she had found the whole process uninteresting. She seemed to like males well enough, but she treated them as she did her horses, with brisk friendliness, immense understanding and cool unsentimentality.

Since my father's accident she had to all intents been in complete charge. The fact that I had been granted a temporary licence to hold the fort made mine the official say-so, but both Etty and I knew I would be lost without her.

It occurred to me, as I watched her capable hands moving quietly across Moonrock's bay hide, that the fat man might find me a pushover, but as an apprentice his son Alessandro was going to run into considerable difficulties han miss Henrietta Craig.

'You better go out with the string, Etty,' I said. 'I'll stay and wait for the vet.'

'Right,' she said, and I guessed she had been on the point of suggesting it herself. As a distribution of labour it was only sense, as the horses were well along in their preparation for the coming racing season, and she knew better than I what each should be doing.

She beckoned to George to come and hold Moonrock's head-collar and keep him soothed. To me she said, stepping out of the box, 'What about this frost? It seems to me it may be thawing.'

'Take the horses over to Warren Hill and use your own judgement about whether to canter.'

She nodded. 'Right.' She looked back at Moonrock and a momentary softness twisted her mouth. 'Mr Griffon will be sorry.'

'I won't tell him yet.'

'No.' She gave me a small businesslike smile and then walked off into the yard, a short neat figure, hardy and competent.

Moonrock would be quiet enough with George. I followed Etty back into the main yard and watched the horses pull out: thirty-three of them in the first lot. The lads led their charges out of the boxes, jumped up into the saddles, and rode away down the yard, through the first double gates, across the lower yard, and out through the far gates into the collecting paddock beyond. The sky lightened moment by moment and I thought Etty was probably right ab⬛⬛⬛ thaw.

After ten minutes or so, when she had sorted them out as she wanted them, the horses moved away out beyond the paddock, through the trees and the boundary fence and straight out on to the Heath.

Before the last of them had gone there was a rushing scrunch in the drive behind me and the vet halted his dusty Land Rover with a spray of gravel. Leaping out with his bag he said breathlessly, 'Every bloody horse on the Heath this morning has got colic or ingrowing toenails . . . You must be Neil Griffon . . . sorry about your father . . . Etty says it's old Moonrock . . . still in the same box?' Without drawing breath he turned on his heel and strode along the outside boxes. Young, chubby, purposeful, he was not the vet I had expected. The man I knew was an older version, slower, twinkly, just as chubby, and given to rubbing his jaw while he thought things over.

'Sorry about this,' the young vet said, having given Moonrock three full seconds' examination. 'Have to put him down, I'm afraid.'

'I suppose that hock couldn't just be dislocated?' I suggested, clinging to straws.

He gave me a brief glance full of the expert's forgiveness for a layman's ignorance. 'The joint is shattered,' he said succinctly.

He went about his business, and splendid old Moonrock quietly folded down on to the straw. Packing his bag again he said, 'Don't look so depressed. He had a better life th████st. And be glad it wasn't Archangel.'

I watched his chubby back depart at speed. Not so very unlike his father, I thought. Just faster.

I went slowly into the house and telephoned to the people who removed dead horses. They would come at once, they said, sounding cheerful. And within half an hour, they came.

Another cup of coffee. Sat down beside the kitchen table and went on feeling unwell. Abduction didn't agree with me in the least.

The string came back from the Heath without Etty, without a two-year-old colt called Lucky Lindsay, and with a long tale of woe.

I listened with increasing dismay while three lads at once told me that Lucky Lindsay had whipped round and unshipped little Ginge over by Warren Hill, and had then galloped off loose and seemed to be making for home, but had diverted down Moulton Road instead, and had knocked over a man with a bicycle and had sent a woman with a pram into hysterics, and had ended up by the clock tower, disorganizing the traffic. The police, added one boy, with more relish than regret, were currently talking to Miss Etty.

'And the colt?' I asked. Because Etty could take care of herself, but Lucky Lindsay had cost thirty thousand guineas and could not.

'Someone caught him down the High Street outside Woolworths.'

I sent them off to their horses and waited for Etty to come back, which she presently did, riding Lucky Lindsay herself and with the demoted and demoralized Ginge slopping along behind on a quiet three-year-old mare.

Etty jumped down and ran an experienced hand down the colt's chestnut legs.

'Not much harm done,' she said. 'He seems to have a small cut there . . . I think he probably did it on the bumper of a parked car.'

'Not on the bicycle?' I asked.

She looked up, and then straightened. 'Shouldn't think so.'

'Was the cyclist hurt?'

'Shaken,' she admitted.

'And the woman with the pram?'

'Anyone who pushes a baby and drags a toddler along Moulton Road during morning exercise should be ready for loose horses. The stupid woman wouldn't stop screaming. It upset the colt thoroughly, of course. Someone had caught him at that point, but he backed off and broke free and went down into the town . . .'

She paused and looked at me. 'Sorry about all this.'

'It happens,' I said. I stifled the small inward smile

at her relative placing of colts and babies. Not surprising. To her, colts were in sober fact more important than humans.

'We had finished the canters,' she said. 'The ground was all right. We went right through the list we mapped out yesterday. Ginge came off as we turned for home.'

'Is the colt too much for him?'

'Wouldn't have thought so. He's ridden him before.'

'I'll leave it to you, Etty.'

'Then maybe I'll switch him to something easier for a day or two . . .' She led the colt away and handed him over to the lad who did him, having come as near as she was likely to admitting she had made an error in putting Ginge on Lucky Lindsay. Anyone, any day, could be thrown off. But some were thrown off more than others.

Breakfast. The lads put straight the horses they had just ridden and scurried to the hostel for porridge, bacon sandwiches and tea. I went back into the house and didn't feel like eating.

It was still cold indoors. There were sad mounds of fir cones in the fireplaces of ten dust-sheeted bedrooms, and a tapestry fire screen in front of the hearth in the drawing-room. There was a two-tier electric fire in the cavernous bedroom my father used and an undersized convector heater in the oak-panelled room where he sat at his desk in the evenings. Not even the kitchen was warm, as the cooker fire had been out for repairs for a month. Normally, having been brought up in it, I did not notice the chill of the house in winter: but then, normally I did not feel so physically wretched.

A head appeared round the kitchen door. Neat dark hair coiled smoothly at the base, to emerge in a triumphant arrangement of piled curls on the crown.

'Mr Neil?'

'Oh . . . good morning, Margaret.'

A pair of fine dark eyes gave me an embracing once-over. Narrow nostrils moved in a small quiver, testing the atmosphere. As usual I could see no further than her neck and half a cheek, as my father's secretary was as economical with her presence as with everything else.

'It's cold in here,' she said.

'Yes.'

'Warmer in the office.'

The half-head disappeared and did not come back. I decided to accept what I knew had been meant as an invitation, and retraced my way towards the corner of the house which adjoined the yard. In that corner were the stable office, a cloakroom, and the one room furnished for comfort, the room we called the owners' room, where owners and assorted others were entertained on casual visits to the stable.

The lights were on in the office, bright against the grey day outside. Margaret was taking off her sheepskin coat, and hot air was blowing busily out of a mushroom-shaped heater.

'Instructions?' she asked briefly.

'I haven't opened the letters yet.'

She gave me a quick comprehensive glance.

'Trouble?'

I told her about Moonrock and Lucky Lindsay. She listened attentively, showed no emotion, and asked how I had cut my face.

'Walked into a door.'

Her expression said plainly, 'I've heard that one before,' but she made no comment.

In her way she was as unfeminine as Etty, despite her skirt, her hairdo and her efficient make-up. In her late thirties, three years widowed and bringing up a boy and a girl with masterly organization, she bristled with intelligence and held the world at arm's length from her heart.

Margaret was new at Rowley Lodge, replacing mouse-like old Robinson who had finally scratched his way at seventy into unwilling retirement. Old Robinson had liked his little chat, and had fritted away hours of working time telling me in my childhood about the days when Charles II rode in races himself, and made Newmarket the second capital of England, so that ambassadors had to go there to see him, and how the Prince Regent had left the town for ever because of an inquiry into the running of his colt Escape, and refused to go back even though the Jockey Club apologized and begged him to, and how in 1905 King Edward VII was in trouble with the police for speeding down the road to London – at forty miles an hour on the straight bits.

Margaret did old Robinson's work more accurately and in half the time, and I understood after knowing her for six days why my father found her inestimable. She demanded no human response, and he was a man who found most human relationships boring. Nothing tired him quicker than people who constantly demanded attention for their emotions and problems, and even social openers about the weather irritated him. Margaret seemed to be a matched soul, and they got on excellently.

I slouched down in my father's revolving office armchair and told Margaret to open the letters herself. My father never let anyone open his letters, and was obsessive about it. She simply did as I said without comment, either spoken or implied. Marvellous.

The telephone rang. Margaret answered it.

'Mr Bredon? Oh yes. He'll be glad you called. I'll put you on to him.'

She handed me the receiver across the desk, and said, 'John Bredon.'

'Thanks.'

I took the receiver with none of the eagerness I would have shown the day before. I had spent three intense days trying to find someone who was free at short notice to take over Rowley Lodge until my father's leg mended, and of all the people whom helpful friends had suggested, only John Bredon, and elderly recently retired trainer, seemed to be of the right experience and calibre. He had asked for time to think it over and had said he would let me know as soon as he could.

He was calling to say he would be happy to come. I thanked him and uncomfortably apologized as I put him off. 'The fact is that after thinking it over I've decided to stay on myself . . .'

I set the receiver down slowly, aware of Margaret's astonishment. I didn't explain. She didn't ask. After a pause she went back to opening the letters.

The telephone rang again. This time, with schooled features, she asked if I would care to speak to Mr Russell Arletti.

Silently I stretched out a hand for the receiver.

'Neil?' a voice barked. 'Where the hell have you got to? I told Grey and Cox you'd be there yesterday. They're complaining. How soon can you get up there?'

Grey and Cox in Huddersfield were waiting for Arletti Incorporated to sort out why their once profitable business was going down the drain. Arletti Incorporated's sorter was sitting disconsolately in a stable office in Newmarket wishing he was dead.

'You'll have to tell Grey and Cox that I can't come.'

'You *what*?'

'Russell . . . count me out for a while. I've got to stay on here.'

'For God's sake, why?'

'I can't find anyone to take over.'

'You said it wouldn't take you more than a week.'

'Well, it has. There isn't anyone suitable. I can't go and sort out Grey and Cox and leave Rowley Lodge rudderless. There is six million involved here. Like it or not, I'll have to stay.'

'Damn it, Neil . . .'

'I'm really sorry.'

'Grey and Cox will be livid.' He was exasperated.

'Go up there yourself. It'll only be the usual thing. Bad costing. Underpricing their product at the planning stage. Rotten cash flow. They say they haven't any militants, so it's ninety per cent to a cornflake that it's lousy finance.'

He sighed. 'I don't have quite your talent. Better ones, mind you. But not the same.' He paused for thought. 'Have to send James, when he gets back from Shoreham. If you're sure?'

'Better count me out for three months at least.'

'Neil!'

'Better say, in fact, until after the Derby . . .'

'Legs don't take that long,' he protested.

'This one is a terrible mess. The bones were splintered and came through the skin, and it was touch and go whether they amputated.'

'Oh *hell*.'

'I'll give you a call,' I said. 'As soon as I look like being free.'

After he had rung off I sat with the receiver in my

35

hand, staring into space. Slowly I put it back in its cradle.

Margaret sat motionless, her eyes studiously downcast, her mouth showing nothing. She made no reference at all to the lie I had told.

It was, I reflected, only the first of many.

CHAPTER THREE

Nothing about that day got better.

I rode out with the second lot on the Heath and found there were tender spots I hadn't even known about. Etty asked if I had toothache. I looked like it, she said. Sort of drawn, she said.

I said my molars were in good crunching order and how about starting the canters. The canters were started, watched, assessed, repeated, discussed. Archangel, Etty said, would be ready for the Guineas.

When I told her I was going to stay on myself as the temporary trainer she looked horrified.

'But you *can't*.'

'You are unflattering, Etty.'

'Well, I mean . . . You don't know the horses.' She stopped and tried again. 'You hardly ever go racing. You've never been interested, not since you were a boy. You don't know enough about it.'

'I'll manage,' I said, 'with your help.'

But she was only slightly reassured, because she was not vain, and she never overestimated her own abilities.

She knew she was a good head lad. She knew there was a lot to training that she wouldn't do so well. Such self-knowledge in the Sport of Kings was rare, and facing it rarer still. There were always thousands of people who knew better, on the stands.

'Who will do the entries?' she asked astringently, her voice saying quite clearly that I couldn't.

'Father can do them himself when he's a bit better. He'll have a lot of time.'

At this she nodded with more satisfaction. The entering of horses in races suited to them was the most important skill in training. All the success and prestige of a stable started with the entry forms, where for each individual horse the aim had to be not too high, not too low, but just right. Most of my father's success had been built on his judgement of where to enter, and when to run, each horse.

One of the two-year-olds pranced around, lashed out, and caught another two-year-old on the knee. The boys' reactions had not been quick enough to keep them apart, and the second colt was walking lame. Etty cursed them coldly and told the second boy to dismount and lead his charge home.

I watched him following on foot behind the string, the horse's head ducking at every tender step. The knee would swell and fill and get hot, but with a bit of luck it would right itself in a few days. If it did not, someone would have to tell the owner. That someone would be me.

That made one horse dead and two damaged in one morning. If things went on at that rate there would soon be no stable left for the fat man to bother about.

When we got back there was a small police car in the drive and a large policeman in the office. He was sitting in my chair and staring at his boots, and rose purposefully to his feet as I came through the door.

'Mr Griffon?'

'Yes.'

He came to the point without preliminaries.

'We've had a complaint, sir, that one of your horses knocked over a cyclist on the Moulton Road this morning. Also a young woman has complained to us that this same horse endangered her life and that of her children.'

He was a uniformed sergeant, about thirty, solidly built, uncompromising. He spoke with the aggressive politeness that in some policemen is close to rudeness, and I gathered that his sympathies were with the complainants.

'Was the cyclist hurt, Sergeant?'

'I understand he was bruised, sir.'

'And his bicycle?'

'I couldn't say, sir.'

'Do you think that a ... er ... a settlement out of court, so to speak, would be in order?'

'I couldn't say, sir,' he repeated flatly. His face was full of the negative attitude which erects a barrier against sympathy or understanding. Into my mind floated one of the axioms that Russell Arletti lived by: in business matters with trade unions, the press, or the police, never try to make them like you. It arouses antagonism instead. And never make jokes: they are anti jokes.

I gave the sergeant back a stare of equal indifference and asked if he had the cyclist's name and address. After only the slightest hesitation he flicked over a page or two of notebook and read it out to me. Margaret took it down.

'And the young woman's?'

He provided that too. He then asked if he might take a statement from Miss Craig and I said, certainly Sergeant, and took him out into the yard. Etty gave him a rapid adding-up inspection and answered his questions in an unemotional manner. I left them together and went back to the office to finish the paper-work with Margaret, who preferred to work straight through the lunch hour and leave at three to collect her children from school.

'Some of the account books are missing,' she observed.

'I had them last night,' I said. 'They're in the oak room . . . I'll go and fetch them.'

The oak room was quiet and empty. I wondered what reaction I would get from the sergeant if I brought him in there and said that last night two faceless men had knocked me out, tied me up, and removed me from my home by force. Also, they had threatened to kill me, and had punched me full of anaesthetic to bring me back.

'Oh yes, sir? And do you want to make a formal allegation?'

I smiled slightly. It seemed ridiculous. The sergeant would produce a stare of top-grade disbelief, and I could hardly blame him. Only my depressing state of health and the smashed telephone lying on the desk made the night's events seem real at all.

The fat man, I reflected, hardly needed to have warned me away from the police. The sergeant had done the job for him.

Etty came into the office fuming while I was returning the account books to Margaret.

'Of all the pompous clods . . .'

'Does this sort of thing happen often?' I asked.

'Of course not,' Etty said positively. 'Horses get loose, of course, but things are usually settled without all this fuss. And I told that old man that you would see he didn't suffer. Why he had to go complaining to the police beats me.'

'I'll go and see him this evening,' I said.

'Now, the old sergeant, Sergeant Chubb,' Etty said forcefully, 'he would have sorted it out himself. He wouldn't have come round taking down statements. But this one, this one is new here. They've posted him here from Ipswich and he doesn't seem to like it. Just promoted, I shouldn't wonder. Full of his own importance.'

'The stripes were new,' Margaret murmured in agreement.

'We always have good relations with the police here,' Etty said gloomily. 'Can't think what they're doing, sending the town someone who doesn't understand the first thing about horses.'

The steam had all blown off. Etty breathed sharply through her nose, shrugged her shoulders, and produced a small resigned smile.

'Oh well . . . worse things happen at sea.'

She had very blue eyes, and light brown hair that went frizzy when the weather was damp. Middle age had roughened her skin without wrinkling it, and, as with most undersexed women, there was much in her face that was male. She had thin lips and bushy unkempt eyebrows, and the handsomeness of her youth was only something I remembered. Etty seemed a sad, wasted person to many who observed her, but to herself she was fulfilled, and was busily content.

She stamped away in her jodhpurs and boots and we heard her voice raised at some luckless boy caught in wrongdoing.

Rowley Lodge needed Etty Craig. But it needed Alessandro Rivera like a hole in the head.

He came late that afternoon.

I was out in the yard looking round the horses at evening stables. With Etty alongside I had got as far round as bay five, from where we would go round the bottom yard before working up again towards the house.

One of the fifteen-year-old apprentices nervously appeared as we came out of one box and prepared to go into the next.

'Someone to see you, sir.'

'Who?'

'Don't know, sir.'

'An owner?'

'Don't know, sir.'

'Where is he?'

'Up by the drive, sir.'

I looked up, over his head. Beyond the yard, out on the gravel, there was parked a large white Mercedes with a uniformed chauffeur standing by the bonnet.

'Take over, Etty, would you?' I said.

I walked up through the yard and out into the drive. The chauffeur folded his arms and his mouth like barricades against fraternization. I stopped a few paces away from him and looked towards the inside of the car.

One of the rear doors, the one nearest to me, opened. A small black-shod foot appeared, and then a dark trouser leg, and then, slowly straightening, the whole man.

It was clear at once who he was, although the resemblance to his father began and ended with the autocratic beak of the nose and the steadfast stoniness of the black eyes. The son was a little shorter, and

43

emaciated instead of chubby. He had sallow skin that looked in need of a sun-tan, and strong thick black hair curving in springy curls round his ears. Over all he wore an air of disconcerting maturity, and the determination in the set of his mouth would have done credit to a steel trap. Eighteen he might be, but it was a long time since he had been a boy.

I guessed that his voice would be like his father's: definite, unaccented, and careful.

It was.

'I am Rivera,' he announced. 'Alessandro.'

'Good evening,' I said, and intended it to sound polite, cool, and unimpressed.

He blinked.

'Rivera,' he repeated. 'I am Rivera.'

'Yes,' I agreed. 'Good evening.'

He looked at me with narrowing attention. If he expected from me a lot of grovelling, he was not going to get it. And something of this message must have got across to him from my attitude, because he began to look faintly surprised and a shade more arrogant.

'I understand you wish to become a jockey,' I said.

'Intend.'

I nodded casually. 'No one succeeds as a jockey without determination,' I said, and made it sound patronizing.

He detected the flavour immediately. He didn't like it. I was glad. But it was a small pin-pricking resistance that I was showing, and in his place I would have taken it merely as evidence of frustrated surrender.

'I am accustomed to succeed,' he said.

'How very nice,' I replied drily.

It sealed between us an absolute antagonism. I felt him shift gear into overdrive, and it seemed to me that he was mentally gathering himself to fight on his own account a battle he believed his father had already won.

'I will start at once,' he said.

'I am in the middle of evening stables,' I said matter-of-factly. 'If you will wait, we will discuss your position when I have finished.' I gave him the politeness of an inclination of the head which I would have given to anybody, and without waiting around for him to throw any more of his slight weight about, I turned smoothly away and walked without haste back to Etty.

When we had worked our way methodically round the whole stable, discussing briefly how each horse was progressing, and planning the work programme for the following morning, we came finally to the four outside boxes, only three busy now, and the fourth full of Moonrock's absence.

The Mercedes still stood on the gravel, with both Rivera and the chauffeur sitting inside it. Etty gave them a look of regulation curiosity and asked who they were.

'New customer,' I said economically.

She frowned in surprise. 'But surely you shouldn't have kept him waiting!'

'This one,' I reassured her with private, rueful irony, 'will not go away.'

But Etty knew how to treat new clients, and making them wait in their car was not it. She hustled me along the last three boxes and anxiously pushed me to return to the Mercedes. Tomorrow, no doubt, she would not be so keen.

I opened the rear door and said to him, 'Come along in to the office.'

He climbed out of the car and followed me without a word. I switched on the fan heater, sat in Margaret's chair behind the desk, and pointed to the swivel arm-chair in front of it. He made no issue of it, but merely did as I suggested.

'Now,' I said in my best interviewing voice, 'you want to start tomorrow.'

'Yes.'

'In what capacity?'

He hesitated. 'As a jockey.'

'Well, no,' I said reasonably. 'There are no races yet. The season does not start for about four weeks.'

'I know that,' he said stiffly.

'What I meant was, do you want to work in the stable? Do you want to look after two horses, as the others do?'

'Certainly not.'

'Then what?'

'I will ride the horses at exercise two or three times

a day. Every day. I will not clean their boxes or carry their food. I only wish to ride.'

Highly popular, that was going to be, with Etty and the other lads. Apart from all else, I was going to have a shop floor–management confrontation, or in plain old terms, a mutiny, on my hands in no time at all. None of the other lads was going to muck out and groom a horse for the joy of seeing Rivera ride it.

However, all I said was, 'How much experience, exactly, have you had so far?'

'I can ride,' he said flatly.

'Racehorses?'

'I can ride.'

This was getting nowhere. I tried again. 'Have you ever ridden in any sort of race?'

'I have ridden in amateur races.'

'Where?'

'In Italy, and in Germany.'

'Have you won any?'

He gave me a black stare. 'I have won two.'

I supposed that that was something. At least it suggested that he could stay on. Winning itself, in his case, had no significance. His father was the sort to buy the favourite and nobble the opposition.

'But you want now to become a professional?'

'Yes.'

'Then I'll apply for a licence for you.'

'I can apply myself.'

I shook my head. 'You will have to have an apprentice licence, and I will have to apply for it for you.'

'I do not wish to be an apprentice.'

I said patiently, 'Unless you become an apprentice you will be unable to claim a weight allowance. In England in flat races the only people who can claim weight allowances are apprentices. Without a weight allowance the owners of the horses will all resist to the utmost any suggestion that you should ride. Without a weight allowance, in fact, you might as well give up the whole idea.'

'My father . . .' he began.

'Your father can threaten until he's blue in the face,' I interrupted. 'I cannot *force* the owners to employ you, I can only persuade. Without a weight allowance, they will never be persuaded.'

He thought it over, his expression showing nothing.

'My father', he said, 'told me that anyone could apply for a licence and that there was no need to be apprenticed.'

'Technically, that is true.'

'But practically, it is not.' It was a statement more than a question: he had clearly understood what I had said.

I began to speculate about the strength of his intentions. It certainly seemed possible that if he read the Deed of Apprenticeship and saw to what he would be binding himself, he might simply step back into his car and be driven away. I fished in one of Margaret's tidy desk drawers, and drew out a copy of the printed agreement.

'You will need to sign this,' I said casually, and handed it over.

He read it without a flicker of an eyelid, and considering what he was reading, that was remarkable.

The familiar words trotted through my mind: '. . . the Apprentice will faithfully, diligently and honestly serve the Master and obey and perform all his lawful commands . . . and will not absent himself from the service of the Master, nor divulge any of the secrets of the Master's business . . . and shall deliver to the Master all such monies and other things that shall come into his hands for work done . . . and will in all matters and things whatsoever demean and behave himself as a good true and faithful Apprentice ought to do . . .'

He put the form down on the desk and looked across at me.

'I cannot sign that.'

'Your father will have to sign it as well,' I pointed out.

'He will not.'

'Then that's an end to it,' I said, relaxing back in my chair.

He looked down at the form. 'My father's lawyers will draw up a different agreement,' he said.

I shrugged. 'Without a recognizable apprenticeship deed you won't get an apprentice's licence. That form there is based on the articles of apprenticeship common to all trades since the Middle Ages. If you alter its intentions, it won't meet the licensing requirements.'

After a packed pause he said, 'That part about delivering all monies to the Master . . . does that mean I would have to give to you all money I might earn in races?' He sounded incredulous, as well he might.

'It does say that,' I agreed, 'but it is normal nowadays for the Master to return half of the race earnings to the apprentice. In addition, of course, to giving him a weekly allowance.'

'If I win the Derby on Archangel, you would take half. Half of the fee and half of the present?'

'That's right.'

'It's wicked!'

'You've got to win it before you start worrying,' I said flippantly, and watched the arrogance flare up like a bonfire.

'If the horse is good enough, I will.'

You kid yourself, mate, I thought; and didn't answer.

He stood up abruptly, picked up the form, and without another word walked out of the office, and out of the house, out of the yard, and into his car. The Mercedes purred away with him down the drive, and I stayed sitting back in Margaret's chair, hoping I had seen the last of him, wincing at the energy of my persisting headache, and wondering whether a treble brandy would restore me to instant health.

I tried it.

It didn't.

*

There was no sign of him in the morning, and on all counts the day was better. The kicked two-year-old's knee had gone up like a football but he was walking pretty soundly on it, and the cut on Lucky Lindsay was as superficial as Etty had hoped. The elderly cyclist, the evening before, had accepted my apologies and ten pounds for his bruises and had left me with the impression that we could knock him down again, any time, for a similar supplement to his income. Archangel worked a half-speed six furlongs on the Sidehill gallop, and in me a night's sleep had ironed out some creases.

But Alessandro Rivera did come back.

He rolled up the drive in the chauffeur-driven Mercedes just as Etty and I finished the last three boxes at evening stables, timing it so accurately that I wondered if he had been waiting and watching from out on Bury Road.

I jerked my head towards the office, and he followed me in. I switched on the heater, and sat down, as before; and so did he.

He produced from an inner pocket the apprenticeship form and passed it towards me across the desk. I took it and unfolded it, and turned it over.

There were no alterations. It was the deed in the exact form he had taken it. There were, however, four additions.

The signatures of Alessandro Rivera and Enso Rivera, with an appropriate witness in each case, sat squarely in the spaces designed for them.

I looked at the bold heavy strokes of both the Riveras' signatures and the nervous elaborations of the witnesses. They had signed the agreement without filling in any of the blanks: without even discussing the time the apprenticeship was to run for, or the weekly allowance to be paid.

He was watching me. I met his cold black eyes.

'You and your father signed it like this,' I said slowly, 'because you have not the slightest intention of being bound by it.'

His face didn't change. 'Think what you like,' he said.

And so I would. And what I thought was that the son was not as criminal as his father. The son had taken the legal obligations of the apprenticeship form seriously. But his father had not.

CHAPTER FOUR

The small private room in the North London hospital where my father had been taken after the crash seemed to be almost entirely filled with the frames and ropes and pulleys and weights which festooned his high bed. Apart from all that there was only a high-silled window with limp floral curtains and a view of half the back of another building and a chunk of sky, a chest-high washbasin with lever-type taps designed to be turned on by elbows, a bedside locker upon which reposed his lower teeth in a glass of water, and an armchair of sorts, visitors for the use of.

There were no flowers glowing against the margarine-coloured walls, and no well-wishing cards brightening the top of the locker. He did not care for flowers, and would have dispatched any that came straight along to other wards, and I doubted that anyone at all would have made the error of sending him a glossy or amusing get-well, which he would have considered most frightfully vulgar.

The room itself was meagre compared with what he

would have chosen and could afford, but to me, during the first critical days, the hospital itself had seemed effortlessly efficient. It did, after all, as one doctor had casually explained to me, have to deal constantly with wrecked bodies prised out of crashes on the A1. They were used to it. Geared to it. They had a higher proportion of accident cases than of the normally sick.

He had said he thought I was wrong to insist on private treatment for my father and that he would find time hanging less heavily in a public ward where there was a lot going on, but I had assured him that he did not know my father. He had shrugged and acquiesced, but said that the private rooms weren't much. And they weren't. They were for getting out of quickly, if one could.

When I visited him that evening, he was asleep. The ravages of the pain he had endured the past week had deepened and darkened the lines around his eyes and tinged all his skin with grey, and he looked defenceless in a way he never did when awake. The dogmatic set of his mouth was relaxed, and with his eyes shut he no longer seemed to be disapproving of nineteen-twentieths of what occurred. A lock of grey-white hair curved softly down over his forehead, giving him a friendly gentle look which was hopelessly misleading.

He had not been a kind father. I had spent most of my childhood fearing him and most of my teens loathing him, and only in the past very few years had I come to understand him. The severity with which he had used me had not after all been rejection and dislike, but lack of imagination and an inability to love. He had not believed in beating, but he had lavishly handed out other punishments of deprivation and solitude, without realizing that what would have been trifling to him was torment to me. Being locked in one's bedroom for three or four days at a time might not have come under the heading of active cruelty, but it had dumped me into agonies of humiliation and shame: and it had not been possible, although I had tried until I was the most repressed child in Newmarket, to avoid committing anything my father could interpret as a fault.

He had sent me to Eton, which in its way had proved just as callous, and on my sixteenth birthday I ran away.

I knew that he had never forgiven me. An aunt had relayed to me his furious comment that he had provided me with horses to ride and taught me obedience, and what more could any father do for his son?

He had made no effort to get me back, and during all the years of my commercial success we had not once spoken to each other. In the end, after fourteen years' absence, I had gone to the Ascot races knowing that he would be there, and wanting finally to make peace.

When I said, 'Mr Griffon . . .', he had turned to me from a group of people, raised his eyebrows, and looked at me enquiringly. His eyes were cool and blank. He hadn't known me.

I had said, with more amusement than awkwardness, 'I am your son . . . I am Neil.'

Apart from surprise he had shown no emotion what-soever, and on the tacit understanding that none would be expected on either side, he had suggested that any day I happened to be passing through Newmarket, I could call in and see him.

I had called three or four times every year since then, sometimes for a drink, sometimes for lunch, but never staying; and I had come to see him from a much saner perspective in my thirties than I had at fifteen. His manner to me was still for the most part forbidding, critical and punitive, but as I no longer depended solely upon him for approval, and as he could no longer lock me in my bedroom for disagreeing with him, I found a perverse sort of pleasure in his company.

I had thought, when I was called in a hurry to Rowley Lodge after the accident, that I wouldn't sleep again in my old bed, that I'd choose any other. But in fact in the end I did sleep in it, because it was the room that had been prepared for me, and there were dust-sheets still over all the rest.

Too much had crowded back when I looked at the unchanged furnishings and the fifty-times-read books on the small bookshelf; and smile at myself as cynically as I would, on that first night back I hadn't been able to lie in there in the dark with the door shut.

I sat down in the armchair and read the copy of *The Times* which rested on his bed. His hand, yellowish, freckled and with thick knotted veins, lay limply on the sheets, still half entwined in the black-framed spectacles he had removed before sleeping. I remembered that when I was seventeen I had taken to wearing frames like those, with plain glass in, because to me they stood for authority, and I had wanted to present an older and weightier personality to my clients. Whether it was the frames or not which did the trick, the business had flourished.

He stirred, and groaned, and the lax hand closed convulsively into a fist with almost enough force to break the lenses.

I stood up. His face was screwed up with pain and beads of sweat stood out on his forehead, but he sensed that there was someone in the room and opened his eyes sharp and wide as if there were nothing the matter.

'Oh . . . it's you.'

'I'll fetch a nurse,' I said.

'No. Be better . . . in a minute.'

But I went to fetch one anyway, and she looked at the watch pinned upside down on her bosom and remarked that it was time for his pills, near enough.

After he had swallowed them and the worst of it had passed, I noticed that during the short time I was out of the room he had managed to replace his lower teeth. The glass of water stood empty on the locker. A great one for his dignity, my father.

'Have you found anyone to take over the licence?' he asked.

'Can I make your pillows more comfortable?' I suggested.

'Leave them alone,' he snapped. 'Have you found anyone to take charge?' He would go on asking, I knew, until I gave him a direct answer.

'No,' I said. 'There's no need.'

'What do you mean?'

'I've decided to stay on myself.'

His mouth opened, just as Etty's had done, and then shut again with equal vigour.

'You can't. You don't know a damn thing about it. You couldn't win a single race.'

'The horses are good, Etty is good, and you can sit here and do the entries.'

'You will not take over. You will get someone who is capable, someone I approve of. The horses are far too valuable to have amateurs messing about. You will do as I say. Do you hear? You will do as I say.'

The pain-killing drug had begun to act on his eyes, if not yet on his tongue.

'The horses will come to no harm,' I said, and thought of Moonrock and Lucky Lindsay and the kicked two-year-old, and wished with all my heart I could hand the whole lot over to Bredon that very day.

'If you think', he said with a certain malice, 'that because you sell antiques you can run a racing stable, you are overestimating yourself.'

'I no longer sell antiques,' I pointed out calmly. As he knew perfectly well.

'The principles are different,' he said.

'The principles of all businesses are the same.'

'Rubbish.'

'Get the costs right and supply what the customer wants.'

'I can't see you supplying winners.' He was contemptuous.

'Well,' I said moderately, 'I can't see why not.'

'Can't you?' he asked acidly. 'Can't you, indeed?'

'Not if you will give me your advice.'

He gave me instead a long wordless stare while he searched for an adequate answer. The pupils in his grey eyes had contracted to micro-dots. There was no tension left in the muscles which had stiffened his jaw.

'You must get someone else,' he said: but the words had begun to slur. I made a non-committal movement of my head halfway between a nod and a shake, and the argument was over for that day. He asked after that merely about the horses. I told him how they had each performed during their workouts, and he seemed to forget that he didn't believe I understood what I had seen. When I left him, a short while later, he was again on the edge of sleep.

I rang the doorbell of my own flat in Hampstead, two long and two short, and got three quick buzzes back, which meant come on in. So I fitted my key into the latch and opened the door.

Gillie's voice floated disembodiedly across the hall. 'I'm in your bedroom.'

'Convenient,' I said to myself with a smile. But she was painting the walls.

'Didn't expect you tonight,' she said, when I kissed her. She held her arms away from me so as not to smear yellow ochre on my jacket. There was a yellow streak on her forehead and a dusting of it on her shining chestnut hair and she looked companionable and easy. Gillie at thirty-six had a figure no model would have been seen dead in, and an attractive lived-in face with wisdom looking out of grey-green eyes. She was sure and mature and much travelled in spirit, and had left behind her one collapsed marriage and one dead child. She had answered an advertisement for a tenant which I had put in *The Times*, and for two and a half years she had been my tenant and a lot else.

'What do you think of this colour?' she said. 'And we're having a cinnamon carpet and green and shocking pink striped curtains.'

'You can't mean it.'

'It will look ravishing.'

'Ugh,' I said, but she simply laughed. When she had taken the flat it had had white walls, polished furniture and blue fabrics. Gillie had retained only the furniture, and Sheraton and Chippendale would have choked over their new settings.

'You look tired,' she said. 'Want some coffee?'

'And a sandwich, if there's any bread.'

She thought. 'There's some crisp-bread, anyway.'

She was permanently on diets and her idea of dieting was to not buy food. This led to a lot of eating out, which completely defeated the object.

Gillie had listened attentively to my wise dictums about laying in suitable protein like eggs and cheese and then continued happily in the same old ways, which brought me early on to believe that she really did not lust after a beauty contest figure, but was content as long as she did not burst out of her forty-inch hip dresses. Only when they got tight did she actually shed half a stone. She could if she wanted to. She didn't obsessively want.

'How is your father?' she asked, as I crunched my way through a sandwich of rye crisp-bread and slices of raw tomato.

'It's still hurting him.'

'I would have thought they could have stopped that.'

'Well, they do, most of the time. And the sister in charge told me this evening that he will be all right in a day or two. They aren't worried about his leg any more. The wound has started healing cleanly, and it should all be settling down soon and giving him an easier time.'

'He's not young, of course.'

'Sixty-seven,' I agreed.

'The bones will take a fair time to mend.'

'Mm.'

'I suppose you've found someone to hold the fort.'

'No,' I said, 'I'm staying there myself.'

'Oh boy, oh boy,' she said, 'I might have guessed.'

I looked at her enquiringly with my mouth full of bits.

'Anything which smells of challenge is your meat and drink.'

'Not this one,' I said with feeling.

'It will be unpopular with the stable,' she diagnosed, 'and apoplectic to your father, and a riotous success.'

'Correct on the first two, way out on the third.'

She shook her head with the glint of a smile. 'Nothing is impossible for the whiz kids.'

She knew I disliked the journalese term, and I knew she liked to use it. 'My lover is a whiz kid,' she said once into a hush at a sticky party: and the men mobbed her.

She poured me a glass of the marvellous Chateau Lafite 1961 which she sacrilegiously drank with anything from caviare to baked beans. It had seemed to me when she moved in that her belongings consisted almost entirely of fur coats and cases of wine, all of which she had precipitously inherited from her mother and father respectively when they died together in Morocco in an earthquake. She had sold the coats because she thought they made her look fat, and had set about drinking her way gradually through the precious bins that wine merchants were wringing their hands over.

'That wine is an *investment*,' one of them had said to me in agony.

'But *someone*'s got to drink it,' said Gillie reasonably, and pulled out the cork on the second of the Cheval Blanc '61.

Gillie was so rich, because of her grandmother, that she found it more pleasing to drink the super-duper than to sell it at a profit and develop a taste for Brand X. She had been surprised that I had agreed until I had pointed out that that flat was filled with precious pieces where painted deal would have done the same job. So we sat sometimes with our feet up on a sixteenth-century Spanish walnut refectory table which had brought dealers sobbing to their knees and drank her wine out of eighteenth-century Waterford glass, and laughed at ourselves, because the only safe way to live with any degree of wealth was to make fun of it.

Gillie had said once, 'I don't see why that table is so special, just because it's been here since the Armada. Just look at those moth-eaten legs . . .' She pointed to four feet which were pitted, stripped of polish, and worn untidily away.

'In the sixteenth century they used to sluice the stone floors with beer because it whitened them. Beer was fine for the stone, but a bit unfortunate for any wood which got continually splashed.'

'Rotten legs proves it's genuine?'

'Got it in one.'

I was fonder of that table than of anything else I possessed, because on it had been founded all my fortunes. Six months out of Eton, on what I had saved out of sweeping the floors at Sotheby's, I set up in business on my own by pushing a barrow round the outskirts of flourishing country towns and buying anything worthwhile that I was offered. The junk I sold to secondhand shops and the best bits to dealers, and by the time I was seventeen I was thinking about a shop.

I saw the Spanish table in the garage of a man from whom I had just brought a late Victorian chest of drawers. I looked at the wrought-iron crossed spars bracing the solid square legs under the four-inch-thick top, and felt unholy butterflies in my guts.

He had been using it as a trestle for paper hanging, and it was littered with pots of paint.

'I'll buy that, too, if you like,' I said.

'It's only an old work table.'

'Well . . . how much would you want for it?'

He looked at my barrow, on to which he had just helped me lift the chest of drawers. He looked at the twenty pounds I had paid him for it, and he looked at my shabby jeans and jerkin, and he said kindly, 'No lad, I couldn't rob you. And anyway, look, its legs are all rotten at the bottom.'

'I could afford another twenty,' I said doubtfully. 'But that's about all I've got with me.'

He took a lot of persuading, and in the end would only let me give him fifteen. He shook his head over me, telling me I'd better learn a bit more before I ruined myself. But I cleaned up the table and re-polished the beautiful slab of walnut, and I sold it a fortnight later to a dealer I knew from the Sotheby's days for two hundred and seventy pounds.

With those proceeds swelling my savings I had opened the first shop, and things never looked back. When I sold out twelve years later to an American syndicate there was a chain of eleven, all bright and clean and filled with treasures.

A short time afterwards, on a sentimental urge, I traced the Spanish table, and bought it back. And I sought out the handyman with his garage and gave him two hundred pounds, which almost caused a heart attack; so I reckoned if anyone was going to put their feet up on that expensive plank, no one had a better right.

'Where did you get all those bruises?' Gillie said, sitting up in the spare-room bed and watching me undress.

I squinted down at the spatter of mauve blotches.

'I was attacked by a centipede.'

She laughed. 'You're hopeless.'

'And I've got to be back at Newmarket by seven tomorrow morning.'

'Stop wasting time, then. It's midnight already.'

I climbed in beside her, and lying together in naked companionship we worked our way through the *Times* crossword.

It was always better like that. By the time we turned off the light we were relaxed and entwined, and we turned to each other for an act that was a part but not the whole of a relationship.

'I quite love you,' Gillie said. 'Believe it or not.'

'Oh, I believe you,' I said modestly. 'Thousands wouldn't.'

'Stop biting my ear, I don't like it.'

'The books say the ear is an A1 erogenous zone.'

'The books can go stuff themselves.'

'Charming.'

'And all those women's lib publications about "The Myth of the Vaginal Orgasm". So much piffle. Of course it isn't a myth.'

'This is not supposed to be a public meeting,' I said. 'This is supposed to be a spot of private passion.'

'Oh well . . . if you insist.'

She wriggled more comfortably into my arms.

'I'll tell you something, if you like,' she said.

'If you absolutely must.'

'The answer to four down isn't hallucinated, it's hallucinogen.'

I shook. 'Thanks very much.'

'Thought you'd like to know.'

I kissed her neck and laid my hand on her stomach.

'That makes it a g, not a t, in twenty across,' she said.

'Stigma?'

'Clever old you.'

'Is that the lot?'

'Mm.'

After a bit she said, 'Do you really loathe the idea of green and shocking pink curtains?'

'Would you mind just concentrating on the matter in hand?'

I could feel her grin in the darkness.

'OK,' she said.

And concentrated.

She woke me up like an alarm clock at five o'clock. It was not so much the pat she woke me up with, but where she chose to plant it. I came back to the surface laughing.

'Good morning, little one,' she said.

She got up and made some coffee, her chestnut hair in a tangle and her skin pale and fresh. She looked marvellous in the mornings. She stirred a dollop of heavy cream into the thick black coffee and sat opposite me across the kitchen table.

'Someone really had a go at you, didn't they?' she said casually.

I buttered a piece of rye crunch and reached for the honey.

'Sort of,' I agreed.

'Not telling?'

'Can't,' I said briefly. 'But I will when I can.'

'You may have a mind like teak,' she said, 'but you've a vulnerable body, just like anyone else.'

I looked at her in surprise, with my mouth full. She wrinkled her nose at me.

'I used to think you mysterious and exciting,' she said.

'Thanks.'

'And now you're about as exciting as a pair of old bedroom slippers.'

'So kind,' I murmured.

'I used to think there was something magical about the way you disentangled all those nearly bankrupt businesses . . . and then I found out that it wasn't magic but just uncluttered common sense . . .'

'Plain, boring old me,' I agreed, washing down the crumbs with a gulp of coffee.

'I know you well, now,' she said. 'I know how you tick . . . And all those bruises . . .' She shivered suddenly in the warm little room.

'Gillie,' I said accusingly. 'You are suffering from intuition,' and that remark in itself was a dead giveaway.

'No . . . from interpretation,' she said. 'And just you watch out for yourself.'

'Anything you say.'

'Because,' she explained seriously, 'I do not want to have the bother of hunting for another ground-floor flat with cellars to keep the wine in. It took me a whole month to find this one.'

CHAPTER FIVE

It was drizzling when I got back to Newmarket. A cold wet horrible morning on the Heath. Also, the first thing I saw when I turned into the drive of Rowley Lodge was the unwelcome white Mercedes.

The uniformed chauffeur sat behind the wheel. The steely young Alessandro sat in the back. When I stopped not far away from him he was out of his car faster than I was out of mine.

'Where have you been?' he demanded, looking down his nose at my silver-grey Jensen.

'Where have you?' I said equably, and received the full freeze of the Rivera speciality in stares.

'I have come to begin,' he said fiercely.

'So I see.'

He wore superbly cut jodhpurs and glossy brown boots. His waterproof anorak had come from an expensive ski shop and his string gloves were clean and pale yellow. He looked more like an advertisement in *Country Life* than a working rider.

'I have to go in and change,' I said. 'You can begin when I come out.'

'Very well.'

He waited again in his car and emerged from it immediately I reappeared. I jerked my head at him to follow, and went down into the yard wondering just how much of a skirmish I was going to have with Etty.

She was in a box in bay three helping a very small lad to saddle a seventeen-hand filly, and with Alessandro at my heels I walked across to talk to her. She came out of the box and gave Alessandro a widening look of speculation.

'Etty,' I said matter-of-factly. 'This is Alessandro Rivera. He has signed his indentures. He starts today. Er, right now, in fact. What can we give him to ride?'

Etty cleared her throat. 'Did you say *apprenticed*?'

'That's right.'

'But we don't need any more lads,' she protested.

'He won't be doing his two. Just riding exercise.'

She gave me a bewildered look. 'All apprentices do their two.'

'Not this one,' I said briskly. 'How about a horse for him?'

She brought her scattered attention to bear on the immediate problem.

'There's Indigo,' she said doubtfully. 'I had him saddled for myself.'

'Indigo will do beautifully,' I nodded. Indigo was a quiet ten-year-old gelding which Etty often rode as lead horse to the two-year-olds, and upon which she liked to give completely untrained apprentices their first riding lessons. I stifled the urge to show Alessandro up by putting him on something really difficult: couldn't risk damaging expensive property.

'Miss Craig is the head lad,' I told Alessandro. 'And you will take your orders from her.'

He gave her a black unfathomable stare which she returned with uncertainty.

'I'll show him where Indigo is,' I reassured her. 'Also the tackroom, and so on.'

'I've given you Cloud Cuckoo-land this morning, Mr Neil,' she said hesitantly. 'Jock will have got him ready.'

I pointed out the tackroom, feedroom and the general layout of the stable to Alessandro and led him back towards the drive.

'I do not take orders from a woman,' he said.

'You'll have to,' I said without emphasis.

'No.'

'Goodbye, then.'

He walked one pace behind me in fuming silence, but he followed me round to the outside boxes and did not peel off towards his car. Indigo's box was the one next to Moonrock's, and he stood there patiently in his saddle and bridle, resting his weight on one leg and looking round lazily when I unbolted his door.

Alessandro's gaze swept him from stem to stern and he turned to me with unrepressed anger.

'I do not ride nags. I wish to ride Archangel.'

'No one lets an apprentice diamond cutter start on the Kohinoor,' I said.

'I can ride any racehorse on earth. I can ride exceptionally well.'

'Prove it on Indigo, then, and I'll give you something better for second lot.'

He compressed his mouth. I looked at him with the complete lack of feeling that always seemed to calm tempers in industrial negotiations; and after a moment or two it worked on him as well. His gaze dropped away from my face; he shrugged, untied Indigo's headcollar, and led him out of his box. He jumped with ease up into the saddle, slipped his feet into the stirrups, and gathered up the reins. His movements were precise and unfussy, and he settled on to old Indigo's back with an appearance of being at home. Without another word he started walking away down the yard, shortening the stirrup leathers as he went, for Etty rode long.

Watching his backview I followed him on foot, while from all the bays the lads led out the horses for the first lot. Down in the collecting paddock they circled round the outer cinder track while Etty on the grass in the centre began the ten-minute task of swapping some of the riders. The lads who did the horses did not necessarily ride their own charges out at exercise: each horse had to be ridden by a rider who could at the least control him and at the most improve him. The lowliest riders usually got the task of walking any unfit horses round the paddock at home: Etty seldom let them loose in canters on the Heath.

I joined her in the centre as she referred to her list. She was wearing a bright yellow sou'wester down which the drizzle trickled steadily, and she looked like a diminutive American fireman. The scrawled list in her hand was slowly degenerating into pulp.

'Ginge, get up on Pullitzer,' she said.

Ginge did as he was told in a sulk. Pullitzer was a far cry from Lucky Lindsay, and he considered that he had lost face.

Etty briefly watched Alessandro plod round on Indigo, taking in with a flick of a glance that he could at least manage him with no problems. She looked at me in a baffled questioning way but I merely steered her away from him by asking who she was putting up on our problem colt Traffic.

She shook her head in frustration. 'It'll still have to be Andy . . . He's a right little devil, that Traffic. All that breed, you can't trust one of them.' She turned and called to him, 'Andy . . . Get up on Traffic.'

Andy, middle-aged, tiny, wrinkled, could ride the sweetest of training gallops: but when years ago he had been given his chances in races his wits had flown out of the window, and his grasp of tactics was nil. He was given a leg-up on to the dark irritable two-year-old, which jigged and fidgeted and buck-jumped under him without remission.

Etty had switched herself to Lucky Lindsay, who

wore a shield over the cut knee and, although sound, would not be cantering; and in Cloud Cuckoo-land she had given me the next best to a hack, a strong five-year-old handicapper up to a man's weight. With everyone mounted, the gates to the Heath were opened, and the whole string wound out on to the walking ground . . . colts as always in front, fillies behind.

Bound for the Southfield gallops beside the race-course, we turned right out of the gate and walked down behind the other stables which were strung out along the Bury Road. Passed the Jockey Club notice board announcing which training areas could be used that day. Crossed the A11, holding up heavy lorries with their windscreen wipers twitching impatiently. Wound across the Severals, along the Watercourse, through St Mary's Square, along The Rows, and so finally to Southfields. No other town in England pro-vided a special series of roads upon which the only traffic allowed was horses; but one could go from one end of Newmarket to the other, only yards behind its bustling High Street, and spend only a fraction of the journey on the public highway.

We were the only string on Southfields that morning, and Etty wasted no time in starting the canters. Up on the road to the racecourse stood the two usual cars, with two men standing out in the damp in the unmistak-able position which meant they were watching us through binoculars.

'They never miss a day,' Etty said sourly. 'And if

they think we've brought Archangel down here they're in for a disappointment.'

The touts watched steadfastly, though what they could see from half a mile away through unrelenting drizzle was anyone's guess. They were employed not by bookmakers but by racing columnists, who relied on their reports for the wherewithal to fill their pages. I thought it might be a very good thing if I could keep Alessandro out of their attention for as long as possible.

He could handle Indigo right enough, though the gelding was an undemanding old thing within the powers of the Pony Club. All the same, he sat well on him and had quiet hands. 'Here, you,' Etty said, beckoning to him with her whip. 'Come over here.'

To me she said, as she slid to the ground from Lucky Lindsay, 'What is his name?'

'Alessandro.'

'Aless . . .? Far too long.'

Indigo was reined to a halt beside her. 'You, Alex,' she said. 'Jump down and hold this horse.'

I thought he would explode. His furious face said plainly that no one had any right to call him Alex, and that no one, but no one, was going to order him about. Especially not a woman.

He saw me watching him and suddenly wiped all expression from his own face as if with a sponge. He shook his feet out of the irons, swung his leg agilely forward over Indigo's withers, and slid to the ground facing us. He took the reins of Lucky Lindsay, which

Etty held out to him, and gave her those of Indigo. She lengthened the stirrup leathers, climbed up into the saddle, and rode away without comment to give a lead to the six two-year-olds we had brought with us.

Alessandro said like a throttled volcano, 'I am not going to take any more orders from that woman.'

'Don't be so bloody silly,' I said.

He looked up at me. The fine rain had drenched his black hair so that the curls had tightened and clung close to his head. With the arrogant nose, the back-tilted skull, the close curling hair, he looked like a Roman statue come to life.

'Don't talk to me like that. No one talks to me like that.'

Cloud Cuckoo-land stood patiently, pricking his ears to watch some seagulls fly across the Heath.

I said, 'You are here because you want to be. No one asked you to come, no one will stop you going. But just so long as you do stay here, you will do what Miss Craig says, and you will do what I say, and you will do it without arguing. Is that clear?'

'My father will not let you treat me like this.' He was rigid with the strength of his outrage.

'Your father', I said coldly, 'must be overjoyed to have a son who needs to shelter behind his skirts.'

'You will be sorry,' he threatened furiously.

I shrugged. 'Your father said I was to give you good horses to ride in races. Nothing was mentioned about bowing down to a spoiled little tin god.'

'I will tell him . . .'

'Tell him what you like. But the more you run to him the less I'll think of you.'

'I don't care what you think of me,' he said vehemently.

'You're a liar,' I said flatly, and he gave me a long tight-lipped stare until he turned abruptly away. He led Lucky Lindsay ten paces off, and stopped and watched the canters that Etty was directing. Every line of the slender shape spoke of injured pride and flaming resentment, and I wondered whether his father would indeed think that I had gone too far. And if I had, what was he going to do about it?

Mentally shrugging off the evil until the day thereof, I tried to make some assessment of the two-year-olds' relative abilities. Scoff as people might about me taking over my father's licence, I had found that childhood skills came back after nineteen years as naturally as riding a bicycle; and few lonely children could grow up in a racing stable without learning the trade from the muck-heap up. I'd had the horses out of doors for company, and the furniture indoors, and I reckoned if I could build one business out of the dead wood I could also try to keep things rolling with the live muscles. But for only as long, I reminded myself, as it took me to get rid of Alessandro.

Etty came back after the canters and changed horses again.

'Give me a leg-up,' she said briskly to Alessandro;

77

for Lucky Lindsay like most young thoroughbreds did not like riders climbing up to mount them.

For a moment I thought the whole pantomime was over. Alessandro drew himself up to his full height, which topped Etty's by at least two inches, and dispatched at her a glare which should have cremated her. Etty genuinely didn't notice.

'Come on,' she said impatiently, and held out her leg backwards, bent at the knee.

Alessandro threw a glance of desperation in my direction, then took a visibly deep breath, looped Indigo's reins over his arm, and put his two hands under Etty's shin. He gave her quite a respectable leg-up, though I wouldn't have been surprised if it had been the first time in his life that he had done it.

I carefully didn't laugh, didn't sneer, didn't show that I thought there was anything to notice. Alessandro swallowed his capitulation in private. But there was nothing to indicate that it would be permanent.

We rode back through the town and into the yard, where I gave Cloud Cuckoo-land back to Jock and walked into the office to see Margaret. She had the mushroom heater blowing full blast, but I doubted that I would have properly dried through by the time we pulled out again for second lot.

'Morning,' she said economically.

I nodded, half smiled, slouched into the swivel chair. 'I've opened the letters again ... was that right?' she said.

78

'Absolutely. And answer them yourself, if you can.'

She looked surprised. 'Mr Griffon always dictates everything.'

'Anything you have to ask about, ask. Anything I need to know, tell me. Anything else, deal with it yourself.'

'All right,' she said, and sounded pleased.

I sat in my father's chair, and stared down at his boots, which I had usurped, and thought seriously about what I had seen in his account books. Alessandro wasn't the only trouble the stable was running into.

There was a sudden crash as the door from the yard was forcibly opened, and Etty burst into the office like a stampeding ballistic missile.

'That bloody boy you've taken on . . . He'll have to go. I'm not standing for it. I'm not.'

She looked extremely annoyed, with eyes blinking fiercely and her mouth pinched into a slit.

'What has he done?' I asked resignedly.

'He's gone off in that stupid white car and left Indigo in his box still with his saddle and bridle on. George says he just got down off Indigo, led him into the box, and came out and shut the door, and got into the car and the chauffeur drove him away. Just like that!' She paused for breath. 'And who does he think is going to take the saddle off and dry the rain off Indigo and wash out his feet and rug him up and fetch his hay and water and make his bed?'

'I'll go out and see George,' I said. 'And ask him to do it.'

'I've asked him already,' Etty said furiously. 'But that's not the point. We're not keeping that wretched little Alex. Not one more minute.'

She glanced at me with her chin up, making an issue of it. Like all head lads she had a major say in the hiring and firing of the help. I had not consulted her over the hiring of Alessandro, and clear as a bell she was telegraphing that I was to acknowledge her authority and get rid of him.

'I'm afraid that we'll have to put up with him, Etty,' I said sympathetically. 'And hope to teach him better ways.'

'He must go,' she insisted vehemently.

'Alessandro's father', I lied sincerely, 'is paying through the nose to have his son taken on here as an apprentice. It is very much worth the stable's while financially to put up with him. I'll have a talk with him when he comes back for second lot and see if I can get him to be more reasonable.'

'I don't like the way he stares at me,' Etty said, unmollified.

'I'll ask him not to.'

'Ask!' Etty said exasperatedly. 'Whoever heard of *asking* an apprentice to behave with respect to the head lad?'

'I'll tell him,' I said.

'And tell him to stop being so snooty with the other

lads, they are already complaining. And tell him he is to put his horse straight after he has ridden it, the same as all the others.'

'I'm sorry, Etty. I don't think he'll put his horse straight. We'll have to get George to do it regularly. For a bonus, of course.'

Etty said angrily, 'It's not a yard man's job to act as a . . . a . . . *servant* . . . to an *apprentice*. It just isn't right.'

'I know, Etty,' I agreed. 'I know it isn't right. But Alessandro is not an ordinary apprentice, and it might be easier all round if you could let all the other lads know that his father is paying for him to be here, and that he has some romantic notion of wanting to be a jockey, which he'll get out of his system soon enough, and when he has gone, we can all get back to normal.'

She looked at me uncertainly. 'It isn't a proper apprenticeship if he doesn't look after his horses.'

'The details of an apprenticeship are a matter of agreement between the contracting parties,' I said regretfully. 'If I agree that he doesn't have to do his two, then he doesn't have to. And I don't really approve of him not doing them, but there you are, the stable will be richer if he doesn't.'

Etty had calmed down but she was not pleased. 'I think you might have consulted me before agreeing to all this.'

'Yes, Etty. I'm very sorry.'

'And does your father know about it?'

'Of course,' I said.

'Oh well, then.' She shrugged. 'If your father wants it, I suppose we must make the best of it. But it won't be at all good for discipline.'

'The lads will be used to him within a week.'

'They won't like it if he looks like getting any chance in races which they think should be theirs.'

'The season doesn't start for a month,' I said soothingly. 'Let's see how he makes out, shall we?'

And put off the day when he got the chances however bad he was, and however much they should have gone to someone else.

Etty put him on a quiet four-year-old mare which didn't please him but was a decided step up from old Indigo. He had received with unyielding scorn my request that he should stop staring so disquietingly at Etty, and sneered at my suggestion that he should let it be understood that his father was paying for him to be there.

'It is not true,' he said superciliously.

'Believe me,' I said with feeling, 'if it were true, you wouldn't be here tomorrow. Not if he paid a pound a minute.'

'Why not?'

'Because you are upsetting Miss Craig and upsetting the other lads, and a stable seething with resentment is not going to do its best by its horses. In fact, if you want the horses here to win races for you, you'll do your best to get along without arousing ill-feeling in the staff.'

He had given me the black stare and hadn't answered, but I noticed that he looked steadfastly at the ground when Etty detailed him to the mare. He rode her quietly along towards the back of the string and completed his allotted half-speed four-furlong canter without incident. On our return to the yard George met him and took the mare away to the box, and Alessandro, without a backward glance, walked to his Mercedes and was driven away.

The truce lasted for two more mornings. On each of them Alessandro arrived punctually for the first exercise, disappeared presumably for breakfast, came back for the second lot, and departed for the rest of the day. Etty gave him middling horses to ride, all of which he did adequately enough to wring from her the grudging comment: 'If he doesn't give us any more trouble, I suppose it could be worse.'

But on his fourth morning, which was Saturday, the defiant attitude was not only back but reinforced. We survived through both lots without a direct confrontation between him and Etty only because I purposely kept parting them. For the second lot, in fact, I insisted on taking him with me and a party of two-year-olds along to the special two-year-old training ground while Etty led the bulk of the string over to Warren Hill.

We got back before Etty so that he should be gone

before she returned, but instead of striding away to his Mercedes he followed me to the office door.

'Griffon,' he said behind me.

I turned; regarded him. The arrogant stare was much in evidence. His eyes were blacker than space.

'I have been to see my father,' he said. 'He says that you should be treating me with deference. He says I should not take orders from a woman and that you must arrange that I do not. If necessary, Miss Craig must leave. He says I must be given better horses to ride, and in particular, Archangel. He says that if you do not see to these things immediately, he will show you that he meant what he said. And he told me to give you this. He said it was a promise of what he could do.'

He produced a flat tin box from an inner pocket of his anorak, and held it out to me.

I took it. I said, 'Do you know what it contains?'

He shook his head, but I was sure he did know.

'Alessandro,' I said. 'Whatever your father threatens, or whatever he does, your only chance of success is to leave the stable unharmed. If your father destroys it, there will be nothing for you to ride.'

'He will make another trainer take me,' he asserted.

'He will not,' I said flatly, 'because should he destroy this stable I will put all the facts in front of the Jockey Club and they will take away your licence and stop you riding in any races whatsoever.'

84

'He would kill you,' he said matter-of-factly. The thought of it did not surprise or appal him.

'I have already lodged with my solicitor a full account of my interview with your father. Should he kill me, they will open that letter. He could find himself in great trouble. And you, of course, would be barred for life from racing anywhere in the world.'

A lot of the starch had turned to frustration. 'He will have to talk to you himself,' he said. 'You do not behave as he tells me you will. You confuse me . . . He will talk to you himself.'

He turned on his heel and took himself stiffly away to the attendant Mercedes. He climbed into the back, and the patient chauffeur, who waited always in the car all the time that his passenger was on the horses, started the purring engine and, with a scrunch of his Michelins, carried him away.

I took the flat tin with me into the house, through into the oak-panelled room, and opened it there on the desk.

Between the layers of cotton wool it contained a small carved wooden model of a horse. Round its neck was tied a label, and on the label was written one word: Moonrock.

I picked the little horse out of the tin. It was necessary to lift it out in two pieces, because the off-hind leg was snapped through at the hock.

CHAPTER SIX

I sat for quite a long time turning the little model over in my hands, and its significance over in my mind, wondering whether Enso Rivera could possibly have organized the breaking of Moonrock's leg, or whether he was simply pretending that what had been a true accident was all his own work.

I did not on the whole believe that he had destroyed Moonrock. What did become instantly ominous, though, was his repeated choice of that word, destroy.

Almost every horse which broke a leg had to be destroyed, as only in exceptional cases was mending them practicable. Horses could not be kept in bed. They would scarcely ever even lie down. To take a horse's weight off a leg meant supporting him in slings. Supporting him in slings for the number of weeks that it took a major bone to mend incurred debility and gut troubles. Racehorses, always delicate creatures, could die of the inactivity, and if they survived were never as good afterwards; and only in the case of valuable stallions and brood mares was any attempt normally made to keep them alive.

If Enso Rivera broke a horse's leg, it would have to be destroyed. If he broke enough of them, the owners would remove their survivors in a panic, and the stable itself would be destroyed.

Alessandro had said his father had sent the tin as a promise of what he could do.

If he could break horses' legs, he could indeed destroy the stable.

But it wasn't as easy as all that, to break a horse's leg.

Fact or bluff.

I fingered the little maimed horse. I didn't know, and couldn't decide, which it represented. But I did decide at least to turn a bit of my own bluff into fact.

I wrote a full account of the abduction, embellished with every detail I could remember. I packed the little wooden horse back into its tin and wrote a short explanation of its possible significance. Then I enclosed everything in a strong manilla envelope, wrote on it the time-honoured words, 'To be opened in the event of my death', put it into a larger envelope with a covering letter and posted it to my London solicitor from the main post office in Newmarket.

'You've done *what*?' my father exclaimed.

'Taken on a new apprentice.'

He looked in fury at all the junk anchoring him to his bed. Only the fact that he was tied down prevented him from hitting the ceiling.

'It isn't up to you to take on new apprentices. You are not to do it. Do you hear?'

I repeated my fabrication about Enso paying well for Alessandro's privilege. The news percolated through my father's irritation and the voltage went out of it perceptibly. A thoughtful expression took over, and finally a grudging nod.

He knows, I thought. He knows that the stable will before long be short of ready cash.

I wondered whether he were well enough to discuss it, or whether even if he were well enough he would be able to talk to me about it. We had never in our lives discussed anything: he had told me what to do, and I either had or hadn't done it. The divine right of kings had nothing on his attitude, which he applied also to most of the owners. They were all in varying degrees in awe of him and a few were downright afraid: but they kept their horses in his stable because year after year he brought home the races that counted.

He asked how the horses were working. I told him at some length and he listened with a sceptical slant to his mouth and eyebrows, intending to show doubt of the worth of any or all of my assessments. I continued without rancour through everything of any interest, and at the end he said, 'Tell Etty I want a list of the work done by each horse, and its progress.'

'All right,' I agreed readily. He searched my face for signs of resentment and seemed a shade disappointed when he didn't find any. The antagonism of an ageing and infirm father towards a fully grown healthy son was a fairly universal manifestation throughout nature, and I wasn't fussed that he was showing it. But all the same, I was not going to give him the satisfaction of feeling he had scored over me; and he had no idea of how practised I was at taking the prideful flush out of people's ill-natured victories.

I said merely, 'Shall I take a list of the entries home, so that Etty will know which races the horses are to be prepared for?'

His eyes narrowed and his mouth tightened, and he explained that it had been impossible for him to do the entries: treatment and X-rays took up so much of his time and he was not left alone long enough to concentrate.

'Shall Etty and I have a go, between us?'

'Certainly not. I will do them . . . when I have more time.'

'All right,' I said equably. 'How is the leg feeling? You are certainly looking more your old self now . . .'

'It is less troublesome,' he admitted. He smoothed the already wrinkle-free bedclothes which lay over his stomach, engaged in his perennial habit of making his surroundings as orderly, as dignified, as starched as his soul.

I asked if there was anything I could bring him. 'A

book,' I suggested. 'Or some fruit? Or some champagne?' Like most racehorse trainers he saw champagne as a sort of superior Coca-Cola, best drunk in the mornings if at all, but he knew that as a pick-me-up for the sick it had few equals.

He inclined his head sideways, considering. 'There are some half bottles in the cellar at Rowley Lodge.'

'I'll bring some,' I said.

He nodded. He would never, whatever I did, say thank you. I smiled inwardly. The day my father thanked me would be the day his personality disintegrated.

Via the hospital telephone I checked whether I would be welcome at Hampstead, and, having received a warming affirmative, headed the Jensen along the further eight miles south.

Gillie had finished painting the bedroom but its furniture was still stacked in the hall.

'Waiting for the carpet,' she explained. 'Like Godot.'

'Godot never came,' I commented.

'That', she agreed with exaggerated patience, 'is what I mean.'

'Send up rockets, then.'

'Fire crackers have been going off under backsides since Tuesday.'

'Never mind,' I said soothingly. 'Come out to dinner.'

'I'm on a grapefruit day,' she objected.

'Well I'm not. Positively not. I had no lunch and I'm hungry.'

'I've got a really awfully nice grapefruit recipe. You put the halves in the oven doused in saccharine and Kirsch and eat it hot . . .'

'No,' I said definitely. 'I'm going to the Empress.'

That shattered the grapefruit programme. She adored the Empress.

'Oh well . . . it would be so boring for you to eat alone,' she said. 'Wait a mo while I put on my tatty black.'

Her tatty black was a long-sleeved Saint Laurent dress that made the least of her curves. There was nothing approaching tatty about it, very much on the contrary, and her description was inverted, as if by diminishing its standing she could forget her guilt over its price. She had recently developed some vaguely socialist views, and it had mildly begun to bother her that what she had paid for one dress would have supported a ten-child family throughout Lent.

Dinner at the Empress was its usual quiet, spacious, superb self. Gillie ordered curried prawns to be followed by chicken in a cream and brandy sauce, and laughed when she caught my ironic eye.

'Back to the grapefruit,' she agreed. 'But not until tomorrow.'

'How are the suffering orphans?' I asked. She worked three days a week for an adoption society which because of the Pill and easy abortion was running out of its raw materials.

'You don't happen to want two-year-old twins, Afro-Asian boys, one of them with a squint?' she said.

'Not all that much, no.'

'Poor little things.' She absent-mindedly ate a bread roll spread with enjoyable chunks of butter. 'We'll never place them. They don't look even averagely attractive . . .'

'Squints can be put right,' I said.

'Someone has to care enough first, to get it done.'

We drank a lesser wine than Gillie's but better than most.

'Do you realize', Gillie said, 'that a family of ten could live for a week on what this dinner is costing?'

'Perhaps the waiter has a family of ten,' I suggested. 'And if we didn't eat it, what would they live on?'

'Oh . . . Blah,' Gillie said, but looked speculatively at the man who brought her chicken.

She asked how my father was. I said better, but by no means well.

'He said he would do the entries,' I explained, 'but he hasn't started. He told me it was because he isn't given time, but the Sister says he sleeps a great deal. He had a frightful shaking and his system hasn't recovered yet.'

'What will you do, then, about the entries? Wait until he's better?'

'Can't. The next lot have to be in by Wednesday.'

'What happens if they aren't?'

'The horses will go on eating their heads off in the stable when they ought to be out on a racecourse trying to earn their keep. It's now or never to put their names down for some of the races at Chester and Ascot and the Craven meeting at Newmarket.'

'So you'll do them yourself,' she said matter-of-factly, 'and they'll all go and win.'

'Almost any entry is better than no entry at all,' I sighed. 'And by the law of averages, some of them must be right.'

'There you are, then. No more problems.'

But there were two more problems, and worse ones, sticking up like rocks on the fairway. The financial problem, which I could solve if I had to; and that of Alessandro, which I didn't yet know how to.

The following morning, he arrived late. The horses for first lot were already plodding round the cinder track, while I stood with Etty in the centre as she changed the riders, when Alessandro appeared through the gate from the yard. He waited for a space between the passing horses and then crossed the cinder track and came towards us.

The finery of the week before was undimmed. The boots shone as glossily, the gloves as palely, and the ski jacket and jodhpurs were still immaculate. On his head, however, he wore a blue and white striped woolly cap with a pom-pom, the same as most of the other lads: but on Alessandro this cosy protection against the stinging March wind looked as incongruous as a bowler hat on the beach.

I didn't even smile. The black eyes regarded me with their customary chill from features that were more gaunt than delicate. The strong shape of the bones showed clearly through the yellowish skin, and more so, it seemed to me, than a week ago.

'What do you weigh?' I asked abruptly.

He hesitated a little. 'I will be able to ride at six stone seven when the races begin. I will be able to claim all the allowances.'

'But now? What do you weigh now?'

'A few pounds more. But I will lose them.'

Etty fumed at him but forebore to point out to him that he wouldn't get any rides if he weren't good enough. She looked down at her list to see which horse she had allotted him, opened her mouth to tell him, and then shut it again, and I literally saw the impulse take hold of her.

'Ride Traffic,' she said. 'You can get up on Traffic.'

Alessandro stood very still.

'He doesn't have to,' I said to Etty; and to Alessandro, 'You don't have to ride Traffic. Only if you choose.'

He swallowed. He raised his chin and his courage, and said, 'I choose.'

With a stubborn set to her mouth Etty beckoned to

Andy, who was already mounted on Traffic, and told him of the change.

'Happy to oblige,' Andy said feelingly, and gave Alessandro a leg-up into his unrestful place. Traffic lashed out into a few preliminary bucks, found he had a less hard-bitten customer than usual on his back, and started off at a rapid sideways trot across the paddock.

Alessandro didn't fall off, which was the best that could be said. He hadn't the experience to settle the sour colt to obedience, let alone to teach him to be better, but he was managing a great deal more efficiently than I could have done.

Etty watched him with disfavour and told everyone to give him plenty of room.

'That nasty little squirt needs taking down a peg,' she said in unnecessary explanation.

'He isn't doing too badly,' I commented.

'Huh.' There was a ten-ton lorry-load of scorn in her voice. 'Look at the way he's jabbing him in the mouth. You wouldn't catch Andy doing that in a thousand years.'

'Better not let him out on the Heath,' I said.

'Teach him a lesson,' Etty said doggedly.

'Might kill the goose, and then where would we be for golden eggs?'

She gave me a bitter glance. 'The stable doesn't need that sort of money.'

'The stable needs any sort of money it can get.'

But Etty shook her head in disbelief. Rowley Lodge

had been in the top division of the big league ever since she had joined it, and no one would ever convince her that its very success was leading it into trouble.

I beckoned to Alessandro and he came as near as his rocking-horse permitted.

'You don't have to ride him on the Heath,' I said.

Traffic turned his quarters towards us and Alessandro called over his shoulder: 'I stay here. I choose.'

Etty told him to ride fourth in the string and everyone else to keep out of his way. She herself climbed into Indigo's saddle, and I into Cloud Cuckoo-land's, and George opened the gates. We turned right on to the walking ground, bound for the canter on Warren Hill, and nothing frantic happened on the way except that Traffic practically backed into an incautious tout when crossing Moulton Road. The tout retreated with curses, calling the horse by name. The Newmarket touts knew every horse on the Heath by sight. A remarkable feat, as there were about two thousand animals in training there, hundreds of them two-year-olds which altered shape as they developed month by month. Touts learned horses like headmasters learned new boys, and rarely made a mistake. All I hoped was that this one had been too busy getting himself to safety to take much notice of the rider.

We had to wait our turn on Warren Hill as we were the fourth stable to choose to work there that morning. Alessandro walked Traffic round in circles a little way apart – or at least tried to walk him. Traffic's idea of walking would have tired a bucking bronco.

Eventually Etty sent the string off up the hill in small clusters, with me sitting halfway up the slope on Cloud Cuckoo-land, watching them as they swept past. At the top of the hill they stopped, peeled off to the left, and went back down the central walking ground to collect again at the bottom. Most mornings each horse cantered up the hill twice, the sharpish incline getting a lot of work into them in a comparatively short distance.

Alessandro started up the hill in the last bunch, one of only four.

Long before he drew level with me I could see that of the two it was the horse who had control. Galloping was hard labour up Warren Hill, but no one had given Traffic the message.

As he passed me he was showing all the classic signs of the bolter in action: head stretched horizontally forward, bit gripped between his teeth, eyes showing the whites. Alessandro, with as much hope of dominating the situation as a virgin in a troop ship, hung grimly on to the neck-strap and appeared to be praying.

The top of the rise meant nothing to Traffic. He swerved violently to the left and set off sideways towards Bury Hill, not even having the sense to make straight for the stable but swinging too far north and missing it by half a mile. On he charged, his hooves thundering relentlessly over the turf, carrying

Alessandro inexorably away in the general direction of Lowestoft.

Stifling the unworthy thought that I wouldn't care all that much if he plunged straight on into the North Sea, I reflected with a bit more sense that if Traffic damaged himself, Rowley Lodge's foundations would feel the tremor. I set off at a trot after him as he disappeared into the distance, but when I reached the Bury St Edmunds Road there was no sign of him. I crossed the road and reined in there, wondering which direction to take.

A car came slowly towards me with a shocked-looking driver poking his head out of the window.

'Some bloody madman nearly ploughed straight into me,' he yelled. 'Some bloody madman on the road on a mad horse.'

'How very upsetting,' I shouted back sympathetically, but he glared at me balefully and nearly ran into a tree.

I went on along the road, wondering whether it would be a dumped-off Alessandro I saw first, and if so, how long it would take to find and retrieve the wayward Traffic.

From the next rise there was no sign of either of them: the road stretched emptily ahead. Beginning to get anxious, I quickened Cloud Cuckoo-land until we were trotting fast along the soft ground edging the tarmac.

Past the end of the Limekilns, still no trace of Alessandro. The road ran straight, down and up its inclines. No Alessandro. It was a good two miles from the training ground that I finally found him.

He was standing at the crossroads, dismounted, holding Traffic's reins. The colt had evidently run himself to a standstill, as he drooped there with his head down, his sides heaving, and sweat streaming from him all over. Flecks of foam spattered his neck, and his tongue lolled exhaustedly out.

I slid down from Cloud Cuckoo-land and ran my hand down Traffic's legs. No tenderness. No apparent strain. Sighing with relief, I straightened up and looked at Alessandro. His face was stiff, his eyes expressionless.

'Are you all right?' I asked.

He lifted his chin. 'Of course.'

'He's a difficult horse,' I remarked.

Alessandro didn't answer. His self-pride might have received a big blow, but he was not going to be so soft as to accept any comfort.

'You'd better walk back with him,' I said. 'Walk until he's thoroughly cooled down. And keep him out of the way of the cars.'

Alessandro tugged the reins and Traffic sluggishly turned, not moving his legs until he absolutely had to.

'What's that?' Alessandro said, pointing to a mound in the grass at the corner of the crossroads where he had been standing. He shoved Traffic further away so that I could see; but I had no need to.

'It's the boy's grave,' I said.

'What boy?' He was startled. The small grave was known to everyone in Newmarket, but not to him. The mound, about four feet long, was outlined with overlapping wire hoops, like the edges of lawns in parks. There were some dirty-looking plastic daffodils entwined in the hoops, and a few dying flowers scattered in the centre. Also a white plastic drinking mug which someone had thrown there. The grave looked forlorn, yet in a futile sort of way, cared for.

'There are a lot of legends,' I said. 'The most likely is that he was a shepherd boy who went to sleep in charge of his flock. A wolf came and killed half of them, and when he woke up he was so remorseful that he hanged himself.'

'They used to bury suicides at crossroads,' Alessandro said, nodding. 'It is well known.'

There didn't seem to be any harm in trying to humanize him, so I went on with the story.

'The grave is always looked after, in a haphazard sort of way. It is never overgrown, and fresh flowers are often put there . . . No one knows exactly who puts them there, but it is supposed to be the gipsies. And there is also a legend that in May the flowers on the grave are in the colours that will win the Derby.'

Alessandro stared down at the pathetic little memorial.

'There are no black flowers,' he said slowly: and Archangel's colours were black, pale blue and gold.

'The gipsies will solve that if they have to,' I said

drily: and thought that they would opt for an easier-to-stage nap selection.

I turned Cloud Cuckoo-land in the direction of home and walked away. When presently I looked back, Alessandro was walking Traffic quietly along the side of the road, a thin straight figure in his clean clothes and bright blue and white cap. It was a pity, I thought, that he was as he was. With a different father, he might have been a different person.

But with a different father, so would I. And who wouldn't.

I thought about it all the way back to Rowley Lodge. Fathers, it seemed to me, could train, feed or warp their young plants, but they couldn't affect their basic nature. They might produce a stunted oak or a luxuriant weed, but oak and weed were inborn qualities, which would prevail in the end. Alessandro, on such a horticultural reckoning, was like a cross between holly and deadly nightshade; and if his father had his way the red berries would lose out to the black.

Alessandro bore Etty's strongly implied scorn with a frozen face, but few of the other lads teased him on his return, as they would have done to one of their own sort. Most of them seemed to be instinctively afraid of him, which to my mind showed their good sense, and the other, less sensitive types had drifted into the defence mechanism of ignoring his existence.

George took Traffic off to his box, and Alessandro followed me into the office. His glance swept over

Margaret, sitting at her desk in a neat navy blue dress with the high curls piled as elaborately as ever, but he saw her as no bar to giving me the benefit of the thoughts that he, evidently, had also had time for on the way back.

'You should not have made me ride such a badly trained horse,' he began belligerently.

'I didn't make you. You chose to.'

'Miss Craig told me to ride it to make a fool of me.'

True enough.

'You could have refused,' I said.

'I could not.'

'You could have said that you thought you needed more practice before taking on the worst ride in the yard.'

His nostrils flared. So self-effacing an admission would have been beyond him.

'Anyway,' I went on, 'I personally don't think riding Traffic is going to teach you most. So you won't be put on him again.'

'But I insist,' he said vehemently.

'You insist what?'

'I insist I ride Traffic again.' He gave me the haughtiest of his selection of stares, and added, 'Tomorrow.'

'Why?'

'Because if I do not, everyone will think it is because I cannot, or that I am afraid to.'

'So you do care', I said matter-of-factly, 'what the others think of you.'

'No, I do not.' He denied it strongly.

'Then why ride the horse?'

He compressed his strong mouth stubbornly. 'I will answer no more questions. I will ride Traffic tomorrow.'

'Well, OK,' I said casually. 'But I'm not sending him on the Heath tomorrow. He'll hardly need another canter. Tomorrow he'll only be walking round the cinder track in the paddock, which will be very boring for you.'

He gave me a concentrated, suspicious, considering stare, trying to work out if I was meaning to undermine him. Which I was, if one can call taking the point out of a Grand Gesture undermining.

'Very well,' he said grudgingly. 'I will ride him round the paddock.'

He turned on his heel and walked out of the office. Margaret watched him go with a mixed expression I couldn't read.

'Mr Griffon would never stand for him talking like that,' she said.

'Mr Griffon doesn't have to.'

'I can see why Etty can't bear him,' she said. 'He's insolent. There's no other word for it. Insolent.' She handed me three opened letters across the desk. 'These need your attention, if you don't mind.' She reverted to Alessandro: 'But all the same, he's beautiful.'

'He's no such thing,' I protested mildly. 'If anything, he's ugly.'

She smiled briefly. 'He's absolutely loaded with sex appeal.'

I lowered the letters. 'Don't be silly. He has the sex appeal of a bag of rusty nails.'

'You wouldn't notice,' she said judiciously. 'Being a man.'

I shook my head. 'He's only eighteen.'

'Age has nothing to do with it,' she said. 'Either you've got it, or you haven't got it, right from the start. And he's got it.'

I didn't pay much attention: Margaret herself had so little sex appeal that I didn't think her a reliable judge. When I'd read through the letters and agreed with her how she should answer them, I went along to the kitchen for some coffee.

The remains of the night's work lay littered about: the various dregs of brandy, cold milk, coffee, and masses of scribbled-on bits of paper. It had taken me most of the night to do the entries; a night I would far rather have spent lying warmly in Gillie's bed.

The entries had been difficult, not only because I had never done them before, and had to read the conditions of each race several times to make sure I understood them, but also because of Alessandro. I had to make a balance of what I would have done without him, and what I would have to let him ride if he were still there in a month's time.

I was taking his father's threats seriously. Part of the time I thought I was foolish to do so; but that abduction a week ago had been no playful joke, and until I was certain Enso would not let loose a thunderbolt it was more prudent to go along with his son. I still had nearly a month before the Flat season started, still nearly a month to see a way out. But, just in case, I had put down some of the better prospects for apprentice races, and had duplicated the entries in many open races, because if two ran there would be one for Alessandro. Also I entered a good many in the lesser meetings, particularly those in the north: because whether he liked it or not, Alessandro was not going to start his career in a blaze of limelight. After all that I dug around in the office until I found the book in which old Robinson had recorded all the previous years' entries, and I checked my provisional list against what my father had done. After subtracting about twenty names, because I had been much too lavish, and shuffling things around a little, I made the total number of entries for that week approximately the same as those for the year before, except that I still had more in the north. But I wrote the final list on to the official yellow form, in block letters as requested, and double checked again to make sure I hadn't entered two-year-olds in handicaps, or fillies in colts-only, and made any other such give-away gaffs.

When I gave the completed form to Margaret to record and then post, all she said was, 'This isn't your father's writing.'

'No,' I said. 'He dictated the entries. I wrote them down.'

She nodded non-committally, and whether she believed me or not I had no idea.

Alessandro rode Pullitzer competently next day at first lot, and kept himself to himself. After breakfast he returned with a stony face that forbade comment, and when the main string had started out for the Heath, was given a leg-up on to Traffic. Looking back from the gate I saw the fractious colt kicking away at shadows as usual, and noticed that the two other lads detailed to stay in and walk their charges were keeping well away from him.

When we returned an hour and a quarter later, George was holding Traffic's reins, the other lads had dismounted, and Alessandro was lying on the ground in an unconscious heap.

CHAPTER SEVEN

'Traffic just bucked him off, sir,' one of the lads said. 'Just bucked him clean off, sir. And he hit his head on the paddock rail, sir.'

'Just this minute, sir,' added the other anxiously.

They were both about sixteen, both apprentices, both tiny, neither of them very bold. I thought it unlikely they would have done anything purposely to upset Traffic further and bring the stuck-up Alessandro literally down to earth, but one never knew. What I did know was that Alessandro's continuing health was essential to my own.

'George,' I said, 'put Traffic away in his box, and Etty . . .' She was at my shoulder, clicking her tongue but not looking over-sorry, 'Is there anything we can use as a stretcher?'

'There's one in the tackroom,' she said, nodding, and told Ginge to go and get it.

The stretcher turned out to be a minimal affair of a piece of grubby green canvas slung between two unevenly shaped poles, which looked as though they might once have been a pair of oars. By the time Ginge returned with it my heartbeat had descended from Everest: Alessandro was alive and not in too deep a coma, and Enso's pistol would not yet be popping me off in revenge to kingdom come.

As far as I could tell, none of his bones was broken, but I took exaggerated care over lifting him on to the stretcher. Etty disapproved: she would have had George and Ginge lift him up by his wrists and ankles and sling him on like a sack of corn. I, more moderately, told George and Ginge to lift him gently, carry him down to the house, and put him on the sofa in the owners' room. Following, I detoured off into the office and asked Margaret to telephone for a doctor.

Alessandro was stirring when I went into the owners' room. George and Ginge stood looking down at him, one elderly and resigned, one young and pugnacious, neither of them feeling any sympathy with the patient.

'OK,' I said to them. 'That's the lot. The doctor's coming for him.'

Both of them looked as if they would like to say a lot, but they ambled out tight-lipped and aired their opinions in the yard.

Alessandro opened his eyes, and for the first time looked a little vulnerable. He didn't know what had happened, didn't know where he was or how he had got there. The puzzlement formed new lines on his face; made it look younger and softer. Then his eyes focused on my face and in one bound a lot of memory came back. The dove dissolved into the hawk. It was like watching the awakening of a spastic, from loose-limbed peace up to tightness and jangle.

'What happened?' he asked.

'Traffic threw you.'

'Oh,' he said more weakly than he liked. He shut his eyes and through his teeth emitted one heartfelt word. 'Sod.'

There was a sudden commotion at the door and the chauffeur plunged into the room with Margaret trying to cling to one arm. He threw her effortlessly out of his way and shaped up to do the same to me.

'What has happened?' he demanded threateningly. 'What are you doing to the son?' His voice set up a shiver in my spine. If he wasn't one of the rubber-faces, he sounded exactly like it.

Alessandro spoke from the sofa with tiredness in his voice: and he spoke in Italian, which thanks to a one-time girlfriend I more or less understood.

'Stop, Carlo. Go back to the car. Wait for me. The horse threw me. Neil Griffon will not harm me. Go back to the car, and wait for me.'

Carlo moved his head to and fro like a baffled bull, but finally subsided and did as he was told. Three sotto voce cheers for the discipline of the Rivera household.

'A doctor is coming to see you,' I said.

'I do not want a doctor.'

'You're not leaving that sofa until I'm certain there is nothing wrong with you.'

He sneered, 'Afraid of my father?'

'Think what you like,' I said; and he obviously did.

The doctor, when he came, turned out to be the same one who had once diagnosed my mumps, measles and chicken-pox. Old now, with overactive lacrymal glands and hesitant speech, he did not in the least appeal to his present patient. Alessandro treated him rudely, and got back courtesy where he deserved a smart kick.

'Nothing much wrong with the lad,' was the verdict. 'But he'd better stay in bed today, and rest tomorrow. That'll put you right, young man, eh?'

The young man glared back ungratefully and didn't answer. The old doctor turned to me, gave me a tolerant smile and said to let him know if the lad had any after effects, like dizziness or headaches.

'Old fool,' said the lad audibly, as I showed the doctor out; and when I went back he was already on his feet.

'Can I go now?' he asked sarcastically.

'As far and for as long as you like,' I agreed.

His eyes narrowed. 'You are not getting rid of me.'

'Pity,' I said.

After a short furious silence he walked a little unsteadily past me and out of the door. I went into the office and with Margaret watched through the window while the chauffeur bustled around, settling him comfortably into the back seat of the Mercedes; and presently, without looking back, he drove 'the son' away.

'Is he all right?' Margaret asked.

'Shaken, not stirred,' I said flippantly, and she laughed. But she followed the car with her eyes until it turned left down Bury Road.

He stayed away the following day but came back on the Thursday morning in time for the first lot. I was up in the top part of the yard talking to Etty when the car arrived. Her pleasant expression changed to the one of tight-lipped dislike which she always wore when Alessandro was near her, and when she saw him erupting athletically from the back seat and striding purposefully towards us she discovered something that urgently needed seeing to in one of the bays further down.

Alessandro noted her flight with a twist of scorn on his lips, and widened it into an irritating smirk as a greeting to me. He held out a small flat tin box, identical with the one he had presented before.

'Message for you,' he said. All the cockiness was back fortissimo, and I would have known even without the tin that he had again been to see his father. He had recharged his malice like a battery plugged into the mains.

'Do you know what is in it, this time?'

He hesitated. 'No,' he said. And this time I believed

him, because his ignorance seemed to annoy him. The tin was fastened round the edge with adhesive tape. Alessandro, with the superior smirk still in place, watched me pull it off. I rolled the tape into a small sticky ball and put it in my pocket: then carefully I opened the tin.

There was another little wooden horse between two thin layers of cotton wool.

It had a label round its neck.

It had a broken leg.

I didn't know what exactly was in my face when I looked up at Alessandro, but the smirk deteriorated into a half-anxious bravado.

'He said you wouldn't like it,' he remarked defiantly.

'Come with me, then,' I said abruptly. 'And see if you do.' I set off up the yard towards the drive, but he didn't follow: and before I reached my destination I was met by George hurrying towards me with a distressed face and worried eyes.

'Mr Neil . . . Indigo's got cast and broken a leg in his box . . . same as Moonrock . . . you wouldn't think it could happen, not to two old'uns like them, not ten days apart.'

'No, you wouldn't,' I said grimly, and walked back with him into Indigo's box stuffing the vicious message in its tin into my jacket pocket.

The nice-natured gelding was lying in the straw trying feebly to stand up. He kept lifting his head and pushing at the floor with one of his forefeet, but all strength seemed to have left him. The other forefoot lay uselessly bent at an unnatural angle, snapped through just above the pastern.

I squatted down beside the poor old horse and patted his neck. He lifted his head again and thrashed to get back on to his feet, then flopped limply back into the straw. His eyes looked glazed, and he was dribbling.

'Nothing to be done, George,' I said. 'I'll go and telephone the vet.' I put only regret into my voice and kept my boiling fury to myself. George nodded resignedly but without much emotion: like every older stableman he had seen a lot of horses die.

The young chubby Dainsee got out of his bath to answer the telephone.

'Not another one!' he exclaimed, when I explained.

'I'm afraid so. And would you bring with you any gear you need for doing a blood test?'

'Whatever for?'

'I'll tell you when you get here . . .'

'Oh,' he sounded surprised, but willing to go along. 'All right then. Half a jiffy while I swap the bath towel for my natty suiting.'

He came in jeans, his dirty Land Rover, and twenty minutes. Bounced out on to the gravel, nodded cheerfully, and turned at once towards Indigo's box. George was along there with the horse, but the rest of the yard stood quiet and empty. Etty, showing distress at the imminent loss of her lead horse, had taken the string down to Southfields on the racecourse side, and Alessandro presumably had gone with her, as he was nowhere about, and his chauffeur was waiting as usual in the car.

Indigo was up on his feet. George, holding him by the headcollar, said that the old boy just suddenly seemed to get his strength back and stood up, and he'd been eating some hay since then, and it was a right shame he'd got cast, that it was. I nodded and took the headcollar from him, and told him I'd see to Indigo, and he could go and get on with putting the oats through the crushing machine ready for the morning feeds.

'He makes a good yard man,' Dainsee said. 'Old George, he was deputy head gardener once at the Viceroy's palace in India. It accounts for all those tidy flowerbeds and tubs of pretty shrubs which charm the owners when they visit the yard.'

I was surprised. 'I didn't know that . . .'

'Odd world.' He soothed Indigo with a touch, and peered closely at the broken leg. 'What's all this about a blood test?' he asked, straightening up and eyeing me with speculation.

'Do vets have a keep-mum tradition?'

His gaze sharpened into active curiosity. 'Professional secrets, like doctors and lawyers? Yes, sure we do. As long as it's not a matter of keeping quiet about a spot of foot and mouth.'

'Nothing like that.' I hesitated. 'I'd like you to run a private blood test . . . could that be done?'

'How private? It'll have to go to the Equine Research Labs. I can't do it myself, haven't got the equipment.'

'Just a blood sample with no horse's name attached.'

'Oh sure. That happens all the time. But you can't really think anyone *doped* the poor old horse!'

'I think he was given an anaesthetic,' I said. 'And that his leg was broken on purpose.'

'Oh glory.' His mouth was rounded into an O of astonishment, but the eyes flickered with the rapidity of his thoughts. 'You seem sane enough,' he said finally, 'so let's have a look see.'

He squatted down beside the affected limb and ran his fingers very lightly down over the skin. Indigo shifted under his touch and ducked and raised his head violently.

'All right, old fellow,' Dainsee said, standing up again and patting his neck. He raised his eyebrows at me, 'Can't say you're wrong, can't say you're right.' He paused, thinking it over. The eyebrows rose and fell several times, like punctuations. 'Tell you what,' he said at length. 'I've got a portable X-ray machine back home. I'll bring it along, and we'll take a picture. How's that?'

'Very good idea,' I said, pleased.

'Right.' He opened his case, which he had parked just inside the door. 'Then I'll just freeze that leg, so he'll be in no discomfort until I come back.' He brought out a hypodermic and held it up against the light, beginning to press the plunger.

'Do the blood test first,' I said.

'Eh?' He blinked at me. 'Oh yes, of course. Golly, yes, of course. Silly of me.' He laughed gently, laid down the first syringe and put together a much larger one, empty.

He took the sample from the jugular vein, which he found and pierced efficiently first time of asking. 'Bit of luck,' he murmured in self-deprecation, and drew half a tumbler full of blood into the syringe. 'Have to give the lab people enough to work on, you know,' he said, seeing my surprise. 'You can't get reliable results from a thimbleful.'

'I suppose not . . .'

He packed the sample into his case, shot the freezing local into Indigo's near fore, nodded and blinked with undiminished cheerfulness, and smartly departed. Indigo, totally unconcerned, went back contentedly to his hay net, and I, with bottled anger, went into the house.

The label on the little wooden horse had 'Indigo' printed in capitals on one side of it, and on the other, also in capitals, a short sharp message.

'To hurt my son is to invite destruction.'

Neither George nor Etty saw any sense in the vet going away without putting Indigo down.

'Er . . .' I said. 'He found he didn't have the humane

killer with him after all. He thought it was in his bag, but it wasn't.'

'Oh,' they said, satisfied, and Etty told me that everything had gone well on the gallops and that Lucky Lindsay had worked a fast five furlongs and afterwards wouldn't have blown out a candle.

'I put that bloody little Alex on Clip Clop and told him to take him along steadily, and he damn well disobeyed me. He shook him into a full gallop and left Lancat standing, and the touts' binoculars were working overtime.'

'Stupid little fool,' I agreed. 'I'll speak to him.'

'He takes every opportunity he can to cross me,' she complained. 'When you aren't there he's absolutely insufferable.' She took a deep, troubled breath, considering. 'In fact, I think you should tell Mr Griffon that we can't keep him.'

'Next time I go to the hospital, I'll see what he says,' I said. 'What are you giving him to ride, second lot?'

'Pullitzer,' she replied promptly. 'It doesn't matter so much if he doesn't do as he's told on that one.'

'When you get back, tell him I want to see him before he leaves.'

'Aren't you coming?'

I shook my head. 'I'll stay and see to Indigo.'

'I rather wanted your opinion of Pease Pudding. If he's to run in the Lincoln we ought to give him a trial this week or next. The race is only three weeks on Saturday, don't forget.'

'We could give him a half-speed gallop tomorrow and see if he's ready for a full trial,' I suggested, and she grudgingly agreed that one more day would do no harm.

I watched the trim jodhpured figure walk off towards her cottage for breakfast, and would have felt flattered that she wanted my opinion had I not known why. Under an umbrella, she worked marvellously: out in the open, she felt rudderless. Even though in her heart she knew she knew more than I did, her shelter instinct had cast me as decision maker. What I needed now was a crash course in how to tell when a horse was fit . . . and that old joke about a crash course for pilots edged itself into a corner of my mind, like a thin gleam in the gloom.

Dainsee came back in his Land Rover when the string had gone out for second lot, and we ran the cable for the X-ray machine through the office window and plugged it into the socket which served the mushroom heater. There seemed to be unending reinforcements of cable: it took four lengths plugged together to reach Indigo's box, but their owner assured me that he could manage a quarter of a mile, if pushed.

He took three X-rays of the dangling leg, packed everything up again, and almost as a passing thought, put poor old Indigo out of his troubles.

'You'll want evidence for the police,' Dainsee said, shaking hands and blinking rapidly.

'No . . . I shan't bother the police. Not yet, anyway.'

He opened his mouth to protest, so I went straight on, 'There are very good reasons. I can't tell you them . . . but they do exist.'

'Oh well, it's up to you.' His eyes slid sideways towards Moonrock's box, and his eyebrows asked the question.

'I don't know,' I said. 'What do you think? Looking back.'

He thought for several seconds, which meant he was serious, and then said, 'It would have taken a good heavy blow to smash that hock. Wouldn't have thought anyone would bother, when a pastern like Indigo's would be simple.'

'Moonrock just provided the idea for Indigo?' I suggested.

'I should think so.' He grinned. 'Mind it doesn't become an epidemic.'

'I'll mind,' I said lightly; and knew I would have to.

Alessandro showed no sign that Etty had given him my message about wanting to see him. He strode straight out of the yard towards his waiting car and it was only because I happened to be looking out of the office window that I caught him.

I opened the window and called to him. 'Alessandro, come here a minute . . .'

He forged straight on as if he hadn't heard, so I added, 'To talk about your first races.'

He stopped in one stride with a foot left in the air in indecision, then changed direction and came more slowly towards the window.

'Go round into the owners' room,' I said. 'Where you were lying on the sofa . . .' I shut the window, gave Margaret a whimsical rueful placating smile which could mean whatever she thought it did, and removed myself from earshot.

Alessandro came unwillingly into the owners' room, knowing that he had been hooked. I played fair, however.

'You can have a ride in an apprentice race at Catterick four weeks today. On Pullitzer. And on condition that you don't go bragging about it in the yard and antagonizing all the other boys.'

'I want to ride Archangel,' he said flatly.

'It sometimes seems to me that you are remarkably intelligent and with a great deal of application might become a passable jockey,' I said, and before his self-satisfaction smothered him, added, 'and sometimes, like today, you behave so stupidly and with such little understanding of what it takes to be what you want to be, that your ambitions look pathetic.'

The thin body stiffened rigidly and the black eyes glared. Since I undoubtedly had this full attention, I made the most of it.

'These horses are here to win races. They won't win races if their training programme is hashed up. If you are told to do a half-speed gallop on Clip Clop and you work him flat out and tire him beyond his capacity, you are helping to make sure he takes longer to prepare. You won't win races unless the stable does, so it is in your own interest to help train the horses to the best of your ability. Disobeying riding orders is therefore just plain stupid. Do you follow?'

The black eyes looked blacker and sank into the sockets. He didn't answer.

'Then there is this fixation of yours about Archangel. I'll let you ride him on the Heath as soon as you show you are good enough, and in particular responsible enough, to look after him. Whether you ever ride him in a race is up to you, more than me. But I'm doing you a favour in starting you off on less well-known horses at smaller meetings. You may think you are brilliant, but you have only ridden against amateurs. I am giving you a chance to prove what you can do against professionals in private, and lessening the risk of you falling flat on your face at Newbury or Kempton.'

The eyes were unwavering. He still said nothing.

'And Indigo,' I went on, taking a grip on my anger and turning it out cold and biting, 'Indigo may have been of no use to you because he no longer raced, but if you cause the death of any more of the horses there will be just one less for you to win on.'

He moved his jaw as if with an effort.

'I didn't . . . cause the death of Indigo.'

I took the tin out of my pocket and gave it to him.

He opened it slowly, compressed his mouth at the contents, and read the label.

'I didn't want ... I didn't mean him to kill Indigo.' The supercilious smile had all gone. He was still hostile, but defensive. 'He was angry because Traffic had thrown me.'

'Did you mean him to kill Traffic, then?'

'No, I did not,' he said vehemently. 'As you said, what would be the point of killing a horse I could win a race on?'

'But to kill harmless old Indigo because you bumped your head off a horse you yourself insisted on riding ...' I protested with bitter sarcasm.

His gaze, for the first time, switched to the carpet. Somewhere, deep down, he was not too proud of himself.

'You didn't tell him,' I guessed. 'You didn't tell him that you insisted on riding Traffic.'

'Miss Craig told me to,' he said sullenly.

'Not the time he threw you.'

He looked up again, and I would have sworn he was unhappy. 'I didn't tell my father I was knocked out.'

'Who did?'

'Carlo. The chauffeur.'

'You could have explained that I did not try to harm you.'

The unhappiness turned to a shade of desperation. 'You have met him,' he said. 'It isn't always possible to tell him things, especially when he is angry. He will give me anything I ask for, but I cannot talk to him.'

He went away and left me speechless.

He couldn't talk to his father.

Enso would give Alessandro anything he wanted . . . would smash a path for him at considerable trouble to himself and would persist as long as Alessandro hungered, but they couldn't talk.

And I . . . I could lie and scheme and walk a tight-rope to save my father's stables for him.

But talk with him, no, I couldn't.

CHAPTER EIGHT

'Did you know,' Margaret said, looking up casually from her typewriter, 'that Alessandro is living down the road at the Forbury Inn?'

'No, I didn't,' I said, 'but it doesn't surprise me. It goes with a chauffeur-driven Mercedes, after all.'

'He has a double room to himself with a private bathroom, and doesn't eat enough to keep a bird alive.'

'How do you know all this?'

'Susie brought a friend home from school for tea yesterday and she turned out to be the daughter of the resident receptionist at the Forbury Inn.'

'Any more fascinating intimate details?' I asked.

She smiled. 'Alessandro puts on a track suit every afternoon and goes off in the car and when he comes back he is all sweaty and has a very hot bath with nice smelly oil in it.'

'The receptionist's daughter is how old?'

'Seven.'

'Proper little snooper.'

'All children are observant . . . And she also said that

he never talks to anyone if he can avoid it except to his chauffeur in a funny language . . .'

'Italian,' I murmured.

'. . . and that nobody likes him very much because he is pretty rude, but they like the chauffeur still less because he is even ruder.'

I pondered. 'Do you think,' I said, 'that via your daughter, via her school chum, via her receptionist parent, we could find out if Alessandro gave any sort of home address when he registered?'

'Why don't you just ask him?' she said reasonably.

'Ah,' I said. 'But our Alessandro is sometimes a mite contrary. Didn't you ask him, when you completed his indentures?'

'He said they were moving, and had no address.'

'Mm,' I nodded.

'How extraordinary . . . I can't see why he won't tell you. Well, yes, I'll ask Susie's chum if she knows.'

'Great,' I said, and pinned little hope on it.

Gillie wanted to come and stay at Rowley Lodge.

'How about the homeless orphans?' I said.

'I could take some weeks off. I always can. You know that. And now that you've stopped wandering round industrial towns living in one hotel after another, we could spend a bit more time together.'

I kissed her nose. Ordinarily I would have welcomed her proposal. I looked at her with affection.

'No,' I said. 'Not just now.'

'When, then?'

'In the summer.'

She made a face at me, her eyes full of intelligence. 'You never like to be cluttered when you are deeply involved in something.'

'You're not clutter,' I smiled.

'I'm afraid so ... That's why you've never married. Not like most bachelors because they want to be free to sleep with any offered girl, but because you don't like your mind to be distracted.'

'I'm here,' I pointed out, kissing her again.

'For one night in seven. And only then because you had to come most of the way to see your father.'

'My father gets visited because he's on the way to you.'

'Liar,' she said equably. 'The best you can say is that it's two cats with one stone.'

'Birds.'

'Well, birds, then.'

'Let's go eat,' I said; opened the front door and closed it behind us, and packed her into the Jensen.

'Did you know that Aristotle Onassis had earned himself a whole million by the time he was twenty-eight?'

'No, I didn't know,' I said.

'He beat you,' she said. 'By four times as much.'

'He's four times the man.'

Her eyes slid sideways towards me and a smile hovered in the air. 'He may be.'

We stopped for a red light and then turned left beside a church with a notice board saying, 'These doth the Lord hate: a proud look, a lying tongue. Proverbs 6.16–17.'

'Which proverb do you think is the most stupid?' she asked.

'Um . . . Bird in the hand is worth two in the bush.'

'Why ever?'

'Because if you build a cage round the bush you get a whole flock.'

'As long as the two birds aren't both the same sex.'

'You think of everything,' I said admiringly.

'Oh, I try. I try.'

We went up to the top of the Post Office Tower and revolved three and a half times during dinner.

'It said in *The Times* today that that paper firm you advised last autumn has gone bust,' she said.

'Well . . .' I grinned. 'They didn't take my advice.'

'Silly old them . . . What was it?'

'To sack ninety per cent of the management, get some new accountants, and make peace with the unions.'

'So simple, really.' Her mouth twitched.

'They said they couldn't do it, of course.'

'And you said?'

'Prepare to meet thy doom.'

'How biblical.'

'Or words to that effect.'

'Think of all those poor people thrown out of work,' she said. 'It can't be funny when a firm goes bust.'

'The firm had hired people all along in the wrong proportions. By last autumn they had only two productive workers for every one on the clerical, executive and maintenance staff. Also, the unions were vetoing automation, and insisting that every time a worker left another should be hired in his place.'

She pensively bit into pate and toast. 'It doesn't sound as if it could have been saved at all.'

'Yes, it could,' I said reflectively, 'but it often seems to me that people in a firm would rather see the whole ship sink than throw out half of the crew and stay afloat.'

'Fairer to everyone if they all drown?'

'Only the firm drowns. The people swim off and make sure they overload someone else's raft.'

She licked her fingers. 'You used to find sick firms fascinating.'

'I still do,' I said, surprised.

She shook her head. 'Disillusion has been creeping in for a long time.'

I looked back, considering. 'It's usually quite easy to see what's wrong. But there's often a stone-wall resistance on both sides to putting it right. Always dozens of reasons why change is impossible.'

'Russell Arletti rang me up yesterday,' she said casually.

'Did he really?'

She nodded. 'He wanted me to persuade you to leave Newmarket and do a job for him. A big one, he said.'

'I can't,' I said positively.

'He's taking me out to dinner on Tuesday evening to discuss, as he put it, how to wean you from the gee-gees.'

'Tell him to save himself the price of a meal.'

'Well, no . . .' she wrinkled her nose. 'I might just be hungry again by Tuesday. I'll go out with him. I like him. But I think I'll spend the evening preparing him for the worst.'

'What worst?'

'That you won't ever be going back to work for him.'

'Gillie . . .'

'It was only a phase,' she said, looking out of the window at the sparkle of the million lights slowly sliding by below us. 'It was just that you'd cashed in your antique chips and you weren't exactly starving, and Russell netted you on the wing, so to speak, with an interesting diversion. But you've been getting tired of it recently. You've been restless, and too full of . . . I don't know . . . too full of power. I think that after you've played with the gee-gees you'll break out in a great gust and build a new empire . . . much bigger than before.'

'Have some wine?' I said ironically.

'. . . and you may scoff, Neil Griffon, but you've been letting your Onassis instinct go to rust.'

'Not a bad thing, really.'

'You could be creating jobs for thousands of people, instead of trotting round a small town in a pair of jodhpurs.'

'There's six million quids' worth in that stable,' I said slowly; and felt the germ of an idea lurch as it sometimes did across the ganglions.

'What are you thinking about?' she demanded, later. 'What are you thinking about at this moment?'

'The genesis of ideas.'

She gave a sigh that was half a laugh. 'And that's exactly why you'll never marry me, either.'

'What do you mean?'

'You like the *Times* crossword more than sex.'

'Not more,' I said. 'First.'

'Do you want me to marry you?'

She kissed my shoulder under the sheet.

'Would you?'

'I thought you were fed up with marriage.' I moved my mouth against her forehead. 'I thought Jeremy had put you off it for life.'

'He wasn't like you.'

He wasn't like you . . . She said it often. Any time her husband's name cropped up. He wasn't like you.

The first time she said it, three months after I met her, I asked the obvious question.

'What was he like?'

'Fair, not dark. Willowy, not compact. A bit taller: six feet two. Outwardly more fun; inwardly, infinitely more boring. He didn't want a wife so much as an admiring audience . . . and I got tired of the play.' She paused. 'And when Jennifer died . . .'

She had not talked about her ex-husband before, and had always shied painfully away from the thought of her daughter. She went on in a careful emotionless quiet voice, half muffled against my skin.

'Jennifer was killed in front of me . . . by a youth in a leather jacket on a motorcycle. We were crossing the road. He came roaring round the corner doing sixty in a built-up area. He just . . . ploughed into her . . .' A long shuddering pause. 'She was eight . . . and super.' She swallowed. 'The boy had no insurance . . . Jeremy raved on and on about it, as if money could have compensated . . . and we didn't need money, he'd inherited almost as much as I had . . .' Another pause. 'So, anyway, after that, when he found someone else and drifted off, I was glad, really . . .'

Though passing time had done its healing, she still had dreams about Jennifer. Sometimes she cried when she woke up, because of Jennifer.

I smoothed her shining hair. 'I'd make a lousy husband.'

'Oh . . .' She took a shaky breath. 'I know that. Two and a half years I've known you, and you've blown in every millennium or so, to say hi.'

'But stayed a while.'

'I'll grant you.'

'So what do you want?' I asked. 'Would you rather be married?'

She smiled contentedly. 'We'll go on as we are . . . if you like.'

'I do like,' I switched off the light.

'As long as you prove it now and again,' she added unnecessarily.

'I wouldn't let anyone else', I said, 'hang pink and green curtains against ochre walls in my bedroom.'

'My bedroom. I rent it.'

'You're in arrears. By at least eighteen months.'

'I'll pay up tomorrow . . . Hey, what are you doing?'

'I'm a businessman,' I murmured. 'Getting down to business.'

Neville Knollys Griffon did not make it easy for me to start a new era in father–son relationships.

He told me that as I did not seem to be making much progress in engaging someone else to take over the stable, he was going to find someone himself. By telephone.

He said he had done some of the entries for the next two weeks, and that Margaret was to type them out and send them off.

He said that Pease Pudding was to be taken out of the Lincoln.

He said that I had brought him the '64 half bottles of Bollinger, and he preferred the '61.

'You are feeling better, then,' I said into the first real gap of the monologue.

'What? Oh yes, I suppose I am. Now did you hear what I said? Pease Pudding is not to go in the Lincoln.'

'Why ever not?'

He gave me an irritated look. 'How do you expect him to be ready?'

'Etty is a good judge. She says he will be.'

'I will not have Rowley Lodge made to look stupid by running hopelessly under-trained horses in important races.'

'If Pease Pudding runs badly, people will only say that it shows how good a trainer you are yourself.'

'That is not the point,' he said repressively.

I opened one of the half bottles and poured the golden bubbles into his favourite Jacobean glass, which I had brought for the purpose. Champagne would not have tasted right to him from a tooth mug. He took a sip and evidently found the '64 was bearable after all, though he didn't say so.

'The point', he explained as if to a moron, 'is the stud fees. If he runs badly, his future value at stud is what will be affected.'

'Yes, I understand that.'

'Don't be silly, how can you? You know nothing about it.'

I sat down in the visitors' armchair, leant back,

crossed my legs, and put into my voice all the reasonableness and weight which I had learned to project into industrial discussions, but which I had never before had the sense to use on my father.

'Rowley Lodge is heading for some financial rocks,' I said, 'and the cause of it is too much prestige-hunting. You are scared of running Pease Pudding in the Lincoln because you own a half share in him, and if he runs badly it will be your own capital investment, as well as Lady Vector's, that will suffer.'

He spilled some champagne on his sheet, and didn't notice it.

I went on, 'I know that it is quite normal for people to own shares in the horses they train. At Rowley Lodge just now, however, you own too many part shares for safety. I imagine you collected so many because you could not bear to see rival stables acquiring what you judged to be the next crop of world beaters, so that you probably said to your owners something like, "If Archangel goes for forty thousand at auction and that's too much for you, I'll put up twenty thousand towards it." So you've gathered together one of the greatest strings in the country, and their potential stud value is enormous.'

He gazed at me blankly, forgetting to drink.

'This is fine,' I said, 'as long as the horses do win as expected. And year after year, they do. You've been pursuing this policy in moderation for a very long time, and it's made you steadily richer. But now, this year, you've over-extended. You've bought too many. As all the part owners only pay part training fees, the receipts are not now covering the expenses. Not by quite a long way. As a result the cash balance at the bank is draining away like bathwater, and there are still three weeks to go before the first race, let alone the resale of the unsuccessful animals for stud. This dicey situation is complicated by your broken leg, your assistant being still in a coma from which he is unlikely to recover, and your stable apparently stagnating in the hands of a son who doesn't know how to train the horses; and all that is why you are scared silly of running Pease Pudding in the Lincoln.'

I stopped for reactions. There weren't any. Just shock.

'You can, on the whole, stop worrying,' I said, and knew that things would never again be quite as they had been between us. Thirty-four, I thought ruefully; I had to be thirty-four before I entered this particular arena on equal terms. 'I could sell your half share before the race.'

Wheels slowly began to turn again behind his eyes. He blinked. Stared at his sloping champagne and straightened the glass. Tightened the mouth into an echo of the old autocracy.

'How ... how did you know all this?' There was more resentment in his voice than anxiety.

'I looked at the account books.'

'No ... I mean, who told you?'

'No one needed to tell me. My job for the last six years has involved reading account books and doing sums.'

He recovered enough to take some judicious sips.

'At least you do understand why it is imperative we get an experienced trainer to take over until I can get about again.'

'There's no need for one,' I said incautiously. 'I've been there for three weeks now . . .'

'And do you suppose that you can learn how to train racehorses in three weeks?' he asked with reviving contempt.

'Since you ask,' I said, 'yes.' And before he turned purple, tacked on, 'I was born to it, if you remember . . . I grew up there. I find, much to my own surprise, that it is second nature.'

He saw this statement more as a threat than as a reassurance. 'You're not staying on after I get back.'

'No.' I smiled. 'Nothing like that.'

He grunted. Hesitated. Gave in. He didn't say in so many words that I could carry on, but just ignored the whole subject from that point.

'I don't want to sell my half of Pease Pudding.'

'Draw up a list of those you don't mind selling, then,' I said. 'About ten of them, for a start.'

'And just who do you think is going to buy them? New owners don't grow on trees, you know. And half shares are harder to sell . . . owners like to see their names in the race cards and in the press.'

136

'I know a lot of businessmen,' I said, 'who would be glad to have a racehorse but who actively shun the publicity. You pick out ten horses, and I'll sell your half shares.'

He didn't say he would, but he did, then and there. I ran my eye down the finished list and saw only one to disagree with.

'Don't sell Lancat,' I said.

He bristled. 'I know what I'm doing.'

'He's going to be good as a three-year-old,' I said. 'I see from the form book that he was no great shakes at two, and if you sell now you'll not get back what you paid. He's looking very well, and I think he'll win quite a lot.'

'Rubbish. You don't know what you're talking about.'

'All right . . . how much would you accept for your half?'

He pursed his lips, thinking about it. 'Four thousand. You should be able to get four, with his breeding. He cost twelve, altogether, as a yearling.'

'You'd better suggest prices for all of them,' I said. 'If you wouldn't mind.'

He didn't mind. I folded the list, put it in my pocket, picked up the entry forms he had written on, and prepared to go. He held out to me the champagne glass, empty.

'Have some of this . . . I can't manage it all.'

I took the glass, refilled it, and drank a mouthful.

The bubbles popped round my teeth. He watched. His expression was as severe as ever, but he nodded, sharply, twice. Not as symbolic a gesture as a pipe of peace, but just as much of an acknowledgement, in its way.

On Monday morning, tapping away, Margaret said, 'Susie's friend's mum says she has just happened to see Alessandro's passport.'

'Which just happened', I said drily, 'to be well hidden away in Alessandro's bedroom.'

'Let us not stare at gift horses.'

'Let us not,' I agreed.

'Susie's friend's mum says that the address on the passport was not in Italy, but in Switzerland. A place called Bastagnola. Is that any use?'

'I hope Susie's friend's mum won't lose her job.'

'I doubt it,' Margaret said. 'She hops into bed with the manager, when his wife goes shopping in Cambridge.'

'How do you know?'

Her eyes laughed. 'Susie's friend told me.'

I telephoned to an importer of cameras who owed me a favour and asked him if he had any contacts in the town of Bastagnola.

'Not myself. But I could establish one, if it's important.'

'I want any information anyone can dig up about

a man called Enso Rivera. As much information as possible.'

He wrote it down and spelled it back. 'See what I can do,' he said.

He rang two days later and sounded subdued.

'I'll be sending you an astronomical bill for European phone calls.'

'That's all right.'

'An awful lot of people didn't want to talk about your man. I met an exceptional amount of resistance.'

'Is he Mafia, then?' I asked.

'No. Not Mafia. In fact, he and the Mafia are not on speaking terms. On stabbing terms, maybe, but not speaking. There seems to be some sort of truce between them.' He paused.

'Go on,' I said.

'Well . . . As far as I can gather . . . and I wouldn't swear to it . . . he is a sort of receiver of stolen property. Most of it in the form of currency, but some gold and silver and precious stones from melted-down jewellery. I heard . . . and it was at third hand from a high-up policeman, so you can believe it or not as you like . . . that Rivera accepts the stuff, sells or exchanges it, takes a large commission, and banks the rest in Swiss accounts which he opens up for his clients. They can collect their money any time they like . . . and it is believed that he has an almost worldwide connection.

But all this goes on behind a supposedly legitimate business as a dealer in watches. They've never managed to bring him to court. They can never get witnesses to testify.'

'You've done marvels,' I said.

'There's a bit more.' He cleared his throat. 'He has a son, apparently, that no one cares to cross. Rivera has been known to ruin people who don't immediately do what the son wants. He only has this one child. He is reputed to have deserted his wife . . . well, a lot of Italian men do that . . .'

'He is Italian, then?'

'By birth, yes. He's lived in Switzerland for about fifteen years, though. Look, I don't know if you're intending to do business with him, but I got an unmistakable warning from several people to steer clear of him. They say he's dangerous. They say if you fall foul of him you wake up dead. Either that, or . . . well, I know you'll laugh . . . but there's a sort of superstition that if he looks your way you'll break a bone.'

I didn't laugh. Not a chuckle.

Almost as soon as I put the receiver down the telephone rang again.

Dainsee.

'I've got your X-ray pictures in front of me,' he said. 'But they're inconclusive, I'm afraid. It just looks a pretty ordinary fracture. There's a certain amount of longitudinal splitting, but then there often is with cannon-bones.'

'What would be the simplest way to break a bone on purpose?' I asked.

'Twist it,' he said promptly. 'Put it under stress. A bone under stress would snap quite easily if you gave it a bang. Ask any footballer or any skater. Stress, that's what does it.'

'You can't see stress on the X-rays . . .'

'Afraid not. Can't rule it out, though. Can't rule it in, either. Sorry.'

'It can't be helped.'

'But the blood test,' he said. 'I've had the results, and you were bang on target.'

'Anaesthetic?'

'Yep. Some brand of promazine. Sparine, probably.'

'I'm no wiser,' I said. 'How would you give it to a horse?'

'Injection,' Dainsee said promptly. 'Very simple intra-muscular injection, nothing difficult. Just punch the needle in anywhere handy. It's often used to shoot into mania patients in mental hospitals, when they're raving. Puts them out for hours.'

Something about promazine rung a highly personal note.

'Does the stuff work instantly?' I asked.

'If you give it intravenously, it would. But intramuscularly, what it's equally designed for, it would take a few minutes, probably. Ten to fifteen minutes on a human; don't know for a horse.'

'If you injected it into a human, could you do it through clothes?'

'Oh sure. Like I said. They use it as a standby in mental hospitals. They wouldn't get people in a manic state to sit nice and quiet and roll their sleeves up.'

CHAPTER NINE

For three weeks the status at Rowley Lodge remained approximately quo.

I heavily amended my father's entry forms and sent them in, and sold six of the half-shares to various acquaintances, without offering Lancat to any of them.

Margaret took to wearing green eye shadow, and Susie's friend reported that Alessandro had made a telephone call to Switzerland and didn't wear pyjamas. Also that the chauffeur always paid for everything, as Alessandro didn't have any money.

Etty grew more tense as the beginning of the season drew nearer, and lines of anxiety seldom left her forehead. I was leaving a great deal more to her judgement than my father did, and she was in consequence feeling insecure. She openly ached for his return.

The horses, all the same, were working well. We had no further mishaps except that a two-year-old filly developed severe sinus trouble, and, as far as I could judge from watching the performances of the other forty-five stables using Newmarket Heath, the Rowley Lodge string was as forward as any.

Alessandro turned up day after day and silently rode what and how Etty told him to, though with a ramrod spine of protest. He said no more about not taking orders from a woman, and I imagined that even he could see that without Etty there would be fewer winners on the horizon. She herself had almost stopped complaining about him and was watching him with a more objective eye; because there was no doubt that after a month's concentrated practice he was riding better than the other apprentices.

He was also growing visibly thinner, and no longer looked well. Small-framed though he might be, the six stone seven pounds that he was aiming to shrink his body down to was punitive for five foot four.

Alessandro's fanaticism was an awkward factor. If I had imagined that by making the going as rough as I dared he would give up his idle fancy and depart, I had been wrong. This was no idle fancy. It was revealing itself all too clearly as a consuming ambition: an ambition strong enough to make him starve himself, take orders from a woman, and perform what were evidently miracles of self-discipline, considering that it was probably the first time in his life that he had had to use any.

Against Etty's wishes I put him one morning on Archangel.

'He's not ready for that,' she protested, when I told her I was going to.

'There isn't another lad in the yard who will take more care of him,' I said.

'But he hasn't the experience.'

'He has, you know. Archangel is only more valuable, not more difficult to ride, than the others.'

Alessandro received the news not with joy but with an 'at last' expression, more scorn than patience. We went down to the Waterhall canter, away from public gaze, and there Archangel did a fast six furlongs and pulled up looking as if he had just walked out of his box.

'He had him balanced,' I said to Etty. 'All the way.'

'Yes, he did,' she said grudgingly. 'Pity he's such an obnoxious little squirt.'

Alessandro returned with an 'I told you so' face which I wiped off by saying he would be switched to Lancat tomorrow.

'Why?' he demanded furiously. 'I rode Archangel very well.'

'Well enough,' I agreed. 'And you can ride him again, in a day or two. But I want you to ride Lancat in a trial on Wednesday, so you can go out on him tomorrow as well, and get used to him. And after the trial I want you to tell me your opinion of the horse and how he went. And I don't want one of your short sneering comments but a thought-out assessment. It is almost as important for a jockey to be able to analyse what a horse has done in a race as ride it. Trainers depend quite a lot on what their jockeys can tell them. So you can tell me about Lancat, and I'll listen.'

He gave me a long concentrating stare, but for once without the habitual superciliousness.

'All right,' he said. 'I will.'

We held the trial on the Wednesday afternoon on the trial ground past the Limekilns, a long way out of Newmarket. Much to Etty's disgust, because she wanted to watch it on television, I had timed the trial to start at exactly the same moment as the Champion Hurdle at Cheltenham. But the stratagem worked. We achieved the well-nigh impossible, a full-scale trial without an observer or a tout in sight.

Apart from the two Etty and I rode, we took only four horses along there: Pease Pudding, Lancat, Archangel, and one of the previous year's most prolific winners, a four-year-old colt called Subito, whose best distance was a mile. Tommy Hoylake drove up from his home in Berkshire to ride Pease Pudding, and we put Andy on Archangel and a taciturn lad called Faddy on the chestnut Subito.

'Don't murder them,' I said, before they started. 'If you feel them falter, just ease off.'

Four nods. Four fidgeting colts, glossy and eager.

Etty and I hacked round to within a hundred yards of where the trial ground ended, and, when we had pulled up in a useful position for watching, she waved a large white handkerchief above her head. The horses started towards us, moving fast and still accelerating, with the riders crouched forward on their withers, heads down, reins very short, feet against the horses' moving shoulders.

They passed us still going all out, and pulled up a little further on. Archangel and Pease Pudding ran the whole gallop stride for stride and finished together. Lancat, from starting level, lost ten lengths, made up eight, lost two again, but still moved easily. Subito was ahead of Lancat at the beginning, behind him when he moved up quickly, and alongside when they passed Etty and me.

She turned to me with a deeply worried expression.

'Pease Pudding can't be ready for the Lincoln if Lancat can finish so near him. In fact the way Lancat finished means that neither Archangel nor Subito is as far on as I thought.'

'Calm down, Etty,' I said. 'Relax. Take it easy. Just turn it the other way round.'

She frowned. 'I don't understand you. Mr Griffon will be very worried when he hears . . .'

'Etty,' I interrupted. 'Did Pease Pudding, or did he not, seem to you to be moving fast and easily?'

'Well, yes, I suppose so,' she said doubtfully.

'Then it may be Lancat who is much better then you expected, not the others which are worse.'

She looked at me with a face screwed up with indecision. 'But Alex is only an apprentice, and Lancat was useless last year.'

'In what way was he useless?'

'Oh . . . sprawly. Babyish. Had no action.'

'Nothing sprawly about him today,' I pointed out.

'No,' she admitted slowly. 'You're right. There wasn't.'

The riders walked towards us, leading the horses, and Etty and I both dismounted to hear more easily what they had to say. Tommy Hoylake, built like a twelve-year-old boy with a forty-three-year-old man's face sitting incongruously on top, said in his comfortable Berkshire accent that he had thought that Pease Pudding had run an excellent trial until he saw Lancat pulling up so close behind him. He had ridden Lancat a good deal the previous year, and hadn't thought much of him.

Andy said Archangel went beautifully, considering the Guineas was nearly six weeks away, and Faddy in his high-pitched finicky voice said Subito had only been a pound or two behind Pease Pudding last year in his opinion, and he could have been nearer to him if he had really tried. Tommy and Andy shook their heads. If they had really tried, they too could have gone faster.

'Alessandro?' I said.

He hesitated. 'I . . . I lost ground at the beginning because I didn't realize . . . I didn't expect them to go so fast. When I asked him, Lancat just shot forward . . . and I could have kept him nearer to Archangel at the end, only he did seem to tire a bit, and you said . . .' He stopped with his voice, so to speak, on one foot.

'Good,' I said. 'You did right.' I hadn't expected him to be so honest. For the first time since his arrival he had made an objective self-assessment, but my faint and even slightly patronizing praise was enough to bring back the smirk. Etty looked at him with uncontrolled dislike, which didn't disturb Alessandro one little bit.

'I hardly need to remind you', I said to all of them, ignoring the displayed emotions, 'to keep this afternoon's doings to yourselves. Tommy, you can count on Pease Pudding in the Lincoln and Archangel in the Guineas, and if you'll come back to the office now we'll go through your other probable rides for the next few weeks.'

Alessandro's smirk turned sour, and the look he cast on Tommy was pure Rivera. Actively dangerous: inured to murder. Any appearance he might have given of being even slightly tamed was suddenly as reliable as sunlight on quicksand. I remembered the unequivocal message of Enso's gun pointing at my chest; that if killing seemed desirable, killing would quite casually be done. I had put Tommy Hoylake in jeopardy, and I'd have to get him out.

I sent the others on ahead and told Alessandro to stay for a minute. When the others were too far away to hear, I said, 'You will have to accept that Tommy Hoylake will be riding as first jockey to the stable.'

I got the full stare treatment, black, wide, and ill-intentioned. I could almost feel the hate which flowed out of him like hot waves across the cool March air.

'If Tommy Hoylake breaks his leg,' I said clearly, 'I'll break yours.'

It shook him, though he tried not to show it.

'Also, it would be pointless to put Tommy Hoylake out of action, as I would then engage someone else. Not you. Is that clear?'

He didn't answer.

'If you want to be a top jockey, you've got to do it yourself. You've got to be good enough. You've got to fight your own battles. It's no good thinking your father will destroy everyone who stands in your way. If you are good enough, no one will stand in your way; and if you are not, no amount of ruining others will make you.'

Still no sound. But fury, yes. Signifying all too much.

I said seriously, 'If Tommy Hoylake comes to any harm whatsoever, I will see that you never ride in another race. At whatever consequence to myself.'

He removed the stare from my face and scattered it over the wide windy spread of the Heath.

'I am accustomed . . .' he began arrogantly, and then stopped.

'I know to what you are accustomed,' I said. 'To having your own way at any expense to others. Your own way, bought in misery, pain and fear. Well . . . you should have settled for something which could be paid for. No amount of death and destruction will buy you ability.'

'All I wanted was to ride Archangel in the Derby,' he said defensively.

'Just like that? Just a whim?'

He turned his head towards Lancat and gathered together the reins. 'It started like that,' he said indistinctly, and walked away from me in the direction of Newmarket.

He came and rode out as usual the following morning and all the days after. News that the trial had taken place got around, and I heard that I had chosen the time of the Champion Hurdle so that I could keep the unfit state of Pease Pudding decently concealed. The ante-post price lengthened and I put a hundred pounds on him at twenty to one.

My father shook the *Sporting Life* at me in a rage and insisted that the horse should be withdrawn.

'Have a bid on him instead,' I said. 'I have.'

'You don't know what you're doing.'

'Yes, I do.'

'It says here ...' He was practically stuttering with the frustration of not being able to get out of bed and thwart me. 'It says here that if the trial was unsatisfactory, nothing more could be expected, with me away.'

'I read it,' I agreed. 'That's just a guess. And it wasn't unsatisfactory, if you want to know. It was very encouraging.'

'You're crazy,' he said loudly. 'You're ruining the stable. I won't have it. I won't have it, do you hear?'

He glared at me. A hot amber glare, not a cold black one. It made a change.

'I'll send Tommy Hoylake to see you,' I said. 'You can ask him what he thinks.'

Three days before the racing season started I walked into the office at two-thirty to see if Margaret wanted me to sign any letters before she left to collect her children, and found Alessandro in there with her, sitting on the edge of her desk. He was wearing a navy-blue track suit and heavy white running shoes, and his black hair had crisped into curls from the dampness of his own sweat.

She was looking up at him with obvious arousal, her face slightly flushed as if someone had given all her senses a friction rub.

She caught sight of me before he did, as he had his back to the door. She looked away from him in confusion, and he turned to see who had disturbed them.

There was a smile on the thin sallow face. A real smile, warm and uncomplicated, wrinkling the skin round the eyes and lifting the upper lip to show good teeth. For two seconds I saw an Alessandro I wouldn't

have guessed existed, and then the light went out inside
and the facial muscles gradually reshaped themselves
into the familiar lines of wariness and annoyance.

He slid his slight weight to the ground and wiped
away with a thumb some of the sweat which stood out
on his forehead and trickled down in front of his ears.

'I want to know what horses I am going to ride this
week at Doncaster,' he said. 'Now that the season is
starting, you can give me horses to race.'

Margaret looked at him in astonishment, for he had
sounded very much the boss. I answered him in a
manner and tone carefully lacking in both apology and
aggression.

'We have only one entry at Doncaster, which is
Pease Pudding in the Lincoln on Saturday, and Tommy
Hoylake rides it,' I said. 'And the reason we have only
one entry', I went straight on, as I saw the anger stoking
up at what he believed to be a blocking movement on
my part, 'is that my father was involved in a motor
accident the week these entries should have been made,
and they were never sent in.'

'Oh,' he said blankly.

'Still,' I said, 'it would be a good idea for you to go
every day to the races, to see what goes on, so that you
don't make any crashing mistakes next week.'

I didn't add that I intended to do the same myself.
It never did to show all your weaknesses to the
opposition.

'You can start on Pullitzer on Wednesday at Catterick,' I said. 'After that, it's up to you.'

There was a flash of menace in the black eyes.

'No,' he said, a bite in his voice. 'It's up to my father.'

He turned abruptly on one toe and without looking back trotted out of the office into the yard, swerved left and set off at a steady jog up the drive towards Bury Road. We watched him through the window, Margaret with a smile tinged with puzzlement and I with more apprehension than I liked.

'He ran all the way to the Boy's Grave and back,' she said. 'He says he weighed six stone twelve before he set off today, and he's lost twenty-two pounds since he came here. That sounds an awful lot, doesn't it? Twenty-two pounds, for someone as small as him.

'Severe,' I said, nodding.

'He's strong, though. Like wire.'

'You like him,' I said, making it hover on the edge of a question.

She gave me a quick glance. 'He's interesting.'

I slouched into the swivel chair and read through the letters she pushed across to me. All of them in economic, good English, perfectly typed.

'If we win the Lincoln,' I said. 'You can have a raise.'

'Thanks very much.' A touch of irony. 'I hear the *Sporting Life* doesn't think much of my chances.'

I signed three of the letters and started reading the fourth. 'Does Alessandro often call in?' I asked casually.

'First time he's done it.'

'What did he want?' I asked.

'I don't think he wanted anything, particularly. He said he was going past, and just came in.'

'What did you talk about?'

She looked surprised at the question but answered without comment.

'I asked him if he liked the Forbury Inn and he said he did, it was much more comfortable than a house his father had rented on the outskirts of Cambridge. He said anyway his father had given up that house now and gone back home to do some business.' She paused, thinking back, the memory of his company making her eyes smile, and I reflected that the house at Cambridge must have been where the rubber-faces took me, and that there was now no point in speculating more about it.

'I asked him if he had always liked riding horses and he said yes, and I asked him what his ambitions were and he said to win the Derby and be Champion Jockey, and I said that there wasn't an apprentice born who didn't want that.'

I turned my head to glance at her. 'He said he wanted to be Champion Jockey?'

'That's right.'

I stared gloomily down at my shoes. The skirmish had been a battle, the battle was in danger of becoming war, and now it looked as if hostilities could crackle on for months. Escalation seemed to be setting in in a big way.

'Did he', I asked, 'ask you anything?'

'No. At least . . . yes, I suppose he did.' She seemed surprised, thinking about it.

'What?'

'He asked if you or your father owned any of the horses . . . I told him your father had half shares in some of them, and he said did he own any of them outright. I said Buckram was the only one . . . and he said . . .' She frowned, concentrating, 'He said he supposed it would be insured like the others, and I said it wasn't, actually, because Mr Griffon had cut back on his premiums this year, so he'd better be extra careful with it on the roads . . .' She suddenly sounded anxious. 'There wasn't any harm in telling him, was there? I mean, I didn't think there was anything secret about Mr Griffon owning Buckram.'

'There isn't,' I said comfortingly. 'It runs in his name, for a start. It's public knowledge that he owns it.'

She looked relieved and the lingering smile crept back round her eyes, and I didn't tell her that it was the bit about insurance that I found disturbing.

One of the firms I had advised in their troubles were assemblers of electronic equipment. Since they had in fact reorganized themselves from top to bottom and were now delighting their shareholders, I rang up their chief executive and asked for help for myself.

Urgently, I said. In fact, today. And it was half past three already.

A sharp 'phew' followed by some tongue clicking, and the offer came. If I would drive towards Coventry, their Mr Wallis would meet me at Kettering. He would bring what I wanted with him, and explain how I was to install it, and would that do?

It would do very well indeed, I said: and did the chief executive happen to be in need of half a racehorse?

He laughed. On the salary cut I had persuaded him to take? I must be joking, he said.

Our Mr Wallis, all of nineteen, met me in a business-like truck and blinded me with science. He repeated the instructions clearly and twice, and then obviously doubted whether I could carry them out. To him the vagaries of the photoelectric effect were home ground, but he also realized that to the average fool they were not. He went over it again to make sure I understood.

'What is your position with the firm?' I asked in the end.

'Deputy Sales Manager,' he said happily, 'and they tell me I have you to thank.'

I quite easily, after the lecture, installed the early warning system at Rowley Lodge: basically a photoelectric cell linked to an alarm buzzer. After dark, when everything was quiet, I hid the necessary ultra-violet light source in the flowering plant in a tub which stood against the end wall of the four outside boxes, and the cell itself I camouflaged in a rose bush outside the office window. The cable from this led through the office window, across the lobby and into the owner's room, with a switch box handy to the sofa.

Soon after I had finished rigging it, Etty walked into the yard from her cottage for her usual last look round before going to bed, and the buzzer rasped out loud and clear. Too loud, I thought. A silent intruder might just hear it. I put a cushion over it, and the muffled buzz sounded like a bumble bee caught in a drawer.

I switched the noise off. When Etty left the yard it started again immediately. Hurrah for the Deputy Sales Manager, I thought, and slept in the owner's room with my head on the cushion.

No one came.

Stiffly at six o'clock I got up and rolled up the cable, and collected and stowed all the gear in a cupboard in the owners' room; and when the first of the lads ambled yawning into the yard, I headed directly to the coffee pot.

Tuesday night, no one came.

Wednesday, Margaret mentioned that Susie's friend had reported two Swiss phone calls, one outgoing by Alessandro, one incoming to the chauffeur.

Etty, more anxious than ever with the Lincoln only three days away, was snapping at the lads, and Alessan-

dro stayed behind after second exercise and asked me
if I had reconsidered and would put him up on Pease
Pudding in place of Tommy Hoylake.

We were outside, in the yard, with the late morning
bustle going on all around. Alessandro looked tense
and hollow-eyed.

'You must know I can't,' I said reasonably.

'My father says I am to tell you that you must.'

I slowly shook my head. 'For your own sake, you
shouldn't. If you rode it, you would make a fool of
yourself. Is that what your father wants?'

'He says I must insist.' He was adamant.

'OK,' I said. 'You've insisted. But Tommy Hoylake
is going to ride.'

'But you must do what my father says,' he protested.

I smiled at him faintly, but didn't answer, and he did
not seem to know what to say next.

'Next week, though,' I said matter-of-factly, 'you can
ride Buckram in a race at Aintree. I entered him there
especially for you. He won first time out last year, so
he should have a fair chance again this time.'

He just stared; didn't even blink. If there was anything to be given away, he didn't give it.

At three o'clock Thursday morning the buzzer went
off with enthusiasm three inches from my ear drum
and I nearly fell off the sofa. I switched off the noise and

got to my feet, and took a look into the yard through the owners' room window.

Moving quickly through the moonless night went one single small light, very faint, directed at the ground. Then, as I watched, it swung round, paused on some of the boxes in bay four and settled inexorably on the one which housed Buckram.

Treacherous little bastard, I thought. Finding out which horse he could kill without the owner wailing a complaint; an uninsured horse, in order to kick Rowley Lodge the harder in the financial groin.

Telling him Buckram might win him a race hadn't stopped him. Treacherous, callous little bastard . . .

I was out through the ready left-ajar doors and down the yard, moving silently on rubber shoes. I heard the bolts drawn quietly back and the doors squeak on their hinges, and homed in on the small flickering light with far from charitable intentions.

No point in wasting time. I swept my hand down on the switch and flooded Buckram's box with a hundred watts.

I took in at a glance the syringe held in a stunned second of suspended animation in the gloved hand, and noticed the truncheon lying on the straw just inside the door.

It wasn't Alessandro. Too heavy. Too tall. The figure turning purposefully towards me, dressed in black from neck to foot, was one of the rubber-faces.

In his rubber face.

CHAPTER TEN

This time I didn't waste my precious advantage. I sprang straight at him and chopped with all my strength at the wrist of the hand that held the syringe.

A direct hit. The hand flew backwards, the fingers opened, and the syringe spun away through the air.

I kicked his shin and punched him in the stomach, and when his head came forward I grabbed hold of it and swung him with a crash against the wall.

Buckram kicked up a fuss and stamped around loose, as rubber-face had not attempted to put the head-collar on. When rubber-face rushed at me with jabbing fists I caught hold of his clothes and threw him against Buckram, who snapped at him with his teeth.

A muffled sound came through the rubber, which I declined to interpret as an appeal for peace. Once away from the horse he came at me again, shoulders hunched, head down, arms stretching forwards. I stepped straight into his grasp, ignored a bash in my short ribs, put my arm tight round his neck, and banged his head on the nearest wall. The legs turned to latex to match the face, and the lids palely shut inside the eye-holes. I gave him another small crack against the wall to remove any lingering doubts, and stood back a pace. He lay feebly in the angle between floor and wall, one hand twisting slowly forwards and backwards across the straw.

I tied up Buckram, who by some miracle had not pushed his way out of the unbolted door and roused the neighbourhood, and in stepping away from the tethering ring nearly put my foot right down on the scattered syringe. It lay under the manger, in the straw, and had survived undamaged through the rumpus.

Picking it up I tossed it lightly in my hand and decided that the gifts of the gods should not be wasted. Pulling up the sleeve of rubber-face's black jersey, I pushed the needle firmly into his arm and gave him the benefit of half the contents. Prudence, not compassion, stopped me from squirting in the lot: it might be that what the syringe held was a flattener for a horse but curtains for a man, and murdering was not going to help.

I pulled off rubber-face's rubber face. Underneath it was Carlo. Surprise, surprise.

The prizes of war now amounted to one rubber mask, one half-empty syringe, and one bone-breaking truncheon. After a slight pause for thought I wiped my fingerprints off the syringe, removed Carlo's gloves, and planted his all over it; both hands. A similar liberal sprinkling went on to the truncheon: then, using the gloves to hold them with, I took the two incriminating articles up to the house and hid them temporarily in a lacquered box under a dust-sheet in one of the ten unused bedrooms.

From the window on the stairs on the way down I caught an impression of a large pale shape in the drive near the gate. Went to look, to make sure. No mistake: the Mercedes.

Back in Buckram's box, Carlo slept peacefully, totally out. I felt his pulse, which was slow but regular, and looked at my watch. Not yet three thirty. Extraordinary.

Carrying Carlo to the car looked too much of a chore, so I went and fetched the car to Carlo. The engine started with a click and a purr, and made too little noise in the yard even to disturb the horses. Leaving the engine running I opened both rear doors and lugged Carlo in backwards. I had intended to do him the courtesy of the back seat, since he had done as much for me, but he fell limply to the floor. I bent his knees up, as he lay on his back, and gently shut him in.

As far as I could tell no one saw our arrival at the Forbury Inn. I parked the Mercedes next to the other cars near the front door, switched off the engine and the side lights, and quietly went away.

By the time I had walked the near mile home, collected the rubber mask from Buckram's box, dismantled the electronic eye and stowed it in the cupboard, it was too late to bother with going to bed.

I slept for an hour or so more on the sofa and woke up feeling dead tired and not a bit full of energy for the first day of the races.

Alessandro arrived late, on foot, and worried.

I watched him, first through the office window and then from the owners' room, as he made his way down into the yard. He hovered in indecision in bay four, and with curiosity overcoming caution, made a crablike traverse over to Buckram's box. He unbolted the top half of the door, looked inside, and then bolted the door again. Unable from a distance to read his reaction, I walked out of the house into his sight without appearing to take any notice of him.

He removed himself smartly from bay four and pretended to be looking for Etty in bay three, but finally his uncertainty got the better of him and he turned to come and meet me.

'Do you know where Carlo is?' he asked without preamble.

'Where would you expect him to be?' I said.

He blinked. 'In his room ... I knock on his door when I am ready ... but he wasn't there. Have you ... have you seen him?'

'At four o'clock this morning,' I said casually, 'he was fast asleep in the back of your car. I imagine he is still there.'

He turned his head away as if I'd punched him.

164

'He came, then,' he said, and sounded hopeless.

'He came,' I agreed.

'But you didn't . . . I mean . . . kill him?'

'I'm not your father,' I said astringently. 'Carlo got injected with some stuff he brought for Buckram.'

His head snapped back and his eyes held a fury that was for once not totally directed at me.

'I told him not to come,' he said angrily. 'I told him not to.'

'Because Buckram could win for you next week?'

'Yes . . . no . . . You confuse me.'

'But he disregarded you,' I suggested, 'and obeyed your father?'

'I told him not to come,' he repeated.

'He wouldn't dare disobey your father,' I said drily.

'No one disobeys my father,' he stated automatically and then looked at me in bewilderment. 'Except you,' he said.

'The knack with your father', I explained, 'is to disobey within the area where retaliation becomes progressively less profitable, and to widen that area at every opportunity.'

'I don't understand.'

'I'll explain it to you on the way to Doncaster,' I said.

'I am not coming with you,' he said stiffly. 'Carlo will drive me in my own car.'

'He'll be in no shape to. If you want to go to the races

165

I think you'll find you either have to drive yourself or come with me.'

He gave me an angry stare and didn't admit he couldn't drive. But he couldn't resist the attraction of the races, either, and I had counted on it.

'Very well, I will come with you.'

After we had ridden back from Racecourse side with the first lot I told him to talk to Margaret in the office while I changed into race-going clothes, and then I drove him up to the Forbury Inn for him to do the same.

He bounded out of the Jensen almost before it stopped rolling and wrenched open one of the Mercedes' rear doors. Inside the car a hunched figure sitting on the back seat showed that Carlo was at least partially awake, if not a hundred per cent receptive of the Italian torrent of abuse breaking over him.

I tapped Alessandro on the back and when he momentarily stopped cursing, said, 'If he feels anything like I did after similar treatment, he will not be taking much notice. Why don't you do something constructive, like getting ready to go to the races?'

'I'll do what I please,' he said fiercely, but the next minute it appeared that what pleased him was to change for the races.

While he was indoors, Carlo made one or two remarks in Italian which stretched my knowledge of the language too far. The gist, however, was clear. Something to do with my ancestors.

Alessandro reappeared wearing the dark suit he had first arrived in, which was now a full size too large. It make him look even thinner, and a good deal younger, and almost harmless. I reminded myself sharply that a lowered guard invited the uppercut, and jerked my head for him to get into the Jensen.

When he had closed the door, I spoke to Carlo through the open window of the Mercedes. 'Can you hear what I say?' I said. 'Are you listening?'

He raised his head with an effort and gave me a look which showed that he was, even if he didn't want to.

'Good,' I said. 'Now, take this in. Alessandro is coming with me to the races. Before I bring him back, I intend to telephone to the stables to make quite sure that no damage of any kind has been done there . . . that all the horses are alive and well. If you have any idea of going back today to finish off what you didn't do last night, you can drop it. Because if you do any damage you will not get Alessandro back tonight . . . or for many nights . . . and I cannot think that Enso Rivera would be very pleased with you.'

He looked as furious as his sorry state would let him.

'You understand?' I said.

'Yes.' He closed his eyes and groaned. I left him to it with reprehensible satisfaction.

*

'What did you say to Carlo?' Alessandro demanded as I swept him away down the drive.

'Told him to spend the day in bed.'

'I don't believe you.'

'Words to that effect.'

He looked suspiciously at the beginnings of a smile I didn't bother to repress, and then, crossly, straight ahead through the windscreen.

After ten silent miles I said, 'I've written a letter to your father. I'd like you to send it to him.'

'What letter?'

I took an envelope out of my inner pocket and handed it to him.

'I want to read it,' he stated aggressively.

'Go ahead. It isn't stuck. I thought I would save you the trouble.'

He compressed his mouth and pulled out the letter. He read:

Enso Rivera,
The following points are for your consideration.
1. While Alessandro stays, and wishes to stay, at Rowley Lodge, the stable cannot be destroyed.

Following any form or degree of destruction, or of attempted destruction, of the stables, the Jockey Club will immediately be informed of everything that has passed, with the result that Alessandro would be banned for life from riding races anywhere in the world.

2. Tommy Hoylake.

Should any harm of any description come to Tommy Hoylake, or to any other jockey employed by the stable, the information will be laid, and Alessandro will ride no more races.

3. Moonrock, Indigo and Buckram.

Should any further attempts be made to injure or kill any of the horses at Rowley Lodge, information will be laid, and Alessandro will ride no more races.

4. The information which would be laid consists at present of a full account of all pertinent events, together with (*a*) the two model horses and their handwritten labels; (*b*) the results of an analysis done at the Equine Research Establishment on a blood sample taken from Indigo, showing the presence of the anaesthetic promazine; (*c*) X-ray pictures of the fracture to Indigo's near foreleg; (*d*) one rubber mask, worn by Carlo; (*e*) one hypodermic syringe containing traces of anaesthetic, and (*f*) one truncheon, both bearing Carlo's fingerprints.

These items are all lodged with a solicitor, who has instructions for their use in the event of my death.

Bear in mind that the case against you and your son does not have to be proved in a court of law, but only to the satisfaction of the Stewards of the Jockey Club. It is they who take away jockeys' licences.

If no further damage is done or attempted at Rowley Lodge, I will agree on my part to give

Alessandro every reasonable opportunity of becoming a proficient and successful jockey.

He read the letter through twice. Then he slowly folded it and put it back in the envelope.

'He won't like it,' he said. 'He never lets anyone threaten him.'

'He shouldn't have tried threatening me,' I said mildly.

'He thought it would be your father . . . and old people frighten more easily, my father says.'

I took my eyes off the road for two seconds to glance at him. He was no more disturbed by what he had just said than when he had said his father would kill me. Frightening and murdering had been the background to his childhood, and he still seemed to consider them normal.

'Do you really have all those things?' he asked. 'The blood test result . . . and the syringe?'

'I do indeed.'

'But Carlo always wears gloves . . .' He stopped.

'He was careless,' I said.

He brooded over it. 'If my father makes Carlo break any more horses' legs, will you really get me warned off?'

'I certainly will.'

'But after that you would have no way of stopping him from destroying the stables in revenge.'

'Would he do that?' I asked. 'Would he bother?'

Alessandro gave me a pitying, superior smile. 'My father would be revenged if someone ate the cream cake he wanted.'

'So you approve of vengeance?' I said.

'Of course.'

'It wouldn't get you back your licence,' I pointed out, 'and anyway I doubt whether he could actually do it, because there would then be no bar to police protection and the loudest possible publicity.'

He said stubbornly, 'There wouldn't be any risk at all if you would agree to my riding Pease Pudding and Archangel.'

'It never was possible for you to ride them without any experience, and if you'd had any sense you would have known it.'

The haughty look flooded back, but diluted from the first time I'd seen it.

'So,' I went on, 'although there's always a risk in opposing extortion, in some cases it is the only thing to do. And starting from there, it's just a matter of finding ways of opposing that don't land you in the morgue empty-handed.'

There was another long pause while we skirted Grantham and Newark. It started raining. I switched on the wipers and the blades clicked like metronomes over the glass.

'It seems to me,' Alessandro said glumly, 'as if you and my father have been engaged in some sort of power struggle, with me being the pawn that both of you push around.'

I smiled, surprised both at his perception and that he should have said it aloud.

'That's right,' I agreed, 'that's how it's been from the beginning.'

'Well, I don't like it.'

'It only happened because of you. And if you give up the idea of being a jockey, it will all stop.'

'But I *want* to be a jockey,' he said, as if that were the end of it. And as far as his doting father was concerned, it was. The beginning of it, and the end of it.

Ten wet miles further on, he said, 'You tried to get rid of me, when I came.'

'Yes, I did.'

'Do you still want me to leave?'

'Would you?' I sounded hopeful.

'No,' he said.

I twisted my mouth. 'No,' he said again, 'because between you, you and my father have made it impossible for me to go to any other stable and start again.'

Another long pause. 'And anyway,' he said, 'I don't want to go to any other stable. I want to stay at Rowley Lodge.'

'And be Champion Jockey?' I murmured.

'I only told Margaret . . .' he began sharply, and then put a couple of things together. 'She told you I asked about Buckram,' he said bitterly. 'And that's how you caught Carlo.'

In justice to Margaret I said, 'She wouldn't have told me if I hadn't directly asked her what you wanted.'

'You don't trust me,' he complained.

'Well, no,' I said ironically. 'I would be a fool to.'

The rain fell more heavily against the windscreen. We stopped at a red light in Bawtry and waited while a lollipop man shepherded half a school across in front of us.

'That bit in your letter about helping me to be a good jockey . . . do you mean it?'

'Yes, I do,' I said. 'You ride well enough at home. Better than I expected, to be honest.'

'I told you . . .' he began, lifting the arching nose.

'That you were brilliant,' I finished, nodding. 'So you did.'

'Don't laugh at me.' The ready fury boiled up.

'All you've got to do is win a few races, keep your head, show a judgement of pace and an appreciation of tactics, and stop relying on your father.'

He was unpacified. 'It is natural to rely on one's father,' he said stiffly.

'I ran away from mine when I was sixteen.'

He turned his head. I could see out of the corner of my eye that he was both surprised and unimpressed.

'Obviously he did not, like mine, give you everything you wanted.'

'No,' I agreed. 'I wanted freedom.'

I judged that freedom was the one thing that Enso wouldn't give his son for the asking: the obsessively

generous were often possessive as well. There was no
hint of freedom in the fact that Alessandro carried
no money, couldn't drive, and had Carlo around to
supervise and report on every move. But then freedom
didn't seem to be high on Alessandro's list of desirables.
The perks of serfdom were habit-forming, and sweet.

I spent most of the afternoon meeting the people who
knew my father: other trainers, jockeys, officials and
some of the owners. They were all without exception
helpful and informative, so that by the end of the day
I had learned what I would be expected (and just as
importantly, not expected) to do in connection with
Pease Pudding for the Lincoln.

Tommy Hoylake, with an expansive grin, put it succinctly. 'Declare it, saddle it, watch it win, and stick
around in case of objections.'

'Do you think we have any chance?'

'Oh, must have,' he said. 'It's an open race, anything
could win. Lap of the gods, you know. Lap of the gods.'
By which I gathered that he still hadn't made up his
mind about the trial, whether Lancat was good or Pease
Pudding bad.

I drove Alessandro back to Newmarket and asked how
he had got on. As his expression whenever I had caught
sight of him during the afternoon had been a mixture

of envy and pride, I knew without him telling me that he had been both titillated to be recognizable as a jockey, because of his size, and enraged that a swarm of others should have started the season without him. The look he had given the boy who had won the apprentice race would have frightened a rattlesnake.

'I cannot wait until next Wednesday,' he said. 'I wish to begin tomorrow.'

'We have no runners before next Wednesday,' I said calmly.

'Pease Pudding.' He was fierce. 'On Saturday.'

'We've been through all that.'

'I wish to ride him.'

'No.'

He seethed away in the passenger seat. The actual sight and sound and smell of the races had excited him to the pitch where he could scarcely keep still. The approach to reasonableness which had been made on the way up had all blown away in the squally wind on Doncaster's Town Moor, and the first half of the journey back was a complete waste, as far as I was concerned. Finally, though, the extreme tenseness left him, and he slumped back in his seat in some species of gloom.

At that stage, I said, 'What sort of race do you think you should ride on Pullitzer?'

His spine straightened again instantly and he answered with the same directness as he had after the trial.

'I looked up his last year's form,' he said. 'Pullitzer was consistent, he came third or fourth or sixth, mostly. He was always near the front for most of the race but then faded out in the last furlong. Next Wednesday at Catterick it is seven furlongs. It says in the book that the low numbers are the best to draw, so I would hope for one of those. Then I will try to get away well at the start and take a position next to the rails, or with only one other horse inside me, and I will not go too fast, but not too slow either. I will try to stay not farther back than two and a half lengths behind the leading horse, but I will not try to get to the front until right near the end. The last sixty yards, I think. And I will try to be in front only about fifteen yards before the winning post. I think he does not race his best if he is in front, so he mustn't be in front very long.'

To say I was surprised is to get nowhere near the queer excitement which rose sharply and unexpectedly in my brain. I'd had years of practice in sorting the genuine from the phoney, and what Alessandro had said rang of pure sterling.

'OK,' I said casually. 'That sounds all right. You ride him just like that. And how about Buckram . . . you'll be riding him in the apprentice race at Liverpool the day after Pullitzer. Also you can ride Lancat at Teesside two days later, on the Saturday.'

'I'll look them up, and think about them,' he said seriously.

'Don't bother with Lancat's form,' I reminded him.

'He was no good as a two-year-old. Work from what you learned during the trial.'

'Yes,' he said. 'I see.'

His eagerness had come back, but more purposefully, more controlled. I understood to some degree his hunger to make a start: he was reaching out to race riding as a starving man to bread, and nothing would deflect him. I found, moreover, that I no longer needed to deflect him, that what I had said about helping him to become a jockey was more true than I had known when I had written it.

As far as Enso was concerned, and as far as Alessandro was concerned, they were both still forcing me to give him opportunities against my will. It privately and sardonically began to amuse me that I was beginning to give him opportunities because I wanted to.

The battle was about to shift to different ground. I thought about Enso, and about the way he regarded his son . . . and I could see at last how to make him retract his threats. But it seemed to me that very likely the future would be more dangerous than the past.

CHAPTER ELEVEN

Every evening during the week before the Lincoln I spent hours answering the telephone. One owner after another rang up, and without exception sounded depressed. This, I discovered, after the fourth in a row had said in more or less identical words, 'Can't expect much with your father chained to his bed,' was because the invalid in question had been extremely busy on the blower himself.

He had rung them all up, apologized for my presence, told them to expect nothing, and promised them that everything would be restored to normal as soon as he got back. He had also told his co-owner of Pease Pudding, a Major Barnette, that in his opinion the horse was not fit to run; and it had taken me half an hour of my very best persuasive tongue to convince the Major that as my father hadn't seen the horse for the past six weeks, he didn't actually know.

Looking into his activities more closely, I found that my father had also written privately every week to Etty for progress reports and had told her not to tell me she was sending them. I practically bullied this last gem out of her on the morning before the Lincoln, having cottoned on to what was happening only through mentioning that my father had told all the owners the horses were unfit. Something guilty in her expression had given her away, but she fended off my bitterness by claiming that she hadn't actually said they were unfit: that was just the way my father had chosen to interpret things.

I went into the office and asked Margaret if my father had telephoned or written to her for private reports. She looked embarrassed and said that he had.

When I spoke about race tactics to Tommy Hoylake that Friday, he said not to worry, my father had rung him up and given him his instructions.

'And what were they?' I asked, with a great deal more restraint than I was feeling.

'Oh . . . just to keep in touch with the field and not drop out of the back door when he blows up.'

'Um . . . If he hadn't rung you up, how would you have planned to ride?' I said.

'Keep him well up all the time,' he said promptly. 'When he's fit, he's one of those horses who likes to make the others try to catch him. I'd pick him up two furlongs out, take him to the front, and just pray he'd stay there.'

'Ride him like that, then,' I said. 'I've got a hundred pounds on him, and I don't usually bet.'

His mouth opened in astonishment. 'But your father . . .'

'Promise you'll ride the horse to win,' I said pleasantly, 'or I'll put someone else up.'

I was insulting him. No one ever suggested replacing Tommy Hoylake. He looked uncertainly at my open expression and came to the conclusion that because of my inexperience I didn't realize the enormity of what I'd said.

He shrugged. 'All right. I'll give it a whirl. Though what your father will say . . .'

My father had not finished saying, not by six or more calls, mostly, it appeared, to the Press. Three papers on the morning of the Lincoln quoted his opinion that Pease Pudding had no chance. He'd have me in before the Stewards, I grimly reflected, if the horse did any good.

Among all this telephonic activity he rang me only once. Although the overpowering bossiness had not returned to his voice, he sounded stilted and displeased, and I gathered that the champagne truce had barely seen me out of the door.

He rang on the Thursday evening after I got back from Doncaster, and I told him how helpful everyone had been.

'Hmph,' he said, 'I'll ring the Clerk of the Course tomorrow, and ask him to keep an eye on things.'

'Have you entirely cornered the telephone trolley?' I asked.

'Telephone trolley? Could never get hold of it for long enough. Too many people asking for it all the time. No, no. I told them I needed my own private extension, here in this room, and after a lot of fuss and delay they fixed one up. I insisted, of course, that I had a business to run.'

'And you insisted often?'

'Of course,' he said without humour, and I knew from long experience that the hospital had had as much chance as an egg under a steamroller.

'The horses aren't as backward as you think,' I told him. 'You don't really need to be so pessimistic.'

'You're no judge of a horse,' he said dogmatically; and it was the day after that that he talked to the Press.

Major Barnette gloomed away in the parade ring and poured scorn and pity on my hefty bet.

'Your father told me not to throw good money after bad,' he said. 'And I can't think why I let you persuade me to run.'

'You can have fifty of my hundred, if you like.' I offered it with the noblest of intentions, but he took it as a sign that I wanted to get rid of some of my losses.

'Certainly not,' he said resentfully.

He was a spare, elderly man of middle height, who stood at the slightest provocation upon his dignity. Sign of basic failure, I diagnosed uncharitably, and remembered the old adage that some owners were harder to train than their horses.

The twenty-nine runners for the Lincoln were stalking long-leggedly round the parade ring, with all the other owners and trainers standing about in considering groups. Strong, cold northwest winds had blown the clouds away and the sun shone brazenly from a brilliant high blue sky. When the jockeys trickled through the crowd and emerged in a sunburst into the parade ring their glossy colours gleamed and reflected the light like children's toys.

The old–young figure of Tommy Hoylake in bright green bounced towards us with a carefree aura of play-it-as-it-comes, which did nothing to persuade Major Barnette that his half share of the horse would run well.

'Look,' he said heavily to Tommy, 'just don't get tailed off. If it looks as if you will be, pull up and jump off, for God's sake, and pretend the horse is lame or the saddle's slipped. Anything you like, but don't let it get around that the horse is no good, or its stud value will sink like a stone.'

'I don't think he'll actually be tailed off, sir,' Tommy said judiciously, and cast an enquiring glance up at me.

'Just ride him as you suggested,' I said, 'and don't leave it all in the lap of the gods.'

He grinned. Hopped on the horse. Flicked his cap to Major Barnette. Went on his light-hearted way.

The Major didn't want to watch the race with me,

which suited me fine. My mouth felt dry. Suppose after all that my father was right . . . that I couldn't tell a fit horse from a letterbox, and that he in his hospital bed was a better judge. Fair enough, if the horse ran stinkingly badly I would acknowledge my mistake and do a salutary spot of grovelling.

The horses had cantered a straight mile away from the stands, circled, lined up, and started back at a flat gallop. Unused to holding race glasses and to watching races head-on from a mile away, I couldn't for a long time see Tommy at all, even though I knew vaguely where to look for him: drawn number twenty-one, almost midfield. I put the glasses down after a while and just watched the mass making its distant way towards the stands, a multi-coloured charge dividing into two sections, one each side of the course. Each section narrowed until the centre of the track was bare, and it looked as though two separate races were being held at the same time.

I heard his name on the commentary before I spotted the colours.

'And now on the stands' side it's Pease Pudding coming to take it up. With two furlongs to go, Pease Pudding on the rails with Gossamer next and Badger making up ground now behind them, and Willy Nilly on the far side followed by Thermometer, Student Unrest, Manganeta . . .' He rattled off a long string of names to which I didn't listen.

That he had been fit enough to hit the front two

furlongs from home was all that mattered. I honestly didn't care from that moment whether he won or lost. But he did win. He won by a short head from Badger, holding his muzzle stubbornly in front when it looked impossible that he shouldn't be caught, with Tommy Hoylake moving rhythmically over the withers and getting out of him the last milligram of balance, of stamina, of utter bloody-minded refusal to be beaten.

In the winner's unsaddling enclosure Major Barnette looked more stunned than stratospheric, but Tommy Hoylake jumped down with the broadest of grins and said, 'Hey, what about that, then? He had the goods in the parcel after all.'

'So he did,' I said, and told the discountenanced Pressmen that anyone could win the Lincoln any old day of the week: any old day, given the horse, the luck, the head lad, my father's stable routine, and the second-best jockey in the country.

About twenty people having suddenly developed a close friendship with Major Barnette, he drifted off more or less at their suggestion to the bar to lubricate their hoarse-from-cheering throats. He asked me lamely to join him, but as I had caught his eye just when, recovering from his surprise, he had been telling the world that he always knew Pease Pudding had it in him, I saved him embarrassment and declined.

When the crowd round the unsaddling enclosure had dispersed and the fuss had died away, I somehow found myself face to face with Alessandro, who had been driven to Doncaster that day, and the previous day, by a partially revitalized chauffeur.

His face was as white as his yellowish skin could get, and his black eyes were as deep as pits. He regarded me with a shaking, strung-up intensity, and seemed to have difficulty in actually saying what was hovering on the edge. I looked back at him without emotion of any sort, and waited.

'All right,' he said jerkily, after a while. 'All right. Why don't you say it? I expect you to say it.'

'There's no need,' I said neutrally. 'And no point.'

Some of the jangle drained out of his face. He swallowed with difficulty.

'I will say it for you, then,' he said. 'Pease Pudding would not have won if you had let me ride him.'

'No, he wouldn't,' I agreed.

'I could see,' he said, still with a shake in his voice, 'that I couldn't have ridden like that. I could see . . .'

Humility was a torment for Alessandro.

I said, in some sort of compassion, 'Tommy Hoylake has no more determination than you have, and no better hands. But what he does have is a marvellous judgement of pace and tremendous polish in a tight finish. Your turn will come, don't doubt it.'

Even if his colour didn't come back, the rest of the rigidity disappeared. He looked more dumbfounded than anything else.

He said slowly, 'I thought . . . I thought you

would . . . what is it Miss Craig says . . .? Rub my nose
in it.'

I smiled at the sound of the colloquialism in his
careful accent.

'No, I wouldn't do that.'

He took a deep breath and involuntarily stretched
his arms out sideways.

'I want . . .' he said, and didn't finish it.

You want the world, I thought. And I said, 'Start on
Wednesday.'

When the horse-box brought Pease Pudding back to
Rowley Lodge that night the whole stable turned out
to greet him. Etty's face was puckered with a different
emotion from worry, and she fussed over the returning
warrior like a mother hen. The colt himself clattered
stiff-legged down the ramp into the yard and modestly
accepted the melon-sized grins and the earthy comments (you did it, you old bugger) which were directed
his way.

'Surely every winner doesn't get this sort of reception,' I said to Etty, after I'd come out of the house to
investigate the bustle. I had reached the house half an
hour before the horse, and found everything quiet: the
lads had finished evening stables and gone round to
the hostel for their tea.

'It's the first of the season,' she said, her eyes shining

in her good plain face. 'And we didn't expect . . . well,
I mean . . . without Mr Griffon and everything . . .'

'I told you to have more faith in yourself, Etty.'

'It's bucked the lads up no end,' she said, ducking
the compliment. 'Everyone was watching on TV. They
made such a noise in the hostel they must have heard
them at the Forbury Inn . . .'

The lads were all spruced up for their Saturday evening out. When they'd seen Pease Pudding safely stowed
away, they set off in a laughing and cheering bunch to
make inroads into the stocks of the Golden Lion; and
until I saw the explosive quality of their pleasure, I
hadn't realized the extent of their depression. But they
had after all, I reflected, read the papers. And they were
used to believing my father rather than their own eyes.

'Mr Griffon will be so pleased,' Etty said, with genuine, unsophisticated certainty.

But Mr Griffon, predictably, was not.

I drove down to see him the following afternoon
and found several of the Sunday newspapers in the
waste basket. He greeted me with a face that made
agate look like putty, and was watchfully determined
that I shouldn't have a chance of crowing.

He needn't have worried. Nothing made for worse
future relations in any field whatsoever than crowing
over losers; and if I knew nothing else, I knew how to
negotiate for the best long-term results.

I congratulated him on the win.

He didn't quite know how to deal with that, but at

least it got him out of the embarrassment of having to admit he'd been made to look foolish.

'Tommy Hoylake rode a brilliant race,' he stated, and ignored the fact that he had given him directly opposite instructions.

'Yes, he did,' I agreed wholeheartedly, and repeated that all the rest of the credit lay with Etty and with his own stable routine, which we had faithfully followed.

He unbent a little more, but I found, slightly to my dismay, that in contrast I admired Alessandro for the straightforwardness of his apology, and for the moral courage which had nerved him to offer it. Moral courage was not something I had ever associated with Alessandro, before that moment.

Since my last visit, my father's room had taken on the appearance of an office. The regulation bedside locker had been replaced by a much larger table which pushed around easily on huge wheel castors, like the bed. On the table was the telephone on which he had broadcast so much blight, also a heap of *Racing Calendars*, copies of the *Sporting Life*, entry forms, a copy of *Horses in Training*, the three previous years' form books and, half hidden, the reports from Etty in her familiar schoolgirl handwriting.

'What, no typewriter?' I said flippantly, and he said stiffly that he was arranging for a local girl to come in and take dictation some time in the next week.

'Fine,' I said encouragingly; but he refused to be friendly. He saw the winning of the Lincoln as a serious threat to his authority, and his manner said plainly that that authority was not passing to me or even to Etty, while he could do anything to prevent it.

He was putting himself in a very ambivalent position. Every winner would be to him personally excruciating, yet at the same time he needed it desperately from the financial angle. Too much of his fortune for safety was still invested in half shares: and if the horses all ran as badly as it seemed he would like them to, their value would curl up like dahlias in a frost.

Understanding him was one thing: sorting him out, quite another.

'I can't wait for you to get back,' I said, but that didn't work either. It seemed that the bones were not mending as fast as had been hoped, and the reminder of the delay simply switched him into a different sort of aggravation.

'Some tommy-rot about elderly bones taking longer to knit,' he said irritably. 'All these weeks . . . and they can't say when I can get out of all these confounded pulleys. I told them I want a plaster cast I can walk on . . . damn it, enough people have them . . . but they say there are lots of cases where it isn't possible, and that I'm one of them.'

'You're lucky to have a leg at all,' I pointed out. 'At first they thought they would have to take it off.'

'Better if they had,' he snorted. 'Then I would have been back at Rowley Lodge by now.'

I had brought some more champagne, but he refused

to drink any. Afraid it might look too much like a celebration, I supposed.

Gillie gave me an uncomplicated hug, and it was she who said, 'I told you so.'

'So you did,' I agreed contentedly. 'And since I won two thousand pounds on your convictions, I'll take you to the Empress.'

The tatty black, however, was tight.

'Just look,' she wailed, pressing into her abdomen with her fingers, 'I wore it only ten days ago and it was perfectly all right. And now, it's impossible.'

'I'm not over addicted to flat-chested ladies with hip bones sticking up like Monts Blancs,' I said comfortingly.

'No . . . but voluptuous plenty can go too far.'

'Grapefruit, then?'

She sighed, considered, went to fetch a cream trench coat which covered a multitude of bulges, and said cheerfully, 'Whoever could do justice to Pease Pudding on a grapefruit?'

We toasted the victory in Chateau Figeac 1964, but out of respect for the tatty black seams ate melon and steak and averted our eyes strong mindedly from the puddings.

Gillie said over the coffee that owing to the continued shortage of orphans she was more or less having time off thrust upon her, and couldn't I think again and let her come to Newmarket.

'No,' I said, more positively than I intended.

She looked a little hurt, which was unusual enough in her to bother me considerably.

'You remember those bruises I had, about five weeks ago?' I said.

'Yes, I do.'

'Well . . . they were the beginning of a rather unpleasant argument I am still having with a man who has a strong line in threats. So far I have resisted some of the threats, and at present there's a sort of stalemate.' I paused. 'I don't want to upset that balance. I don't want to give him any levers. I've no wife, no children, and no near relatives except a father well protected in hospital. There's no one the enemy can threaten . . . no one for whose sake I will do anything he says. But you see . . . if you come to Newmarket, there would be.'

She looked at me for a long time, taking it in, but the hurt went away at once.

Finally she said, 'Archimedes said that if he could find somewhere to stand he could shift the world.'

'Huh?'

'With a lever,' she said, smiling. 'You uneducated goose.'

'Let's not give Archimedes a foothold.'

'No.' She sighed. 'Set your tiny mind at rest. I'll pay you no visits until invited.'

Back at the flat, lying side by side in bed and reading

the Sunday papers in companionable quiet, she said, 'You do see what follows from allowing him no levers?'

'What?'

'More bruises.'

'Not if I can help it.'

She rolled her head on the pillow and looked at me. 'You know damn well. You're no great fool.'

'It won't come to that,' I said.

She turned back to the *Sunday Times*. 'There's an advertisement here for travel on a cargo boat to Australia ... Would you feel safer if I went on a cruise on a cargo boat to Australia? Would you like me to go?'

'Yes, I would,' I said. 'And no, I wouldn't.'

'Just an offer.'

'Declined.'

She smiled. 'Don't leave this address lying about, then.'

'I haven't.'

She put the paper down. 'Just how much of a lever do you suppose I am?'

I threw the *Observer* on to the floor. 'I'll show you, if you like.'

'Please do,' she said; and switched off the light.

CHAPTER TWELVE

'I would like you to come in my car to the races,' I said
to Alessandro on Wednesday morning, when he turned
up for the first lot. 'Give Carlo a day off.'

He looked back dubiously to where Carlo sat as
usual in the Mercedes, staring watchfully down the
yard.

'He says I talk with you too much. He will object.'

I shrugged. 'All right,' I said, and walked off to
mount Cloud Cuckoo-land. We took the string down
to Waterhall, where Alessandro rode a pipe opener on
both Buckram and Lancat, and Etty grudgingly said
that they both seemed to be going well for him. The
thirty or so others that we took along there didn't seem
to be doing so badly either, and the Lincoln booster
was still fizzing around in grins and good humour. The
whole stable, that week, had come alive.

Pullitzer had set off to Catterick early in the smaller
of the stable's two horse-boxes, accompanied by his
own lad and the travelling head lad, Vic Young, who
supervised the care of the horses while they were away

from home. Second in command to Etty, he was a resourceful, quick-witted Londoner grown too heavy in middle age to ride most of the young stable inmates; but the weight came in useful for throwing around. Vic Young was a great one for getting his own way, and it was just good luck that his own way was usually to the stable's advantage. He was, like all the best older lads, deeply partisan.

When I went out after changing, ready to follow to the races, I found Alessandro waiting beside the Jensen, with Carlo glowering in the Mercedes six feet away.

'I will come in your car,' announced Alessandro firmly. 'But Carlo will follow us.'

'Very well,' I nodded.

I slid down into the driving seat and waited while he got in beside me. Then I started up, moved down the drive, and turned out of the gate with Carlo following in convoy.

'My father ordered him to drive me everywhere . . .' Alessandro explained.

'And he doesn't care to disobey your father,' I finished for him.

'That is right. My father also ordered him to make sure I am safe.'

I slid a glance sideways.

'Don't you feel safe?'

'No one would dare to hurt me,' he said simply.

'It would depend what there was to gain,' I said, speeding away from Newmarket.

'But my father . . .'

'I know,' I said. 'I know. And I have no wish to harm you. None at all.'

Alessandro subsided, satisfied. But I reflected that levers could work both ways, and Enso, unlike me, did have someone for whose sake he could be forced to do things against his will. Suppose, I daydreamed idly, that I abducted Alessandro and shut him up in the convenient cellar in the flat in Hampstead. I would then have Enso by the short and curlies in a neat piece of tit for tat.

I sighed briefly. Too many problems that way. And since all I wanted from Enso was for him to get off my back and out of my life before my father came out of hospital, abducting Alessandro didn't seem the quickest way of doing it. The quickest way to the dissolution of Rowley Lodge, more like. Pity, though . . .

Alessandro was impatient for the journey to be over, but was otherwise calmer than I had feared. Determination, however, shouted forth from the arrogant carriage of his head down to the slender hands which clenched and unclenched at intervals on his knees.

I avoided an oncoming oil tanker whose driver seemed to think he was in France, and said casually, 'You won't be able to threaten the other apprentices with reprisals if you don't get it all your own way. You do understand that, don't you?'

He looked almost hurt. 'I will not do that.'

'The habits of a lifetime,' I said without censure, 'are apt to rear their ugly heads at moments of stress.'

'I will ride to win,' he asserted.

'Yes . . . But do remember that if you win by pushing someone else out of the way, the Stewards will take the race away from you, and you'll gain nothing.'

'I will be careful,' he said, with his chin up.

'That's all that is required,' I confirmed. 'Generosity is not.'

He looked at me with suspicion. 'I do not always know if you are meaning to make jokes.'

'Usually,' I said.

We drove steadily north.

'Did it never occur to your father to buy you a Derby prospect, rather than to insert you into Rowley Lodge by force?' I enquired conversationally, as we sped past Wetherby.

He looked as if the possibility were new to him. 'No,' he said. 'It was Archangel I wanted to ride. The favourite. I want to win the Derby, and Archangel is the best. And all the money in Switzerland would not buy Archangel.'

That was true, because the colt belonged to a great sportsman, an eighty-year-old merchant banker, whose lifelong ambition it had been to win the great race. His horses had in years gone by finished second and third, and he had won every other big race in the Calendar, but the ultimate peak had always eluded him. Archangel was the best he had ever had, and time was running short.

'Besides,' Alessandro added, 'my father would not spend the money if a threat would do instead.'

As usual when referring to his father's modus operandi, he took it entirely for granted and saw nothing in it but logic.

'Do you ever think objectively about your father?' I asked. 'About how he achieves his ends, and about whether the ends themselves are of any merit?'

He looked puzzled. 'No . . .' he said uncertainly.

'Where did you go to school, then?' I said, changing tack.

'I didn't go to school,' he said. 'I had two teachers at home. I did not want to go to school. I did not want to be ordered about and to have to work all day . . .'

'So your two teachers spent a lot of time twiddling their thumbs?'

'Twiddling . . .? Oh, yes. I suppose so. The English one used to go off and climb mountains and the Italian one chased the local girls.' There was no humour, however, in his voice. There never was. 'They both left when I was fifteen. They left because I was then riding my two horses all day long and my father said there was no point in paying for two tutors instead of one riding master . . . so he hired one old Frenchman who had been an instructor in the cavalry, and he showed me how to ride better. I used to go and stay with a man my father knew and go hunting on his horse . . . and that is when I rode a bit in races. Four or five races. There were not many for amateurs. I liked it, but I didn't feel as I do now . . . And then, one day at home when I was saying I was bored, my father said, "Very well, Alessandro, say what you want and I will get it for you," and into my head came Archangel, and I just said, just like that, without really thinking, "I want to win the English Derby on Archangel . . ." and he just laughed, how he sometimes does, and said, so I should.' He paused. 'After that, I asked him if he meant it, because the more I thought about it the more I knew there was nothing on earth I wanted more. Nothing on earth I wanted at all. He kept saying, "All in good time," but I was impatient to come to England and start, so when he had finished some business, we came.'

For about the tenth time he twisted round in his seat to look out of the back window. Carlo was still there, faithfully following.

'Tomorrow,' I said, 'he can follow us again, to Liverpool. After Buckram for you tomorrow we have five other horses running at the meeting, and I'm staying there for the three days. I won't be coming with you to Teesside for Lancat.'

He opened his mouth to protest, but I said, 'Vic Young is going up with Lancat. He will do all the technical part. It's the big race of the afternoon, as you know, and you'll be riding against very experienced jockeys. But all you've got to do is get quietly up on that colt, point it in the right direction, and tell it where to accelerate. And if it wins, for God's sake don't brag about how brilliant you are. There's nothing puts backs up quicker than a boastful jockey, and if you want the Press on your side, which you most certainly do, you will give the credit to the horse. Even if you don't feel in the least modest, it will pay to act it.'

He digested this with a stubborn look which gradually softened into plain thoughtfulness. I deemed I might as well take advantage of a receptive mood, so I went on with the pearls of wisdom.

'Don't despair if you make a right mess of any race. Everyone does, sometime. Just admit it to yourself. Never fool yourself, ever. Don't get upset by criticism ... and don't get swollen-headed from praise ... and keep your temper on a racecourse, all of the time. You can lose it as much as you like on the way home.'

After a while he said, 'You have given me more instructions on behaviour than on how to win races.'

'I trust your social manners less than your horsemanship.'

He worked it out, and didn't know whether to be pleased or not.

After the glitter of Doncaster, Catterick Bridge racecourse disappointed him. His glance raked the simple stands, the modest weighing room, the small-meeting atmosphere, and he said bitterly, 'Is this ... all?'

'Never mind,' I said, though I hadn't myself known

what to expect. 'Down there on the course are seven important furlongs, and they are all that matters.'

The parade ring itself was attractive with trees dotted all around. Alessandro came out there in yellow and blue silks, one of a large bunch of apprentices, most of whom looked slightly smug or self-conscious or nervous, or all of them at once.

Alessandro didn't. His face held no emotion whatsoever. I had expected him to be excited, but he wasn't. He watched Pullitzer plod round the parade ring as if he were of no more interest to him than a herd of cows. He settled into the saddle casually, and without haste gathered the reins to his satisfaction. Vic Young stood holding Pullitzer's rug and gazing up at Alessandro doubtfully.

'Jump him off, now,' he said admonishingly. 'You've got to keep him up there as long as you can.'

Alessandro met my eyes over Vic's head. 'Ride the way you've planned,' I said, and he nodded.

He went away without fuss on to the course and Vic Young, watching him go, exclaimed to me, 'I never did like that snooty little sod, and now he doesn't look as though he's got his heart in the job.'

'Let's wait and see,' I said soothingly. And he waited. And we saw.

Alessandro rode the race exactly as he'd said he would. Drawn number five of sixteen runners he made his way over to the rails in the first two furlongs, stayed steadfastly in fifth or sixth place for the next three, moved up slightly after that, and in the last sixty yards found an opening and some response from Pullitzer, and shot through the leading pair of apprentices not more than ten strides from the post. The colt won by a length and a half, beginning to waver.

He hadn't been backed and he wasn't much cheered, but Alessandro didn't seem to need it. He slid off the horse in the unsaddling enclosure and gave me a cool stare quite devoid of the arrogant self-satisfaction I had been expecting. Then suddenly his face dissolved into the smile I'd only seen him give that once to Margaret, a warm, confident, uncomplicated expression of delight.

'I did it,' he said, and I said, 'You did it beautifully,' and he could certainly see that I was as pleased as he was.

Pullitzer's win was not popular with the lads. No one had had a penny on it, and when Vic got back and reported that the old horse must have developed a lot with age as Alessandro hadn't ridden to instructions, they were all quick to deny him any credit. As he seldom talked to any of them, however, I doubted whether he knew.

He was highly self-contained when he came to Rowley Lodge the following morning. Etty had gone down to the Flat on Racecourse side with the first lot to give them some longish steady canters, which, because of the distance I had to drive, I couldn't stay to watch. She seemed content to be left in charge for the three days, and had assured me that Lancat and Lucky Lindsay (bound for a two-year-old five-furlongs with an experienced northern jockey) would arrive safely at Teesside on the Saturday.

Alessandro came with me in the Jensen, with Carlo following as before. On the way we mostly discussed the tactics he would need on Buckram and Lancat, and again there was that odd lack of excitement, only this time more marked. Where I would have expected him to be strung up and passionate, he was totally relaxed. Now that he was actually racing, it seemed as if his impatient fever had evaporated.

Buckram didn't win for him, but not because he didn't ride the race he had meant to. Buckram finished third because two other horses were faster, and Alessandro accepted it with surprising resignation.

'He did his best,' he explained simply. 'But we couldn't get there.'

'I saw,' I said; and that was that.

During the rest of the three-day meeting I came to know a great many more racing people and began to get the feel of the industry. I saddled our other four runners, which Tommy Hoylake rode, and congratulated him when one of them won.

'Funny thing,' he said, 'the horses are as forward this year as I've ever known them.'

'Is that good or bad?' I asked.

'Are you kidding? But the next trick will be to keep them going till September.'

'My father will be back to do that,' I assured him.

'Oh . . . yes. I suppose he will,' Tommy said without the enthusiasm I would have expected, and took himself off to weigh out for the next race.

On Saturday Lancat cruised home by four lengths at Teesside at twenty-five to one, which increased my season's winnings from two thousand to four thousand five hundred. And that, I imagined, would be the last of the easy pickings: Lancat was the third winner from the stable out of nine runners, and no one was any longer going to suppose that Rowley Lodge was in the doldrums.

Alessandro's and Vic Young's accounts of what had happened at Teesside were predictably different.

Alessandro said, 'You remember, in the trial, that I made up a lot of ground . . . but I did it too soon, because I had been left behind, and then he got tired . . . Well, he did produce that burst of speed again, just as we thought, and it worked well. I got him going a little before the last furlong pole and he simply zoomed past the others. It was terrific.'

But Vic Young said, 'He left it nearly too late. Got shut in. The others could ride rings round him, of course. That Lancat must be something special, winning in spite of being ridden by an apprentice having only his third race.'

During the next week we had eight more runners,

of which Alessandro rode three. Only one of his was
in an apprentice race, and none of them won. In one
race he was quite clearly outridden in a tight finish by
the champion jockey, but all he said about that was
that he would improve, he supposed, with practice.

The owners of all three horses turned up to watch,
and raised not a grumble between them. Alessandro
behaved towards them with sense and civility, though
I gathered from an unguarded sneer that he let loose
when he thought no one was looking that he was acting
away like crazy.

One of the owners was an American, who turned
out to be one of the subscribers to the syndicate which
had bought out my shops. It amused him greatly to find
I was Neville Griffon's son, and he spent some time in
the parade ring before the race telling Alessandro that
this young fellow here, meaning me, could teach everyone he knew a thing or two about how to run a business.

'Never forgot how you summed up your recipe for
success, when we bought you out: "Put an eyecatcher in
the window, and deal fair." We'd asked you, remember?
And we were expecting a whole dose of the usual
management-school jargon, but that was all you said.
Never forgot it.'

It was his horse on which Alessandro lost by a head,
but he had owned racehorses for a long time and knew
what he was seeing, and he turned to me on the stands
immediately they had passed the post, and said, 'Never

a disgrace to be beaten by the champion ... and that boy of yours, he's going to be good.'

The following week, Alessandro rode in four races and won two of them, both against apprentices. On the second occasion he beat the previous season's star apprentice discovery on the home ground at Newmarket, and the Press began to ask questions. Four wins in three weeks had put him high on the apprentice list ... Where had he come from, they wanted to know. One or two of them spoke to Alessandro himself, and to my relief he answered them quietly. Strictly eyes down, even if tongue in cheek. The old habitual arrogance was kept firmly out of sight.

He usually came to the races in the Jensen, but Carlo never gave up following. The arrangement had become routine.

He talked quite a lot on the journeys. Talked naturally, unselfconsciously, without strain. Mostly we discussed the horses and their form and possibilities in relation to the opposition, but sometimes I had another glimpse or two of his extraordinary home life.

He had not seen his mother since he was about six, when she and his father had had a last appalling row which had seemed to him to go on for days. He said he had been frightened because they were both so violent, and he hadn't understood what it was all about. She kept shouting one word at his father, taunting him, he said, and he had remembered it, though for years he didn't know what it meant. Sterile, he said. That had been the word. His father was sterile. He had had some sort of illness shortly after Alessandro's birth, to which his mother had constantly referred. He couldn't remember her features, only her voice beginning sentences to his father, bitterly and often, with, 'Since your illness . . .'

He had never asked his father about it, he added. It would be impossible, he said, to ask.

I reflected that if Alessandro was the only son Enso could ever have, it explained in some measure the obsessive side of his regard for him. Alessandro was special to Enso in a psychologically disturbing way, and Enso, with well-developed criminal characteristics, was not a normal character in the first place.

As Alessandro's riding successes became more than coincidences, Etty unbent to him a good deal: and Margaret unbent even more. For a period of about four days there was an interval of peaceful, constructive teamwork in a friendly atmosphere. Something which, looking back to the day of his arrival, one would have said was as likely as snow in Singapore.

Four days, it lasted. Then he arrived one morning with a look of almost apprehension, and said that his father was coming to England. Was flying over, that same afternoon. He had telephoned, and he hadn't sounded pleased.

CHAPTER THIRTEEN

Enso moved in to the Forbury Inn and the very next day the prickles were back in Alessandro's manner. He refused to go to Epsom with me in the Jensen: he was going with Carlo.

'Very well,' I said calmly, and had a distinct impression that he wanted to say something, to explain, to entreat ... perhaps something like that ... but that loyalty to his father was preventing it. I smiled a bit ruefully at him and added, 'But any day you like, come with me.'

There was a flicker in the black eyes, but he turned away without answering and walked off to where Carlo was waiting: and when we arrived at Epsom I found that Enso had travelled with him as well.

Enso was waiting for me outside the weighing room, a shortish chubby figure standing harmlessly in the April sunshine. No silenced pistol. No rubber-faced henchmen. No rope round my wrists, needles in my arm. Yet my scalp contracted and the hairs on my legs rose on end.

He held in his hand the letter I had written him, and the hostility in his puffy lidded eyes beat anything Alessandro had ever conjured up by a good twenty lengths.

'You have disobeyed my instructions,' he said, in the sort of voice which would have sent bolder men than I scurrying for shelter. 'I told you that Alessandro was to replace Hoylake. I find that he has not done so. You have given my son only crumbs. You will change that.'

'Alessandro', I said, with as unmoved an expression as I could manage, 'has had more opportunities than most apprentices get in their first six months.'

The eyes flashed with a thousand-kilowatt sizzle. 'You will not talk to me in that tone. You will do as I say. Do you understand? I will not tolerate your continued disregard of my instructions.'

I considered him. Where on the night he had abducted me he had been deliberate and cool, he was now fired by some inner strong emotion. It made him no less dangerous. More, possibly.

'Alessandro is riding a very good horse in the Dean Swift Handicap this afternoon,' I said.

'He tells me this race is not important. It is the Great Metropolitan which is important. He is to ride in that race as well.'

'Did he say he wanted to?' I asked curiously, because our runner in the Great Met was the runaway Traffic, and even Tommy Hoylake regarded the prospect without joy.

'Of course,' Enso insisted, but I didn't wholly believe him. I thought he had probably bullied Alessandro into saying it.

'I'm afraid,' I said with insincere regret, 'that the owner could not be persuaded. He insists that Hoylake should ride. He is adamant.'

Enso smouldered, but abandoned the lost cause. He said instead, 'You will try harder in future. Today, I will overlook. But there is to be no doubt, no shadow of doubt, do you understand, that Alessandro is to ride this horse of yours in the Two Thousand Guineas. Next week he is to ride Archangel, as he wishes. Archangel.'

I said nothing. It was still as impossible for Alessandro to be given the ride on Archangel as ever it was, even if I wanted to, which I didn't. The merchant banker was never going to agree to replacing Tommy Hoylake with an apprentice of five weeks' experience, not on the starriest Derby prospect he had ever owned. And for my father's sake also, Archangel had to have the best jockey he could. Enso took my continuing silence for acceptance, began to look less angry and more satisfied, and finally turned his back on me in dismissal.

Alessandro rode a bad race in the Handicap. He knew the race was the Derby distance, and he knew I was giving him practice at the mile and a half because I hoped he would win the big apprentice race of that length two days later: but he hopelessly misjudged things, swung really wide at Tattenham Corner, failed to balance his mount in and out of the dip, and never produced the speed that was there for the asking.

He wouldn't meet my eyes when he dismounted, and after Tommy Hoylake won the Great Met (as much to Traffic's surprise as to mine) I didn't see him for the rest of the day.

Alessandro rode four more races that week, and in none of them showed his former flair. He lost the apprentices' race at Epsom by a glaringly obvious piece of mistiming, letting the whole field slip him half a mile from home and failing to reach third place by a neck, though travelling faster than anything else at the finish.

At Sandown on the Saturday the two owners he rode for both told me after he trailed in mid-field on their fancied and expensive three-year-olds that they did not agree that he was as good as I had made out, that my father would have known better, and that they would like a different jockey next time.

I relayed these remarks to Alessandro by sending into the changing room for him and speaking to him in the weigh room itself. I was now given little opportunity to talk to him anywhere else. He was wooden in the mornings and left the instant he dismounted, and at the races he was continuously flanked by Enso and Carlo, who accompanied him everywhere like guards.

He listened to me with desperation. He knew he had ridden badly, and made no attempt to justify himself. All he said, when I had finished, was, 'Can I ride Archangel in the Guineas?'

'No,' I said.

His black eyes burned in his distressed face.

'Please,' he said with intensity, 'please say I can ride him. I beg you.'

I shook my head.

'You don't understand.' It was an entreaty; but I wouldn't and couldn't give him what he wanted.

'If your father will give you anything you ask,' I said slowly. 'Ask him to go back to Switzerland and leave you alone.'

It was he then who shook his head, but helplessly, not in disagreement.

'Please,' he said again, but without any hope in his voice, 'I must . . . ride Archangel. My father believes that you are going to let me, even though I told him you wouldn't . . . I am so afraid that if you don't, he really will destroy the stable . . . and then I will not be able to race again . . . and I can't . . . bear . . .' He limped to a stop.

'Tell him,' I suggested without emphasis, 'that if he destroys the stable you will hate him for ever.'

He looked at me numbly. 'I think I would,' he said.

'Then tell him so, before he does it.'

'I'll . . .' He swallowed. 'I'll try.'

He didn't turn up to ride out the next morning, the first he had missed since his bump on the head. Etty suggested it was time some of the other apprentices had more chances than the very few I had given them, and indicated that their earlier ill-feeling towards Alessandro had all returned with interest.

I agreed with her for the sake of peace, and drove off for my Sunday visit south.

My father was bearing the stable's successes with fortitude and finding some comfort in its losses. He did however genuinely seem to want Archangel to win the Guineas, and told me he had had long telephone talks with Tommy Hoylake about how it should be ridden.

He said that his assistant trainer was finally showing signs of coming out of his coma, though the doctors feared irreparable brain damage. He thought he would have to find a replacement.

His own leg also was mending properly at last, he said. He hoped to be home in time for the Derby; and he wouldn't be needing me after that.

The hours spent with Gillie were the usual oasis of peace and amusement, and bedtime was even more satisfactory than usual.

Most of the newspapers that day carried summings-up of the Guineas, with varying assessments of Archangel's chances. They all agreed that Hoylake's big-race temperament was a considerable asset.

I wondered if Enso read the English papers.
I hoped he didn't.

There were to be no race meetings for the next two days, not until Ascot and Catterick on Wednesday, followed by the Newmarket Guineas meeting on Thursday, Friday and Saturday.

Monday morning, Alessandro appeared on leaden feet with charcoal shadows round his eyes, and said his father was practically raving because Tommy Hoylake was still down to ride Archangel.

'I told him,' he said, 'that you wouldn't let me ride him. I told him I understood why you wouldn't. I told him I would never forgive him if he did any more harm here. But he doesn't really listen. I don't know . . . he's different, somehow. Not how he used to be.'

But Enso, I imagined, was what he had always been. It was Alessandro himself who had changed.

I said merely, 'Stop fretting over it and bend your mind to a couple of races you had better win for your own sake.'

'What?' he said vaguely.

'Wake up, you silly nit. You're throwing away all you've worked so hard for. It soon won't matter a damn if you're warned off for life, you're riding so atrociously you won't get any rides anyway.'

He blinked, and the old fury made a temporary comeback. 'You will not speak to me like that.'

'Want to bet?'

'Oh . . .' he said in exasperation. 'You and my father, you tear me apart.'

'You'll have to choose your own life,' I said matter-of-factly. 'And if it still includes being a jockey, mind you win at Catterick. I'm running Buckram there in the apprentice race, and I should give one of the other lads the chance, but I'm putting you up again, and if you don't win they will likely lynch you.'

The ghost of the arrogant lift of the nose did its best. His heart was no longer in it.

'And on Thursday, here at Newmarket, you can ride Lancat in the Heath Handicap. It's a straight mile, for three-year-olds only, and I reckon he should win it, on his Teesside form. So get cracking, study those races and know approximately what the opposition might do. And you bloody well win them both. Understand?'

He gave me a long stare in which there was all of the old intensity but none of the old hostility.

'Yes,' he said finally. 'I understand I am to bloody well win them both.' A faint smile rose and died in his eyes over the first attempt at a joke I had ever heard him make.

Etty was tight-lipped and angry over Buckram. My father would not approve, she said; and another private report was clearly on its way.

I sent Vic Young up to Catterick and went myself with three other horses to Ascot, telling myself that I was in duty bound to escort the owners at the bigger meeting, and that it had nothing to do with wanting to avoid Enso.

Out on the Heath during the wait at the bottom of Side Hill for two other stables to complete their canters, I discussed with Alessandro the tactics he proposed using. Apart from the shadows which persisted round his eyes he seemed to have regained some of his former race-day icy calm. It had yet to survive a long drive in his father's company, but it was a hopeful sign.

Buckram finished second. I felt distinctly disappointed when I saw his name on the 'Results from Other Meetings' board at Ascot, but when I got back to Rowley Lodge Vic Young was just returning with Buckram, and he was, for him, enthusiastic.

'He rode a good race,' he said, nodding. 'Intelligent, you might say. Not his fault he got beat. Not like those stinking efforts last week. He didn't look the same boy, not at all.'

The boy walked into the Newmarket parade ring the following afternoon with all the inward-looking self-possession I could want.

'It's a straight mile,' I said. 'Don't get tempted by the optical illusion that the winning post is much nearer than it really is. You'll know where you are by the furlong posts. Don't pick him up until you've passed the one with two on it, by the bushes, even if you think it looks wrong.'

'I won't,' he said seriously. And he didn't.

He rode a copybook race, cool, well paced,

unflustered. From looking boxed-in two furlongs out he suddenly sprinted through a split-second opening and reached the winning post an extended length ahead of his nearest rival. With his 5 lb apprentice allowance and his Teesside form he had carried a lot of public money, and he earned his cheers.

When he slid down from Lancat in the winner's unsaddling enclosure he gave me again the warm rare smile, and I reckoned that as well as too much weight and too much arrogance, he was going to kick the worst problem of too much father.

But his focus shifted to somewhere behind me and the smile changed and disintegrated, first into a deprecating smirk and then into plain apprehension.

I turned round.

Enso stood inside the small white-railed enclosure.

Enso, staring at me with the towering venom of the dispossessed.

I stared back. Nothing else to do. But for the first time, I feared I couldn't contain him.

For the first time, I was afraid.

I dare say it was asking for trouble to work at the desk in the oak room after I'd seen round the stables and poured myself a modest Scotch. But this time it was a fine light evening on the last day in April, not midnight in a freezing February.

The door opened with an aggressive crash and Enso

walked through it with his two men behind him, the stony-faced familiar Carlo and another with a long nose, small mouth and no evidence of loving kindness.

Enso was accompanied by his gun, and the gun was accompanied by its silencer.

'Stand up,' he said.

I slowly stood.

He waved the gun towards the door.

'Come,' he said.

I didn't move.

The gun steadied on the central area of my chest. He handled the wicked-looking thing as coolly, as familiarly, as a toothbrush.

'I am close to killing you,' he said in such a way that I saw no reason not to believe him. 'If you do not come at once, you will go nowhere.'

This time there were no little jokes about only killing people if they insisted. But I remembered; and I didn't insist. I moved out from behind the desk and walked woodenly towards the door.

Enso moved back to let me pass, too far away from me for me to jump him. But with the two now barefaced helpers at hand, I would have had no chance at all if I had tried.

Across the large central hall of Rowley Lodge the main front door stood open. Outside, through the lobby and the further doors, stood a Mercedes. Not Alessandro's. This one was maroon, and a size larger.

I was invited inside it. The American ex-rubber-face

drove. Enso sat on my right side in the back, and Carlo on the left. Enso held the gun in his right hand, balancing the silencer on his rounded knee, and his fingers never relaxed. I could feel the angry tension in all his muscles whenever the moving car swayed his weight against me.

The American drove the Mercedes northwards along the Norwich road, but only for a short distance. Just past the Limekilns and before the bridge over the railway line he swung off to the left into a small wood, and stopped as soon as the car was no longer in plain sight of the road.

He had stopped on one of the regular and often highly populated walking grounds. The only snag was that as all horses had to be off the Heath by four o'clock every afternoon, there was unlikely to be anyone at that hour along there to help.

'Out,' Enso said economically; and I did as he said.

There was a short pause while the American, who seemed to be known as Cal to his friends, walked around to the back of the car and opened the boot. From it he took first a canvas grip, which he handed to Carlo. Next he produced a long darkish grey gaberdine raincoat, which he put on although the weather was as good as the forecast. Finally he picked out with loving care a Lee Enfield 303.

Protruding from its underside was a magazine for ten bullets. He very deliberately worked the bolt to bring the first of them into the breech. Then he pulled back the short lever which locked the firing mechanism in the safety position.

I looked at the massive rifle which he handled so carefully yet with such accustomed precision. It was a gun to frighten with as much as to kill, though from what I knew of it, a bullet from it would blow a man to pieces at a hundred yards, would pierce the brick walls of an average house like butter, would penetrate fifteen feet into sand and if unimpeded would carry accurately for five miles. Compared with a shotgun, which wasn't reliably lethal at a range of more than thirty yards, the Lee Enfield 303 was a dambuster to a peashooter. Compared with the silenced pistol, which couldn't be counted on even as far as a shotgun, it gave making a dash for it over the Heath as much chance of success as a tortoise in the Olympics.

I raised my eyes from the source of those unprofitable thoughts and met the unwinking gaze of its owner. He was obscurely amused, enjoying the effect his pet had had on me. I had never as far as I knew met an assassin before; but without any doubt, I knew then.

'Walk along there,' Enso said, pointing with his pistol up the walking ground. So I walked, thinking that a Lee Enfield made a lot of noise, and that someone would hear, if they shot me with it. The only thing was, the bullet travelled one and half times as fast as sound, so that you'd be dead before you heard the bang.

Cal had calmly put the big gun under the long raincoat and was carrying it upright with his hand through what was clearly a slit, not a pocket. From even a very short distance away, one would not have known he had it with him.

Not that there was anyone to see. My gloomiest assessments were quite right: we emerged from the little wood on to the narrow end of the Railway Land, and there wasn't a horse or rider in sight.

Across the field, alongside the railway, there was a fence made of wooden posts with a wooden top rail and plain wire strands below. There were a few bushes bursting green round about, and a calm peaceful late-spring evening sunshine touching everything with red gold.

When we reached the fence, Enso said to stop.

I stopped.

'Fasten him up,' he said to Carlo and Cal; and he himself stayed quietly pointing his pistol at me while Cal laid his deadly treasure flat on the ground and Carlo unzipped the canvas hold-all.

From it he produced nothing more forbidding than two narrow leather belts, with buckles. He gave one of them to Cal, and without allowing me the slightest hope of escape, they turned my back towards the fence and each fastened one of my wrists to the top wooden rail.

It didn't seem much. It wasn't even uncomfortable, as the rail was barely more than waist high. It just seemed professional, as I couldn't even turn my hands inside the straps, let alone slide them out.

They stepped away, behind Enso, and the sunlight threw my shadow on the ground in front of me . . . Just a man leaning against a fence on an evening stroll.

Away in the distance on my left I could see the cars going over the railway bridge on the Norwich road, and further still, down towards Newmarket on my right, there were glimpses of the traffic in and out of the town.

The town, the whole area, was bursting with thousands of visitors to the Guineas meeting. They might as well have been at the South Pole. From where I stood, there wasn't a soul within screaming distance.

Just Enso and Carlo and Cal.

I had watched Cal in his efforts on my right wrist, but it seemed to me shortly after they had finished that it was Carlo who had been rougher.

I turned my head and understood why I thought so. He had somehow turned my arm over the top of the rail and strapped it so that my palm was half facing backwards. I could feel the strain taking shape right up through my shoulder and I thought at first he had done it by accident.

Then with unwelcome clarity I remembered what Dainsee had said: the easiest way to break a bone is to twist it, to put it under stress.

Oh Christ, I thought: and my mind cringed.

CHAPTER FOURTEEN

I said, 'I thought this sort of thing went out with the Middle Ages.'

Enso was not in the mood for flippant comment.

Enso was stoking himself up into a proper fury.

'I hear everywhere today on the racecourse that Tommy Hoylake is going to win the Two Thousand Guineas on Archangel. Everywhere, Tommy Hoylake, Tommy Hoylake.'

I said nothing.

'You will correct that. You will tell the newspapers that it is to be Alessandro. You will let Alessandro ride Archangel on Saturday.'

Slowly I said, 'Even if I wanted to, I could not put Alessandro on the horse. The owner will not have it.'

'You must find a way,' Enso said. 'There is to be no more of this blocking of my orders, no more of these tactics of producing unsurmountable reasons why you are not able to do as I say. This time, you will do it. This time you will work out how you *can* do it, not how you cannot.'

I was silent.

'Also you will not entice my son away from me.'

'I have not.'

'Liar.' The hatred flared up like magnesium and his voice rose half an octave. 'Everything Alessandro says is Neil Griffon this and Neil Griffon that and Neil Griffon says, and I have heard your name so much that I could cut . . . your . . . throat.' He was almost shouting as he bit out the last three words. His hands were shaking, and the gun barrel wavered round its target. I could feel the muscles tighten involuntarily in my stomach, and my wrists jump uselessly against the straps.

He took a step nearer and his voice was loud and high.

'What my son wants, I will give him. I . . . I . . . will give him. I will give him what he wants.'

'I see,' I said, and reflected that comprehending the situation went no way at all towards getting me out of it.

'There is no one who does not do as I say,' he shouted. 'No one. When Enso Rivera tells people to do things, they do them.'

Whatever I said was as likely to enrage as to calm him, so I said nothing at all. He took a further step near me, until I could see the glint of gold-capped back teeth and smell the sweet heavy scent of his after-shave.

'You too,' he said. 'You will do what I say. There is no one who can boast he disobeyed Enso Rivera. There is no one alive who has disobeyed Enso Rivera.' The pistol moved in his grasp and Cal picked up his Lee Enfield, and it was quite clear what had become of the disobedient.

'You would be dead now,' he said. 'And I want to kill you.' He thrust his head forward on his short neck, the strong nose standing out like a beak and the black eyes as dangerous as napalm. 'But my son . . . my son says he will hate me for ever if I kill you . . . And for that I want to kill you more than I have ever wanted to kill anyone . . .'

He took another step and rested the silencer against my thin wool sweater shirt, with my heart thumping away only a couple of inches below it. I was afraid he would risk it, afraid he would calculate that Alessandro would in time get over the loss of his racing career, afraid he would believe that things would somehow go back and be the same as on the day his son casually said, 'I want to ride Archangel in the Derby.'

I was afraid.

But Enso didn't pull the trigger. He said, as if the one followed inexorably from the other, as I suppose in way it did, 'So I will not kill you . . . but I will make you do what I say. I cannot afford for you not to do what I say. I am going to make you . . .'

I didn't ask how. Some questions are so silly they are better unsaid. I could feel the sweat prickling out on my body and I was sure he could read the apprehension on my face: and he had done nothing at all yet, nothing but threaten.

'Alessandro will ride Archangel,' he said. 'The day after tomorrow. In the Two Thousand Guineas.'

His face was close enough for me to see the black-heads in the unhealthy putty skin.

I said nothing. He wasn't asking for a promise. He was telling me.

He took a pace backwards and nodded his head at Carlo. Carlo picked up the holdall and produced from it a truncheon very like the one I had removed from him in Buckram's box.

Promazine first?

No promazine.

They didn't mess around making things easy, as they had for the horses. Carlo simply walked straight up to me, lifted his right arm with truncheon attached, and brought it down with as much force as he could manage. He seemed to be taking a pride in his work. He concentrated on getting the direction just right. And it wasn't any of the fearsome things like my twisted elbow that he hit, but my collar-bone.

Not too bad, I thought confusedly in the first two seconds of numbness, and anyway steeplechase jockeys broke their collar-bones any bloody day of the week, and didn't make a fuss of it . . . but the difference between a racing fall and Carlo's effort lay in the torque and tension all the way up my arm. They acted like one of Archimedes' precious levers and pulled the ends of my collar-bone apart. When sensation returned with ferocity, I could feel the tendons in my neck tighten into strings and stand out taut with the effort of keeping my mouth shut.

I saw on Enso's face a grey look of suffering: narrow eyes, clamped lips, anxious, contracted muscles, lines showing along his forehead and round his eyes; and realized with extraordinary shock that what I saw on his face was a mirror of my own.

When his jaw relaxed a fraction I knew it was because mine had. When his eyes opened a little and some of the overall tension slackened, it was because the worst had passed with me.

It wasn't sympathy, though, on his part. Imagination, rather. He was putting himself in my place, to savour what he'd caused. Pity he couldn't do it more thoroughly. I'd break a bone for him any time he asked.

He nodded sharply several times, a message of satisfaction. There was still a heavy unabated anger in his manner and no guarantee that he had finished his evening's work. But he looked regretfully at the pistol, unscrewed the silencer, and handed both bits to Cal, who stowed them away under the raincoat.

Enso stepped close to me. Very close. He ran his finger down my cheek and rubbed the sweat from it against his thumb.

'Alessandro will ride Archangel in the Guineas,' he said. 'Because if he doesn't, I will break your other arm. Just like this.'

I didn't say anything. Couldn't, really.

Carlo unfastened the strap from my right wrist and put it with the truncheon in the holdall, and they all three turned their backs on me and walked away across the field and through the wood to the waiting Mercedes.

It took a long inch-by-inch time to get my right hand round to my left, to undo the other strap. After that I sat on the ground with my back against one of the posts, to wait until things got better. They didn't seem to, much.

I looked at my watch. Eight o'clock. Time for dinner, down at the Forbury Inn. Enso probably had his fat knees under the table, tucking in with a good appetite.

In theory it had seemed reasonable that the most conclusive way to defeat him had been to steal his son away. In practice, as I gingerly hugged to my chest my severly sore left arm, I doubted if Alessandro's soul was worth the trouble. Arrogant, treacherous, spoilt little bastard . . . but with guts and determination and talent. A mini battlefield, torn apart by loyalty to his father and the lure of success on his own. A pawn, pushed around in a power struggle. But this pawn was all . . . and whoever captured the pawn won the game.

I sighed, and slowly, wincing, got back to my feet. No one except me was going to get me home and bandaged up.

I walked. It was less than a mile. But far enough.

The elderly doctor was fortunately at home when I telephoned.

'What do you mean, you fell off a horse and broke your collar-bone?' he demanded. 'At this hour? I thought all horses had to be off the Heath by four?'

'Look,' I said wearily. 'I've broken my collar-bone. Would you come and deal with it?'

'Mm,' he grunted. 'All right.'

He came within half an hour, equipped with what looked like a couple of rubber quoits. Clavical rings, he said, as he proceeded to push one up each of my shoulders and tie them together behind my back.

'Bloody uncomfortable,' I said.

'Well, if you will fall off horses . . .'

His heavy eyes assessed his handiwork with impass-ive professionalism. Tying up broken collar-bones in Newmarket was as regular as dispensing coughdrops.

'Take some codeine,' he said. 'Got any?'

'I don't know.'

He clicked his tongue and produced a packet from his bag. 'Two every four hours.'

'Thank you. Very much.'

'That's all right,' he said, nodding. He shut his bag and flipped the clips.

'Have a drink?' I suggested, as he helped me into my shirt.

'Thought you'd never ask,' he said smiling, and dealt with a large whisky as familiarly as with his bandages. I kept him company, and the spirit helped the codeine along considerably.

'As a matter of interest,' I said as he reached the

second half of his glassful. 'What illnesses cause sterility?'

'Eh?' He looked surprised, but answered straight-forwardly. 'Only two, really. Mumps and venereal disease. But mumps very rarely causes complete ster-ility. Usually affects one testicle only, if it affects any at all. Syphilis is the only sure sterility one. But with modern treatment, it doesn't progress that far.'

'Would you tell me more about it?'

'Hypothetical?' he asked. 'I mean, you don't think you yourself may be infected? Because if so . . .'

'Absolutely not,' I interrupted. 'Strictly hypothetical.'

'Good . . .' He drank efficiently. 'Well. Sometimes people contract both syphilis and gonorrhoea at once. Say they get treated and cured of gonorrhoea, but the syphilis goes unsuspected . . . Right? Now syphilis is a progressive disease, but it can lie quiet for years, doing its slow damage more or less unknown to its host. Sterility could occur a few years after infection. One couldn't say exactly how many years, it varies enorm-ously. But before the sterility occurs, any number of infected children could be conceived. Mostly, they are stillborn. Some live, but there's almost always some-thing wrong with them.'

Alessandro had said his father had been ill after he was born, which seemed to put him in the clear. But venereal disease would account for Enso's wife's extreme bitterness, and the violent break up of the marriage.

'Henry VIII,' the doctor said, as if it followed naturally on.

'What?' I said.

'Henry VIII,' he repeated patiently. 'He had syphilis. Katherine of Aragon had about a dozen stillborn children and her one surviving child, Mary, was barren. His sickly son Edward died young. Don't know about Elizabeth, not enough data.' He polished off the last drop in his glass.

I pointed to the bottle. 'Would you mind helping yourself?'

He got to his feet and refilled my glass, too. 'He went about blaming his poor wives for not producing sons, when it was his fault all the time. And that extreme fanaticism about having a son ... and cutting off heads right and left to get one ... that's typical obsessive syphilitic behaviour.'

'How do you mean?'

'The pepper king,' he said, as if that explained all.

'What had he got to do with pepper, for heaven's sake?'

'Not Henry VIII,' he said impatiently. 'The pepper king was someone else ... Look, in the medical textbooks, in the chapter on the advanced complications which can arise from syphilis, there's this bit about the pepper king. He was a chap who had megalomania in an interim stage of GPI, and he got this obsession about pepper. He set out to corner all the pepper in the world and make himself into a tycoon, and because of his compulsive fanaticism, he managed it.'

I sorted my way through the maze. 'Are you saying that at a further stage than sterility, our hypothetical syphilitic gent can convince himself that he can move mountains?'

'Not only convince himself,' he agreed, nodding. 'But actually do it. There is literally no one more likely to move mountains than your megalomaniac syphilitic. Not that it lasts for ever, of course. Twenty years, perhaps, in that stage, once it's developed.'

'And then what?'

'GPI.' He took a hefty swallow. 'General paralysis of the insane. In other words, descent to cabbage.'

'Inevitable?'

'After this megalomania stage, yes. But not everyone who gets syphilis gets GPI, and not everyone who gets GPI gets megalomania first. They're only branch lines . . . fairly rare complications.'

'They would need to be,' I said with feeling.

'Indeed yes. If you meet a syphilitic megalomaniac, duck. Duck quickly, because they can be dangerous. There's a theory that Hitler was one . . .' He looked at me thoughtfully over the top of his glass, and his old damp eyes slowly widened. His gaze focused on the sling he had put round my arm, and he said as if he couldn't believe what he was thinking. 'You didn't duck quick enough . . .'

'A horse threw me,' I said.

He shook his head. 'It was a direct blow. I could see that ... but I couldn't believe it. Thought it very puzzling, as a matter of fact.'

'A horse threw me,' I repeated.

He looked at me in awakening amusement. 'If you say so,' he said. 'A horse threw you. I'll write that in my notes.' He finished his drink and stood up. 'Don't stand in his path any more, then. And I'm serious, young Neil. Just remember that Henry VIII chopped off a lot of heads.'

'I'll remember,' I said.

As if I could forget.

I rethought the horse-threw-me story and substituted a fall down the stairs for Etty's benefit.

'What a damn nuisance,' she said in brisk sympathy, and obviously thought me clumsy. 'I'll drive you along to Waterhall in the Land Rover, when we pull out.'

I thanked her, and while we were waiting for the lads to lead the horses out of the boxes ready for the first lot, we walked round into bay one to check on Archangel. Checking on Archangel had become my most frequent occupation.

He was installed in the most secure of high-security boxes, and since Enso's return to England I had had him guarded day and night. Etty thought my care excessive, but I had insisted.

By day bay one was never left unattended. By night the electric eye was positioned to trap unwanted visitors. Two specially engaged security men watched all the time, in shifts, from the owners' room, whose window looked out towards Archangel's box: and their Alsatian dog on a long tethering chain crouched on the ground outside the box and snarled at everyone who approached.

The lads had complained about the dog, because each time they had to see to any horse in bay one, they had to fetch the security guard to help them. All other stables, they had pointed out, only had a dog on duty at night.

Etty waved an arm to the guard in the window. He nodded, came out into the yard, and held his dog on a short leash so that we could walk by safely. Archangel came over to the door when I opened the top half, and poked his nose out into the soft Mayday morning. I rubbed his muzzle and patted his neck, admiring the gloss on his coat and thinking that he hadn't looked better in all the weeks I'd been there.

'Tomorrow,' Etty said to him with a gleam in her eyes. 'We'll see what you can do, boy, tomorrow.' She smiled at me in partnership, acknowledging finally that I had taken some share in getting him ready. During the past month, since the winners had begun mounting up, her constant air of worry had mostly disappeared, and the confidence I had remembered in her manner had all come back. 'And we'll see how much more we'll have to do with him, to win the Derby.'

'My father will be back for that,' I said, intending to reassure her. But the spontaneity went out of her smile, and she looked blank.

'So he will,' she said. 'Do you know . . . I'd forgotten.'

She turned away from his box and walked out into the main yard. I thanked the large ex-policeman guard and begged him and his mate to be especially vigilant for the next thirty-four hours.

'Safe as the Bank of England, sir. Never you fear, sir.' He was easy with certainty, but I thought him optimistic.

Alessandro didn't turn up to ride out, not for either lot. But when I climbed stiffly out of the Land Rover after the second dose of Etty's jolting driving, he was standing waiting for me at the entrance to the yard. When I walked towards the door of the office he came to meet me and stopped in my way.

I stopped also, and looked at him. He held himself rigidly, and his face was thin and white with strain.

'I am sorry,' he said jerkily. 'I am sorry. He told me what he had done . . . I did not want it. I did not ask it.'

'Good,' I said casually. I thought about the way I was carrying my head on one side because it was less painful like that. I felt it was time to straighten up. I straightened.

'He said you would now agree to me riding Archangel tomorrow.'

'And what do you think?' I asked.

He looked despairingly, but he answered without doubt. 'I think you will not.'

'You've grown up a lot,' I said.

'I have learned from you . . .' He shut his mouth suddenly and shook his head. 'I mean . . . I beg you to let me ride Archangel.'

I said mildly, 'No.'

The words burst out of him, 'But he will break your other arm. He said so, and he always does what he says. He'll break your arm again, and I . . . and I . . .' He swallowed and took a grip on his voice, and said with much more control, 'I told him this morning that it is right that I do not ride Archangel. I told him that if he hurt you any more you would tell the Stewards about everything, and I would be warned off. I told him I do not want him to do any more. I want him to leave me here with you, and let me get on on my own.'

I took a slow deep breath. 'And what did he say to that?'

He seemed bewildered as well as distraught. 'I think it made him even more angry.'

I said in explanation. 'He doesn't so much care about whether or not you ride Archangel in the Guineas. He cares only about making me let you ride it. He cares about proving to you that he can give you everything you ask, just as he always has.'

235

'But I ask him now to leave you alone. Leave me here. And he will not listen.'

'You are asking him for the only thing he won't give you,' I said.

'And what is that?'

'Freedom.'

'I don't understand,' he said.

'Because he did not want you to have freedom, he gave you everything else. Everything . . . to keep you with him. As he sees it, I have recently been holding out to you the one thing he doesn't want you to have. The power to make a success of life on your own. So his fight with me now is not really about who rides Archangel tomorrow, but about you.'

He understood all right. It drenched him like a revelation.

'I will tell him he has no fear of losing me,' he said passionately. 'Then he will do you no more harm.'

'Don't you do that. His fear of losing you is all that's keeping me alive.'

His mouth opened. He stared at me with the black eyes, a pawn lost between the rooks.

'Then what . . . what am I to do?'

'Tell him that Tommy Hoylake rides Archangel tomorrow.'

His gaze wandered down from my face to the hump made by the clavicle rings and the outline of my arm in its sling inside my jersey.

'I cannot,' he said.

I half smiled. 'He will find out soon enough.'

Alessandro shivered slightly. 'You don't understand. I have seen . . .' His voice trailed away and he looked back to my face with a sort of awakening on his own. 'I have seen people he has hurt. Afterwards, I've seen them. There was fear in their faces. And shame, too. I just thought . . . how clever he was . . . to know how to make people do what he wanted. I've seen how every-one fears him . . . and I thought he was marvellous . . .' He took a shaky breath. 'I don't want him to make you look like those others.'

'He won't,' I said, with more certainty than I felt.

'But he will not just let Tommy ride Archangel, and do nothing about it. I know him . . . I know he will not. I know he means what he says. You don't know what he can be like . . . You must believe it. You must.'

'I'll do my best,' I said drily, and Alessandro almost danced with frustration.

'Neil,' he said, and it was the only time he had used my first name, 'I'm afraid for you.'

'That makes two of us,' I said without seriousness, but he was not at all cheered. I looked at him with compassion. 'Don't take it so hard, boy.'

'But you don't . . . you don't understand.'

'I do indeed understand,' I said.

'But you don't seem to care.'

'Oh I care,' I said truthfully. 'I'm not mad keen on another smashing up session with your father. But I'm even less keen on crawling along the ground to lick his

237

boots. So Tommy rides Archangel, and we keep our fingers crossed.'

He shook his head, intensely troubled. 'I know him,' he said. 'I know him . . .'

'Next week at Bath,' I said, 'you can ride Pullitzer in the apprentice race, and Clip Clop at Chester.'

His expression said plainly that he doubted we would ever reach next week.

'Did you ever have any brothers or sisters?' I asked abruptly.

He looked bewildered at the unconnected question. 'No . . . My mother had two more children after me, but they were both born dead.'

CHAPTER FIFTEEN

Saturday morning, May 2nd. Two Thousand Guineas day.

The sun rose to another high golden journey over the Heath, and I inched myself uncomfortably out of bed with less fortitude than I would have admired. The thought that Enso could inflict yet more damage was one I hastily shied away from: yet I myself had blocked all his tangents and left him with only one target to aim at. Having engineered the full-frontal confrontation, so to speak, it was too late to wish I hadn't.

I sighed. Were eighty-five thoroughbreds, my father's livelihood, the stable's future, and perhaps Alessandro's liberation worth one broken collar-bone?

Well, yes, they were.

But *two* broken collar-bones?

God forbid.

Through the buzz of my electric razor I considered the pros and cons of the quick getaway. A well-organized, unfollowed retreat to the fastnesses of Hampstead. Simple enough to arrange. The trouble was, some time or other I would have to come back; and while I was away the stable would be too vulnerable.

Perhaps I could fill the house with guests and make sure I was never alone ... but the guests would depart in a day or two, and Enso's idea of vengeance would be like Napoleon brandy, undiluted by passing time.

I struggled into a sweater and went down into the yard hoping that even Enso would see that revenge was useless if it lost you what you prized most on earth. If he harmed me any more, he would lose his son.

It had long been arranged that Tommy Hoylake should take the opportunity of his overnight stay in Newmarket to ride a training gallop in the morning. Accordingly, at seven o'clock he drove his Jaguar up the gravel and stopped with a jerk outside the office window.

'Morning,' he said, stepping out.

'Morning.' I looked at him closely. 'You don't look terribly well.'

He made a face. 'Had a stomach-ache all night. Threw up my dinner, too. I get like that, sometimes. Nerves, I guess. Anyway, I'm a bit better now. And I'll be fine by this afternoon, don't worry about that.'

'You're sure?' I asked with anxiety.

'Yeah.' He gave a pale grin. 'I'm sure. Like I told you, I get this upset now and again. Nothing to worry about. But look, would you mind if I don't ride this gallop this morning?'

'No,' I said. 'Of course not. I'd much rather you

didn't . . . We don't want anything to stop you being all right for this afternoon.'

'Tell you what, though. I could give Archangel his pipe opener. Nice and quiet. How about that?'

'If you're sure you're all right?' I said doubtfully.

'Yeah. Good enough for that. Honest.'

'All right, then,' I said, and he took Archangel out accompanied by Clip Clop, and they cantered a brisk four furlongs, watched by hundreds of the thousands who would yell for him down on the racecourse that afternoon.

Etty was taking the rest of the string along to Waterhall, where several were due for a three-quarter-speed mile along the Line gallop.

'Who shall we put on Lucky Lindsay, now we haven't got Tommy?' Etty said. And it presented a slight problem, because we were short of enough lads with good hands.

'I suppose we had better swap them around,' I said, 'and put Andy on Lucky Lindsay and Faddy on Irrigate, and . . .'

'No need,' Etty interrupted looking towards the drive. 'Alex is good enough, isn't he?'

I turned round. Alessandro was walking down the yard, dressed for work. Long gone were the dandified clothes and the pale washed gloves: he now appeared regularly in a camel-coloured sweater with a blue shirt underneath, an outfit he had copied from Tommy Hoylake on the basis that if that was what a top jockey wore to ride out in, it was what Alessandro Rivera should wear too.

There was no Mercedes waiting behind him in the drive. No watchful Carlo staring down the yard. Alessandro saw my involuntary search for his faithful attendant and he said awkwardly, 'I skipped out. They said not to come, but Carlo's gone off somewhere, so I thought I would. May I . . . I mean, will you let me ride out?'

'Why ever not?' said Etty, who didn't know why ever not.

'Go ahead,' I agreed. 'You can ride the gallop on Lucky Lindsay.'

He was surprised. 'But it said in all the papers that Tommy was riding that gallop this morning.'

'He's got stomach-ache,' I said, and as I saw the wild hope leap in his face, added, 'And don't get excited. He's better, and he will definitely be OK for this afternoon.'

'Oh.'

He smothered the shattered hope as best he could and went off to fetch Lucky Lindsay. Etty was riding Cloud Cuckoo-land along with the string, but I had arranged to have George drive me down later in the Land Rover in time to watch the gallops. The horses pulled out, circled in the paddock to sort out the riders, and went away out of the gate, turning left along the walking ground towards Waterhall.

With them went Lancat, but he, after his hard race

two days earlier, was just to go as far as the main road crossing, and then turn back.

I watched them all go, glossy and elegant creatures on one of those hazy May mornings like the beginning of the world. I took a deep regretful breath. It was strange . . . but in spite of Enso and his son, I had enjoyed my spell as a racehorse trainer. I was going to be sorry when I had to leave. Sorrier than I had imagined. Odd, I thought. Very odd.

I walked back up the yard, talked for a few minutes to Archangel's security guard, who was taking the opportunity of his absence to go off to the canteen for his breakfast, went into the house, made some coffee, and took it into the office. Margaret didn't come on Saturdays. I drank some of the coffee and opened the morning's mail by holding the envelopes between my knees and slitting them with a paper-knife.

I heard a car on the gravel, and the slam of a door, and just missed seeing who was passing the window through misjudging the speed at which I could turn my head. Any number of people would be coming to visit the stable on Guineas' morning. Any of the owners who were staying in Newmarket for the meeting. Anyone.

It was Enso who had come. Enso with his silenced leveller. He was waving it about as usual. So early in the morning, I thought frivolously. Guns before breakfast. Damn silly.

The end of the road, I thought. The end of the damn bloody road.

If Enso had looked angry before, he now looked explosive. The short thick body moved like a tank round the desk towards where I sat, and I knew what Alessandro meant about not knowing what he could be like. Enso up in Railway Field had been an appetizer: this one was a holocaust.

He waded straight in with a fierce right jab on to the elderly doctor's best bandaging, which took away at one stroke my breath, my composure and most of my resistance. I made a serious stab at him with the paper-knife and got my wrist bashed against the edge of the filing cabinet in consequence. He was strong and energetic and frightening, and I was not being so much beaten by Enso as overwhelmed. He hit me on the side of my head with his pistol and then swung it by the silencer and landed the butt viciously on my shoulder, and by that time I was half sick and almost past caring.

'Where is Alessandro?' he shouted, two centimetres from my right ear.

I sagged rather spinelessly against the desk. I had my eyes shut. I was doing my tiny best to deal with an amount of feeling that was practically beyond my control.

He shook me. Not nice. 'Where is Alessandro?' he yelled.

'On a horse,' I said weakly. Where else? 'On a horse.'

'You have abducted him,' he yelled. 'You will tell me where he is. Tell me . . . or I'll break your bones. All of them.'

'He's out riding a horse,' I said.

'He's not,' Enso shouted. 'I told him not to.'

'Well . . . he is.'

'What horse?'

'What does it matter?'

'*What horse?*' He was practically screaming in my ear.

'Lucky Lindsay,' I said. As if it made any difference. I pushed myself upright in the chair and got my eyes open. Enso's face was only inches away and the look in his eyes was a death warrant.

The gun came up. I waited numbly.

'Stop him,' he said. 'Get him back.'

'I can't.'

'You must. Get him back or I'll kill you.'

'He's been gone twenty minutes.'

'*Get him back.*' His voice was hoarse, high-pitched, and terrified. It finally got through to me that his rage had turned into agony. The fury had become fear. The black eyes burnt with some unimaginable torment.

'What have you done?' I said rigidly.

'Get him back,' he repeated, as if shouting alone would achieve it. 'Get him back.' He lifted the gun, but I don't think even he knew if he intended to shoot me or to hit me with it.

'I can't,' I said flatly. 'Whatever you do, I can't.'

'He will be killed,' he yelled wildly. 'My son . . . my son will be killed.' He waved his arms wide and his whole body jerked uncontrollably. 'Tommy Hoylake . . .

It says in the newspapers that Tommy Hoylake is riding Lucky Lindsay this morning . . .'

I shifted to the front of the chair, tucked my legs underneath it, and made the cumbersome shift up on to my feet. Enso didn't try to shove me back. He was too preoccupied with the horror trotting through his mind.

'Tommy Hoylake . . . Hoylake is riding Lucky Lindsay.'

'No,' I said roughly. 'Alessandro is.'

'Tommy Hoylake . . . Hoylake . . . It has to be, it has to be . . .' His eyes were stretching wider and his voice rose higher and higher.

I lifted my hand and slapped him hard in the face.

His mouth stayed open but the noise coming out of it stopped as suddenly as if it had been switched off.

Muscles in his cheeks twitched. His throat moved continuously. I gave him no time to get going again.

'You were planning to kill Tommy Hoylake.'

No answer.

'How?' I said.

No answer. I slapped his face again, with everything I could manage. It wasn't very much.

'*How?*'

'Carlo . . . and Cal . . .' The words were barely distinguishable.

Horses on the Heath, I thought. Tommy Hoylake riding Lucky Lindsay. Carlo, who knew every horse in the yard, who watched all the horses every day and knew Lucky Lindsay by sight as infallibly as any tout. And Cal . . . I felt my own gut contract much as Enso's must have done. Cal had the Lee Enfield 303.

'Where are they?' I said.

'I . . . don't . . . know.'

'You'd better find them.'

'They . . . are . . . hiding.'

'Go and find them,' I said. 'Go out and find them. It's your only chance. It's Alessandro's only chance. Find him before they shoot him . . . you stupid murdering sod.'

He stumbled as if blind round the desk and made for the door. Still holding the pistol he bashed into the frame and rocked on his feet. He righted himself, crashed down the short passage and out through the door into the yard, and half ran on unsure legs to his dark-red Mercedes. He took three shots at starting the engine before it fired. Then he swept round in a frantic arc, roared away up the drive and turned right on to the Bury Road with a shriek of tyres.

Bloody, murdering sod . . . I followed him out of the office but turned down the yard.

Couldn't run. The new hammering he'd given my shoulder made even walking a trial. Stupid, mad, murdering bastard . . . Twenty minutes since Alessandro rode out on Lucky Lindsay . . . twenty minutes, and the rest. They'd be pretty well along at Waterhall. Circling round at the end of the Line gallop, forming up into groups. Setting off . . .

Damn it, I thought. Why don't I just go and sit down and wait for whatever happens. If Enso kills his precious son, serve him right.

I went faster down the yard. Through the gates into the bottom bays. Through the far gate. Across the little paddock. Out through the gate to the Heath. Turned left.

Just let him be coming back, I thought. Let him be coming back. Lancat, coming back from his walk, saddled and bridled and ready to go. He was there, coming towards me along the fence, led by one of the least proficient riders, sent back by Etty as he was little use in the gallops..

'Help me take this jersey off,' I said urgently.

He looked surprised, but lads my father had trained never argued. He helped me take off the jersey. He was no Florence Nightingale. I told him to take the sling off as well. No one could ride decently in a sling.

'Now give me a leg up.'

He did that too.

'OK,' I said. 'Go on in. I'll bring Lancat back later.'

'Yes, sir,' he said. And if I'd told him to stand on his head he would have said yes, sir, just the same.

I turned Lancat back the way he had come. I made him trot along the walking ground. Too slow. Much too slow. Started to canter, breaking the Heath rules. It felt horrible. I twitched him out on to the Bury Hill ground which wasn't supposed to be used for another fortnight and pointed him straight at the Bury Road crossing.

Might as well gallop . . . I did the first five furlongs on the gallop and the next three along the walking ground without slowing down much, and frightened a couple of early-morning motorists as I crossed the main road.

Too many horses on Waterhall. I couldn't from more than half a mile away distinguish the Rowley Lodge string from others. All I could see was that it wasn't yet too late. The morning scene was peaceful and orderly. No appalled groups bending over bleeding bodies.

I kept Lancat going. He'd had a hard race two days earlier and shouldn't have been asked for the effort I was urging him into . . . He was fast and willing, but I was running him into the ground.

It was technically difficult, riding in clavicle rings, let alone anything else. However, the ground looked very hard and too far down. I stayed in the saddle as the lesser of two considerable evils. I did wish most fervently that I had stayed at home. I knew all about steeplechase jockeys riding races with broken collarbones. They were crazy. It was for the birds.

I could see Etty. See some of the familiar horses.

I could see Alessandro on Lucky Lindsay.

I was too far away to be heard even if I'd had any breath for shouting, and neither of them looked behind them.

Alessandro kicked Lucky Lindsay into a fast canter

and with two other horses accelerated quickly up the Line gallop.

A mile away, up the far end of it, there were trees and scrub, and a small wood.

And Carlo. And Cal.

I had a frightful feeling of inevitable disaster, like trying to run away through treacle in a nightmare. Lancat couldn't possibly catch the fresh Lucky Lindsay up the gallop. Interception was the only possibility, yet I could misjudge it so terribly easily.

I set off straight across Waterhall, galloping across the cantering ground and then charging over the Middle Canter in the opposite direction to the horses working there. Furious yells from all sides didn't deter me. I hoped Lancat had enough sense not to run head on into another horse, but apart from that my only worry, my sole, embracing, consuming worry, was to get to Alessandro before a bullet did.

Endless furlongs over the grass . . . only a mile, give or take a little . . . but endless. Lancat was tiring, finding every fresh stride a deeper effort . . . his fluid rhythm had broken into bumps . . . he wouldn't be fit again to race for months . . . I was asking him for the reserves, the furthest stores of power . . . and he poured them generously out.

Endless furlongs . . . and I wasn't getting the angle right . . . Lancat was slowing and I'd reach the Line gallop after Alessandro had gone past. I swerved more to the right . . . swayed perilously in the saddle, couldn't even hold the reins in my left hand and I wanted to hold on to the neck-strap with my right, wanted to hold on for dear life, and if I held on, I couldn't steer . . . It wasn't far, not really. No distance at all on a fresh horse. No distance at all for Lucky Lindsay.

All the trees and bushes up ahead . . . somewhere in there lay Carlo and Cal . . . and if Enso didn't know where, he wasn't going to find them. People didn't lie about in full sight, not with a Lee Enfield aimed at a galloping horse; and Cal would have to be lying down. Have to be, to be accurate enough. A Lee Enfield was as precise as any gun ever made, but only if one aimed and fired while lying down. It kicked too much to be reliable if one was standing up.

Enso wouldn't find them. He might find the car. Alessandro's Mercedes. But he wouldn't find Carlo and Cal until the thunderous noise gave away their position . . . and no one but Enso would find them even then, before they reached the car and drove away. Everyone would be concentrating on Alessandro with a hole torn in his chest, Alessandro in his camel jersey and blue shirt which were just like Tommy Hoylake's.

Carlo and Cal knew Alessandro . . . they knew him well . . . but they thought he had obeyed his father and stayed in the hotel . . . and one jockey looked very like another, from a distance, on a galloping horse . . .

Alessandro, I thought. Galloping along in the golden May morning . . . straight to his death.

I couldn't go any faster. Lancat couldn't go any

251

faster. Didn't know about the horse's breath, but mine was coming out in great gulps. Nearer to sobs, I dare say. I really should have stayed at home.

Shifted another notch to the right and kicked Lancat. Feeble kick. Didn't increase the speed.

We were closing. The angle came sharper suddenly as the Line gallop began its sweep round to the right. Lucky Lindsay came round the corner to the most vulnerable stretch . . . Carlo and Cal would be there . . . they would be ahead of him, because Cal would be sure of hitting a man coming straight towards him . . . there weren't the same problems as in trying to hit a crossing target . . .

They must be able to see me too, I thought. But if Cal was looking down his sights, levelling the blade in the ring over Alessandro's brown sweater and black bent head, he wouldn't notice me . . . wouldn't anyway see any significance in just another horse galloping across the Heath.

Lancat swerved of his own volition towards Lucky Lindsay and took up the race . . . a born and bred competitor bent even in exhaustion on getting his head in front.

Ten yards, ten feet . . . and closing.

Alessandro was several lengths ahead of the two horses he had started out with. Several lengths ahead, all on his own.

Lancat reached Lucky Lindsay at an angle and threw up his head to avoid a collision . . . and Alessandro

turned his face to me in wide astonishment . . . and although I had meant to tell him to jump off and lie flat on the ground until his father succeeded in finding Carlo and Cal, it didn't happen quite like that.

Lancat half rose up into the air and threw me, twisting, on to Lucky Lindsay, and I put my right arm out round Alessandro and scooped him off, and we fell like that down on to the grass. And Lancat fell too, and lay across our feet, because brave, fast, determined Lancat wasn't going anywhere any more.

Half of Lancat's neck was torn away, and his blood and his life ran out on to the bright green turf.

Alessandro tried to twist out of my grasp and stand up.

'Lie still,' I said fiercely. 'Just do as I say, and lie still.'

'I'm hurt,' he said.

'Don't make me laugh.'

'I have hurt my leg,' he protested.

'You'll have a hole in your heart if you stand up.'

'You are mad,' he said.

'Look at Lancat . . . What do you think is wrong with him? Do you think he is lying there for fun?' I couldn't keep the bitterness out of my voice, and I didn't try. 'Cal did that. Cal and his big bloody rifle. They came out here to shoot Tommy Hoylake, and you rode Lucky Lindsay instead, and they couldn't tell the difference, which should please you . . . and if you stand up now they'll have another go.'

253

He lay still. Speechless. And quite, quite still.

I rolled away from him and stuffed my fist against my teeth, for if the truth were told I was hurting far more than I would have believed possible. Him and his damn bloody father ... the free sharp ends of collarbone were carving new and unplanned routes for themselves through several protesting sets of tissue.

A fair amount of fuss was developing around us. When the ring of shocked spectators had grown solid and thick enough I let him get up, but he only got as far as his knees beside Lancat, and there were smears of the horse's blood on his jodhpurs and jersey.

'Lancat ...' he said hopelessly, with a sort of death in his voice. He looked across at me as a couple of helpful onlookers hauled me to my feet, and the despair on his face was bottomless and total.

'Why?' he said. 'Why did he do it?'

I didn't answer. Didn't need to. He already knew.

'I hate him,' he said.

The people around us began to ask questions but neither Alessandro nor I answered them.

From somewhere away to our right there was another loud unmistakable crack. I and half the gathering crowd involuntarily ducked, but the bullet would already have reached us if it had been coming our way.

One crack, then silence. The echoes died quickly over Waterhall, but they shivered for ever through Alessandro's life.

CHAPTER SIXTEEN

Enso had found Carlo and Cal hidden in a clump of bushes near the Boy's Grave crossroads.

We found them there too, when we walked along to the end of the Line gallop to flag down a passing motorist to take Etty quickly into Newmarket. Etty, who had arrived frantic up the Gallop, had at first like all the other onlookers taken it for granted that the shooting had been an accident. A stray bullet loosed off by someone being criminally careless with a gun.

I watched the doubt appear on her face when she realized that my transport had been Lancat and not the Land Rover, but I just asked her matter-of-factly to buzz down to Newmarket and ring up the dead horse removers, then to drive herself back. She sent Andy off with instructions to the rest of the string, and the first car that came along stopped to pick her up.

Alessandro walked off the training ground into the road with a stunned, stony face, and came towards me. He was leading Lucky Lindsay, which someone had caught, but as automatically as if unaware he was there. Three or four paces away, he stopped.

'What am I to do?' he said. His voice was without hope or anxiety. Lifeless. I didn't answer immediately, and it was then that we heard the noise.

A low distressed voice calling unintelligibly.

Startled, I walked along the road a little and through a thin belt of bushes, and there I found them.

Three of them. Enso and Carlo and Cal.

It was Cal who had called out. He was the only one capable of it. Carlo lay sprawled on his back with his eyes open to the sun and a splash of drying scarlet trickling from a hole in his forehead.

Cal had a wider, wetter, spreading stain over the front of his shirt. His breath was shallow and quick, and calling out loud enough to be found had used up most of his energy.

The Lee Enfield lay across his legs. His hand moved convulsively towards the butt, but he no longer had the strength to pick it up.

And Enso ... Cal had shot Enso with the Lee Enfield at a range of about six feet. It wasn't so much the bullet itself, but the shock wave of its velocity: at that short distance it had dug an entrance as large as a plate.

The force of it had flung Enso backwards, against a tree. He sat there now at the foot of it with the silenced pistol still in his hand and his head sunk forward on his chest. There was a soul-sickening mess where his

paunch had been, and his back was indissoluble from the bark.

I would have stopped Alessandro seeing, but I didn't hear him come. I heard only the moan beside me, and I turned abruptly to see the nausea spring out in sweat on his face.

For Cal his appearance there was macabre.

'You . . .' he said. 'You . . . are dead.'

Alessandro merely stared at him, too shocked to understand, too shocked to speak.

Cal's eyes opened wide and his voice grew stronger with a burst of futile anger.

'He said . . . I had killed you. Killed his son. He was . . . out of his senses. He said . . . I should have known it was you . . .' He coughed, and frothy blood slid over his lower lip.

'You did shoot at Alessandro,' I said. 'But you hit a horse.'

Cal said with visibly diminishing strength, 'He shot Carlo . . . and he shot me . . . so I let him have it . . . the son of a bitch . . . he was out . . . of his senses . . .'

The voice stopped. There was nothing anyone could do for him, and presently, imperceptibly, he died.

He died where he had lain in wait for Tommy Hoylake. When I knelt beside him to feel his pulse, and lifted my head to look along the Gallop, there in front of me was the view he had had: a clear sight of the advancing horses, from through the sparse low branches of a concealing bush. The dark shape of

Lancat lay like a hump on the grass three hundred yards away, and another batch of horses, uncaring, were sweeping round the far bend and turning towards me.

An easy shot, it had been, for a marksman. He hadn't bothered even with a telescopic sight. At that range, with a Lee Enfield, one didn't need one. One didn't need to be of pinpoint accuracy: anywhere on the head or trunk would do the trick. I sighed. If he had used a telescopic sight, he would probably have realized that what he was aiming at was Alessandro.

I stood up. Clumsily, painfully, wishing I hadn't got down.

Alessandro hadn't fainted. Hadn't been sick. The sweat had dried on his face, and he was looking steadfastly at his father.

When I moved towards him he turned, but he needed two or three attempts before he could get his throat to work.

He managed it, finally. His voice was strained; different; hoarse: and what he said was as good an epitaph as any.

'He gave me everything,' he said.

We went back to the road, where Alessandro had tethered Lucky Lindsay to a fence. The colt had his head down to the grass, undisturbed.

Neither of us said anything at all.

Etty clattered up in the Land Rover, and I got her to turn it round and take me straight down to the town.

'I'll be right back,' I said to Alessandro, but he stared silently at nothing, with eyes that had seen too much.

When I went back, it was with the police. Etty stayed behind at Rowley Lodge to see to the stables, because it was, still, and incredibly, Guineas day, and we had Archangel to look to. Also, in the town, I made a detour to the doctor, where I bypassed an outraged queue waiting in his surgery, and got him to put the ends of my collar-bone back into alignment. After that it was a bit more bearable, though nothing still to raise flags about.

I spent most of the morning up at the crossroads. Answered some questions and didn't answer others. Alessandro listened to me telling the highest up of the police who had arrived from Cambridge that Enso had appeared to me to be unbalanced.

The police surgeon was sceptical of a layman's opinion.

'In what way?' he said without deference.

I paused to consider. 'You could look for spiro-chaetes,' I said, and his eyes widened abruptly before he disappeared back into the bushes.

They were considerate to Alessandro. He sat on somebody's raincoat on the grass at the side of the road, and later on the police surgeon gave him a sedative.

It was an injection, and Alessandro didn't want it. They wouldn't pay attention to his objections, and when

259

the needle went into his arm I found him staring fixedly at my face. He knew that I too was thinking about too many other injections; about myself, and Carlo, and Moonrock and Indigo and Buckram. Too many needles. Too much death.

The drug didn't put him out, just made him look even more dazed than before. The police decided he should go back to the Forbury Inn and sleep, and steered him towards one of their cars.

He stopped in front of me before he reached it, and gazed at me in awe from hollow dark sockets in a grey gaunt face.

'Look at the flowers,' he said. 'On the Boy's Grave.'

When he had gone I walked over to the raincoat where he had been sitting, close to the little mound.

There were pale yellow polyanthus, and blue forget-me-nots coming into flower round the edge: and all the centre was filled with pansies. Dark purple velvet pansies, shining black in the sun.

It was cynical of me to wonder if he could have planted them himself.

Enso was in the mortuary and Alessandro was asleep when Archangel and Tommy Hoylake won the Guineas.

Not what they had planned.

A heaviness like thunder persisted with me all afternoon, even though there was by then no reason for it.

The defeat of Enso no longer directed half my actions, but I found it impossible in one bound to throw off his influence. It was not until then that I understood how intense it had become.

What I should have felt was relief that the stable was safe. What I did feel was depression.

The merchant banker, Archangel's owner, was practically incandescent with happiness. He glowed in the unsaddling enclosure and joked with the Press in shaky pride.

'Well done, my boy, well done indeed,' he said to me, to Tommy, and to Archangel impartially, and looked ready to embrace us all.

'And now, my boy, now for the Derby, eh?'

'Now for the Derby,' I nodded, and wondered how soon my father would be back at Rowley Lodge.

I went to see him, the next day.

He was looking even more forbidding than usual because he had heard all about the multiple murders on the gallops. He blamed me for letting anything like that happen. It saved him, I reflected sourly, from having to say anything nice about Archangel.

'You should never have taken on that apprentice.'

'No,' I said.

'The Jockey Club will be seriously displeased.'

'Yes.'

'The man must have been mad.'

'Sort of.'

'Absolutely mad to think he could get his son to ride Archangel by killing Tommy Hoylake.'

I had had to tell the police something, and I had told them that. It had seemed enough.

'Obsessed,' I agreed.

'Surely you must have noticed it before? Surely he gave some sign?'

'I suppose he did,' I agreed neutrally.

'Then surely you should have been able to stop him.'

'I did stop him . . . in a way.'

'Not very efficiently,' he complained.

'No,' I said patiently, and thought that the only one who had stopped Enso efficiently and finally had been Cal.

'What's the matter with your arm?'

'Broke my collar-bone,' I said.

'Hard luck.'

He looked down at his still-suspended leg, almost but not quite saying aloud that a collar-bone was chicken feed compared with what he had endured. What was more, he was right.

'How soon will you be out?' I asked.

He answered in a smug satisfaction tinged with undisguisable malice. 'Sooner than you'd like, perhaps.'

'I couldn't wish you to stay here,' I protested.

He looked faintly taken aback: faintly ashamed.

'No . . . well . . . They say not long now.'

'The sooner the better,' I said, and tried to mean it.

'Don't do any more work with Archangel. And I see from the Calendar that you have made entries on your own. I don't want you to do that. I am perfectly capable of deciding where my horses should run.'

'As you say,' I said mildly, and with surprisingly little pleasure realized that I now no longer had any reason for amending his plans.

'Tell Etty that she did very well with Archangel.'

'I will,' I said. 'In fact, I have.'

The corners of his mouth turned down. 'Tell her that I said so.'

'Yes,' I said.

Nothing much, after all, had changed between us. He was still what I had run away from at sixteen, and it would take me a lot less time to leave him again. I couldn't possibly have stayed on as his assistant, even if he had asked me to.

'He gave me everything,' Alessandro had said of his father. I would have said of mine that he gave me not very much. And I felt for him something that Alessandro had never through love or hate felt for his.

I felt . . . apathy.

'Go away, now,' he said. 'And on your way out, find a nurse. I need a bedpan. They take half an hour, sometimes, if I ring the bell. And I want it now, at once.'

*

The driver of the car I had hired in Newmarket was quite happy to include Hampstead in the itinerary.

'A couple of hours?' I suggested, when I had hauled myself out on to the pavement outside the flat.

'Sure,' he said. 'Maybe there's somewhere open for tea, even on Sunday.' He drove off hopefully, optimistic soul that he was.

Gillie said she had lost three pounds, she was painting the bathroom sludge green, and how did I propose to make love to her looking like a washed-out edition of a terminal consumptive.

'I don't', I said, 'propose.'

'Ah,' she said wisely. 'All men have their limits.'

'And just change that description to looking like a racehorse trainer who has just won his first Classic.'

She opened her mouth and obviously was not going to come across with the necessary compliment.

'OK,' I interrupted resignedly. 'So it wasn't me. Everyone else, but not me. I do so agree. Whole-heartedly.'

'Self-pity is disgusting,' she said.

'Mm.' I sat gingerly down in a blue armchair, put my head back, and shut my eyes. Didn't get much sympathy for that, either.

'So you collected the bruises,' she observed.

'That's right.'

'Silly old you.'

'Yes.'

'Do you want some tea?'

264

'No thank you,' I said politely. 'No sympathy, no tea.'

She laughed. 'Brandy, then?'

'If you have some.'

She had enough for the cares of the world to retreat a pace: and she came across, in the end, with her own brand of fellow-feeling.

'Don't wince,' she said, 'when I kiss you.'

'Don't kiss so damned hard.'

After a bit she said, 'Is this shoulder the lot? Or will there be more to come?'

'It's the lot,' I said, and told her all that had happened. Edited, and flippantly; but more or less all.

'And does your own dear dad know all about this?'

'Heaven forbid,' I said.

'But he will, won't he? When you get this Alessandro warned off? And then he will understand how much he owes you?'

'I don't want him to understand,' I said. 'He would loathe it.'

'Charming fellow, your dad.'

'He is what he is,' I said.

'And was Enso what he was?'

I smiled lopsidedly. 'Same principle, I suppose.'

'You're a nut, Neil Griffon.'

I couldn't dispute it.

'How long before he gets out of hospital?' she asked.

'I don't know. He hopes to be on his feet soon. Then a week or two for physiotherapy and walking practice with crutches, or whatever. He expects to be home before the Derby.'

'What will you do then?'

'Don't know,' I said. 'But he'll be three weeks at least, and leverage no longer applies . . . so would you still like to come to Rowley Lodge?'

'Um,' she said, considering. 'There's a three-year-old Nigerian girl I'm supposed to be settling with a family in Dorset . . .'

I felt very tired. 'Never mind, then.'

'I could come on Wednesday.'

When I got back to Newmarket I walked round the yard before I went indoors. It all lay peacefully in the soft light of sundown, the beginning of dusk. The bricks looked rosy and warm, the shrubs were out in flower, and behind the green painted doors the six million quids' worth were safely chomping on their evening oats. Peace in all the bays, winners in many of the boxes, and an air of prosperity and timelessness over the whole.

I would be gone from there soon; and Enso had gone, and Alessandro. When my father came back it would be as if the last three months had never happened. He and Etty and Margaret would go on as they had been before; and I would read about the familiar horses in the newspapers.

I didn't yet know what I would do. Certainly I had

grown to like my father's job, and maybe I could start a stable of my own, somewhere else. I wouldn't go back to antiques, and I knew by then that I wasn't going to work any more for Russell Arletti.

Build a new empire, Gillie had said.

Well, maybe I would.

I looked in at Archangel, now no longer guarded by men, dogs and electronics. The big brown colt lifted his head from his manger and turned on me an enquiring eye. I smiled at him involuntarily. He still showed the effects of his hard race the day before, but he was sturdy and sound, and there was a very good chance he would give the merchant banker his Derby.

I stifled a sigh and went indoors, and heard the telephone ringing in the office.

Owners often telephoned on Sunday evenings, but it wasn't an owner, it was the hospital.

'I'm very sorry,' the voice said several times at the other end. 'We've been trying to reach you for some hours now. Very sorry. Very sorry.'

'But he *can't* be dead,' I said stupidly. 'He was all right when I left him. I was with him this afternoon, and he was all right.'

'Just after you left,' they said. 'Within half an hour.'

'But how?' My mind couldn't grasp it. 'He only had a broken leg . . . and that had mended.'

Would I like to talk to the doctor in charge, they said. Yes, I would.

'He was all right when I left him,' I protested. 'In fact he was yelling for a bedpan.'

'Ah. Yes. Well,' said a high-pitched voice loaded with professional sympathy. 'That's ... er ... that's a very common preliminary to a pulmonary embolus. Calling for a bedpan ... very typical. But do rest assured, Mr Griffon, your father died very quickly. Within a few seconds. Yes, indeed.'

'What', I said, with a feeling of complete unreality, 'is a pulmonary embolus?'

'Blood clot,' he said promptly. 'Unfortunately not uncommon in elderly people who have been bedridden for some time. And your father's fracture ... well, it's tragic, tragic, but not uncommon. I'm afraid. Death sitting up, some people say. Very quick, Mr Griffon. Very quick. There was nothing we could do, do believe me.'

'I believe you.'

But it was impossible, I thought. He couldn't be dead. I had been talking to him just that afternoon ...

The hospital would like instructions, they delicately said.

I would send someone from Newmarket, I said vaguely. An undertaker from Newmarket, to fetch him home.

Monday I spent in endless chat. Talked to the police. Talked to the Jockey Club. Talked to a dozen or so

owners who telephoned to ask what was going to happen to their horses.

Talked and talked.

Margaret dealt with the relentless pressure as calmly as she did with Susie and her friend. And Susie's friend, she said, had incidentally reported that Alessandro had not left his room since the police took him there on Saturday morning. He hadn't eaten anything, and he wouldn't talk to anyone except to tell them to go away. Susie's chum's mum said it was all very well, but Alessandro never had any money, and his bill had only been paid up to the previous Saturday, and they were thinking of asking him to go.

'Tell Susie's chum's mum that Alessandro has money here, and also that in Switzerland he will be rich.'

'Will do,' she said, and rang the Forbury Inn at once.

Etty took charge of both lots out at exercise, and somehow or other the right runners got dispatched to Bath. Vic Young went in charge of them and said later that the apprentice who had the ride on Pullitzer instead of Alessandro was no effing good.

To the police I told the whole of what had occurred on Saturday morning, but nothing of what had occurred before it. Enso had recently arrived in England, I said, and had developed this extraordinary fixation. There was no reason for them not to accept this abbreviated version, and nothing to be gained by telling them more.

Down at the Jockey Club I had a lengthy session

with a committee of Members and a couple of Stewards left over on purpose from the Guineas meeting, and the outcome of that was equally peaceful.

After that I told Margaret to let all enquiring owners know that I would be staying on at Rowley Lodge for the rest of the season, and they could leave or remove their horses as they wished.

'Are you really?' she said. 'Are you staying?'

'Not much else to do, is there?' I said. But we were both smiling.

'Ever since you told that lie about not being able to find anyone to take over, when you had John Bredon lined up all the time, ever since then I've known you liked it here.'

I didn't disillusion her.

'I'm glad you're staying,' she said. 'I suppose it's very disloyal to your father, as he only died yesterday, but I have much preferred working for you.'

I was not so autocratic, that was all. She would have worked efficiently for anyone.

Before she left at three, she said that none of the owners who had so far telephoned were going to remove their horses; and that included Archangel's merchant banker.

When she had gone I wrote to my solicitors in London and asked them to send back to me at New-market the package I had instructed them to open in case of my sudden death.

After that I swallowed a couple of codeines and

wondered how soon everything would stop aching, and from five to six-thirty I walked round at evening stables with Etty.

We passed by Lancat's empty box.

'Damn that Alex,' Etty said, but with a retrospective anger. The past was past. Tomorrow's races were all that mattered. Tomorrow at Chester. She talked of plans ahead. She was contented, fulfilled, and busy. The transition from my father to me had been too gradual to need any sudden adjustment now.

I left her supervising the evening feeds for the horses as usual, and walked back towards the house. Something made me look up along the drive, and there, motionless and only half visible against the tree trunks, stood Alessandro.

It was as if he had got halfway down the drive before his courage deserted him. I walked without haste out of the yard and went to meet him.

Strain had aged him so that he now looked nearer forty than eighteen. Bones stood out sharply under his skin, and there was little in the black eyes except no hope at all.

'I came,' he started. 'I need . . . I mean, you said, at the beginning, that I could have half the money I earned racing . . . Can I still . . . have it?'

'You can,' I said. 'Of course.'

He swallowed. 'I am sorry to come. I had to come. To ask you about the money.'

'You can have it now,' I said. 'Come along into the office.'

I half turned away from him but he didn't move.

'No. I . . . can't.'

'I'll send it along to the Forbury Inn for you,' I said.

He nodded. 'Thank you.'

'Do you have any plans?' I asked him.

The shadows in his face if anything deepened.

'No.'

He visibly gathered every shred of resolution, clamped his teeth together, and asked me the question which was tearing him to shreds.

'When will I be warned off?'

Neil Griffon was a nut, as Gillie had said.

'You won't be warned off,' I told him. 'I talked to the Jockey Club this morning. I told them that you shouldn't lose your licence because your father had gone mad, and they saw that point of view. You may not of course like it that I stressed your father's insanity, but it was the best I could do.'

'But . . .' he said in bewilderment, and then in realization, 'Didn't you tell them about Moonrock and Indigo . . . and about your shoulder?'

'No.'

'I don't understand . . . why you didn't.'

'I don't see any point in revenging myself on you for what your father did.'

'But . . . he only did it . . . in the beginning . . . because I asked.'

'Alessandro,' I said, 'just how many fathers would do as he did? How many fathers, if their sons said they wanted to ride Archangel in the Derby, would go as far as murder to achieve it?'

After a long pause, he said, 'He was mad, then. He really was.' It was clearly no comfort.

'He was ill,' I said. 'That illness he had after you were born. It affected his brain.'

'Then I ... will not ...?'

'No,' I said. 'You can't inherit it. You're as sane as anyone. As sane as you care to be.'

'As I care to be,' he repeated vaguely. His thoughts were turned inward. I didn't hurry him. I waited most patiently, because what he cared to be was the final throw in the game.

'I care to be a jockey,' he said faintly. 'To be a good one.'

I took a breath. 'You are free to ride races anywhere you like,' I said. 'Anywhere in the world.'

He stared at me with a face from which all the arrogance had gone. He didn't look the same boy as the one who had come from Switzerland three months ago, and in fact he wasn't. All of his values had been turned upside-down, and the world as he had known it had come to an end.

To defeat the father, I had changed the son. Changed him at first only as a solution to a problem, but later also because the emerging product was worth it. It seemed a waste, somehow, to let him go. I said abruptly, 'You can stay on at Rowley Lodge, if you like.'

Something shattered somewhere inside him, like a glass breaking. When he turned away I could have sworn that against all probability there were tears in his eyes.

He took four paces, and stopped.

'Well?' I said.

He turned round. The tears had drained back into the ducts, as they do in the young.

'What as?' he said apprehensively, looking for snags.

'Stable jockey,' I said. 'Second to Tommy.'

He walked six more paces away down the drive as if his ankles were springs.

'Come back,' I called. 'What about tomorrow?'

He looked over his shoulder. 'I'll be here to ride out.'

Three more bouncing steps.

'You won't,' I shouted. 'You get a good sleep and a good breakfast and be here at eleven. We're flying over to Chester.'

'Chester?' He turned and shouted in surprise, and went two more steps, backwards.

'Clip Clop,' I yelled. 'Ever heard of him?'

'Yes,' he yelled back, and the laughter took him uncontrollably, and he turned and ran away down the drive, leaping into the air as if he were six.